From Love's Ashes

Frances Patton Statham

Bocage Books

Also by Frances Patton Statham

Bright Sun, Dark Moon

Flame of New Orleans

Jasmine Moon

Daughters of the Summer Storm

Phoenix Rising

On Wings of Fire

To Face the Sun

The Roswell Women

The Roswell Legacy

Trail of Tears

Mary Musgrove, Queen of Savannah

(former title: Call the River Home)

The Silk Train

Mountain Legacy

Murder, al fresco

From Love's Ashes

Library of Congress Control Number: 2013917666

ISBN: 0-9675233-6-2
13 digit: 978-0-9675-2336-1
(Previously ISBN: 0-449-90096-7)

First Trade Edition: February 1984 by Ballantine Books
Mass Market Edition: February 1986 by Ballantine Books
Second Edition: November 2013 by Bocage Books

Cover Design by Steve McAfee

10 9 8 7 6 5 4 3 2

Bocage Books

bocagebooks@mindspring.com
www.bocagebooks.com

"Love is of the phoenix kind,
That burns itself with self-made fire;
To breed still new birds in the mind,
From ashes of the old desire."
—Fulke Greville

Chapter 1

March 1935
Atlanta, Georgia

Creag Trent paced anxiously before the library doors in his rustic stucco-and-timber house and gazed out at the sleet—hard, pelting—as it battered the silvery landscape.

He would never get used to Atlanta in March, with its warm spring weather turning and snarling without warning, like a tamed wolf that suddenly remembers its wild heritage.

Already the telephone line was down and the electricity, erratic and flickering, would go soon too, as it had the previous March, paralyzing the city with not so much as a trolley car running.

In the darkness, the sound that he had waited to hear for the past hour finally emerged—the noise of a plane engine overhead. Creag threw open the library doors and rushed onto the terrace. He looked upward, but the icy trees blocked his view. Yet it didn't matter; for he knew it was his pilot, Babcock, buzzing his house, as usual, to let him know he had gotten through. Only an idiot would fly a mail plane in such weather.

Creag listened until the noise disappeared. Then

satisfied that the plane would make it the rest of the way to Candler Field, he brushed the sleet from the shoulders of his brown velvet smoking jacket and turned to go inside.

The sudden movement of white between iced trees in the distance stopped him. Startled to see a figure silhouetted in the dim light, he walked to the end of the terrace, and as quickly as the slippery ice would allow him, Creag worked his way through the dense mat of vines and rhododendrons, toward the low evergreen hedge that separated his property from that of his neighbor.

Who else, besides Babcock, would be foolish enough to venture out in such foul weather? Closer now, Creag paused and watched while the clash of branch brushing against frozen branch provided an eerie wind-chime accompaniment to the nebulous floating form.

It was a woman, dressed in a thin, white nightgown, with one flimsy slipper to protect her feet from the ice. Stephanie Wexford. He recognized her now, even as he had recognized her four nights earlier, running from the terrace after the gunshot that had killed her husband.

Creag stepped forward and his anger at seeing her spilled over into his speech. "What are you doing out in this weather?" he growled, blocking her way.

The sound of his voice, his sudden appearance had no effect upon her. Creag reached out and laid his hand on her arm to stop her. "Steppie."

Her wild brown eyes gazed beyond him to the crab apple trees. "He's lying on the stones. Neal's hurt. I have to go to him," she said, speaking more to herself than to the man beside her.

Creag tightened his hold on her arm. "He's not out here, Steppie."

For the first time, she acknowledged the man beside her. "Let me go to Neal," she protested, attempting to wrench her arm from his grasp.

"Steppie," he repeated, louder this time. "Neal's dead. Dead and buried."

His brutal words produced a small whimper in her throat. "No," she cried, her head moving from side to side in denial.

A tree branch, coated with ice, broke and narrowly missed Creag as it fell to the ground. He swore at the close call and, not wasting any more time trying to reason with her, he lifted her into his arms to carry her back to her house. The family should watch over her better than this, and he would tell them, too.

She fought against the man who had thwarted her, but Creag ignored her. Finally Steppie gave up the struggle and, as if exhausted, she leaned her head against his shoulder while he spanned the distance to the gray French Normandy house.

Rising out of the darkness, with the tip of its round gray turret partially obscured by the sleet, the house had a medieval appearance. Massive stone lions guarded the heavy oak double doors at the entrance. Yet the side door, left ajar, was vulnerable to the elements and to anyone who wished to trespass beyond the terrace.

Creag crossed the threshold and kicked the door closed. Already the red and blue Persian carpet covering the parquet floor was damp from exposure. He walked into the entrance hall and stopped at the foot of the stairs.

"Verbena," he called, and waited. There was no answer.

"Where's your housekeeper?" he asked, gazing down at the dazed Steppie, clad only in the thin nightgown.

She looked at him with blank eyes.

"Belline," he called out impatiently. Again there was no reply.

Finally, an exasperated Creag, searching for someone to whom he could relinquish his burden, began to walk through the downstairs hall. "Is anyone here?" he called out in a loud voice. The deserted house mocked the words he spoke.

Steppie's teeth began to chatter. "So cold," she croaked.

Of course she was cold, with almost nothing on, Creag thought. He stared at her bare feet. She had lost the other slipper, too, he noticed. The sneeze that escaped her lips decided him. He couldn't stand around, waiting for someone who might never come. She could take pneumonia and die if she didn't get warm soon.

The globe light hanging in the entrance hall flickered, and Creag, aware of the buildup of ice on the power lines, hurriedly shifted the weight in his arms and walked up the winding staircase, his shoes leaving a wet imprint upon each carpeted tread.

At the head of the stairs, Creag saw the remnants of a fire through an open bedroom door. He walked into the room and dumped Steppie into the small, chintz-covered chair before the hearth. On the floor lay a crocheted afghan. Creag stooped to pick it up and hastily draped it over Steppie. A hot bath was what she needed to counteract the chill, and so Creag left her, to look for the nearest bathroom.

He found it adjacent to the bedroom, with dark mahogany paneling and mirrors reflecting the gold dolphin fixtures of the tub. His feet sank into the soft white lambswool carpeting, and the odors of lavender and jasmine, permeating the space, hinted of spring, despite the cold, icy winter outside.

Creag reached out, grasped the dolphin handles, and turned on the water. A spray splashed against the white marble sides of the tub and ricocheted back onto his chin. He straightened and quickly brushed the water from his face.

While the tub filled with water, he walked back into the bedroom. Stephanie Wexford hadn't moved. She still sat in the same position in the chair, her wet brown hair plastered to her well-shaped head.

He didn't know why that should make him angry, seeing her like that, appearing so vulnerable, and yet so aloof from everything that was happening.

"Get up," he ordered, his voice rougher than he intended. "Your bath is ready."

She obeyed him, moving from the chair toward the bath, her bare feet making no noise on the floor. He followed her into the mahogany-paneled bath, shut off the water, and tested it with his hand. Not hot enough to burn her skin—he'd made sure of that. He straightened and without bothering to close the door between the bath and the bedroom, he left her, to attend to the dying fire.

Creag removed the fire screen, placed the last two logs into position and, with the black iron poker, he stirred the embers. Kneeling on the hearth beside a large white ceramic cat, he listened for sounds from the bath. An occasional splash indicated that at least she had gotten into the tub.

He had been a fool to buy the house next to Neal Wexford. But from the moment he had met Stephanie, he realized he could purchase no other. It didn't matter that she belonged to another man and wasn't even aware that Creag Trent was alive. He had to be near her, just to watch her whenever he could; for the vision that he had nurtured in his mind for so many years, and had used as a measuring stick for each woman he met, had finally appeared before him. Creag had made an altar of his heart and lifted the unattainable Steppie Wexford above all mortals.

But she had plummeted from her position with a rudeness that shattered his entire being. She was not the angel he had made of her. She evidently had plotted to have her husband murdered. How else could she explain talking with her accomplice in the shadow of the trees a few short moments before she'd sent Neal outside to his death?

Standing up and brushing his hands against each other, Creag left the fire. The Widow Wexford would need a dry nightgown before he put her to bed.

Through one drawer and another he searched until he finally came to the gowns. It was strange that the drawers held only her things. She hadn't wasted much time, Creag thought, his jaw tightening, to remove all reminders of her dead husband. There was no sign of him, except the picture on the table beside the bed.

With a pale pink gown slung over his arm, Creag walked closer to the table. He stared down at the picture of the serious, blond-haired man and at the prescription box beside it. He might have known why Steppie was acting so strangely. They'd given her something to calm her, but the sedative had backfired, producing the opposite effect. Curiously, Creag picked up the box and shook it. It was empty. How many pills had Steppie taken?

His head jerked upward and he listened for some sign of activity from the bath. He was greeted by silence and the odor of lavender and jasmine. His eyes returned to the empty prescription box in his hand. There was no name on it, no indication of the drug it contained. His heart began to beat against his chest in alarm. If she had taken all the pills at once, then she could be in trouble.

Creag dropped the box and the wispy gown on the floor and began to run toward the bath. "Steppie," he shouted. With trembling hands he thrust back the curtain that had been drawn to screen the tub from view.

She was almost completely submerged, her hair no longer plastered to her head, but floating in every direction. Stifling a frantic groan in his throat, Creag plunged his arms into the water to rescue her.

She was limp and the wetness of her body caused Creag's hands to slip. Quickly, he circled her waist with his arms and lifted her out of the water.

He placed her over his knees, like a limp sack of goods. And with a rolling motion he began the painful process of forcing the water from her lungs.

She couldn't have been submerged for long. Not long enough to drown, he kept telling himself. Why, then, wasn't there some sound, some movement from her?

Every shred of anger in him was directed at her, for of all her sins, this coming so close to death herself was the worst. It never occurred to him that she might be dead already.

"Cough," he said, his fierce voice demanding, but she was slow in responding.

Finally, a gurgling sound of water came, and with the sound, Creag renewed his rolling motion, forgetting his awkward position and the strain to his muscles. A great whooping noise filled the room, while the water rushed from her lungs. It was as if she had drunk the whole damned tubful, he thought.

On and on, Creag continued the rolling motion, making her rid herself of the water and any pills not already absorbed by her body. She coughed; she choked. With every movement, she protested his harsh treatment of her. At last, when her lungs were clear, when there was no more water to be forced out, nothing left in her stomach, Steppie looked up at him with accusing eyes.

He clasped her to him, his hoarse voice rasping. "What were you trying to do? Kill yourself, too?"

She weakly shook her head. "No," she whispered.

Averting his eyes, Creag quickly covered her with a towel, but he was loath to give her up. Aware of the softness of her trembling body, he held her in his arms a moment longer, their images fused in the reflecting mirrors.

Later, Creag leaned over the bed where Steppie lay. He looked down at the woman clad in the wispy pink gown. His eyes traveled from her porcelain face to her small hand touching the raglan sleeve of the blue robe he now wore.

"Neal?" she said, hesitantly.

Creag shook his head. "No, I'm Creag. Creag Trent," he added.

He bore no resemblance to the aristocratic Neal Wexford. Creag was earthy, with dark golden hair curling from the dampness. His eyes were the color of burnt sienna, giving the impression that he had seen much of life. The permanent frown line, etched like a V between his eyes, indicated that he had not always liked what he'd seen. Yet his expression, faintly cynical and knowing, was immediately softened by the deep cleft in his chin—a whimsical touch that worked to his advantage in his dealings with other men. Too late, his adversaries realized that he was far more astute than his deceptively benign face showed.

Steppie, still touching the sleeve, moved her finger back and forth over the material and the caress of her hand caused a tightening in Creag's muscles.

The robe. It was the blue robe, of course. He had found it hanging on the other side of the bath, and it belonged to Neal. Probably the one item she had missed when she'd disposed of Neal's clothes. And it was lucky for him that she'd missed it; for his smoking jacket and the rest of his clothes were drenched, not so much from the sleet as from rescuing the woman from drowning.

"Are you feeling better?" Creag questioned, removing her hand from his sleeve and placing it on the coverlet of the bed.

"Yes," Steppie replied.

He felt the power of her questioning brown eyes, luminous and liquid, great pools of darkness drawing him to her—enchantment that threatened to make him forget his anger, his disillusionment. At that moment he wanted to hold her in his arms as he had dreamed of doing ever since he met her. But then his anger took precedence over his desire. Abruptly, he moved from the bedside. "I'm going downstairs for more wood," he announced tersely, with a wave of his hand toward the empty log holder by the hearth. She made no comment as Creag left the room.

He hurried downstairs to the back porch where a supply of hickory logs, placed by Wash, the Wexford gardener and yardman, lay neatly stacked in a corner. The wind swept the porch while outside, the ground, frozen solid, was a mirror—hard, reflective, treacherous. But at least the sleet was no longer coming down. Loading the logs in his arms, Creag wound his way through the kitchen and up the stairs.

"The sleet has stopped—for a while, at least," he commented, aiming his voice in the general direction where Stephanie Wexford lay.

Creag walked to the hearth, unloaded the logs, and added one to the diminishing fire. But before he had time to set the fire screen in place again, he saw a small, bare foot on the hearth beside him.

"You shouldn't be out of bed," he growled, standing up immediately The scolding words stuck in his throat.

In the saffron glow of the fire, he stared openly at her, seeing the slender legs, the soft dark mound of hair, the firm, round breasts pushing the flimsy material of the gown outward. Nothing in her appearance proclaimed the disastrous accident of the previous hour. She stood, an open invitation in her seductive gown, her wanton eyes begging for love.

He had heard how recently bereaved women reached out to the first willing man for comfort. If love was what she wanted, then he was more than willing.

Creag moved, suddenly enveloping her in his strong arms and holding her desperately against him. He leaned down to cover her mouth with his own, not gently, but in a harsh, demanding manner, holding all the bitterness of love denied by propriety, by marriage vows, and his reverence for a woman beyond his reach.

Stephanie Wexford was no longer an enshrined image, but tarnished; a widow freed from marriage by her own hand. She was no longer beyond his reach, but in his arms. "Stephanie," he whispered, and then pressed his lips against hers, gentler this time, his anger losing itself in the softness of her response.

He lifted her and placed her on the bed, where he lay beside her, only the fleece blue material of the robe and the flimsy pink nightgown separating them.

Cut off from the outside world, the French Normandy house with its steep slate roof rose into the mist, with a thicket of ice blocking and protecting it from view. And inside the bedroom at the head of the stairs, Creag Trent made love to Stephanie, the woman who had fallen so abruptly from her position of honor.

The lights went out once and for all, leaving the room bathed dimly in the hearthlight—an orange glow, with an underglaze of blue, where no air could penetrate the flame's innermost citadel.

The robe fell to the floor. The gown was removed by impatient hands. Now flesh against flesh, the two became one—silken heat and desire clothing them, as no woven garment was ever capable of doing.

But something was wrong. The woman, wrapped in the closeness of his arms, bringing him to the edge of ecstasy and beyond, had been wife to no man for a long time. The awful truth rose to his consciousness too late— far too late for him to make amends. Down, down, beyond reason, Creag went, fighting the tight, almost impenetrable defense of a body long denied the ways of love.

"Steppie," he moaned, mingling his breath with hers, feeling his passion roar and then subside, to be replaced by a sense of inordinate sadness.

The enormity of his deed overwhelmed him. He was

in a place he had no right to be; with the widow of a man who had been buried less than two days. Creag moved, attempting to break the embrace. But Steppie, sensing his withdrawal, tightened her arms about him and refused to give up the closeness of their bodies.

Creag braced himself to withstand the lips that kissed him on the brow and moved to the cleft of his chin. Steppie's fingers ran through the still damp, golden curls and lingered at the nape of his neck.

Unable to bear the intimacy any longer, he pushed her from him and leaned over to retrieve the blue robe that had been discarded in a heap by the bed. He put it on, tied the tasseled rope around his waist, and escaped to the window, where he stood, breathing hard and gazing out into the vast darkness. He waited for the recriminations that were sure to follow.

The silence built, but the censure he expected to hear did not materialize. Creag straightened his shoulders and took a step closer. "Steppie," he said. "I'm sorry."

She didn't answer, and Creag, staring down at her with the soft shadows on her face, saw that her eyes were closed. He frowned, and the V-shaped line between his eyes deepened. Could she have gone to sleep as quickly as that—casually dismissing what had happened between them? Perhaps. On the other hand, what if the pills had worked their insidious damage before he'd gotten to her? What if she were lapsing into a coma? How could he tell? With the telephone line down, he couldn't even call a doctor for advice.

Damn! Should he try to wake her and pour some coffee into her? Creag tried to recall what old Doc Massey had told him about Babcock. "Pinch him or pull his hair, Trent. See if he moves. If he does, then you can bet he's not in a coma."

Of course, Babcock's trouble had been alcohol, not pills, but they probably had the same effect on the body. Creag placed his hand on Steppie's arm and squeezed it gently. She stirred and mumbled something unintelligible before turning on her side. So she was merely asleep. Creag felt relief. But the knowledge that she had not been affected by his lovemaking nearly so much as he rankled him.

Feeling compelled, nevertheless, to watch over her the rest of the night, Creag Trent moved from the bedside to the chair in front of the fire. He stayed awake for a long time, while Stephanie slept quietly a short distance from him.

At intervals during the night, he placed more logs on the fire. At first light, Creag dressed in his own clothes, now dry. Casting one last glance at the sleeping Steppie, he left the bedroom and slipped out the side door to his own house.

Chapter 2

Steppie awoke slowly, with a sense that something was wrong—terribly wrong. Her mouth was lined with cotton; every bone in her body ached.

She reached over to turn on the bedside lamp, but there was no electricity. What time was it? What day? Adjusting her eyes to the dimness of the room, Steppie peered at the clock on the mantel. Twenty minutes past ten. So it was morning. Thursday morning.

Melting ice, breaking loose from the trees, fell on the roof with a clattering noise. Steppie climbed out of bed and walked to the window, where she pushed aside the drapery and rubbed a clear spot on the glass so she could see out. Moving her left hand brought pain, and she stared at her wrist, which showed the beginning sign of a bruise. She didn't remember injuring herself. In fact, she remembered little after swallowing the pills the night before, to blur the nightmare and the loneliness when she found herself stranded, with Verbena gone and Kathryn, her friend, unable to reach the house because of the insidious ice storm.

Steppie, widening the circle on the windowpane with her other hand, studied the trees bent over with ice. On the ground lay large limbs that had already broken under the weight. She shivered at the coldness and turned toward the hearth, to rebuild the fire that had dwindled to ashes sometime during the night.

The blue robe lay across the chair beside the hearth. A startled Steppie stopped and touched it. "Neal?" Her voice quivered as she said his name aloud, for at once the room shouted of his presence, as if he had been sitting in the chair, warming himself and watching her. But that was impossible. Neal was dead. He was buried in the family mausoleum at Oakland Cemetery. That had been two—no, three days ago.

The desperate, haunted feeling began all over again, the dreadful emptiness with nothing to assuage her grief. Distraught, she walked to the dressing table and picked up the mother-of-pearl hairbrush that her husband had given her in Paris. So long ago...before the gradual estrangement that had lengthened like a shadow between them.

All the wasted years. But it had not been Neal's fault. It had been the war and his head injury—and the things he couldn't cope with except by an unalterable sense of right and truth, regardless of how his words affected others. For Neal, there was no space for compromise, for softening the blow, when he decided to speak.

At first, it hadn't mattered. He was a hero and the family treated him as such. Cousin Axel, giving him a job at the bank, had known that he might never be well again. But in providing a place for him to go each day, Axel St. John had given her husband self-respect, and Steppie was grateful to her influential cousin for that.

But then, things had gradually gotten worse. How many times had Steppie been forced to smooth ruffled feelings that threatened to tear the family apart. Only with their daughter, Belline, had Neal remained the same, but finally, that relationship had come under his scrutiny, on the same night that he was murdered.

"No, Neal. Please don't tell Belline. We promised we'd never tell."

"She's fifteen, Stephanie. Old enough to know."

Neal's face showed the stubborn resolve that was so familiar to Steppie. With his action, her feelings as a mother superceded her need to placate her husband.

"I won't have it, Neal. You've done enough to Belline already."

Surprised at Steppie's accusation, Neal countered, "What are you talking about? Haven't I treated her the same as if she were my own flesh and blood?"

"That's just the problem. Ever since she was a baby, you've filled her with such pride in being a Wexford. Can't you realize the terrible blow for her to be told now, without warning, that she's really not a Wexford , after all, but a foundling? I beg of you, Neal. Don't destroy her."

Neal shook his head. "She needs to know the truth."

Steppie's eyes mirrored her bitterness. "Just as Daniel needed to know the truth about Christmas when he was four? No, Neal. I won't let you devastate Belline. Especially now."

"You can't stop me from telling her, Stephanie."

Neal deliberately turned his back to Steppie and walked toward the window. In the silence, Steppie struggled to hold back the tears. What was she going to do—what *could* she do—to stop Neal?

While Steppie's thoughts were on Belline, Neal, peering out the window, narrowed his gaze. His face turned white and he abruptly whirled toward Steppie. "Who was that?" Neal demanded. His stubbornness had vanished.

Alert to the sudden change in his voice, Steppie looked at him. And she knew that the conversation about Belline had been forgotten.

"Who was that?" Neal demanded again.

"Where?"

"Out there—on the terrace."

Steppie looked toward the window and sighed. "The gardener was here a few minutes ago," she replied in the same soothing tone that she always used to calm Neal's fears.

But Neal, choosing not to be calmed, walked to the desk and unlocked the lower drawer. He took the German Luger pistol from its hiding place and, like a sleepwalker, began to move toward the door.

"Where are you going?"

"To see who's out there."

Steppie followed him. "The war's over, Neal. You don't have any enemies. Give me the gun, please."

Steppie held out her hand, but Neal, pushing her aside, thrust open the door and stumbled onto the terrace.

Steppie hurried back to the chair for the beige sweater draped over the cushion. It was then she heard the muffled shot. She grabbed her sweater and dashed toward the open terrace door. What if Neal should shoot Wash, the gardener? Or injure himself? She had to stop him.

Slowing so that he would not be alarmed, Steppie strolled toward the end of the faintly lit terrace where Neal stood, his gun raised toward the rhododendron bushes in the distance. Without thinking of the danger to herself, Steppie confronted her husband.

"Give me the gun, Neal." Quietly insistent, she stood in front of him until he finally obeyed her and laid the gun in her hands. With a strangling, gutteral noise, the tall, severe, blond-headed man slowly crumpled at her feet.

"Neal," she screamed. The only answer came from the wind sweeping a path over the terraced garden.

She would never be able to erase the horror—red blood in the cold, winter moonlight, with its beams casting a glow on the newly swollen buds of the crab apple trees, the first sign that winter was dying. And on the stones lay her husband, who would never again see the coming of spring and the blossoming of the trees he had nurtured.

Steppie shuddered at the memory, so etched in her brain—that of the German Luger in her hands, her husband's blood on her sweater and dress, and Belline's reaction to the dreadful sight.

"Murderer! You killed my father. I'll never forgive you. Never!"

"Belline, it was an accident. A terrible accident."

Quickly, Steppie laid the hairbrush in place on the dressing table. She had to see to the fire before she caught cold.

The sound of knocking downstairs, barely perceptible at first, gradually grew louder. Had Verbena gotten through the storm, after all? Steppie, unable to find her own robe immediately, grabbed the one in the chair and rushed down the stairs. "I'm coming, Verbena," she called.

She opened the side door, but instead of the housekeeper, her neighbor Creag Trent stood before her.

"Yes?"

For a moment, Creag said nothing but continued to stare at Steppie. Finally, with his emotions in check, his eyes showing no sign of recognizing the robe, Creag said, "I wanted to make certain that you were all right this morning."

The cold air pushed through the open door and Steppie moved back quickly. "I'm...fine, thank you," she replied, self-consciously tightening the tasseled rope.

He remained standing before her, making no move to leave. Puzzled at his lingering, she asked, "Did you want something else, Mr. Trent?"

Her innocent brown eyes looked through him, and her formality struck him like a blow in the face. With a sharp intake of breath, Creag thundered, "No. Nothing else, thank you. Good morning!" He abruptly turned his back to her and began the treacherous return to his own house.

Faust, the gray Persian cat, brushed against Steppie's legs and streaked past her, making a run for an unsuspecting bird near the steps. While she waited for the cat to come back inside, Steppie held the door ajar and watched until Creag Trent disappeared.

* * *

In a red-brick Georgian house on Peachtree Road, Belline Wexford sat at the breakfast table with her cousins, Rennie and Axel St. John, and their eighteen-year-old son, Ben Mark. Her long red hair was pulled back from her narrow face, and her tall, slender fifteen-year-old figure was hidden by the heavy woolen lavender sweater that she'd put on to combat the cold.

Here, in the St. John house, with Axel as her legal guardian, she would be safe until summer. They could hardly do anything but invite her to stay the rest of the school year, especially since she had threatened to run away rather than remain in the house with her mother. And if her brother Daniel didn't come home from Europe by summer, she would think of something else to keep from going back then.

Belline stared at Axel, whose massive bald head was set atop a short, stout body. At that moment his bushy eyebrows expressed his displeasure at Ben Mark's elbows on the table.

Unconcerned, Ben Mark lifted one elbow, picked at a loose thread on his sweater, and then replaced his arm in the same spot on the table. Belline, amused at the unspoken challenge between father and son, watched displeasure grow and sweep over Axel's face and finally settle in a cloud of red on his cheeks.

"Just look at the trees, Axel," a flustered Rennie, gauging the extent of her husband's anger, said in an attempt to divert him. She pointed to the frozen spires outside the breakfast room window. "Aren't they beautiful?"

"I don't see anything beautiful about them," he replied grumpily, taking a cursory look at the landscape. "Damned dangerous with all that ice. One could fall on the house at any minute."

"Axel, please watch your language in front of the children," the plump Rennie chastened, gazing in Belline's direction.

"How long do you think the electric power will be off?" Belline broke in, joining in the conspiracy to take Axel's mind from Ben Mark.

He blinked at her sudden interest in continuing the discussion of the storm. Ponderous and deliberate, he replied, "Depends on the damage and how long it takes for the ice to melt."

"I hope it takes at least another day, so we won't have to go to school until Monday," Ben Mark offered.

Axel frowned and started to say something, but at the clearing of Rennie's throat, he changed his mind. Instead, he pushed himself from the table. "I'll be in the library," he announced before stalking from the breakfast room.

"And I think I'll call Steppie and see how it is on the other side of town," Rennie said, getting up also.

"The telephone lines are down, Mama. Don't you remember?" Ben Mark reminded her.

Rennie put her hand to her forehead. "I forgot," she said, sitting down again in the white Chippendale chair that faced the window, and toying with her half-filled teacup. "Ben Mark, why don't you show Belline your new collection of arrowheads?"

"Yes. Come on, Ben Mark," Belline said. And without offering to help with the dishes, she excused herself from the table and left the room with her cousin.

"You really want to see the arrowheads?" Ben Mark asked, grinning at Belline.

"No. I just wanted to get away from the table," Belline answered candidly. "I *would* like to hear your new records, though." As soon as the words were out, she made a face. "But the power's off. I'm as bad as Cousin Rennie."

"We can go up to the recreation room anyway," Ben Mark suggested.

They walked up two flights of stairs and as they climbed beyond the second level, the steps narrowed into a steep, twisting stairway that finally ended in a third-story alcove. A green suede-covered pool table stood solidly in the space, with a faint outline of a dozen wooden cue sticks on the wall.

Belline, walking ahead, ignored the game table and proceeded into the massive recreation room on the right. Meager sunlight fanned itself from the overhead skylight, and spread frugally in short, stiff rays, touching the squares of parquet flooring directly beneath the domed glass.

The hint of a smile touched Belline's lips as she saw the small raised stage at the end. With the tapping of her shoes reverberating in the emptiness of the large room, she quickly mounted the three steps and turned to face Ben Mark, who stood at the threshold with a cue stick in his hand.

"Do you remember, Ben Mark," she called out, "the Christmas program we gave when I was ten?"

Ben Mark walked halfway in the room. "How could I forget?" he said with a short laugh. "I was black and blue for days after that. You really went overboard, hitting me with the stick."

"Well, after all, you *were* the villain of the piece." Belline smiled in remembrance. "You were so short and fat then, and you had such straight black hair. I thought you were going to grow up to look just like Cousin Axel. But you really have changed, you know. You're quite handsome now."

Ben Mark grimaced. "And you were all arms, legs, and teeth. I can see you now, with those red pigtails and freckles."

"I didn't have fresckles," she denied, stepping down from the stage and heading toward him. "I've never had freckles in my life. You're making that up."

He laughed and held the cue stick defensively, as if to ward off her blow.

A thunderous noise stopped their horseplay. "What was that?" Belline asked, frowning.

"Sounded like one of the trees falling," Ben Mark said.

They both rushed to the dormer window to peer out at the hard concrete courtyard below. The broken top of a pine tree lay on the ground, with splinters of ice resembling shattered glass in all directions.

"At least it didn't fall on the house," Belline commented.

"My father must be dreadfully disappointed," Ben Mark replied, and waited for Belline to laugh.

Instead, the red-haired Belline shivered and a tear suddenly appeared on her cheek, as she stared at the dreary landscape. "*My* father's dead."

The quivering voice, the sudden sobriety, made Ben Mark uncomfortable. It was hard enough getting through the funeral. He wanted no more sad, dull times, especially on this day that had miraculously turned into a holiday because of the weather. He didn't relish the discipline at the military school that he attended at the edge of town. And any chance he had to stay out of school he heartily welcomed.

"Don't think about it, Belline," he urged.

"How can I help it?" she answered, her wounded blue-green eyes staring at him. "He's dead and it's all my mother's fault."

"Your father was killed by a burglar," Ben Mark countered, "not your mother."

"*She* had the gun in her hands; his blood was all over her dress."

Ben Mark made an impatient noise. "I know you

don't get along with your mother right now, but it's sort of tacky to accuse her of murder."

"Well, *somebody* killed him."

"The burglar," Ben Mark reiterated.

Belline shook her head. "I don't believe there was ever a burglar in the garden. It was only after Cousin Axel and Julian got there that they locked the pistol back into the desk and concocted that story," Belline argued. "When I first saw my mother out on the terrace, she actually confessed that it was an accident. She knew that she'd killed him."

"Uncle Julian said that the German Luger hadn't been fired."

"He's a doctor, not a gun expert. He only said that to protect her. My parents were having a terrible argument that night. I could hear it all the way upstairs. And by the time I got downstairs, my father was dead and my mother had the gun in her hands."

"All right, Belline," Ben Mark said irritably. "Let's suppose that Steppie did kill him. Would you be happy if your own mother went to jail?"

"She needs to be punished."

"Really, Belline, I would have thought—"

"I don't want to talk about it anymore. I'm cold, and I want to go downstairs to the fire."

Chapter 3

The crab apple trees, unhurt by the ice, blossomed like clouds of chiffon, sprinkling their delicate pink petals on the stepping stones next to the terrace, and then covered their bare branches with puritan green leaves, as if repentant of the vulgar, riotous display of color.

One day followed another; the sun rose and set, and Steppie, with Verbena, her housekeeper, measured the passing of weeks by the letters that Daniel sent from Paris.

"I worry about you, Steppie," he wrote, "staying alone in the house so much of the time. I still think you should have let me come home, even though I wouldn't have gotten there in time for Father's funeral."

Steppie held the letter in her hands as she reread it. At nineteen, he sounded so mature, so serious with his advice to her. She continued reading.

"As for Belline, the best thing you can do at the moment is absolutely nothing. She'll eventually come home, but only when she's ready."

How well Daniel knew Belline. A great feeling of love rose in Steppie's breast for this adopted son whom she and Neal had rescued from the battlefields of Europe and brought home to Atlanta after the war.

It hadn't been easy for Daniel, growing up under the stigma of uncertain parentage. Although he had been given the Wexford name, people were cruel with their whisperings. Daniel was at the age when he needed a sense of who he was, a pride in the land of his birth. And the old Vicomtesse d'Arcy, family friend through the years, was the very one who could implant this in him. Yes, it was good for Daniel to be in France to study and to come to terms with his heritage.

In a way, he was luckier than Belline. Her past had been sworn to secrecy, on the day of her birth, by all concerned—natural mother, physician, Steppie, and Neal. Only Neal had determined to break the covenant.

Steppie sighed and folded Daniel's letter back into the envelope. It was already dark and time to go. Automatically, Steppie walked to the bedroom mirror and concentrated on her appearance. Dark brown eyes held no reflection of light; an unrecognizable stranger stared back at her, impersonally recording the ebony brown hair encircling a porcelain white face.

She had never looked her age. At thirty-eight, Steppie could easily have passed for a woman in her twenties. That was, until six weeks ago. Now she was ageless—like a Kabuki mask placed purposely between the actor and the audience. A black dress, relieved only by the single strand of matched pearls, hung loosely on her small frame.

Steppie turned from the mirror and walked to the closet. She reached up to the shelf, took down a box that held the crocheted shawl that Daniel had sent her for Christmas. Hurriedly, she shook it out, placed it around her shoulders, and then walked downstairs to wait for Axel's chauffeur to come for her. Stationing herself by the paneled glass at the side door, she watched for the car coming up her driveway.

In a few minutes she saw the headlights shining through the cedars along the drive. She didn't give the chauffeur time to get out and knock. Instead, Steppie walked onto the graveled entryway and proceeded toward the car as it stopped.

"Good evening, String," she said when he hopped out

of the car to hold the door for her.

"Good evenin', Miz Wexford," he replied, waiting for her to seat herself before closing the car door.

Steppie smiled at his uncanny resemblance to her gardener, Wash. Identical twins they were—big, brown men with gentle black eyes—named for presidents of the United States. Yet, no one ever called them by those illustrious names—George Washington and Theodore Roosevelt Turner. They had been Wash and String for as long as she could remember.

Steppie sat back, drew the shawl around her, and closed her eyes. She tried to compose her thoughts, to slow the anxious beating of her heart. That night wouldn't be easy for her, seeing Belline for the first time since Neal's funeral, with the entire family present.

The long black limousine traveled from Ponce de Leon Avenue to Peachtree Street, and Steppie, opening her eyes, took no notice of the traffic on the street or the signs proclaiming the next religious revival. Her mind was on Belline.

The car turned north on Peachtree, and for the next two miles, only one car passed them, impatiently honking its horn. As the battered yellow car went by, String muttered to himself. "Po' white trash, jus' tryin' to show off." Unflustered, he kept up his slow, steady pace until he came to a stop in the driveway of the familiar Georgian red-brick house, its welcoming lights ablaze across the front.

The cousins were all there when Steppie arrived—Axel and Rennie, Julian and his wife Carey, and the lawyer, Reed, who'd come alone as usual because his invalid wife never went anywhere with him.

"Hello, Steppie," Carey said, the first to greet her, with a kiss on her cheek. "You're looking well," she lied.

"Thank you, Carey. So are you," Steppie responded, with her eyes searching for some sign of Belline.

As if she could read her thoughts, Carey said, "If

you're looking for Belline, she and Martha and Ben Mark are still up in the recreation room. They're going to put on one of their famous plays for us after dinner." A knowing smile flitted across her face and then was gone.

Rennie, coming into the parlor with a tray of nuts, saw the look and frowned. She had never cared for Carey, her sister-in-law, who always delighted in making other people uncomfortable. Rennie, walking across the room to Steppie, smiled and said, "Let me take your wrap, Steppie, while I get something for you to drink. Would you like a tomato juice?"

"She might prefer a gin and tonic, instead," Axel pointed out to Rennie as he joined them both.

"Now you know Steppie doesn't care for your strong liquor, Axel," Rennie replied.

"A tomato juice will be fine," Steppie affirmed quickly to avoid any further argument. And to Axel, she said, "I think I'll keep my shawl. I'm still a little cool."

Assessing the thin figure hidden under the wrap, Axel admonished, "You'd do well to drink some gin to warm you up. Put a little weight on you, too."

"Not everybody likes to be plump," Carey said, snidely, glancing in Rennie's direction as she walked from the room. "Some of us like to keep our figures. Right, Steppie?"

Axel, liking Carey even less than his wife did, immediately defended, "If you're talking about Rennie, she's exactly the right size, as far as I'm concerned."

Rennie, hearing the exchange from the doorway, quickly glanced over her shoulder toward her husband. She wore a pleased expression. Carey shrugged and sat down near Reed, her other brother-in-law.

Dr. Julian St. John, the youngest of the three brothers, observed with a clinical eye the members of his family. Carey, his wife, had better watch her step. Crossing swords with Axel or Reed was not wise. One or the other could annihilate her at anytime he chose to do so, in either words or actions.

Rennie returned with the glass for Steppie and left again. Axel relaxed in the rust-colored high-backed chair, and as the conversation flowed on a shallow surface, denying the seriousness of family events, Julian's eyes narrowed as he assessed Neal's widow. She was far too thin—almost as thin as Carey. Her eyes held a solemn look, belying the slight smile about her lips as she lifted the priceless crystal goblet to her mouth. Yes, there was something different about Stephanie tonight, something about the eyes, beyond their look of gravity.

Caught by Steppie's sudden turning toward him, Julian quickly asked, "How is your garden, Stephanie?"

She hesitated, and then becoming an accomplice to his idle chatter, she replied, "The crab apple trees have finished shedding, but the azaleas that Wash planted last year on the hill above the terrace are in full bloom. You must come and see them, Julian. Carey, too," she added.

"The food will be ready in a few minutes," Rennie announced, coming back into the room. "Axel, you'd better go upstairs and tell the children everyone's here."

Lumbering from the chair, Axel did his wife's bidding. And Steppie, listening for the sound of returning footsteps, found it hard to make small talk.

"Have you seen your handsome neighbor lately?" Carey asked, looking at Steppie.

"You mean Mr. Trent?"

"Yes. I would hardly call old Mrs. Barber handsome," Carey replied with amusement in her voice.

Steppie chose to ignore the last comment. "Not since the ice storm."

"Here're the young people now," Axel said, returning with them to the living room.

With her back to the door, Steppie was at a disadvantage. Hungry for the sight of her fifteen-year-old red-headed daughter, Steppie turned and half-rose from her chair. "Hello, Belline," she said. Something in

Belline's face caused her to sink back in her chair.

Silence permeated the room, and it seemed as if a moving picture camera had suddenly stopped on one frame, freezing the action. Finally, a girlish voice answered, "Hello, Mother." Belline immediately brushed past Steppie and headed toward Carey.

"I like your dress, Carey," she said. "Is it a Paris original?"

"Yes. Leonard brought it back from New York for me."

Julian winced inwardly when he heard the name of the man who dressed half of Atlanta. He would receive a substantial bill for the dress, he was sure. In his mind, Julian saw the bedroom that Carey had converted into a giant closet, with racks for her dresses and coats, cupboards for her dozens of shoes. She was insatiable in her acquisition of goods to go on her back.

Carey, not concerned for her husband's thoughts, patted a place beside her on the sofa for Belline to join her.

At her daughter's preference for Carey, Steppie quickly disguised the hurt. Why should she expect Belline to behave any differently from the past weeks?

Ben Mark paused before Steppie's chair. "Hello, cousin," he said and moved farther into the room with fourteen-year-old Martha at his side.

A replica of her mother, Martha had Carey's curly brown hair, the small almost oriental eyes that contrasted with the rather snub nose, giving the appearance of a certain pedigreed canine. Martha lifted her hand in greeting and walked toward the window seat with Ben Mark.

The black man who had served as chauffeur now stood at the living room door in his butler's white coat.

"Dinner is served," he announced in his deep bass voice.

"Thank you, String," Rennie said. She turned to Reed.

"Will you take Steppie into the dining room?" she asked, leaving Axel to squire Carey. Rennie latched onto Julian's arm. "The three children want to eat on the sun porch," she said, "so they can get ready for their performance after dinner."

From Rennie's words, Steppie realized that Belline had effectively separated them for the entire evening. They would not have a single moment together, for when the play was over, it would be time for Steppie to go home. Denying her disappointment and pretending that nothing was amiss, Steppie continued walking into the dining room with Reed.

String, serving the meal, moved from chair to chair with the silver tray piled high with roast beef, slices of turkey, and fresh vegetables surrounding the meat.

The food held no appeal for Steppie. She ate one bite, laid down her fork, and took a sip of water from the sterling silver goblet. The metallic taste further discouraged her appetite.

Axel, brushing a bread crumb from his mouth with a large white monogrammed linen napkin, took notice of Steppie's lack of enthusiasm for her food. "Told you, you should have had a gin and tonic to improve your appetite," he admonished. "Eat up, Steppie." He took his own advice and speared another piece of roast beef.

Steppie smiled at Axel and once again reclaimed her fork. The conversation went on about her, ultimately coming to the topic that had occupied most Americans ever since the tragic March day when the Lindbergh baby had been kidnapped. After two years, a suspect had been caught, brought to trial and convicted, but still the case wasn't over.

"I don't understand why the New Jersey governor is protecting that murderer," Axel complained. "If the trial had been in Georgia, old Eugene would have pulled the juice himself."

"Governor Hoffman isn't absolutely certain that they

have the right man," Reed argued. "It was only circumstantial evidence that—"

"Hell, Reed, how much more evidence do you need?" Axel interrupted. "Hauptmann had the ransom money. They even matched the piece of wood from the ladder he used to the missing piece of wood in his attic."

"No one saw him do it, though," Julian intervened, seeing Axel's face turn red at Reed's argument. "It wasn't like the man who kidnapped you last year, Axel. You were able to identify him."

"Damned right I did," Axel muttered.

"Axel, please watch your language," Rennie begged.

"Well, I'm still mad about it," Axel said in a chastened voice. "Putting you through all that worry—to get the ransom money. Not knowing whether I was dead or alive. And all the time I was tied to that da—" He stopped, looked sheepishly at Rennie. "Tied to that tree," he finished.

"That was a strange epidemic, those running-board kidnappings," Reed commented. "You weren't the only one to get caught at a red light downtown and forced to drive to a lonely road. At least, *you* didn't have to walk back, like Ottley."

"But Axel got a terrible case of poison ivy," Rennie said.

"Why does crime seem to get much worse during a depression, Reed?" Steppie asked.

"As many reasons as there are crimes, Stephanie. Greed. Lack of food. A man's moral sense seems to disintegrate when his pocket is empty."

"That doesn't explain why Neal—" Carey began, but Julian, frowning at his wife, broke in.

"You notice that since Al Capone has left the Federal Pen, there's less crime in Atlanta. Probably just a coincidence, though."

Looking from Carey to Steppie, Rennie asked, "Did either one of you ever see *Mrs.* Capone?"

"Once," Steppie replied, "when I was shopping at Rich's. She had her daughter with her. And I felt sorry for them both."

"Sorry? For a gangster's family?" an incredulous Carey asked.

"It must have been hard on them, living at the Briarcliff for two whole years, with only his henchmen for company," Rennie admitted. "Just think of the disgrace. I…I don't think I could live with that."

"What would you do, Rennie—if, say, *I* were put in jail?"

"Oh, Axel, you haven't done anything… *criminal,* have you?" Rennie's distressed voice inquired.

Axel laughed heartily. "I was merely teasing you, dear. Since you and Steppie seemed to be wasting all that concern on such an unworthy family."

"My sentiments, exactly," Carey joined in, looking down her nose at her sister-in-law.

Ben Mark, Belline, and Martha chose that moment to traipse through the dining room on their way upstairs. "We're going to set up the play now," Belline said. "Come as soon as you can."

"After we've finished our dessert, dear," Rennie said, and Steppie, following her daughter with anxious eyes, watched until the three young people had disappeared.

Twenty minutes later, when String had removed the dessert plates and it was time to climb the stairs to the recreation room, Steppie could no longer ignore the way she felt. All she could think of was to get home and lie down. As she rose from the table, she swayed and reached out to steady herself. Carey, seeing her awkward motion, laughed and said, "I do believe Steppie got into the gin and tonic after all."

Steppie forced herself to smile, as if she had merely caught her heel in the carpet. But she lingered behind the others and waited for Rennie. "Do forgive me, Rennie," she said softly, "but I don't think I can stay any longer. Would you mind if String took me home now?"

"Oh, my dear, I'm sorry. Of course he can take you home. Are you not feeling well?"

"I'm extremely...tired," Steppie confessed, refusing to admit how she actually felt.

"I'll take you home, Stephanie." Julian's voice startled her.

She looked at the man who had quietly returned to the dining room. "That's too much trouble, Julian. I'll ride with String."

Julian turned to Rennie. "Let String finish cleaning up. I don't mind taking Stephanie home." Looking at Steppie, he said, "My car's in the driveway." Julian held her arm and guided her out of the dining room. Glancing back toward Rennie, Steppie said, "Give my apologies to the others for leaving so soon. And...thank you for inviting me."

With her solemn blue eyes showing her concern, Rennie nodded. "I hope you're going to feel better, Steppie."

By the time they reached the house on Castlemeade Road and Julian had opened the heavy oak door for Steppie, he said, "I want to see you in my office tomorrow, Stephanie. I'll tell my nurse you're coming in."

Steppie's lips trembled. "I only need a good night's sleep, Julian. That's all that's wrong with me."

Julian shook his head. "Tomorrow, Stephanie," he repeated, no longer the cousin, but the professional, with his eyebrows meeting to give his ascetic face the look of authority that brooked no opposition.

"All right, Julian. Tomorrow."

Chapter 4

A week later, Stephanie sat in Julian's office again.

"Pregnant! That's impossible, Julian." She clutched the arm of the chair and leaned toward the desk where Dr. Julian St. John sat pensively with his hands locked.

"I know it's a shock to you, Stephanie, after all these years. But the tests came back this morning. You're going to have a baby." Julian waited while Steppie absorbed the news.

There had to be some mistake, she thought. The tests had gotten mixed up. Julian was speaking of another patient, not her.

"You're… certain?" she asked, finding her voice again.

"The tests don't lie, Stephanie."

He still waited, as if he had a whole day to spend with her. Yet Steppie knew he had a roomful of patients waiting to see him.

"How soon?" she inquired. She stared at the diplomas on the wall while she listened for his reply.

"Probably sometime the first of December. It couldn't have been more than a few days before Neal's death," he said, "when you became pregnant."

Groping for something to say—anything at all—she asked, "There's a danger, isn't there, at my age?"

Julian hesitated. "Thirty-eight isn't that old, Stephanie. It would be safer, I'll admit, if it weren't your first pregnancy, but if you're careful and take good care of yourself…"

"I didn't mean danger to *me,* Julian. I meant to the baby."

He picked up the metal paperweight on his desk and examined it before replying. "I keep forgetting that you've had nurse's training," he said. "Yes, Stephanie, there's always a greater risk that a woman over thirty-five might deliver a Mongoloid child."

Suddenly he smiled reassuringly. "But we won't worry about that. There've been none in either your family or Neal's family. So we can assume that you'll have a healthy baby." He added, "It's a pity, though, that Neal couldn't have lived long enough to see his own child."

Neal's child. Julian didn't know that she and Neal had long ceased to be man and wife.

Steppie, rising from her chair, went through the motions of leaving Julian's office and walking into the waiting room where Kathryn Mansour, her best friend, sat reading a back issue of *Woman's Home Companion.*

"What's the matter, Steppie?" Kathryn asked, putting down the magazine when she saw the expression on Steppie's face. "Bad news?"

"No. I'm…fine. Let's go home."

Steppie bolted toward the door, with a startled Kathryn grabbing her purse and following. They walked in silence to the elevator, while the arrow above the door pointed downward. As the door opened on the fifth floor, Steppie nodded to the operator and, joining the others in the elevator, she and Kathryn rode to the ground floor. They exited through the side door of the building and walked to the covered parking lot where Kathryn's car stood.

Once inside the car, Kathryn broke the silence. "If there's something wrong, Steppie, you can tell me."

Glancing at Kathryn, Steppie saw the small spot of

blue pigment below Kathryn's hairline. "You have paint on your neck," she said.

Kathryn groaned. "As long as it's not on my new dress," she replied. "I'm as bad as Whistler, ruining every new suit."

"What are you working on now?" Steppie asked. From her question Kathryn realized that her friend had no wish to discuss her visit to Julian's office.

"A canvas for old Mr. Epwile. He brought a sepia tone of his dead wife, and wants me to turn it into a life-size portrait. The old goat. He thinks I can make the woman into some ethereal creature, with *that* face to work with. It's impossible. But I need the money," she confessed.

Steppie knew that Kathryn was exaggerating. If there were anyone at all who had no need of extra money, it was Kathryn; her father had left her a sizable trust.

Steppie watched Kathryn as they left the parking lot and pulled onto the street. Her long, slender artist's fingers hugged the steering wheel of the low-slung Astin-Martin.

Kathryn had never married. During her teens and twenties she had been extremely attractive, and if she would pay a little more attention to her grooming, she could be attractive again. Her brown hair, twisted into a granny knot on top of her head, was at odds with the rest of her face—fine-boned, with high cheeks and slanted blue eyes.

Kathryn's fingers tightened on the wheel as she quickly veered to the left to avoid a car jutting too far from a side street. She stayed on Peachtree Street until she reached the familiar intersection with Ponce de Leon. Turning right, she drove several more blocks, past the fine mansions set far back from the street. Finally, the Druid Hills Golf Club emerged through the trees on the left.

"You want to stop for lunch?" Kathryn asked, slowing the car by the club entrance.

"Not really, Kathryn. If you don't mind, I'd rather go home."

Kathryn gathered speed, leaving behind a small group of men with their caddies on the green. She continued down Castlemeade Road, the car hugging the curve of the pavement. The turret of the French Normandy house appeared on the right. Kathryn pulled off the street at the cedared driveway and stopped in the graveled courtyard.

Faust, the large gray cat, was curled up on the side of the courtyard. He stretched and yawned, and brushed against Steppie as she got out of the car. "I can fix us both a sandwich, if you'd like to come in, Kathryn." Steppie tried hard to sound hospitable, but Kathryn declined, sensing that she would rather be alone.

"I'd better go on back to the studio. Take care, Steppie. And I'll see you another time."

"Thank you, Kathryn, for taking me to Julian's."

The woman waved, started the engine of her automobile, and wound down the meandering drive and onto the street again.

The control that Steppie had tried so hard to maintain began to dissolve. As soon as she walked inside the house, she put her head in her hands. Pregnant. It couldn't be true. But while she denied it with her lips, her body gave truth to Julian's diagnosis. Steppie thought her grief had caused her body to react—the moments of early morning nausea, the drowsiness, the vague discomfort and dizziness. She had even attributed the episode at Axel's to her anxiety at seeing Belline.

"A few days before the ice storm," Julian had said. Steppie remembered clearly those last days before Neal died—his determination to tell Belline that she was an adopted child, his dismissing her entreaty not to burden Belline with another problem just at the time she was struggling with so many other problems of growing up and finding herself. No. One thing was certain. Neal was not the father of her unborn child.

The house seemed too dark and so Steppie, fleeing from the walls that threatened to close about her, walked outside to the terrace where the crab apple trees had begun to bear fruit. She shivered despite the warmth of the day. Something about the trees triggered her recollection of the ice storm and the strange dreams that had plagued her the night after Neal's funeral.

Dreams. Had they merely been dreams as she had thought, or were they reality — stark, frightening reality?

Suddenly she remembered the blue robe lying across the chair when she awoke that morning. Steppie twisted her gold wedding band back and forth. Her heart knew with a certainty that she had spent the night in a man's arms. There had been a man's body next to hers, but his face remained elusive — unknown.

The night kept nagging at her, gnawing at her memory, torturing her, revealing nothing. If only she hadn't taken the pills. Poor baby, with no name.

That wasn't true, though. Julian had assumed it was Neal's child. The baby would have Neal's name. Dead, beautiful Neal, resting in the family mausoleum at Oakland Cemetery, while in his wife's womb the seed of another man grew.

Steppie left the terrace and walked inside the house. And with her came Faust, following her to the kitchen for a bowl of milk.

On the same afternoon in downtown Atlanta, Ben Mark stalked out of the Peachtree Trust Bank building and headed for his Stutz Bearcat in the back lot. As usual, his father had not understood his need for more money.

When he was smaller, he had actually enjoyed coming to the bank; having the large, brass-trimmed front door opened for him by the guard disguised as a doorman; all the tellers in their cages speaking to him as he gazed up at the marble columns supporting his father's empire. How many times he had stood in the middle of the marble floor with its circular design resembling a rare Roman coin edged in gold, with its raised figure of the Roman Wolf and Twins. He had hopped on each strange letter surrounding it until he had become dizzy. *Montalcino, ascendi, 1556.*

It inspired trust, his father always said, to have something old and classical in design, to make the bank look as if it had been there forever. Then, the public wouldn't get scared and draw out its money at the first sign of panic.

His father had always prided himself on that — being able to keep the bank open, despite so many others closing their doors permanently.

But the bank's vaults had been closed to Ben Mark that day by his father. "No, I told you yesterday, Ben Mark, that money doesn't grow on trees. You won't get a cent more from me until the first of the month."

"But I owe — "

"That doesn't make any difference. If you've run up debts that you can't pay, you'll have to make your own arrangements."

Mulling over what he could pawn on Decatur Street until his father came through with the money, he almost stumbled over the small figure sitting on the marble bench near the hitching post at the back door. Green eyes stared up at him through a mass of tangled red hair.

"Belline?" he said, startled at her appearance.

"No, I'm Alpharetta," the girl said, pushing her long mop of hair behind her ears and exposing the rest of her face to view.

He laughed. "Alpharetta. That's the name of a *town*, not a girl."

She drew herself up in a defensive gesture. "We're *all* named for towns in our family," she said.

He stared at the uncanny resemblance to his cousin, and his boredom and disgust at his insolvency vanished. "Who are you, really?" he asked. "And what are you doing here?"

Acting as if she thought he didn't believe her, she became indignant.

"I already told you my name. And as to what I'm doin' here, I'm waitin' on my pa who has business with Mr. St. John."

She looked the other way, dismissing him by her action. Just like Belline in her haughty airs, too. He stood, taking in every inch of the girl, assessing her from every angle while she ignored him.

She wore a clean white blouse and a dark skirt, and her skin, exposed to the sun, had a golden glow with the hint of a freckle or two across her turned-up nose.

"And your father? What's his name?" Ben Mark finally demanded.

"That's none of your business," she replied, changing her position and looking toward the Stutz Bearcat a few feet away.

"Let me guess," Ben Mark said aloud. "Your father's name is Tucker Beaumont."

All at once, Alpharetta lifted her head, turning her attention from the car to the tall, black-haired boy standing over her. "How did you know?"

With a twinkle in his eye, he answered, "The same way I know that my father won't be seeing anyone for the next half-hour. I'm Ben Mark St. John," he said, waiting for the name to impress her.

It took only two seconds. "You're Mr. Axel St. John's boy?" she asked.

"Not a boy," he denied. "I'm eighteen."

Alpharetta stood. She was taller than Belline, but just as slender. "I'm sixteen," she offered. She gazed again at the sports car. "Is that yours?" she asked.

"Yes. Would you like to ride in it?"

She hesitated, looking toward the door of the bank building.

"I told you. It will be at least a half-hour. Come on."

Alpharetta followed him to the car and stood back while he opened the door for her; for she didn't want to display her ignorance of the catch. Then she settled herself on the black leather upholstery while Ben Mark walked to the other side. He started the engine and, with a roar, he shot out of the bank parking lot.

Like streamers flapping in the breeze, Alpharetta's long red hair trailed behind her, while the breeze cooled her flushed, excited cheeks. Her brothers, Duluth and Conyer, would never believe her. Surreptitiously, she glanced at the boy. Tall, with dark hair and a slightly spoiled look about his mouth. But handsome.

Alpharetta sighed, shut her eyes, and forgot everything but the feel of the wind in her hair, the roar of the sports car that belonged to Ben Mark St. John, and the fortune-teller's prophecy at the county fair the year before.

Axel, still irritated with his son, took his time in looking over the requests for loans. He wasn't getting any younger, and that was why he rested each afternoon from four to four-thirty. By that time, the bank had closed its doors, the tellers were busy checking their day's transactions, and by five o'clock when he left for home, he was refreshed.

He thought of Rennie, his wife, waiting at home for him. God, how he loved that woman. He loved her small, dainty hands and feet, her little plump loving body, never denying him, even at his age.

He was lucky—far luckier than his brothers—Julian, with that snobbish, stringbean Carey for a wife, with only bones to pat where soft flesh should be, soft flesh like Rennie's. And then Reed, who was even worse off with Anna Clare. The whole family knew what was the matter with her, yet no one spoke aloud of her need for morphine every few hours, the whining and begging when she didn't get it. It was enough to make a man sick, seeing a woman disintegrate before his very eyes. And Anna Clare could live like that for years.

Rennie. Yes, he was mighty lucky to have a woman like Rennie. That was why he'd do anything to make sure she was kept happy, no matter the cost....

The knock at the door startled him. "Mr. St. John," his assistant's voice called from the other side of the door. "Mr. Beaumont is still waiting to see you."

Axel fumed inwardly. What was the man doing at the bank? Hadn't he told him to stay away during business hours? Disguising his anger, he said, "Send him in, Mr. Bussey." He rose from his oversized mahogany desk in the middle of his dark-paneled office to open the door.

Axel stood at the door and waited for the man to appear. Underneath his bushy eyebrows, his eyes narrowed at the sight of the man walking toward him.

"That will be all, Mr. Bussey," Axel said and motioned for Tucker Beaumont to come into his office. He was wearing a suit and looked no different from any other farmer who came to him for a loan. Nevertheless, Axel knew he had to put a stop to his appearances at the bank.

Axel closed the door and glared at the man. "I thought I told you—"

"It's an emergency," the man said, towering over Axel. "The county sheriff smashed the still."

Alarmed at the news, Axel left off his reprimand. "Did anyone get caught?"

"No. Duluth heard them coming and ran."

"How long will it take for you to repair it?"

"Can't. It's smashed for good. Besides, I'll have to move to another place, now that the sheriff's found it."

"How long will it take to set it up somewhere else

and get it running?"

"A week, at least. That is, if we can find another spot right away."

"Damn it, man. That's too long. I promised another shipment by the end of the week."

"Then, we'll have to use the reserve jugs stored at the cemetery," Tucker advised.

"That's too dangerous, with Mrs. Wexford going back and forth to the mausoleum," Axel protested, wondering now if it had been such a good idea to store the contraband liquor in the Wexford family vault. But then, he hadn't reckoned on Steppie's using the old mausoleum for Neal.

"We could go at night," Tucker suggested.

"No. The gates are locked at sundown. It would be too hard to take anything out."

"Then, you'll have to keep her away while we get it out. Unless you come up with a better idea."

Axel remained silent for a moment, pushing his plump fingers together and then pulling them apart in a nervous gesture. Finally he said, "We need to get the jugs. I'll think of something to keep her away. Maybe Rennie could invite her for the afternoon."

Now that he had made up his mind, Axel's thoughts turned to the still. "How much will it take to set up another still?"

"You have to have the land, first," Tucker cautioned. "Then, if you want the same size still— about five hundred dollars."

The information made Axel glum. He was running low on funds. That's why he'd been so hard on Ben Mark. And yet—if he didn't come up with the money and the land within a few minutes, he really would be in trouble.

The bank could give Tucker a loan. But the land. Where could he get land in a hurry, with the necessary creek for draining; the cover with which to disguise the still from the air? The damned revenuers had recently taken to the airways to track down the stills, which made it harder on everybody.

Axel drummed his fingers on his desk while the big, red-haired man, Tucker Beaumont, sat infuriatingly quiet in front of him.

Land. Now where could he get the land? Suddenly, the frown relaxed on Axel's plump face. Of course — the James trust — the land on the other side of Stone Mountain — sufficiently isolated; the owner sufficiently dead, with the heirs sufficiently disinterested. And with the work stopped on the Confederate Memorial at the mountain, no one would be about to stumble onto the property.

Axel smiled and, without bothering to tell Tucker Beaumont his decision, he took a loan application from his desk and began filling it in.

"Here, sign it," Axel said, thrusting the paper in front of the man on the other side of the desk.

"What is it?" Tucker inquired.

"A loan for the five hundred dollars — for your new tractor."

"But—"

"Don't waste time, Beaumont. The bank's about to close. If you want your money—"

"You'll have to pay back half of it, Mr. St. John."

"I know that, man. We're partners, aren't we?"

Reluctantly, Tucker took the pen and began signing his name. In a hurry, Axel rang for Mr. Bussey. And when his assistant entered, Axel said, "Mr. Bussey, I'm letting Mr. Beaumont have five hundred dollars for a tractor. Bring me the cash right away and we'll process the application tomorrow."

"Yes, sir, Mr. St. John."

While they waited for Mr. Bussey to go downstairs for the money, Axel drew a map for Tucker. Ten minutes later, with the cash in his coat pocket, along with the map, Tucker Beaumont walked past the doorman-guard at the back door and hurried out the closed bank building.

"Let's go, girl," he said to Alpharetta, who sat primly on the stone bench by the door.

Hurrying to match her father's long stride, she trotted alongside him for several blocks as they headed for the wagon yard opposite the police station on Decatur Street, where Duluth and Conyer waited by the specially designed farm wagon with its false bottom covered in straw.

Ben Mark was late for dinner. He roared into the St. John driveway, drove through the *porte cochère*, and came to a stop near the kitchen steps at the back. Hopping over the low-slung door of his automobile, he ran into the kitchen of the red-brick house and barely missed bumping into String coming through the butler's pantry. A quick swipe at a white towel hanging on the pantry door took care of washing his hands.

"I'm sorry I'm late," he apologized to his mother as he entered the dining room, slid into his chair, and spread the napkin on his lap. "I got held up."

"You know we have dinner right at six o'clock, Ben Mark," Axel admonished.

Ben Mark flushed. He didn't like to be reprimanded in front of his cousin Belline. "I *said* I'm sorry," he repeated. All at once, Ben Mark looked at the empty place at the table. "Looks like Belline is late, too."

Rennie, glancing first at Axel, said, "I sent Belline home this afternoon."

"To stay?"

"Yes. Her mother isn't well," Rennie replied.

"What's wrong with her?"

Rennie hesitated. "Your father will tell you later."

Ben Mark felt disappointed. He had wanted to see Belline's face when he told her about her look-alike. His disappointment was short-lived, however, for String now stood at his elbow with the platter of fried chicken. Ben Mark took both legs and a thigh.

"Pass the rice, Mama," he said. Axel lifted one bushy eyebrow at him. "Please," Ben Mark added hurriedly, and soon his mind was on nothing else but assuaging his hunger.

Less than an hour before Ben Mark got home, his cousin, Belline Wexford, opened the door to the French Normandy house on Castlemeade Road and dragged her suitcase inside. Steppie, hearing the commotion, walked into the hallway. She saw her red-haired daughter and, thinking that she had come home voluntarily, she smiled. "Welcome home, Belline."

The girl raised her defiant blue-green eyes and glared at Steppie. "Cousin Rennie threw me out," she complained. "She said I *had* to come home."

Belline bent down, picked up the suitcase and, bumping it on each stair tread, she made her way upstairs to the bedroom at the opposite end of the house. Steppie, standing below and watching Belline, said nothing. At least her daughter had not run away. That was a start.

Chapter 5

Creag Trent stopped his car at the end of the deserted road and for a long while he sat, looking up at the mountain of granite in front of him.

The monolith rose relentlessly toward the sky, like some prehistoric beast spewed from the smoking cauldrons of Hell. Stretching its great granite hump as far as the eye could measure, the monolith had taken root, clothed itself with a thin, patchy garment of vegetation, and waited over the centuries for human hands to find a use for it, beyond the pagan altars of the Indians.

Suddenly, Creag felt a need to stand on the rock ledges at the mountain's base, to handle the stones — and to remember. For it was here that he had first seen Stephanie Wexford, and it was here that his entire life had changed. Eleven years ago — when he was merely Creag, the stonecutter, working for the sculptor, John Gutzon de la Mothe Borglum.

Creag closed the car door and began to wend his way through the tall, coarse clumps of grass and the outcroppings of granite that served as a snare to the trespasser's boot.

Closer now he came, shading his eyes from the brilliant rays of the sun; dismissing the unfinished carving on the scarp of the mountain, and searching for traces of the earlier sculpture, magnificent in design;

desecrated by the inferior work beneath it.

The years shed themselves like the copperhead's brown, mottled skin hidden under the rock where Creag stood. And the lonely cry of the bobwhite was heard, not by Creag Trent, millionaire and entrepreneur, but by the stonecutter, stopping to gaze at the magnificent carving to be unveiled in the ceremony the very next day.

The work had gone well, so far, and Creag smiled as he thought of the commemoration of Lee's birthday on January 19, 1924. What a fitting time to unveil the head of General Robert E. Lee, carved in stone over a thousand feet in the air. He gazed at the few clouds gathering to the east, and hoped that no rain would come to spoil the day.

Creag's burnt sienna eyes sought out the heavy tables anchored to the massive ledge of stone that formed General Lee's shoulders. He laughed aloud at the sheer drama of it, envisioning the people who had accepted Borglum's invitation to eat breakfast in the sky before the ceremony celebrating the Confederate War Memorial.

Borglum came to stand beside him, at the base of the mountain where a specially constructed wooden elevator lodged. "Is everything in order, Trent? You've checked the pulleys and made certain they're safe?"

"Everything's in order," he replied tersely, and went back to set up the platform for the formal unveiling.

Borglum, standing at the base of the mountain, envisioned a design far grander than the simple carving of Robert E. Lee. For he saw the entire Confederate Army marching around the mountain—artillery, infantry, and cavalry—and riding at their head, Lee, Jackson, and Davis, on horses carved in stone, visible for miles. It would be an appropriate memorial to the heroic hours of the South.

In the dim light of early morning, while Creag Trent waited for the crowd to assemble at Stone Mountain, Stephanie Wexford awoke in the gray French Normandy house on Castlemeade Road. She began to dress quietly; for the children, sleeping in the nursery adjacent to the master bedroom, were easily awakened.

Steppie's sense of excitement caused her brown eyes to sparkle like the effervescence of the golden champagne she and Neal had drunk the previous night at the speakeasy on Moreland Avenue.

"I'll be downstairs," Neal whispered, leaning over to nibble on her ear.

Steppie giggled and whirled around, seeing her husband in full uniform, with the French *croix de guerre* on prominent display. "You're so handsome," she mouthed silently, her eyes following him to the door.

She ran to the closet and pulled out the long, luxurious beige winter coat trimmed in a shawl collar of red fox fur with cuffs to match. It would be cold on the mountainside. They were idiots to have accepted Mr. Borglum's invitation.

The close-fitting cloche of beige wool hid the shingled bob of her rich brown hair. Looking in the mirror, Steppie pinched her cheeks for color, grabbed up her purse, and hurried downstairs.

They were halfway to Stone Mountain when the sun came up. The black Buick protested the bumps and slides in the red Georgia clay road, the grades and curves.

"Ouch," Steppie complained, as she was thrown against Neal's shoulder.

"Sorry, darling," he replied, drawing her close to him in a protective manner. "Wash is doing the best he can," he said. Their gardener-chauffeur was at that moment trying hard to see through a windshield bombarded with dazzling fragments of sun.

They came to the mountain in a long, slow procession—cars of every size, from the new models by Mr. Ford; the Reos, the Packards, and the sportier coupes with rumble seats; some open to the weather, and others, chauffeur-driven and enclosed—cars that proclaimed, like the Wexford car, the wealth of its occupants. And up on the ledge, the breakfast tables had already been set.

Creag Trent was ready when they arrived. Separating the guests in groups of four, he began to hoist them to the stone shoulders of General Lee.

She stood apart from the others and waited her turn—beautiful, richly dressed in her fox-trimmed coat, her small, slender figure a contrast to the tall blond man at her side. She smiled at her husband and placed her hand on his arm. For the second time in his life, Creag felt a blinding jealousy tearing him apart. He looked down at his workman's shoes, his callused hands, and then back to the man in uniform, with the French medal hung around his neck.

Now he understood the sin of David; the longing for another man's wife and the rage to possess her. Yes, even to kill, if that were necessary. Bathsheba—with her brown eyes promising the honeyed delights of a thousand years. He swallowed the bile stuck in his throat and called out, "Next, please—if you will step inside…"

Seven times he took the cage up and down the mountainside and deposited the guests. Now, out of thirty, only two remained to be taken up—Steppie and Neal.

Why had they stood back, he wondered, waiting to be last, when they were among the first to arrive? Was she afraid? Was she going to change her mind and not go up, after all?

"It's quite safe," he assured her, motioning her to step onto the wooden flooring. Without hesitation she stepped inside, with the man behind her. Out of the corner of his eye, Creag watched her as they left the ground.

"Look, Neal," she said, her eyes sparkling with delight. "You can actually see the little church in the village.

Oh, isn't it lovely up here?"

"It resembles the French countryside from the air," he responded. "Except for the red slate roofs."

"My husband was in the Flying Service," Steppie volunteered to the man taking them up.

Creag nodded, making no attempt to join in their conversation. He continued the ascent, aware of the very breathing of the woman beside him, the subtle scent of lavender and jasmine on the cold, crisp winter air.

The cage came to a stop. "You can get out now," Creag told them. "Just be careful not to go beyond the roped off area."

"Well, who's going to go first?" Steppie asked, laughing a little. "You, Neal?"

Her husband stepped onto the stone ledge and held out his hand for Steppie. Single file, they began to walk almost two thousand feet above sea level, toward the other guests already seated at the tables.

Laughter rang out and reverberated in the caves at the top of the mountain, where legends swore of hidden gold and mystical rites of passage into another world. Rock crevices held fairy shrimp that hatched and then died in a never-ending cycle of death and resurrection, three hundred miles from their coastal habitat.

When Steppie and Neal reached the others, a cheering applause greeted them; for now all thirty were on the scarp of the mountain, to enjoy the breakfast so lavishly served, with the host, Gutzon Borglum, directing it all.

"Neal, are you all right?" Steppie looked anxiously toward her husband. His face had that faraway look that presaged one of his spells. She gazed down at his plate, untouched, and her concern muted the sparkle of her dark brown eyes. Please, no. Not here. Don't let Neal become ill again.

He stood up. "The wing's on fire," he said. "You'll have to bail out, Pierre."

"It's all right, Neal," Steppie said, rising with him. "It's over. You're home."

"No," he said, twisting from her. "You take the parachute. I'll ride the plane down."

Creag Trent, watching from below, sensed that something was wrong. He started the cage upward, his muscles bulging under the stress of ropes and pulleys.

Thank God, Steppie said under her breath when she saw the elevator in motion and coming toward them.

"Jump, Pierre," Neal shouted.

"No, Neal," Steppie cried out as her husband gave her a push.

Steppie, in a desperate effort to save herself, reached out for the rope, but it eluded her. Nothing could save her now. She was falling off the mountain. But then a callused hand grasped her arm.

The chill of that winter day gave way to the heat of August. Perspiration ran down Creag's neck, dampening the collar of his freshly starched white shirt. The bobwhite sang its mating call again from the tall clump of grass in the distance.

Creag had saved Steppie Wexford from the mountain that day. She had duly thanked him, but her eyes never really saw him. Her concern had been for her husband, Neal.

A bittersweet smile curved Creag's lips. Unknowingly, Steppie had touched him as no other human being had done. Because of her, his ambition had been ignited. Eleven years ago.

Creag, the stonecutter, left the base of the mountain, and Trent, the millionaire entrepreneur, started the engine of his long black car and took the road to the old James property on the other side of the mountain.

Chapter 6

Tucker Beaumont finished loading the last of the jugs into the black hearse.

"Alpharetta, are you ready?" he called out.

"Yes, Papa. I'm coming." She pinned the black lace veil to the hat, put it on to cover her red hair and, smoothing the dark, matronly dress to her slender form, she hurried out of the cabin.

Some fortune teller, she mused, with a disgusted look passing over her face. In a year, the gypsy had said, she would be wearing beautiful clothes and living in one of the finest houses in Atlanta. Alpharetta was a fool to have believed her. She was stuck, cooking and cleaning and taking care of her father and her two older brothers. And it would be even worse when the new cabin was finished; for it was completely isolated. Why, oh why did her mother have to die when she was born?

"You look sad already," her father commented as she climbed beside him in the hearse.

"I'm practicin'," she answered.

Tucker started the engine and backed out of the dirt yard. "You'll be the lookout, just like the last time," he instructed, "and if you see someone getting too close, you can start bawling loud enough for me to hear."

"Yes, Papa."

Tucker had deliberately chosen the latter part of the day to replace the jugs at Oakland Cemetery, when the place would be deserted. It was safer now that they no longer stored their liquor in the Wexford mausoleum, but rather in a more secluded one at the far end of the wall.

The jugs, cushioned in the casket in the back, had been unloaded from the wagon by Conyer before he'd started for Stone Mountain to relieve Duluth at the still. Tucker would feel a lot better when their new cabin was finished and they could move in. He didn't like the boys carting liquor over the roads. They were more apt to be caught by the revenuers at a blockade. That was a job for the trippers. Tucker conceded that he could make a great deal more money delivering, but it wasn't worth the risk. It was enough that he had made the golden nectar.

As Tucker continued driving, a man walking down the road with his spotted dog respectfully stopped and took off his hat as the hearse passed by.

Tucker was no good at making small talk with Alpharetta, so he remained silent. The boys now—he could talk to Duluth and Conyer about politics and women, and even the Monkey Trial. But somehow, none of those things was fitting for Alpharetta's ears.

He was aware of the way his daughter sat beside him—composed, with her hands in her lap. And despite the drab costume she wore, anyone looking could tell she was fine-boned and delicate, with an air of breeding. Heaven knows she didn't get it from either him or Edna. It must have come from his mother's family—the Carletons. The only thing he could claim was the red hair.

Alpharetta, with her eyes straight ahead, gave no indication that she was miles away in spirit. She sat on the old patched seat, but for her, the hearse had become a Stutz Bearcat with fine black leather seats, and her father had suddenly turned into the handsome Ben Mark St. John. Alpharetta felt the breeze through the window. She closed her eyes, and her thoughts flew far from the squalid cabin and her two large, raw-boned brothers.

The prime timberland on the other side of Stone Mountain was far too large in acreage for Creg Trent to see it all on foot. But an hour of walking had convinced him. He wanted the land. Now he only had to persuade the owners to sell.

Heading for his house on Castlemeade Road with the car windows rolled down, Creag felt the sting of the hot, dry air on his face. His wet shirt stuck to his back and he longed for a cold shower, a cooling drink as relief from the August heat he thought was as searing as that of the jungle. No, he'd take that back. Only Hell was hot as the jungle.

Twenty minutes later, Creag slowed the car when he went by the Decatur courthouse, with its Civil War cannon, painted green, standing on the lawn. Already, he loved the sleepy, snobbish little town that had turned up its nose at the offer of the railroad terminus—the terminus that, when installed six miles away, had made Atlanta into a brawling, rowdy place, attracting every form of humanity during those early years.

Westward, Creag's car traveled. Despite the heat, lawns and flowers, huge shade trees—oaks and poplars—lined the street where houses gradually changed from modest to substantial. Close to his own street, Decatur gave way to the city of Atlanta with a simple sign between one house and another.

As he turned onto Castlemeade Road and approached his driveway, he automatically searched for some sign of Steppie Wexford. Actually, he had seen her only once or twice the entire summer, and fleetingly at that. But her daughter, Belline, was a different story. She had taken to sitting with him on his terrace in the early summer evenings. She was a spoiled little brat, used to being pampered, but he had been tolerant, realizing that the girl had lost her father and missed him dreadfully.

At fifteen Belline needed a man to be amused at her childish ploys while, at the same time, aware of the woman she was becoming.

Creag knew, though, that however amused he might be, no amount of teenaged flirting could erase the memory of her mother, the woman he had held in his arms for one impossible night — and loved.

If he thought he would see the mother more often because of the daughter, he was wrong. Steppie kept to herself, sending Verbena to collect her daughter when it grew late — never joining them. Steppie had effectively put a barrier between them and not even Belline, with her visits, could bridge the chasm.

Yet each day the possibility was there that he might see her again. Riding down his driveway, Creag automatically glanced at the house where Steppie lived. The courtyard and side terrace were deserted. With a feeling of disappointment, Creag stopped his car by the front door of his stucco-and-timber house, reached for his briefcase, and climbed out of the car.

Creag left his boots at the door and walked through the house to the kitchen, where he went to the refrigerator and pulled out a beer. If he wanted something stronger, all he had to do was walk down Decatur Street, and when the police weren't looking , buy a fruit jar of moonshine. The only trouble was, no one could be certain where it came from — there was the rub.

Creag thought of the old, abandoned still that had been partially hidden by undergrowth on the timberland he'd walked over that afternoon. The rusted truck radiator had drawn his attention to it. Any man would be a fool to risk lead poisoning and death for a drink of liquor. But plenty of men did it. He'd done it himself, but now he was more cautious.

Creag walked up the stairs with the beer bottle in his hand. In the bedroom, he removed his clothes, walked into the bath, and turned on the shower.

The cool water ran down his chest in rivulets, taking away the sweaty stickiness. He lathered himself while his mind saw not the whiteness of the tile around him, but dark mahogany paneling and a woman reflected in the mirrors.

He turned off the shower and began to towel himself dry. As he did so, he gazed out the window at his neighbor's terrace. Creag stopped his toweling and stood quite still and watched. For Steppie Wexford, with a straw basket at her feet, was busy cutting the yellow roses that entwined themselves around a tree near the terrace. He took note of her every motion—bending, clipping, straightening—as she filled the basket with roses.

The flimsy black organdy dress she wore swirled around her with each step. Then, she too stood quite still, like a doe in the forest who suddenly senses that she is being observed. He moved back from the window but continued to watch the woman whose full figure was outlined by the sun.

Creag frowned. She had gained weight since he'd last seen her. Not in her face or limbs, but in her body. He stared at the rounded stomach, faintly disguised by the folds of her dress. Steppie Wexford looked pregnant. The realization pierced him—nail hard. He began to count the months since the ice storm. April, May, June, July, August—five months. Long enough. If Steppie Wexford, still dressed in mourning for her dead husband, were pregnant, that could mean only one thing. *He* was the father of her child.

With his mouth dry, his senses awry, he slowly walked to the closet for fresh clothes. He would have to confront her; to see if what he suspected was true. Before he finished dressing, he heard the sound of an engine starting up. He walked to the window just in time to see the black Buick sedan leaving the driveway. Disappointment registered in his brain. Steppie Wexford had gone. Well, he had waited for five months. He could wait another hour or so until she came home.

Creag took the boar-bristle brush and ran it through his still damp, golden curls. Walking to the table by the window, he picked up the beer bottle and took a sip. It tasted flat. He poured out the remainder of the brew and dropped the empty bottle into the trash bin hidden under the basin in the bath. Then he went downstairs to the library, to think and wait for the black Buick to return.

Belline sat on the front seat of the car with her mother and stared straight ahead. She refused to look at Steppie with her body broadcasting her father's betrayal. All her friends knew her mother was going to have a baby, even though they said nothing to Belline. But she could tell by their behavior when she came near. It was bad enough enduring their whispers and giggles during the summer, but it would become intolerable by the time school started again.

Suddenly making up her mind, Belline said aloud, "I don't want to go back to Washington Seminary this year."

Steppie, surprised at her comment, took her eyes from the road a split second to look at her daughter. "I thought you loved it at the seminary."

"Not anymore. I want to go away to school."

Steppie's hands tightened on the steering wheel. And then she inquired, "Is there a particular school you're interested in?"

"Salem Academy. Martha will be going there a year from now. I...I've been talking with her, and it sounds like a great place."

Actually, she didn't care where she went, if she could only get away.

"It's rather late to be changing schools, Belline," Steppie argued, "less than a month before the year starts."

"But Carey could get me in. I know she could."

Steppie tried hard not to say anything that she'd regret. Yet, there was the money to consider. Reed was still trying to find out what Neal had done with his money. He had suddenly drawn out a large sum from the bank, leaving little in his checking account. She barely had enough for Daniel's tuition. And until her finances were straightened out, Steppie knew she couldn't afford to send Belline to a boarding school.

"Belline, I'd rather you stayed at the seminary this year. Perhaps later…"

"Can't you understand, Mother? I don't *want* to stay. I want to go away immediately."

The headache that had been threatening Steppie all afternoon came to fruition. And with it, her patience with Belline ended.

"It costs money, Belline," she said, "to go away to school. With Daniel in Europe—"

"Daniel is a bastard."

"Belline, don't you dare utter such a word!"

"But it's true. Ben Mark told me. His mother was a French girl and his father was a German officer. And they weren't married."

"Daniel is your brother."

Belline shook her red hair. "No, Mother. You and Daddy might have adopted him, but that doesn't make him my brother. He isn't a true Wexford, like me. Of course," she added, "you've always preferred him to your own daughter."

"That's not true, Belline."

"But Daddy loved *me* the most. If he were alive, he'd let me do what I wanted."

Unable to drive and think at the same time, Steppie said, "We'll talk about it later."

Belline's face tightened in anger. She hunched over in the seat and let the silence build between them.

An unhappy Steppie guided the car down Jackson Street and turned left to follow the square to the cobblestoned entrance at the cemetery. To the right, the cotton mill's smokestacks belched gray clouds into the air. She drove past the gates and stopped the car a short distance from the mausoleum. Looking at Belline, she said, "Would you like to come with me?"

Belline shook her head. "I'll wait."

Steppie got out, leaving the keys in the Buick's ignition. She opened the rear door and removed the cascade of yellow roses wrapped in damp newspaper. Following the path, she left Belline behind.

In the honeyed glaze of late afternoon, thick and sweet with the scent of gardenias, Alpharetta waited for her father. She was hot, but she knew better than to move too far from her position where she could see not only the hearse, partially hidden by wrought-iron fencing, but also the entrance to the cemetery. Actually, where she was standing was her favorite place, next to the statue of the cherubs. Just looking at it could bring tears to her eyes. Poor little babies, buried underneath— ANTHONY COLIN BRADSHAW, AGED 18 MONTHS; BABY ANGELA, AGED 1 WEEK. She traced the letters in the chiseled stone, now algaed with age.

Only one car had driven into the cemetery since she'd been keeping watch. It had turned in the other direction, though, so her father was still safe.

Daylight saving time confused Alpharetta. In the winter, she could look at the sun and tell almost exactly what time it was, but not in the summer. Yet she knew it was late. She peered nervously toward the hearse. Her father had better hurry if he didn't want to get locked up for the night.

In his house across the street, the sexton gazed at his pocket watch. It was time to check the cemetery and close the gates. Grateful for his job when so many men were out of work, he limped across the street. As he went past the brick wall, he pulled one of the gates closed, leaving just enough room for any vehicle remaining in the cemetery to squeeze by. That way, nobody else would drive in while he was checking.

Alpharetta saw the man coming. Quickly, she dropped to the little bench beside the stone statue and pulled out her grandmother's yellowed lace handkerchief. With a loud snort, she began crying.

The sexton, hearing her, stopped walking in her direction. It was always awkward to interrupt a woman in her grief. He'd just walk to the bell tower and then come back. Maybe she'd be gone by then.

Belline Wexford, wandering through the monumented green of grass and stone, stood near the road that traversed the cemetery and watched Alpharetta. As quickly as the tears had started, they stopped. The girl patted the lace handkerchief back in place in the sleeve of her black dress. And taking off her hat with the heavy veil, Alpharetta laid it on the seat beside her. There. It was just too hot to keep it on any longer. She shook her long, red-gold hair and ran her fingers through it, finally pushing it behind her ears.

Belline's mouth dropped open. She was staring at herself. No, that was impossible. She took another look. The girl had the same red hair, the same facial features. But why was she dressed in a garment old enough to be her mother's — with that funny, old-fashioned hat?

She had to know the girl's name; for somehow, Belline, seeing her, felt intuitively that her own destiny was tied to the girl in black. Belline began to walk toward her as a motor turned over in the distance. Alpharetta stood and when the hearse reached the road beside her, she hopped onto the high running board and climbed in beside the driver.

No. The girl couldn't leave now. She might never see

her again. But the hearse was already headed for the gate. Belline ran to the Buick and started it. If she hurried, she could catch up with her.

The hearse drove past the gate, followed a moment later by the black Buick. The bell in the tower began to chime, signaling the locking of the gates. The echoes hung heavily over the consecrated ground as the sexton, with one last look toward the cemetery, closed the gates with a bang and, wrapping the chain in its place, locked them for the night.

Chapter 7

Chased by the moon rising on the wind, the sun speared the darkness with one last golden thrust and then was gone. Creag Trent, waiting and listening for the sound of Steppie's car, heard only the rumble of thunder in the distance. A summer storm was brewing.

Deciding to wait no longer, he went to the telephone. Maybe Steppie had come home without his hearing her drive in.

"Wexford residence," Verbena's voice answered.

"Verbena, has Mrs. Wexford come home yet?"

"Is that you, Mr. Creag?" the woman inquired.

"Yes."

Verbena became noticeably upset, her voice shaky and tearful. "Somethin' must've happened to 'er, Mr. Creag. She's never stayed away this long before. I was jus' gettin' ready to call Mr. Axel."

"Where did she go, Verbena?"

"To Oakland. She and Belline—with some flowers. She shouldn't have gone so late in the day, but…"

"I'll go and look for her, Verbena," Creag interrupted abruptly. "There's no need for you to call Mr. St. John."

Before Verbena could respond, Creag hung up the telephone and hurried out to his car, still parked in the driveway.

Verbena didn't like telephones. Her heart always jumped into her throat when one rang. Eyeing the black instrument as she would some monster, she stationed herself beside it and waited for it to ring again.

"Papa, I think that black car is following us," Alpharetta warned. "It looks like the same one that was parked at the cemetery."

Tucker gazed into the rearview mirror. "We'll turn off at the next intersection," he said. "Watch and see if it turns, too."

They veered right at the light, and the black car followed in the same direction. "You think it's a revenuer, Papa?"

"If it is, we'll give him the slip easy enough." Tucker throttled the hearse and picked up speed, sending the vehicle hurtling over the streets. The black car sped up also, sticking closely behind the hearse.

"It's following us," Alpharetta said.

Faster now, with the trolley tracks jarring Alpharetta's teeth, the hearse began an elusive route, finally leaving the main thoroughfares to wander through a maze of back alleys.

"Is it still behind us?" Tucker asked.

"The red light caught it," Alpharetta replied, relaxing a little. If it had been a revenuer, he would have run the light.

Like a bird circling in flight, each arc growing smaller and smaller, the hearse finally came to rest at the rear of a shabby funeral home called Heavenly Acres. Three black vehicles sat side by side under a deserted shed. One empty space remained. Tucker pulled into the space, cut off the engine, and waited in the dark. He wanted no government agent examining the empty hearse or following him home.

A nervous Alpharetta sat beside her father. She knew better than to talk. Instead, she listened to the sound of rain on the tin roof of the shed. Fifteen minutes later, Tucker Beaumont backed out and started for home.

* * *

Belline had lost it. Sitting in the Buick on the side street, she deplored her bad luck. For a long time she had been able to keep up with the hearse. But then it disappeared, almost as if the driver knew Belline was following and had deliberately eluded her. Well, not actually her, personally, but someone. Why? What reason for acting that way, unless they were doing something unlawful. But what? Belline worried the corner of her mouth with her tongue. A vast disappointment enveloped her. She might never see the girl again. But there was nothing to do but turn around and go home.

Rain spattered the windshield. The sun had completely disappeared. As she started the car, Belline remembered her mother. She had left her at the cemetery. Stranded. Resentment slowly crept over Belline. She knew she had to go back for her mother. But Belline was in no hurry. She would catch the dickens anyway, for taking the car. Let her mother wait.

Belline thought of her cousin, Ben Mark, who had helped her out of scrapes before. She'd ask him to go with her to the cemetery. And then she wouldn't be alone to face her mother's brown eyes boring into her, reprimanding her for going off without her. Then, too, she admitted to herself that she was just plain scared of going into a dark cemetery alone.

The mausoleum rested on the highest plateau for miles around, not far from the spot where homeless citizens had once stood and watched Sherman's fiery destruction of Atlanta. And below, at the bottom of the hill, lay row upon row of military crosses, proclaiming the white heat of battle grown cold.

Steppie, sitting on the concrete floor of the mausoleum, watched the shadows of the trees lengthen as the day grew tired. She was tired, too, waiting for Belline to come back for her. Whatever had made Belline drive off without her, Steppie knew that she would eventually return. At least, she kept telling herself that; had consoled herself with it for the last hour.

Steppie felt hoarse from her futile calling for help. How had it happened, that she was locked inside the mausoleum? The wind must have slammed the metal door shut. And the lock was rusty. Oh, however it had happened, she was effectively locked in. Cramped and uncomfortable, she shifted positions, and the baby protested with a kick.

In the distance, a rumble of thunder answered the sudden flash across the sky that illuminated the miniature Grecian temple, with its red, steep roof, its fluted columns flanking each side of the intricately worked metal doors. A giant elm, standing alone on the hill, began to sway with the wind in answer to the thunderous tympani, rhythmic, gathering in intensity. Then the rain began, pelting the roof of the structure, slanting its sheets of water through the metal-grilled doors.

Steppie quickly stood up and backed away to avoid the water. But the cloudburst came too rapidly for the earth to absorb it immediately. The rain spilled over and in horror, Steppie watched water trickle down the small aisle, following the path of the Greek-tiled border, the water heading straight for her.

She hugged her arms around her. Her teeth began to chatter. Wet. Cold—despite the heat outside. She was going to drown. No, she mustn't be silly. The ground was too high for that. Where was Belline? Why didn't she come back?

Ebony velvet slowly smothered all light, wrapping itself about her, and the rising terror of the dark, pulsating visibly in her throat, took over. No amount of logic, of rationalization could wipe out the sensation; for within Steppie, as in each man, each woman who had ever lived, lay the child who remembers in dreams the vikings of the night.

"Belline," she screamed, her voice carrying no farther than the roof. She rushed toward the doors, and rattling them, she cried out, "Belline, please come back for me. Don't leave me here all night."

She stood at the mausoleum entrance, with the water swirling about her delicate black sandals, her heart beating far too fast, while in the niche at the back of the chamber, an urn of yellow roses presided over her terror.

She was a prisoner, with only the ghost of her husband Neal for company. To keep her sanity, Steppie began to speak aloud to Neal, as if he could hear her, could share in the memories of their times together, when she and his sister, Kenna, had journeyed to Paris to find him.

"Neal, I loved you then," she said, her voice trembling, "more than I thought possible. You were so frail—so brave. And far too hard on yourself when you couldn't remember events from the past.

"I wanted to take care of you for the rest of my life. It was the least I could do—after the things you'd been through."

Steppie laid her cheek against the cold vault, and her warm, sorrowful tears escaped from tragic brown eyes.

"Do you remember that day in the Bois de Bologne, Neal, when we went riding on horseback? When Kenna rode on ahead, and we stopped for a few minutes by the fountain? I knew you were going to propose to me. It was in your eyes.

"And later, when we returned to the Vicomtesse d'Arcy's apartment, I thought surely that Kenna would be able to tell what had happened between us. I failed her, too, Neal—to let this happen to you when she was so far away."

Steppie stopped speaking, her eyes, even in the darkness, mentally tracing the words of the letter that had finally arrived from Egypt two months after it was written.

"My dearest Steppie— How I wish I could be with you in our sorrow, but it's impossible. If Irish should leave before the factories are completed, I'm afraid King Fuad would have his head." The last words of the letter still haunted her. "I shall pray for you during these two years that we are apart."

The deafening sound of lightning close at hand brought Steppie out of her reverie. Once again, her fear returned; for the memories of the past were not sufficient to protect her from the present danger.

Chapter 8

"I swear, Belline. You've got to have rocks in your head," Ben Mark accused, glowering at his cousin in the car beside him.

"But I couldn't let her get away, Ben Mark. She was a carbon copy of *me*."

"Not quite. Alpharetta's eyes are green."

"What?"

"I said she has different color eyes."

"You called her 'Alpharetta.' You mean you know who I'm talking about?"

"Sure. She's a Beaumont. Tucker Beaumont's daughter."

"Who's Tucker Beaumont?"

"He's supposed to be a farmer. But everyone on Decatur Street knows he makes the best moonshine in the state of Georgia." Ben Mark tried to appear sophisticated at his knowledge.

"That…that's illegal," Belline responded.

Ben Mark shrugged. "That doesn't bother the politicians at the Henry Grady Hotel. They're supposed to be his best customers."

"Wouldn't it be awful to be a moonshiner's daughter."

"No need to be so snooty about it. In fact, I've been wondering ever since I saw Alpharetta if maybe you and she might be sisters."

"How can you say such a thing?" Belline cried.

Ben Mark, seeing he had made her uncomfortable, replied, "Well, Daniel's adopted. Have you ever thought that maybe you are, too?"

The remark, intended to tease, produced a far more serious reaction. Fear closed in again. What if it were true—that she wasn't a Wexford after all, but like Daniel, illegitimate, adopted. In a low voice, Belline replied, "If I found out I was the daughter of a moonshiner, I think I would kill myself."

Ben Mark, sorry now that he had teased her, said, "Well, you're not. You're a Wexford. With your mother expecting again, that pretty well proves it. And for your sake, I hope she's all right." Glancing over at her, he added, "You've paid her back, Belline. You know that, don't you?"

"I didn't leave her on purpose," Belline protested, pushing her hair back with her slender hand.

"So you say," Ben Mark replied. "But you blamed her for your father. If you've done something to make her lose the baby..." He didn't finish.

Belline glowered at him. "It's not the same."

Although she had gotten her license the year before, on her fourteenth birthday, Belline was not experienced at driving in the rain. And so, when Ben Mark had parked his Stutz Bearcat and proceeded to climb in on the driver's seat of the sedan, she had moved over without protesting.

Ben Mark now concentrated on the slick, wet streets. It was raining harder and the street lights reflected themselves in the pools of water that had accumulated in the low places. He took the same route that Steppie had taken, driving down Jackson Street and finally stopping the car at the Fair Street gates of the cemetery. He kept the motor running while he got out and checked the chain wrapped around the gates. Then he ran back to the car and slid behind the wheel.

"They're locked," he said, looking at Belline. "What now?" He tapped the steering wheel with the thumb of his right hand while he waited for an answer.

Belline shrugged. "She probably got a ride home before it started raining."

"Don't you think you'd better call home and make sure?"

"If you can find a telephone," Belline replied, not too enthusiastically. "The service station is closed."

They sat for a moment while Ben Mark thought. "There's a guy I went to school with. His father has a restaurant not too far from here. We could use his telephone." He shifted gears and, driving faster than he should, left the Fair Street gates.

Inside the windows at the corner of Luckie and Cone Streets, the lights signaled that the French restaurant had not closed for the night. Parking in front, Ben Mark said, "Come on. I'll go inside with you."

"Could you call, Ben Mark? There's no need for both of us to get wet."

He laughed. "You're chicken," he accused. "You're actually afraid of catching hell from your mother, aren't you?"

"It's not my mother," Belline admitted. "It's Verbena."

He laughed again. "Oh, all right. It'll only take a minute."

A short time later, Ben Mark came out of the restaurant. "You're in luck, Belline. Your neighbor, Mr. Trent, went to pick her up."

The news should have made her glad—that her mother had gotten a ride home. But Belline, hearing Creag Trent's name, made a face. "She's probably crying on his shoulder right this minute, telling him what a terrible daughter I am."

Looking at Belline, Ben Mark suddenly felt sorry for his cousin. With an impish grin, he said, "Well, terrible daughter, you'll just have to take your medicine. Which flavor? Chocolate or vanilla?"

Belline smiled. "Chocolate," she replied and, ignoring the thunder and lightning, they sped away to the Dairy Malt, the local teenagers' hangout.

"Nobody was left in the cemetery, Mr. Trent," the sexton said, shaking his head. "I saw the last car drive out myself, before I locked the gates. A young girl was at the wheel. And she looked like she was in a pretty big hurry."

"How long ago was that?"

"Almost two hours ago."

Creag frowned. "Was there a woman in the car with her?"

"No, sir. She was alone."

At the expression on Creag's face, the sexton said, "I'll be glad to give you the key, if you want to go inside to look."

"Please," Creag said. "And a flashlight. You have one I can use?"

"Just a minute. I'll get it for you."

Creag Trent drove into the cemetery, slowly, carefully, his eyes seeking out all the dark places, the forms of angels and urns and symbols of eternal sleep planted in marble among the trees. Down one lane and up the other he went, the car headlights picking up each movement of tree, wind, and rain. He drove to the Hunter Street gate, and then doubled back past the tall rocks of Moses, with their strange inscriptions proclaiming a new promised land; beyond the sheltered porch of the bell tower. Steppie Wexford was not in any part of the cemetery. He was ready to drive out when he thought of taking one last look. Creag backed the car and started again toward the Wexford mausoleum.

Having given up all hope of rescue, Steppie peered past the metal design of acanthus leaves and grapes, and saw the car's headlights. Belline had come back.

The engine cut off, but the headlights stayed on, lighting a path through the rain. At the sound of a loud crack of thunder, Steppie jerked her hand from the metal door. Finally she heard the squeak of the rusty hinges, forced open from the outside.

"Be careful, Belline," she called out. "Don't keep your hand on the metal. It's dangerous, with the lightning."

Steppie rushed toward the open door. "Belline?"

Steppie gave a start, for in front of her stood, not her daughter, but Creag Trent. With the flashlight in his hand, Creag looked at the woman before him and, remembering another time that he had rescued her from the elements, he felt anger. But this time, his anger included her daughter, as well.

"Did Belline do this to you?" he demanded.

"No, it was my fault," Steppie replied, refusing to condemn Belline. "The wind must have blown the door shut."

"But she drove off and left you," Creag roared above the rain.

Steppie's face, white, hurting, pleaded with him not to question her. Her luminous brown eyes filled with tears. "Please…"

The sound was so small, like the whimper of some kitten trapped in the eaves of a house. Creag denied his need to take her in his arms to comfort her. Instead, he took off his raincoat, draped it over her shoulders and, being careful to guide her so that she wouldn't stumble, he led her back to the car.

They left the cemetery. Creag locked the gates behind him and drove across the street to the little white house where the sexton lived.

"I'll be back in a minute," he said to Steppie. He took the flashlight and the key and walked onto the porch.

"You found her?" the sexton asked, opening the door.

"Yes. She was locked inside."

"I'm sorry. I had no idea." His voice showed his concern. "She's...all right?"

"Yes. But I need to use your telephone."

"Help yourself. It's in the hallway."

The rain, coming down in torrents now, taxed the windshield wipers that speeded up as the car engine slowed and then died with a touch of the accelerator. The condensation fogged the glass and Creag, having difficulty seeing, pushed a handkerchief into Steppie's hands. "Here, wipe the glass," he ordered.

Steppie moved closer to Creag to reach the windshield directly in front of him. Even in profile, the cleft in the man's chin was visible. Steppie's hand reached out, as if to trace the indentation, and then realizing what she had almost done, she took the handkerchief and erased the fog from the glass.

Finally, the rain lessened. "You can stop now," Creag said. Steppie dropped the damp handkerchief onto the floor board and moved away from him.

In silence she rode, with no wish for conversation. Creag, with his hands on the steering wheel, occasionally glanced toward Steppie. He had seen her close up, and now he knew that he had not been mistaken. She was going to have a child. *His* child.

Creag slowed the car and pulled to the side of the wooded road in the park. He cut off the motor and reached for his packet of cigarettes. It was wet, and so without taking one out, Creag tossed the packet on the dashboard. He rolled his window down and the soft, sweet scent of pine from the woods wafted into the car on the wings of the cooling breeze.

"Why didn't you tell me about the baby?"

Steppie, surprised when Creag stopped the car, was unaware of the intense anger building steadily in the man. "I beg your pardon?"

"The baby," he repeated in a harsh, clipped manner.

"Why did you wait for me to discover it, myself?"

"It's…it's none of your business," she answered, incensed at his question.

"Are you planning to pass the child off as Neal's?"

In alarm, Steppie's eyes widenend. "Take me home, please."

"Not until we've settled this, once and for all."

She reached for the door handle, but Creag stopped her. "You can't run away from it, Steppie."

In desperation, she answered, "You have no right to question me."

His harsh laugh cut through her words. "I have every right to question you. The baby is mine. Admit it, Steppie." He grasped her wrist and, leaning close to her, demanded, "Admit that Neal was no husband to you. Admit that I'm the only man you've slept with in years."

She jerked her hand from his clasp. "No. I don't know what you're talking about," she cried. "Take me home, Creag. Please."

Creag ignored the anguish in her throat. "You knew I'd find out eventually," Creag went on, his voice softening. "Why, in heaven's name, didn't you come to me earlier?"

She sank back onto the seat of the car, all fight taken out of her. "Tell me what happened, Creag."

Her quiet request took him by surprise. He stared at her without saying anything until comprehension slowly seeped into his brain. The discovery was startling.

"You mean you don't remember — the night of the ice storm?"

"Was that…when it happened?" she faltered.

Creag nodded. In a suddenly gentle tone, he asked, "Don't you remember anything at all about that night?"

Her voice, tired and fatalistic, was barely above a whisper. "I remember taking the sedatives Julian left me. Nothing else — until I woke the next morning."

Creag felt sick. "I thought you knew. All the time, I

thought you knew."

While Steppie listened, Creag slowly began to tell the story, omitting nothing. "You were outside, on the terrace…"

When it was over, Creag looked at Steppie. Staring down at her hands, she twisted her wedding band on her finger.

"What do you want me to do, Steppie?"

She lifted her head and with embarrassed brown eyes searched his face for some sign of emotion. It revealed nothing. Steppie looked down at her hands again. "All I want you to do right now is to take me home. I…I'm too tired to think."

Creag nodded. There would be plenty of time in the next few days to talk. He rolled up the window of the car, pulled out from the park, and took Steppie home, as she had requested.

Later that night, after Steppie had gone to bed, Ben Mark followed Belline home. She waved to him from the edge of the driveway and proceeded to the garage where she put up the car. Now, her main concern lay in tiptoeing into the house without waking either Verbena or her mother. But when she entered the kitchen, Verbena was waiting for her, with fire in her eyes.

"You march yourself right up to your mama's room, missy," she said. Verbena clucked the back of her throat in disgust. "You've got some powerful explainin' to do, drivin' off and leavin' your mama—in her condition."

"I…"

"Don't bother tryin' to falderal *me*," Verbena said, cutting her off. "Save your fine words for somebody who'll listen to 'em."

"She's still awake?"

"Have you ever known her to go to sleep while you were still out?"

Belline, anxious to escape Verbena, raced up the

stairs and then slowed, pausing before going into her mother's room. She had hoped that, for once, her mother would already be asleep by the time she got home. But that evidently had been too much to hope for.

The bedroom door at the head of the stairs was partially open. Belline tapped on the door and walked in. A subdued Steppie, propped up in bed, closed the book she was reading, or more accurately, was staring at, when she saw Belline.

Slowly dragging one foot after the other, like a recalcitrant child, Belline approached the bed.

"I'm sorry, Mother."

Belline waited for her mother to speak, to acknowledge her apology. In a soft, non-committal voice, Steppie said, "Tell me what happened, Belline." And she listened for Belline's explanation.

"I...saw this girl at the cemetery. She was dressed in a tacky old black dress. But Mother, she was just like *me*, with the same red hair, the same face. You can imagine how I felt, seeing her. I was going to speak to her, but she rode away. And all I could think to do was to follow her, to find out who she was."

Belline swallowed nervously and pushed her hair from her face. "But I lost her in the rain, and by then, it was already dark. I was scared to go back to the cemetery by myself," she admitted, making a mournful moue with her mouth, "so I got Ben Mark to go with me. The...the gates were locked. I *did* go back for you, Mother," Belline vowed. "Honestly, I did."

Steppie's eyes softened and Belline, seeing the expression, knew that she had won.

"Ben Mark suggested that this girl might be my sister—that I could be adopted too, like Daniel. Have you ever heard of anything so ridiculous?"

Steppie tightened her hand on the book by her side. "Everybody has a double somewhere in this world, Belline." Steppie forced herself to smile. "I remember in

Paris, right after the war, I saw a French girl on the street. She looked so much like me that your father mistook her for me. Luckily, I arrived a few seconds later, or he would have taken *her* to lunch."

Belline laughed. "It's slightly disheartening, though, to realize that you resemble a moonshiner's daughter. At least Ben Mark says that's who she is."

"How did he know that? Did Ben Mark see her, too?"

"Not at the cemetery, of course. But he'd met her earlier at the bank, when she was waiting for her father, Tucker Beaumont."

The name, long filed away in the back of Steppie's brain, translated itself into a sudden sense of alarm. It was the same name that Kathryn had confided to her years ago—the soldier whose wife had run off with another man, abandoning her baby and two little boys.

"This girl," Steppie began warily. "How old is she?"

"A year older than I am—sixteen."

That would be the right age. Sixteen. Steppie quickly looked away from Belline to the clock on the mantel. "It's late, Belline. Run on to bed. We'll finish talking in the morning."

"Yes, Mother," Belline said. She left her mother's bedroom and flitted down the hall, humming as she went and congratulating herself on another victory.

Verbena, waiting to lock the doors and retire to her room above the carriage house, heated the milk, sprinkling it with sugar and nutmeg. Pouring the liquid into a glass, she trudged up the stairs and, unlike Belline, walked into Steppie's room without knocking, the prerogative of a trusted servant who saw and knew everything going on in the house.

"I brought you some warm milk to help you sleep," Verbena said, offering the glass to Steppie, who quickly brushed the tears from her eyes.

"Miss Belline needs a swat, square on her bottom," Verbena announced, noticing Steppie's action.

"No, Verbena. She's too old for that. What she really needs is to go away to school."

Verbena snorted. "You can't afford it. You're barely makin' ends meet as it is."

"I'll just have to find the money somehow," Steppie said, realizing how imperative it was to keep Belline from making further contact with the Beaumont girl.

"Well, don't you go worryin' over that tonight, Miss Steppie. You been through enough for one day. You just drink your warm milk and go on to sleep."

Verbena was right. She had been through enough today. More than Verbena would ever know.

Chapter 9

The next day, Julian St. John closed the door to the upstairs sitting room. "Carey, I want a word with you."

"Not now, Julian," Carey said, busy addressing the supper party invitations. She smiled to herself, thinking of the new outfit she would wear for the occasion — green crêpe de chine, with an ecru lace top and ecru lace shoes. She'd been particularly lucky to find those shoes. Well, actually, Leonard had found them for her. They were extremely expensive, but it couldn't be helped. Her long, narrow feet just wouldn't fit into cheap shoes.

She had begun to address another invitation when Julian demanded in a stern voice, "Carey, put the pen down. We have to talk. Now."

Surprised, Carey looked up. In his hands Julian held a bill from the dress shop. So he was going to be difficult again. Carey sighed. "I know. I've spent far too much money this month. I'm sorry."

"You promised me, Carey."

"I know, Julian. But Leonard found — "

"Damn Leonard," Julian said, interrupting her.

"Julian," she said nervously touching the pearls around her throat, "you don't have to talk as vulgar and common as Axel does."

"You've driven me to it. We're having a real money problem, and you're doing nothing to help. Only sending us to the poor house as fast as you can."

Carey sniffed. "I don't believe that for a minute, Julian. You forget, I've seen all the patients in your waiting room. You must have plenty of money coming in to pay Leonard and anybody else."

"Would Leonard take a pound of sausage or a basket of peaches for one of your dresses?"

"Why would you suggest such a silly thing?"

"Because that's how I'm paid by a lot of my patients. They simply don't have the cash."

"You mean, those things you keep bringing home are given to you in *place* of money?"

"Yes."

"That's ridiculous. You'll just have to put a stop to it, Julian."

"No, Carey. I can't."

"Then you're crazy."

"I've been crazy to allow you to become such a spendthrift. But that's going to change," he said. "Immediately. Tomorrow, I'm going to Leonard and inform him that I will no longer pay your bills."

"But I'm your *wife*," Carey protested, tears springing to her eyes.

"Exactly," Julian replied and walked out of the sitting room.

Alarm spread over Carey as she realized the crêpe de chine dress, the lace shoes were lost to her unless she found money for them in a hurry. Her eyes narrowed. Perhaps it was time to pay Kathryn another little visit. Yes. Tomorrow. Everything would be all right. Carey relaxed and picked up her pen to address the next invitation.

At two o'clock the following afternoon, Carey St. John, in a summery seersucker dress and white open-toed shoes, left her dogwood lined street beyond the golf course and drove toward Kathryn Mansour's brown brick house facing Briarcliff. On the left, she passed the closed gates of a private estate where an African giraffe raised its head to nibble on the leaves of the laurel tree. A Bengal tiger, pacing in its cage, gave a hungry roar, and two large mynah birds set up a nervous shriek that pierced the stillness of the afternoon.

Already the neighbors had gotten up a petition to make the owner remove the menagerie from the quiet residential area, and several lawsuits were pending from the last escape of one of the animals, which had terrorized the vicinity before being caught and put back in its cage.

Carey parked her small Vickie Ford in front of Kathryn's house and got out. On the opposite side of the street, two workers from the estate were combing the neighborhood. A man, watering his lawn, watched while the men peered between shrubs and beat under the thicker vegetation of azaleas and photinia.

"What's the matter, Keppie?" the man asked, recognizing one of the men. "Trouble at the zoo?"

"Yes, sir," Keppie answered. "Mr. Asa's baboon done got out again."

The man quickly turned off the water sprinkler and fled inside the house.

Carey walked onto Kathryn's porch. Through the screen door she could see all the way down the entrance hall to the back. She knocked on the wooden partition of the screen and called out, "Hello! Anybody home?"

Soon she heard the sound of footsteps and a big mocha-colored woman with white hair slowly made her way to the door.

"Is Miss Kathryn at home?" Carey inquired, visibly disgusted at Bertha's snuff-filled lower lip. She never allowed her Trudy to dip snuff during working hours.

"She's in the studio at the back," Bertha informed her. "Jus' take the steppin' stones to the side of the house, and you'll get there soon enough."

"Thank you," Carey said in her imperious voice. She stepped off the porch and, walking past the birdbath and the fig tree in the side yard, was careful to stay on the stones to protect her white, open-toed shoes.

Kathryn, unaware that she was being observed, sat at the easel, her back to the door. Overhead, a skylight sent beams of light into the studio, while the old oak tree filtered the heat of the summer afternoon with its massive limbs.

Kathryn dipped her brush into the mixture of turpentine and linseed oil and then, dabbing the brush several times into the cadmium yellow softened with white, she put brush to canvas.

"Hello, Kathryn."

The woman at the easel jumped. She turned and recognized Carey, and her face took on a set, closed expression.

"What do *you* want, Carey?" she inquired.

"Oh, just to talk, Kathryn. I haven't seen you lately."

"I'm busy."

"It won't take long, what I have to say."

Kathryn laid down her brush and took up a cloth to wipe her hands. "If you've come for more money, Carey, you're out of luck. I'm broke."

"That certainly is a shame, Kathryn. Particularly with Belline so grief-stricken over Neal. Wonder what it would do to her—finding out who her real parents are, especially at a time like this?"

"You're a rotten bitch," Kathryn accused, but Carey ignored her response.

"I need three hundred dollars, Kathryn. By tomorrow. Or I swear I'll tell Belline your little secret. Have the money by three o'clock."

Kathryn turned her back to Carey. She was far too angry to say anything. She picked up her sable brush and began to paint—blindly, badly. But she didn't care.

The screen door of the studio closed. So Carey had come and gone—just like that—issuing her threat and then leaving. Suddenly, a scream rent the air. Kathryn, rushing to the door, gazed out. Carey St. John sat on the ground, her foot twisted under her, with one white, open-toed shoe beside her on the grass. Confronting her from the shade of the fig tree was the escaped baboon, spitting and hissing.

"Carey?"

"Call for help," Carey shouted. "Can't you see this wild thing is ready to tear me apart?" She picked up a stone and threw it toward the baboon.

"Don't, Carey," Kathryn cautioned. "You'll only make him madder."

The animal, as if on cue, jumped up and down, snarling and spitting.

"You've got to do something, Kathryn," Carey whined.

"Can't you get up?"

"No. I think I've broken my foot. You'll have to help me."

Looking for a weapon to ward off the baboon, Kathryn retrieved a large wooden dowel by the door, cautiously closed the screen, and stepped into the garden. From the back porch of the brown brick house, Bertha's frightened voice screeched, "Don't you go messin' with that baboon, Miss Kathryn. You get yourself back in that studio right now."

Relieved to hear the woman's voice, Kathryn instructed, "Call the fire department, Bertha."

"Yes'm."

The animal, eating a fig, threw down the outer skin and headed toward Carey's white, open-toed shoe, which lay on the grass. Quickly, he snatched it up, turning it upside down and sticking his nose into it.

"He's got my shoe." Carey cried. "My brand-new shoe."

"Maybe it will keep him occupied long enough for you to get up," Kathryn said as she proceeded slowly toward Carey, with the wooden dowel ready to be used at a moment's notice.

She helped the woman from the ground and Carey, clutching Kathryn's arm, hobbled as fast as she could to the safety of the tiny studio. White and tight-lipped, Carey eased into a chair. While her foot throbbed with pain, she waited. Kathryn, ignoring her, stood at the screen door and kept her eye on the baboon.

The trumpet of an elephant and a cacophony of bird sounds from the menagerie answered the wail of sirens as two red fire trucks passed along Briarcliff Road, slowed, and came to a stop behind Carey's small Vickie. Firemen hopped off the laddered trucks; the fire chief's car turned into the driveway. Bertha, standing at the front door, directed them all to the backyard and hurried down the hallway to watch the summer afternoon drama continue.

The firemen surrounded the fig tree and began to close in, a large tarpaulin held by two of the men. Kathryn watched the performance of firemen and baboon, each one taking the measure of the other, as in some primitive, stylized ritual of the jungle. One step forward, and then back. Closer now, the firemen ventured. The baboon, as if sensing its imminent capture, began to dart in one direction and then another; his movements answered by a rush and the trample of feet, until at last the primal scream of the captured animal, caught up in the tarpaulin, sent a shiver down Kathryn Mansour's spine.

"I won't ever forget this, Kathryn—what I've been through," Carey warned when the struggle was over. "You'll pay for it, too. Every month. Just consider the three hundred dollars the first installment."

The fire chief, opening the door to the studio, said, "I'll take you home, now, Mrs. St. John, if you're ready. And we'll have one of my men drive your car behind us."

"Thank you, Captain," Carey said.

As he lifted her from the chair, Kathryn heard Carey say, "This afternoon has been such a terrible experience. It's enough to give one a heart attack."

"I understand, Mrs. St. John," he said, soothingly, carrying her through the garden. "Especially for someone of your sensibilities."

Kathryn slammed the screen door and walked over to the easel. With her sturdy shoes, she kicked the easel and the canvas flew to the floor. Stuck in her throat was the same primal scream of the animal. Her very survival had been challenged by Carey St. John. And for the moment, there seemed to be no way out.

Chapter 10

On the third floor of the William-Oliver Building, Reed St. John took off his spectacles and stretched his arms upward to relieve the tension in his back. He was tired, from working long past the hour that a senior law partner ought to work. But he didn't mind, really. He had built Albee, St. John and Grant into one of the most prestigious law firms in Atlanta by working those long hours for the past fifteen years. What else had there been for him to do, under the circumstances?

Helping other people with their problems made it easier for him to deny his own, relegating them to the small space in his brain that he examined only occasionally. But seeing Kathryn Mansour had triggered the switch and recalled his dismal personal life.

All those years of grief. Anna Clare had never been able to live beyond the tragedy of that night when their two-year-old had died of whooping cough. Like a veil, her mind had shut out the real world and she had regressed to the days she had been happiest...before Reed had become her husband; before their son had come into the world.

"Papa, don't you like my debutante dress?"

"It's lovely, Anna Clare."

Reed wasn't sure how much longer he would be able to take it—seeing Anna Clare each evening in the tattered old dress, its white lace dingy and frayed and coming loose from the hem.

Would life have been different if he had taken the baby, Belline, home rather than allowing Steppie and Neal to adopt her? Perhaps caring for another child would have snapped Anna Clare out of her depression. But it was too late. No need to think of what he might have done fifteen years ago.

Outside, the streetlight came on and Reed heard a door open into the outer office. He smiled. Hagar, the cleaning girl, had come to sweep and mop. She was always so prompt, he had no need to check the time, but Reed took out his gold watch and squinted at the numbers anyway. Seven o'clock. Time for him to go home.

He closed the law books on his desk, took his dark coat from the rack beside the door, and put it on. Reed glanced around his office, methodically smoothed the papers on the left side of the desk made from the old oak that Sherman's troops had felled on his grandfather's land outside Savannah, and closed the window.

With the books in his arms, he shut the door to his office and headed for the room where the best law library in Atlanta was housed. He was extremely proud of the books; for they contained most of the important cases and judgments ever heard in the courts of the United States.

At the open door, he stopped. Hagar, unaware that anyone was around, sat at the long refectory table, her mop bucket at her side. She leaned over a leather-bound book, her hazel eyes bright with wonder and excitement. Reed, curious to see what the cleaning girl found so interesting in one of his legal tomes, stood and observed her.

Her face, especially her eyes, showed intelligence. He'd noticed that about her before. She was a curious mixture—tall, with a certain regal look, like some Zulu, but with a lighter skin and more Caucasian facial structure, gotten perhaps from some white ancestor.

Reed cleared his throat, and the look of pleasure in Hagar's eyes swiftly changed to fear. She jumped from the table and began to stammer an apology. "I—I didn't know you were still here, Mr. St. John. I was just dusting the book before putting it on the shelf."

She closed the book and energetically dusted it with the black turkey feathers held together by a strap of yellow leather.

"Were you reading the book, Hagar?" he asked.

"Reading it?" she repeated.

"Were you?" He waited for her answer.

The fear in her eyes turned to despair and, weighing her words carefully, as if her very existence depended on the right ones, she began: "I...have six brothers and sisters, Mr. St. John. They all stay hungry. If you don't fire me, I promise I won't ever read one of your books again."

He dismissed her entreaty. "Did you understand what you were reading, Hagar?"

She glanced up at him and, seeing the slight twinkle in his eyes, gave a nervous little laugh. "Yes, sir."

"You've done this before?"

The fear returned to her face. Her head, covered with a clean white cloth, drooped as she replied in a subservient voice, "Yes, sir."

Reed walked to the table and put down the books he was holding. "I'm not going to fire you, Hagar. And I have no objections to your reading any of the books. But I suggest you finish your cleaning first."

Her even, white teeth flashed a grateful smile. "Thank you, Mr. St. John."

He nodded. "Be sure to cut out all the lights when you leave, Hagar."

He walked down the two flights of stairs; for Giles, the elevator boy, had gone for the evening. His car, parked in the space reserved for him, shone a strange shade of green in the streetlight. The conversation with Hagar was forgotten as his thoughts returned to Kathryn Mansour.

Reed was almost certain that Kathryn was being blackmailed. The woman was not one to spend money foolishly. Yet this afternoon, she had requested part of the principal of her trust, and she refused to tell Reed why she needed it. To deny her had been hard, but his hands were tied. The trust would not permit dipping into the principal.

Why, after all these years, would anyone want to blackmail Kathryn? Someone must have uncovered her secret; someone beyond the families involved. He could count on one hand the number of people present when Belline was born—Julian, of course, as the doctor; Steppie, Bertha, Kathryn's servant, and Kathryn's father, now dead. Not even the father of the child knew. In fact, Kathryn refused to reveal the father's name—only that he was a returning soldier who came home to discover his wife had run off with another man while he was overseas. Kathryn, working in the USO canteen, had comforted him in his grief. One night. And that one night had cost her dearly—and was still costing her.

In physical appearance, Reed was the link between Axel and Julian, taking the best characteristics of each— the height of Julian, the twinkling dark eyes of Axel. But his hair was his own—completely white and full. It was strange, though, that lately when Reed looked into the mirror to shave each morning, he seemed to see both brothers staring back at him. He supposed it had to do with getting older. Family characteristics became stronger then. Forty-eight. God, he felt old. In two more years, he would be an old man. And what would he have to show for his life, besides the sign on the office door? When he died, even his name would be removed from the door. Reed shook his head. He had to get over this morbid feeling before he reached his house.

The West Paces Ferry mansion, built in the style of an

Italian villa with its yellow stucco walls and pantile roof, sat regally beyond the allée of dogwood trees. As Reed turned into the allée and drove past the leafy branches on either side of the pavement, he saw only one light, visible in an upstairs bedroom. He drove past the main building and on to the carriage house, where he parked. As he opened the door of his car, he saw the side entrance light come on.

By the time Reed walked up the steps, the Chinese houseboy, Min-yo, stood at the door.

"Good evening, Min-yo," Reed said, divesting himself of his coat and briefcase and relegating them to the houseboy's care.

"Good evening, Mr. Reed," Min-yo answered, slurring over his r's. "You have good day, sir?"

"Yes, a good day," he replied. "And Mrs. St. John. How is she?"

Min-yo hesitated. "Meez Jenson spoiled day for her," he said with a shrug, his shoulders expressing what his face did not.

Reed realized that Min-yo and the nurse for Anna Clare didn't get along. Each was jealous of the other, afraid that their territorial rights would be usurped. Reed sighed. "Is dinner almost ready, Min-yo?"

The houseboy smiled and nodded. "In ten minutes, Mr. Reed. I have game hen with special lemon sauce."

"Good. I'm hungry." Reed walked up the curving double stairs to Anna Clare's suite of rooms. The door was closed and, feeling like a guest in his own house, he knocked on the door.

Mrs. Jenson, dressed in her immaculate white uniform, with her black hair hidden underneath the starched cap, opened the door. She was almost as tall as Reed, and her blue eyes, sterile of all emotion, gazed at him. "Oh, it's you, Mr. St. John. I'm afraid we're not very happy right now," she confided, glancing toward Anna Clare on the sofa.

She stood aside for Reed to enter, and when he walked to the small, flame-stitched sofa, with its tatted antimacassars protecting the arms, he saw that his wife was quietly weeping into her lace handkerchief.

"Anna Clare?"

At the sound of his voice, she looked up. Then, removing herself from the sofa, she fled into Reed's arms. "Oh, Papa, I'm so glad you're home. Mrs. Jenson has been such a beast to me." She stared belligerently in the nurse's direction. "She hid my dress and I had to wear my housecoat all day."

Reed smoothed the stray curl from Anna Clare's forehead. "Everything's all right now," he said. "Dry your eyes. Mrs. Jenson will get your dress for you."

"Yes, Papa," Anna Clare replied, the brightness in her eyes restored.

Mrs. Jenson went to her own room and, with her lips pursed in disapproval, pulled the dress from its hiding place behind a large box at the end of the walk-in closet. She hated the dress. She'd like to burn it, but she knew she might lose her job if she did that. And where could she find such an easy, plush position? But Anna Clare had caused more trouble than usual lately and she'd had to increase the dosage of morphine to keep her quiet.

With the dress over her arm, Lola Jenson walked into the adjoining bedroom, the one occupied by the woman she had been hired to care for.

The dress was old, tattered, a mere ghost of its former beauty, like the woman who owned it. Lola remembered the dress when it was new—the most beautiful dress she had ever seen in her life—for her own mother had been the seamstress, making all the clothes for the Carleton sisters.

They wouldn't remember her. She had never gone to their house, only her mother. But in the evenings at the little house in Cabbagetown, her mother had stayed up late each night, sewing by the dim lamplight until her eyes were ruined.

When the new dress was finished, with the seed pearls sewn around the neckline and the sleeves, Lola had slipped into the room and held the gown close to her body, imagining that her mother had made it for her.

She would never forget the scolding. "That's Miss Anna Clare's debutante dress. I'll tan your hide, Lola, if you've put smudgy fingerprints on it."

Her mother snatched it from her and gave the dress a close scrutiny. Then, satisfied that it wasn't harmed, she'd hung it up again with the clean white sheet covering it.

The diminutive Anna Clare waited, like a child, to be helped with her dress. Lola, noticing the gray in the woman's blonde hair, felt a sense of satisfaction. With birdlike movements, Anna Clare walked to the dressing table, picked up the small tiara, and set it on the top of her head. She was ready by the time Reed returned.

Lola closed the door after them, went to her own room, and turned on the radio. She had an hour to relax before putting Anna Clare St. John to bed.

"You like my dress, Papa?" Anna Clare asked, pirouetting in front of Reed at the base of the stairs.

"Yes, it's lovely, Anna Clare," he replied absentmindedly. "Come, let's go into the dining room. Min-yo is waiting to serve us."

"Mrs. Jenson doesn't like Min-yo," Anna Clare confided in a whisper to Reed as he held the chair for her to be seated. She spread her dress carefully around her, pushing the tattered lace under the chair with her foot.

In silence, Reed ate the leek soup, while his wife took one taste and laid down the spoon. "Don't you want to know why she doesn't like him?"

She looked at Reed and reluctantly he asked, "Why?"

"Because his skin is yellow," she repeated. "Mrs. Jenson says only people with liver disease and Chinese have yellow skin."

"Mrs. Jenson talks too much," Reed said.

"Not to *me*," Anna Clare said, pouting. "Sometimes she doesn't talk to me for a whole day."

Min-yo removed the soup bowls and brought the game hens in lemon sauce, garnished with small potatoes, watercress, and chestnuts.

Reed watched Anna Clare pick at her food, tasting and taking a bite or so, exhibiting little interest in Min-yo's creation. Reed remembered the dinner at Axel's house and how Steppie had also picked at her food, as if it were distasteful. But then, Steppie was pregnant. She was expecting Neal's baby. Strange, after all those years, for Steppie to become pregnant. He looked again at Anna Clare and the sense of sadness he had fought for the past several hours overwhelmed him. Would to God that Anna Clare was pregnant, too. But that was an impossibility. He had not slept with her for twelve years. And now she was too old to conceive. The last time he had gone to her bed, she had made him feel as if he were committing incest. He should have taken a mistress then. But his Calvinist upbringing had precluded that. Yet he had taken no vow of celibacy. He was a man, with yearnings to hold a woman in his arms, to bury his face in her hair. Soon it would be too late. He was already forty-eight years old.

Anna Clare continued to chat away, obviously not minding that she didn't get an answer. Her eyes seemed unusually bright and glittering. Reed frowned. He would have to check with old Dr. Martin to see if he had been able to cut down on the dosage of her medicine.

Chapter 11

Steppie was awakened by the sound of birds at the open window. She climbed out of bed to raise the shade. A slight breeze moved the curtains as she looked out. Already the sun was hot, but the white clouds, so large and plump — August clouds — promised respite from the heat by late afternoon.

For two days now, she had been planning what she must do to protect Belline and to assure her unborn child a chance for survival. Creag's child. But she must erase that knowledge, as if she had never become privy to that information; for no offer of marriage, no avowal of love had accompanied Creag Trent's confession. It would be hard, living next door to the man. But he needn't worry. She would ask no help from him.

Steppie glanced at her watch. Eight o'clock. In another hour, Mr. Whitmire would send his truck for the pair of Chinese Chippendale cabinets that had belonged to her grandmother. Yes, she'd get a good price for them at auction — enough to send Belline away to school. And although the fine old silver service wouldn't bring that much money, she would consign that to the auction, too, for good measure.

An hour later, Steppie heard the furniture truck rumbling up the driveway. She gave a last loving touch to one of the cabinets and her mouth trembled, as if she were saying good-bye to an old familiar friend.

For fifteen years, the cabinets had sat in the large hallway, bordering each side of the door to the living room—splendid mahogany, each piece perfect, from the bamboo cluster legs to the pagoda finials on top. She traced the delicate fretwork with her hand, and then with the chamois cloth she polished the wood where her fingers had lingered.

The brass knocker sounded and Steppie, still holding the chamois cloth in her hand, walked to the door. Mr. Whitmire stood before her. His baggy summer suit, gray with a darker gray stripe, looked as if it too were an antique, discovered in the Union Mission barrel on Ellis Street.

"We've come for the cabinets, Mrs. Wexford," he said, indicating with his hand the man standing behind him.

"Yes. Come in. They're ready, Mr. Whitmire," Steppie said; for the shelves were bare of the collection of ivory elephants and Canton ware.

"You wouldn't want to auction the opium pillows, too, would you?" he asked, his eyes coveting the early Chinese porcelain on the hall table.

"No. The only other item to go is the silver service."

Carefully, the two men tied quilts around the cabinets to hold the glass doors in place.

"I can't promise you how much we'll get for them," Mr. Whitmire said, before loading them on the truck. "If this were New York instead of Atlanta, you'd be more apt to get what they're worth."

"I won't take less than a thousand for the pair, Mr. Whitmire." Steppie's voice was firm.

"Oh, that'll be no problem," he hastened to assure her. "We both know that matching cabinets like these don't come up for auction every day."

Trying not to appear too anxious, Steppie asked, "How…how soon will they be put up?"

"Probably in about ten days," he answered. "I'll let you know."

She tried not to show her disappointment at his answer. It would be September then, before she received the money—barely in time.

She stood in the hallway, now strangely empty, and examined the space that the cabinets had occupied. The Oriental wallpaper along the hall looked faded in comparison to the two large rectangles that had been hidden from the light.

The door knocker sounded again and Steppie, thinking what she could move into place to hide the bare spots, opened the door. Her hand went to her throat; for an angry Creag Trent brushed past her without being invited inside.

"We have to talk, Steppie," he said, striding into the hallway. His eyes immediately went to the empty spaces and Steppie, in a defensive gesture, moved in front of him, as if to block out his view.

"There's nothing to discuss."

His eyes, blazing with sparks of anger, ignored her reply. He walked into the formal living room and, motioning for her to take a seat on the white camel-backed sofa, demanded, "Why are you selling off your furniture?"

Refusing to sit, she said, "You have no right..."

He dismissed her reply with a quelling look. "You're bearing my child, Steppie. That gives me the right to get some answers from you; for what affects you affects my child. Do you need money?"

Steppie's chin was raised in deliberate defiance. "If I do, I'm perfectly capable of attending to it myself."

"Call the man back. Tell him you've changed your mind. I'll give you the money you need."

She shook her head. "It's too late. I've already signed the papers." She looked away from him so that he could not see the tears that threatened to spill over.

"Steppie." His voice, soft and gentle, coaxed her to

look again in his direction. "I wanted to give you time to sort out your feelings after our talk the other night. But I see that I should have said more than I did, to give you some assurance that I was committed to your welfare, that I wasn't going to leave you alone to cope with all this. Won't you sit down, so we can discuss this like two intelligent human beings?"

She obeyed, taking her place on the sofa. He sat beside her.

"I want to marry you, Steppie."

"That's impossible," Steppie replied, not wanting him to finish. "For the baby's sake, there must be no hint of scandal. I'm still in mourning for my husband. And you mustn't forget that he was murdered. That would give a motive for murder, my bearing another man's child."

Creag nodded. He had forgotten. Steppie had to be careful not to be suspected of murdering Neal. He looked at the woman gazing up at him and he felt an overpowering need to protect her, regardless of her guilt.

"How much?"

"What?"

"How much money do you need immediately?"

She hesitated, her pride forcing her to remain silent. But Mr. Whitmire's voice whispered again in her ear. "Ten days." Faced with such a delay, she knew she could not afford her pride. "I need…a thousand dollars," Steppie finally acknowledged, "mostly for Belline's tuition at Salem Academy."

"Belline isn't continuing at the seminary?" he asked in surprise.

"No, she wants to go away to school."

"When did she decide this?"

"Several days ago."

Creag stared at Steppie, who dropped her gaze to her hands.

"I see," he said, as if he had just discovered something that had been puzzling him. "You had an argument over it that afternoon at the cemetery, and she drove off without you."

"No," Steppie protested. "It wasn't like that at all."

"And you decided to sell the cabinets so Belline could have her own way again."

Steppie shook her head. "It was my decision, too," she affirmed. "It's best for Belline—to leave Atlanta for the time being."

Creag stared at Steppie for a few seconds without saying anything. It was an enigma that a daughter could behave in such a malicious manner to a mother as beautiful and kind as Steppie. Yet he knew from experience that all the love—all the kindness in the world—couldn't change people from their basic characters. Perhaps Steppie was too indulgent—not firm enough with Belline.

"You're probably right," he agreed finally. Then, standing up, he said, "I'll go to the bank for the money this morning. It will be better for you to deposit cash to your account. I'll be back in an hour."

She followed him to the door. She didn't know why it was so difficult to talk with him. "Creag, I…"

"Yes?"

"Thank you."

The frown lessened and a telltale muscle near the corner of Creag's mouth moved and then was subdued, leaving his face unfathomable once more.

Belline stood by the door of the dining room and strained to hear the voices. But they had faded into the distance. Her blue-green eyes, far older than her fifteen years, resembled the ancient arctic waters of the North—dangerous and cold. She heard the front door close. Slowly, stealthily, Belline crept back to the breakfast room where she picked up her cup of tea. It, too, was cold, but she hardly noticed; for her mind was busy sorting out the information she had overheard.

She had thought Creag Trent was her friend, but he was her mother's lover, instead. In a way, though, she was relieved; for that meant her father had not betrayed her. The baby wasn't his. Belline smiled. In discovering their secret, Belline began to realize the enormous power she had over both Creag and her mother. She wasn't sure yet how she was going to use the information. But one thing was certain. She would make them both pay for her father's murder.

Steppie stopped short when she saw Belline sitting at the breakfast table. "Belline, I didn't know you were up."

"The furniture truck woke me," she complained, "so I came downstairs for some toast and tea. Is he gone?"

"Who?"

"Mr. Whitmire."

A look of relief erased the frown from Steppie's face. "Yes. He took the cabinets." Steppie sat down at the table. Belline, still in her blue flowered housecoat and blue satin scuffs, curled her feet around the rung of the chair. She removed the tea cozy from the Wedgwood pot and poured another cup of tea.

"Would you like some tea, Mother?" she asked, looking up.

"Yes, Belline. I'll get another cup."

"I'll get it for you, " she offered, hopping up to go to the cupboard near the window. Coming back to the table with the cup, Belline said, "Regina's coming for me in a few minutes. We're going to the library." She sat down and finished her tea in several gulps. "I won't be home until afternoon," she informed Steppie. "We're going to Regina's house after we return our books." She stood up. "Got to hurry."

The breakfast-room door swung back and forth on its hinges, making a squeaking sound. Faust, the cat, ran through the open door, his long, fluffy tail barely escaping being caught in the door. He jumped onto the window ledge, stretched in the sun, and settled down for a nap between the potted geraniums.

Steppie held her teacup while she began to plan the journey to North Carolina. She could ship Belline's trunk ahead by rail. That way, they wouldn't be so crowded in the car.

The hour passed swiftly and Creag Trent, armed with two thousand dollars in cash, knocked at the side door rather than walk around to the more formal entrance to Steppie's house.

"I have the money," he announced in a low tone, looking over Steppie's shoulder to make sure she was alone.

"Come into the library, Creag. I've made out an IOU to repay you when the cabinets are sold."

"Steppie, that isn't necessary."

"Yes, it is," she stubbornly insisted. She walked down the hallway and into the room where the red and blue Persian carpet covered the parquet floor. She seldom used the library. It was Neal's room—a place of memories best forgotten. But as if drawn by a magnet, her eyes stared at the desk drawer where the German Luger was still hidden. Creag tossed two neat packages of money onto the desk, breaking the spell.

"I have the IOU made out, except for the amount," Steppie said. She looked at Creag to supply the information, for something forbade her to stand there and count the money.

"Two thousand."

"That's too much, Creag. I only need a thousand."

He shook his head. "Just deposit the full amount. There's no need for you to run short."

Steppie sighed. Slowly, she filled in the IOU for two thousand dollars. She would deposit only one thousand and put the other in a safe place somewhere in the house. Then, she'd give it back to him, untouched, when she returned the other money.

Steppie held out the IOU for Creag to take. His hand touched hers in the exchange. Creag didn't glance once at the paper in his hand. With his eyes staring into the earnest brown eyes of the woman before him, he tore the paper to bits. He looked away only as he finally dropped the torn IOU into the large glass ashtray on the desk.

Steppie's mouth trembled. "Why did you do that?"

"I need no IOU to remind me of obligations—yours *or* mine."

"If I offended you, I'm sorry."

"Forget it," he said. "We have more important things to discuss. When does Belline leave for school?"

"She registers on the fifth of September, so we'll drive up on the third."

"I had thought I would get Babcock to take her in the plane."

"We're going in the car," she replied.

"I won't let you go, Steppie. It's too dangerous, riding over rough roads in your condition."

"My condition? Stop making it sound as if I have some dread disease, Creag. I'm merely going to have a baby."

"*My* baby, Steppie. And I forbid you to do anything to endanger the child. It would be sheer idiocy for you to travel now. No, Babcock can take Belline."

"She may not want to fly," Steppie resisted. "Have you thought of that?"

Creag laughed. "Amelia Earhart is getting ready to fly around the world. What young girl wouldn't love to be in her place, even for a few minutes—Belline included? No, Steppie, I'll make arrangements with Babcock. And I don't think we'll have any trouble with Belline."

"Do you always get your way?"

"Eventually."

Creag glanced at his watch. He was due again at the bank at eleven o'clock to discuss the James trust with

Axel St. John. There should be no problem in his acquiring the land, if an equitable price could be reached
between him and the James heirs.

Although he could not claim Steppie's child as his
own for a while longer, he knew that one day the child
would bear his name; would inherit all his worldly
goods. Now he had reason to be more successful than
ever.

When Creag had gone for the second time, Steppie
unlocked the desk drawer containing the gun. She
moved the weapon aside to place the package of bills
underneath. Then she hid the key in a small
compartment behind the top drawer on the left and she
walked upstairs to place the other packet of bills in her
black purse.

Chapter 12

"That's impossible, Trent. The land isn't for sale." Axel St. John recalled the words spoken earlier in the day. They had come out of his throat far more harshly and vehemently than he'd intended, but Creag Trent had caught him off guard.

"I've talked with Dempsey James," Creag said, ignoring Axel's sharp response. "I would appreciate it if you would contact the other heirs and let me know something by next week."

Axel wiped his bald head with his handkerchief while Creag sat across the desk from him, gazing at him in that cool, benign way, as if he knew every secret hidden behind the double-lensed glasses Axel wore on his nose.

He didn't like having his hand forced. But Creag Trent had done just that. Now he would have to take up the issue of the James property with the board of directors.

The constant drone of the ceiling fan added to Axel's irritation. He felt no relief from the incessant heat; for the blades merely circulated the satanic breath of the hot pavement upward to the second-story office of the Peachtree Trust Bank.

Axel tugged at his tie, loosening it as he sat at the carved mahogany desk and waited for Mr. Bussey to let him know when the other board members arrived. He was aware of the dramatic impact of making all the men wait for him to appear in the board room. It gave him a sense of power to see his brothers, Reed and Julian, stand when he entered. Like Joseph and the sheaves of wheat—he rather liked the analogy, the more he thought of it. If it hadn't been for him, the money inherited from their grandfather would have dwindled to nothing during the Depression years, so it was only right that his brothers bow to his financial genius.

He had made only one serious mistake and that was in selling the Coca-Cola stock. If he had kept it, then he would have the financial leverage he needed. And he could have told Creag Trent to go to hell.

Why had the man chosen the very piece of granite-cropped timberland where Tucker Beaumont had built his cabin and the moonshine still? Creag Trent was nothing but a trouble-maker, coming into town, buying up property that had lain fallow for years. Every direction he turned, Trent was visible with his money.

It was rumored that he had been Vargas's right-hand man in Brazil—a soldier of fortune, getting rich on the revolution. Axel wished to heaven he'd never found his way out of the jungle.

Now Axel would be forced to circumvent the bid for the James property. He could put a stop to its sale, at least for a year. But it would look much better in the records if he brought up Trent's request later, at another board meeting.

A knock sounded on the open door. "They're all here, Mr. St. John," Mr. Bussey announced.

Axel looked up. Slowly rising from his chair, he gathered his papers, handed them to the man waiting at the door, and began to walk down the marble hallway to the board room.

Inside the board room, a massive brass chandelier hung directly above the rectangular conference table.

With his hands folded pensively, Julian St. John sat at the table, his eyes observing his surroundings. He had gone through this same ritual time and again, thinking little of it until today—this monthly obeisance to his brother, this rite of primogeniture. The room was the shrine Axel had built to himself over the years.

The shrine's walls told the story of a man who had gradually gotten fatter over the years. The portrait hanging over the large fireplace must have been painted when Axel was about forty, showing a slight plumpness but nothing in comparison to the framed pictures lining the wall.

Julian looked at the one of Axel taken with Bobby Jones the year he'd won the Grand Slam in golf—1930. Five years ago. It hardly seemed possible. His eyes scanned the other pictures along the row. Axel had added a new one, Julian noticed, evidently taken at the graduation exercises at Oglethorpe College in May, with Dr. Florence Sabin on one side, Amelia Earhart on the other. Julian, seeing it, made up his mind to talk with Axel about his excess weight. It wasn't good for a man to keep adding pounds to his frame each year.

"Axel is late," Reed complained to Julian.

At that instant, the door opened and Axel stopped at the threshold. Automatically, Julian and Reed stood, and the bald-headed man with the short, stout body entered the room, nodding, and took his place at the head of the table. Caldwell, the cashier, and Egan, the assistant cashier, were the only outsiders, except for Bussey, Axel's assistant who sat at his elbow. Otherwise, Peachtree Trust was represented by the three St. John brothers and one empty chair that Neal had occupied in the past for his wife, Stephanie, who owned fifteen percent of the stock in the family-owned bank.

Julian, sleepy from his middle-of-the-night delivery of the Johnson baby, let his mind wander while the financial report was read, with the cashier explaining the complicated tangle of figures. He had no interest in the inner workings of the bank. He left such things to Axel. But Reed sat forward, with a frown on his face, and periodically questioned Caldwell about the figures.

Axel showed no impatience with his brother. He could override anything that Reed and Julian brought up; for he controlled sixty percent of the stock, counting Steppie's share. As a courtesy, Axel always sent notices of the meetings to her, but Steppie had never tried to barge into the male world of finance, like his cousin, Cricket Soames.

With the thousand dollars stuffed in her black purse, Steppie sat in the back seat of the car while Wash drove to town. She mentally practiced walking up to the teller with the money.

It wouldn't be easy, depositing Creag's money into her own account, but she had no choice. She was penniless and pregnant. How many other women had found themselves in the same situation? Her face grew hot as she remembered her humiliation. Surely, if she racked her brain hard enough, she would come up with some clue as to what Neal had done with their money.

Could he have bought land with it? Put it in another bank? But if so, wouldn't he get some type of notice? No business mail had come to the house on Castlemeade Road except the notice of the bank board meeting. In actuality, it had come to *her;* for she, not Neal, was the stockholder. She had merely let Neal represent her through the years. But Neal was dead. And she had not designated anyone else to vote for her.

Steppie had a sudden need to know what was happening at the bank. Even a small dividend could ease her financial dilemma for the moment. One thing was certain. She wanted no more charity from Creag Trent.

She was on her own now, with Daniel and Belline looking to her until their inheritance could be found.

And the baby —

She had purposely worn the black empire dress; its massive folds would hide the evidence of her pregnancy. The slight trepidation she felt at appearing in public was offset by her need to deposit Creag's money; to see for herself the state of her own finances.

The teller, recognizing Steppie, smiled at her from behind the wire cage. "Good afternoon, Mrs. Wexford," he said. "What can I do for you?"

"Good afternoon, Mr. Cruikshank," she replied, opening her purse and drawing out the packet of bills. "I wish to deposit...one thousand dollars to my account, please." She rushed the words together and quickly laid the money on the counter. In the silence, she stared down at the catch on her purse, snapping it in place.

"Do you want to put any of it in savings?" he asked, trying not to appear surprised at the large amount of money before him.

"No, Mr. Cruikshank. My daughter is going off to school. I shall be spending it soon enough."

She glanced at him in time to see the mask slip from his face. His eyes twinkled in understanding.

"Children cost a lot of money these days, don't they? My boy's at Riverside Academy. He'll be graduating this next year."

"I'm sure you're quite proud of him, Mr. Cruikshank."

"Indeed, I am."

Like a professional gambler, the man flipped through the bills as if they were a new deck of cards—counting and recounting. "One thousand dollars," he repeated. "I'll credit the money to your account immediately, Mrs. Wexford."

"Thank you, Mr. Cruikshank." She turned her back to leave and then stopped. "The board meeting," she inquired, turning around. "Has it started already?"

"Yes, ma'am."

What would happen, Steppie wondered, if she took her place at the conference table with Axel, Reed, and Julian? Cricket Soames, the cousin from whom she had inherited the stock, always attended the family board meetings when she was alive.

"Sometimes it's your blood kin that you have to worry about," Cricket had once remarked, "when it comes to money. I may not recognize a duck bill from a Treasury bill, but they don't know that. They only know I'm there, seeing my money isn't squandered on some harebrained scheme or two."

Impulsively, Steppie walked up the stairs to the second floor and followed the sound of voices down the hallway. But when she reached the open door of the conference room, she stopped. She couldn't brave the male bastion after all.

Mr. Bussey, hurrying back to the board room with a document that Axel had inadvertently left in his office, stopped when he saw the woman. "Oh, Mrs. Wexford," he began. "May I help you?"

For a moment, Steppie wanted to mumble some excuse and flee in the opposite direction. But it was too late for that. Making up her mind not to capitulate to her own timidity, she whispered, "I've come for the board meeting."

All action, all talk were suspended when Steppie Wexford walked into the dark-paneled room. She nodded to Axel as she went by, and before she knew it, all men were standing. Reed indicated the empty chair on his left. By the time Steppie took her place and the men had found their chairs again, Axel had outwardly recovered from his surprise.

He continued the meeting without looking in her direction. Mr. Bussey handed the missing document to Axel, and Reed, sharing his copy of the agenda with Steppie, pointed to the next item of business.

Ten minutes later, Axel nervously cleared his throat.

"We have only one additional minor item to take up—the leasing of some acreage in the James Trust at Stone Mountain. I've been approached by a farmer who wants to rent the land. As you know, the soil is poor but there is water on the property. To offset the taxes, I propose to lease the land for sixty dollars a year, the lease to be renewed yearly. Do I hear any objections?"

"Who is the farmer?" Reed asked.

Axel cleared his throat again. He picked at a piece of lint on the corner of the paper in front of him, as he said the name. "Tucker Beaumont. Do I hear any objection?"

The name meant nothing to anyone in the room, except Steppie. Caldwell, the cashier, said, "Seems like a good move since no one wants to buy it."

Looking around the table, Axel said, "Then I'll tell the man he has the property. Meeting adjourned."

Steppie picked up a copy of the financial statement from the table, folded it, and slipped it into her purse as she left the board room. Reed and Julian, solicitous of her health, walked with her to the automobile parked behind the bank building. Watching from an upstairs window, Axel saw Wash emerge from the shade to open the car door. For some inexplicable reason, a sense of foreboding overwhelmed Axel as the Wexford car left the bank parking lot.

Chapter 13

At the base of the mountain where a tributary of the Yellow River began, the telltale scent of moonshine mash floated upward through scrub pines and hardwood trees. The copper still, well hidden from overhead by the tree limbs, could be reached either by water or by the small rocky trail behind Tucker Beaumont's new cabin.

The Beaumont family had moved into the new cabin the evening before, and Alpharetta had worked hard all morning, arranging their few pieces of furniture—the iron bedsteads, a rocker, a rag rug, and the small antique clock that had long ceased to run, but served as a decoration on the mantelpiece in the main room.

When they arrived in the wagon with their worldly goods, the great mountain seemed only a giant shadow over the land. Now, by day, the vast hulk of granite, visible for miles, intimidated the land around it.

"Glory! Glory!" Alpharetta said, her green eyes widening at the sight of the mountain.

"It's a real hunker, ain't it?" Duluth commented, seeing his sister's reaction to the huge monolith.

"I've never seen anything like it," Alpharetta admitted.

"Me and Conyer went all the way to the top the other day," Duluth confessed. "It's got an old Indian fort on the very tiptop, and the only way you can get up there, higher than an eagle's nest, is by crawling through a narrow passageway of rock. 'Course, you have to be careful you're not crawling into the Panther's Hole, instead."

"You mean there're panthers on the mountain?"

"Used to be, I reckon."

The wind, whistling through the caverns, made a strange, mournful sound and Alpharetta, gathering the remains from the lunch bucket she had brought to Duluth at the still, jumped. "Was that a panther?"

"No. A panther has a cry like a baby," Duluth informed her. "Sounds more like that old pair of hounds. They've been up there for more'n a hundred years."

Alpharetta put down the luncheon bucket and made a face at her brother. "You don't have to make fun of me, Duluth."

"I'm not doin' that, 'Rhetta, I swear. There's this legend," he hastened to explain, "about two old hounds ages ago. They chased an animal up the rock, but then they couldn't get down again. They howled for two whole days, and then they finally slipped and fell. Wasn't a piece of bone or a penny's worth of hide left when the owner came to look for them. Sometimes at night, when I'm out here alone in the woods, I actually think I hear them up on the mountain, howlin' to get down."

The still made a bubbling noise and Duluth rushed toward it. "Go on home, 'Rhetta. You're makin' me forget what I'm doin'. Pa would take a strap to me if this thing broke at the worm while I was busy talkin' to you."

Alpharetta looked at the copper tubing formed like a hiss of s's. She had been around stills long enough to know that when the proof began to fall, the tub had to be pulled away quickly.

While Duluth took a bead of the moonshine to test its strength, she gathered up her bucket and proceeded cautiously back toward the new cabin. As she walked on, she brushed the pine bough across her tracks at intervals, so no one could trace the path to the still.

* * *

From the vantage point of the porch, Alpharetta could see all the way down the hollow. She sat in the rocking chair with her basket of beans and, using the needle and good strong thread, sewed the tender green beans together, pushing the needle through the center of each bean, until she had a long necklace of the legumes. As soon as she finished, she would hang them up to dry so that they would have leather breeches beans to eat in the winter.

She had stripped the entire garden behind the old house just before leaving for the new cabin. And Alpharetta knew she had to hurry to preserve the fruits and vegetables before they spoiled. In the kitchen, a large wooden tub already contained apples that she had sliced, along with the saucer of sulphur, set on fire under a clean cloth. She would take the sulphur saucer out that night, repeat the process for two more days, and then transfer the bleached apples to jars.

Duluth and Conyer had big appetites and it took Alpharetta the entire summer to tend her garden and preserve for the rest of the year the food they could not eat fresh. Even if life did get boring, she never had to go hungry. She never had to worry about her father being out of a job, either, like all those men standing in line at the soup kitchen downtown.

Alpharetta smiled as she thought of the new calico cloth — black with little sprigs of flowers — just waiting to be made into a new dress. Dixie silk — that's what she called the material. One of these days, though, she would have a dress made of real silk, instead of calico. But the idea of having a new dress was the exciting thing. She had already gotten down the Godey ladies' pattern book, and she knew just how she would make it, once she had the time.

"You'd better sew yourself another dress, Alpharetta.

Looks like that one's gettin' a mite too tight for you," her father said, throwing down a quarter bolt of material on the kitchen table, two weeks ago.

Alpharetta looked down at the old dress she was wearing. She took a deep breath. Papa was right. It *did* feel too tight.

She continued to spear each green bean in the middle with her needle, pushing each one down the string to make way for the next. A cloud of dust down the small, winding road alerted Alpharetta that a car was coming. Immediately she laid the beans in the basket at her side, picked up her broom and, facing in the direction of the still, began to sweep the steps vigorously and to sing at the top of her voice. "Oh, Mary, don'cha weep, don'cha mourn…"

Duluth, hearing her warning and fearing revenuers, ran from the still site, to hide in the canebrake along the creek.

Ben Mark St. John felt pleased with himself. Inadvertently, he had found out from Mr. Bussey where Alpharetta Beaumont was living. Ever since the episode behind the bank, he had wanted to see Alpharetta again. He had lain awake at night, wondering what it would be like to make love to her. She intrigued him, looking so much like his cousin, Belline. And maybe that was part of the attraction—something forbidden, taboo. In less than a month he would be going off to college, and he had never done much more than kiss a girl goodnight. Ben Mark, driving up the road, decided it was past time for him to prove his manhood. And Alpharetta was the girl he had chosen to do it with.

The Stutz Bearcat slowed and came to a stop in the dirt yard of the cabin. Alpharetta's voice trailed into a whisper, and as Ben Mark hopped over the car door, she kept sweeping the same spot on the step.

"Hello, Alpharetta," he said. "I thought I'd come and

see how you like your new cabin."

Alpharetta's fingers loosened from around the broom handle. So it was all right. Ben Mark knew.

"I like it fine, thank you," she replied, staring at him, seeing his teasing dark eyes, his ebony hair twisting into damp curls at the base of his shirt collar.

"May I come in?"

"Only as far as the porch. My pa's not home."

"You mean, I came all this way to see the new cabin and you won't invite me inside?"

Alpharetta looked distressed. "I'm sorry, Ben Mark. If you'd like to look through the front window…"

His smile brought creases to the corner of his eyes. "That's all right, Alpharetta. I really drove out to ask if you'd come to watch me race my car on Saturday afternoon."

"Where?" she asked cautiously.

"At Candler Field."

"I've never been to Candler Field," she said, her voice sounding wistful.

"Then that settles it. After the car race, we'll go up in a plane. How would you like that?"

"I think I'd rather stay on the ground," she replied.

Ben Mark laughed. "Well, we'll wait and see. Maybe you'll change your mind."

"Maybe."

There was an awkward silence while Ben Mark gazed at Alpharetta. Her cheeks turned pink and she deliberately lifted her head and looked past him.

"Oh, I almost forgot. I have a little house-warming gift for you, Alpharetta," Ben Mark finally said. "It's in the car. Wait right here and I'll get it."

She watched him hurry back to the Stutz Bearcat and lift a box from the seat. He walked up the steps and on to the porch.

"Where shall I put it?" he asked.

Completely dismissing her father's orders from her

mind, Alpharetta said, "Let's take it into the kitchen." Her sparkling eyes showed her excitement as he proceeded into the house and set the box on the table next to the window that looked out upon the back of the house. A pile of newly stacked wood was visible from the window.

A glass hurricane lamp—white with pink Victorian roses—emerged from the nest of newspapers wrapped around it for protection. Ben Mark crumpled the papers into the box and set it on the floor, leaving the lamp alone on the table.

"You have some kerosene?" Ben Mark inquired.

"Yes. It's in the can on the porch. I'll get it for you."

Ben Mark poured the liquid into the base of the lamp, set the wick high and struck a match to it. As the flame took hold, flickering and then growing, he turned the wick down and placed the fluted glass over it.

Awestruck, Alpharetta stood back. "It's…it's the most beautiful lamp I've ever seen," she said reverently.

"I'm glad you like it," he said. "And I have something else—just for you." He reached into the box on the floor and brought out a small book. "Can you read, Alpharetta?"

"Of course I can," she replied, disconcerted that Ben Mark might think her illiterate. She had gone to school for nine whole years—more than anybody else in her family, except for her Grandmother Carleton. She had read the family Bible all the way through, and parts of it twice. And the one book she possessed, *The Rise and Fall of the Roman Empire* she had made dog-eared from use.

"It's a book of poems," Ben Mark said, "all about nature. *Leaves of Grass* by Whitman."

Her hands trembled as she took possession of the slim volume. "I'll treasure it forever, Ben Mark."

Seeing her eyes brimming with tears and her supple young figure, encased in the tight-fitting dress, moving with her sensuous breathing, Ben Mark tightened his hold on her hand and drew her to him, until his lips touched her mouth.

She jerked her hand from his grasp, the action causing the volume of poetry to fall to the floor. Ben Mark smiled, picked up the book, and laid it on the table beside the burning lamp.

"I'll see you on Saturday, Alpharetta. At the wagon yard at two o'clock. All right?"

"All right, Ben Mark," she replied. The stone chimes hanging on the porch played their music at his leaving. Alpharetta, still standing by the kitchen table, fingered the volume of poetry. Her father would not be pleased if he caught her reading rhymes. She took the book to the small room sheltered from the rest of the house—her very own bedroom—and hid it under the mattress stuffed with corn shucks. Then she stood in the doorway and admired the hurricane lamp on the table. With a light, springing step, she hastened to the lamp and turned the wick down so that the flame flickered and died.

The stone chimes began their strange music again and all at once, Alpharetta remembered Duluth. She had not given him the signal that the coast was clear. He was probably still hiding in the canebrake.

Feeling guilty, Alpharetta walked onto the porch. She began to sing, "On top of old Smokey…" Her clear soprano voice traveled on the wind to the creek.

Ben Mark, slowing his car for the rabbit that ran across the road, heard Alpharetta's voice. She had acted like a scared little rabbit herself a few moments ago when he had kissed her. But after Saturday… Amused, he thought of the lamp that he had spirited away from the attic. No one would miss the old thing, and it evidently would be put to good use at the country cabin. As for the book of poetry, that was sheer genius on his part, giving her a book that he'd been forced to buy for

English class, but never bothered to read. The right romantic touch, he decided.

If he felt disappointed at his brief encounter, he was still philosophical about it. He had to sow the seed before he could enjoy the harvest. Today, he'd done just that.

"Where did the lamp come from?" Tucker Beaumont demanded early that evening.

"It's a housewarming present—from the St. Johns," Alpharetta replied, waiting to see what her father would say to that.

He grunted and began to eat the stewed squirrel with gravy that Alpharetta had cooked for their supper.

"Pretty lamp," Conyer commented. That was the extent of the dinner conversation. As soon as Conyer finished eating, he left the cabin to relieve Duluth at the still for the night.

Later that night, winged moths beat against the shuttered window near Alpharetta's bed. She listened and prayed that the light from the new lamp she had brought into her bedroom would not wake her father. Reaching under the mattress, she withdrew the volume of poetry and began reading—dreaming with her green eyes wide open, reveling in the excitement of new words, new ideas leaping from the page she held in her hands as her imagination soared far beyond the mountain.

Chapter 14

Belline, dressed in a yellow piqué suit with a gored skirt that swirled about her slim figure, ran her comb through the mass of golden red hair. She twisted it into one giant curl and tied it with a strand of yellow satin ribbon.

Taking one last glance at herself in the mirror, she walked toward the door of her pink and white bedroom. The organdy priscilla curtains framing the open window moved with the slight morning breeze. How often Belline had sat, curled in the window seat while she studied. But she wouldn't be sitting there anymore. In a few minutes, she would be on her way to the airport. She was leaving Atlanta behind, all because of her mother.

The words spoken so hastily by Belline on the trip to the cemetery that day had entrapped her. Now that it was time to go, she didn't really want to leave.

What if she hated the school? What if she didn't like the other girls? If only things hadn't changed. She was happy enough before her father died. It was all her mother's fault—everything that had happened.

She blamed Creag Trent, too. The cabinets still had not been put up for auction. Without the money from them, it would have been impossible for her to go to the academy. But Creag had given her mother the tuition money. And she couldn't back down. It would make her look ridiculous.

"Miss Belline, it's time to get goin'."

Verbena's voice at the door caused Belline to jump. She turned around and, frowning at the old black woman, she said, "I'm not ready yet, Verbena. Tell Mother I'll be down in five or ten minutes."

Belline turned her back on the woman and, ignoring the soft scuffing of shoes as Verbena disappeared, she walked toward her dresser, opened the top drawer, and searched for the letter she had written two nights earlier. Belline didn't really expect it to do much damage. But the idea of leaving town without striking a blow for her father was more than she could bear. Let her mother and Creag Trent have a few unpleasant moments with the police. It would serve them both right. Hurriedly she reread the letter, folded it again and sealed the stamped envelope. With it securely tucked into her shoulder bag, she left the bedroom.

Creag Trent waited downstairs with Steppie. Belline's small suitcase was already in his car, parked in the graveled courtyard.

Belline suffered through her mother's kiss. "Write me, darling, as soon as you can," Steppie said.

Belline nodded. "Good-bye, Mother." With no show of emotion on her face, she airily walked toward the heavy oak door.

"Tell Babcock to take good care of her, Creag."

"I will, Steppie." Creag's voice—low, intimate—disgusted Belline. She glanced toward the pair, standing together, her mother's brown eyes looking trustingly into his. Belline grabbed the brass door handle, wrenched open the door, and stepped outside. Not waiting for Creag to open the car door, she climbed into the front seat. She looked neither to the right nor the left when Creag started the motor. Staring straight ahead, she didn't look back to see if Steppie were waving.

When the car reached Ponce de Leon Avenue, Belline turned toward Creag. "I have a letter to mail. Do you mind stopping at the mailbox on the next corner?"

* * *

Still known as Candler Field, despite its recent purchase by Atlanta, the municipal airport stood on three hundred dusty acres of land south of the city. New York, Chicago, and Atlanta — those were the big three of aviation.

Creag Trent had reason to be proud of his airways — sixteen planes in all, with contracts for air-mail service all the way from New York to Miami and Dallas. Roosevelt had given him a scare, though, in the winter of '33, when he'd canceled all mail contracts with private companies and used army pilots instead. But that had proved a fiasco, with one pilot after another crashing in the fog and ice. It was good that Roosevelt had listened to Lindbergh and stopped the needless slaughter of the inexperienced army pilots. It took a special breed — like Babcock and Johnson — specifically trained for the job, and with a sixth sense for danger.

The weather was balmy, a good day to fly. Creag's eyes searched the skies as he drove toward the hangar that housed his planes. Babcock, he knew, would be waiting for them, as arranged. Creag came to a stop on the concrete apron in front of the hangar, with its wind sock indicating easterly currents.

"Well, Belline, are you still game?"

"Of course," she replied. "Did you think I'd back out at the last minute, Creag?"

Her eyes challenged his as she answered. Something about Belline troubled him. He couldn't put his finger on it, but the same feeling was there, at the back of his neck — a prickling sensation — the same response he'd felt many times in the jungle when banditos had sat in wait for him.

Creag reached up and brushed his neck. He looked at Belline, sitting coolly beside him, her girlish pony tail tied with its yellow ribbon. A typical schoolgirl. Creag relaxed and smiled. "Let's go and find Babcock," he said, his hand reaching for the door handle.

Elliot Babcock wasn't used to playing nursemaid to a schoolgirl. He much preferred his mail route. Nevertheless, he did as he was told. He delivered Belline, safe and sound, to the school officials who met the girl at the airport nestled in the valley in the Blue Ridge Mountains of North Carolina. With his chore accomplished, he flew south along the spiny ridge and on to Atlanta, where he put the plane to bed and reported to Creag.

Early the next morning, he taxied the same twin-engined Fokker onto the runway. He had waited for over an hour to get started and, finally growing impatient for the fog to lift, he decided to leave anyway. Once he got past the Atlanta plateau, he'd be safe, the tower assured him.

The airport was built in a low place, so that the river mist and foggy haze enveloped it when the rest of the city was clear. And that fog had made him unbearably late.

As the wings lifted from the ground, great drifts of billowing white waited to meet the aircraft, temporarily hiding the landmarks on all sides. But Babcock, having taken off a hundred times, had no cause to worry. He could fly the route blind, if need be. He didn't mind taking a chance when he had no passengers—just the pouch of mail lodged in the mail compartment. Now yesterday, it would have been different, with the girl as a passenger.

Belline Wexford. She was a strange girl—haughty, like so many of the young girls from the city's elite families. Babcock laughed. The less illustrious backgrounds they had, though, the haughtier they acted. Atlanta was a johnny-come-lately, compared to Charleston or New Orleans. And for this reason he was amused at the inordinate amount of pride that glued together the bits and pieces of questionable family background.

Money. That was the key. It didn't matter if a man came from the cotton fields of Alabama or the bootlegging hills of Tennessee. Once he'd made the money, banked it, bought land, and built a fine house, he could buy his way into the right clubs, the proper Atlanta society. Of course, he got there a little faster if he married the right woman. But what a terrible sentence, Babcock allowed, to look across the breakfast table every morning at an ugly woman. He thought of Dolores, waiting in Richmond for him. He grinned and banked the plane through the next cover of cloud and fog.

Down below, the early morning firing of the moonshine produced a telltale puff of smoke that rose to meet the hazy clouds.

Tucker Beaumont and his two sons had just finished cleaning the copper pot of the backins and now they were ready to start a new run. Tucker took pride in his moonshine—a recipe as old as the hills themselves. It was man's inalienable right to brew his own whiskey, Tucker opined—and sometimes it was the only cash crop a farmer had to buy things that couldn't be swapped or bartered. It wasn't always illegal, either. But between Prohibition and Al Capone, moonshine had gotten a bad name. And now, the revenuers, just like the hated excisemen in England, threatened to stamp out a man's livelihood.

The sputter of a plane engine overhead caused Tucker to look upward, but he could see nothing beyond the limbs of the trees.

"Sounds like a plane's in trouble, Pa," Conyer commented.

"He'd better be careful not to get too close to the mountain," Tucker said.

Duluth, stirring the mash, stopped for a moment to

listen. The engine stalled, sputtered again, and then reverted to its normal purr. At the sound, Duluth went back to his stirring.

In the cabin, Alpharetta began to cut out the black calico material. She had gotten up extra early that morning to finish her chores, so that she could spend the rest of the day making the dress; for today was Friday, and tomorrow she would be with Ben Mark St. John again. If she worked fast, she could have the dress finished by Saturday morning. A scooped princess neckline, puffed sleeves and a slender skirt cut on the bias—she had already planned how it would look. She had some rickrack, too—pink and white—to match the sprigs of flowers in the material. It would be a beautiful dress, she vowed.

For Alpharetta, lost in her sewing, the morning passed swiftly. Occasionally, she stopped sewing on the old treadle machine to listen to outside noise. But the bird songs and the stone chimes were the only sounds recorded by her ears. Soon, she would have to stop to prepare the lunch buckets for her father and brothers. She continued sewing, the treadle making a rhythmic whirr as she sewed one seam and then another.

"Hello. Anybody home?" A man's voice, deep, startling, boomed through the chinked logs of the cabin wall. Frantically, Alpharetta looked up. She had heard no one drive up. The sewing machine must have drowned out the sound of the approaching car. The broom. Where was the broom?

A heavy footstep outside on the porch caused her heart to sink. It was too late to sound a warning. No one could hear her singing inside the house. Alpharetta, glancing toward the door with the bar stretched across it, tiptoed to the back window. To limit the loss of heat in winter, the cabin had few windows and just one door— at the front. The only thing left to do was to climb out the window and run as fast as she could to the still.

Trying to make as little noise as possible, she held her skirt high, lifted one leg and then the other over the sill, and jumped to the ground. Unknown to Alpharetta, a uniformed deputy, standing behind the tall stack of wood, watched her escape. He stepped in front of her just as she reached the woodpile.

"Oh," she said, stopping immediately, her breath coming in short, strange gasps.

"Were you going somewhere?" he asked.

"I...I was frightened. There's a man at the door," she defended, pointing in the direction of the porch.

His look, stern at first, softened. "He won't hurt you, miss. He's a lawman, too. We're looking for someone."

"S-someone?" she repeated.

"Yes. A pilot—from the plane wreckage. Did you see the crash?"

Alpharetta shook her head from side to side.

"We'd like to use your cabin as headquarters, while we comb the area. Do you mind?"

Alpharetta's mouth moved but no sound came forth. She looked toward the open window, high off the ground. "The door is barred—from the inside," she protested.

"You want me to help you back through the window?"

Lamely, she said, "Thank you—if you don't mind."

The man, large, with a bearlike mien, hoisted her up to the window. She climbed inside and, with her face flushed, walked to the door. As she opened it, she saw the entire yard filled with men, but there was no sign of a car or truck.

The deputy, walking onto the porch, turned in the direction of the men swarming in the yard. "All right, men," he said, speaking from the height of the porch, "I want all of you to fan out around the mountain. If you find a piece of the plane—or the body of the pilot—

sound your whistles immediately. Otherwise, I'll see all of you in" — he looked at his watch — "three hours."

When everyone but the deputy had gone, Alpharetta, standing at the door, said, "I...I can help, too." She still had time to warn her father if she could leave the house without arousing suspicion, but the man shook his head at her suggestion.

"You'd better stay here, miss. This is a man's job. Wouldn't want to see a pretty girl like you bitten by a copperhead."

He took his seat on the steps and began to whittle a piece of wood. Evidently, the man didn't intend joining the search himself. Dejectedly, Alpharetta walked back inside the cabin. She stared at the scraps of the calico cloth on the floor near the sewing machine. With no desire to finish the dress, she cleaned up around the machine — putting the small scraps of material into the trash. Then she walked to the black iron stove, lifted the lid, placed pieces of pine kindling inside. When she had poured a small amount of kerosene over them, she threw a lighted match into the cavity. As she jumped back, the flames shot up immediately. With the poker in her hand, Alpharetta pushed the iron lid in place.

Not knowing whether anyone would eat the food, she began to cook, simmering the water on the stove for the vegetables, and getting out the large round skillet to make cracklin' cornbread, her father's favorite.

Creag Trent, joining the search party, tramped through the wooded area next to the mountain. Babcock, damn his hide, had no business taking off in the early fog. Creag wiped the mist from his eyes. Old friend — old soldier — they had been together for ten years. Like brothers, always watching after each other. But Babcock had always had that impulsive streak — too much booze, too many women, too many narrow escapes. Yet Creag had trusted the man with his very life, his soul.

With no hope of finding Babcock alive, Creag trudged along the meandering path of the creek. At his feet, the sun shone on a small piece of metal. He stooped and picked it up. It looked like part of the gasoline gauge from the cockpit. With the metal in his hand, he walked toward the canebrake on the bank of the creek. Dividing its long green shoots with his hands, Creag peered down the bluff where the creek widened and fed into the lake. Staring up at him was a portion of the Fokker tail, jutting from the water.

With a choking sound in his throat, Creag took the whistle hanging around his neck and signaled for help. He scaled the slippery bank and edged into the water. He dove near the wreckage, but he could see nothing beneath the water; for the recent rains had stirred up the strange yellow mud from the bottom. Creag surfaced, wiped the water from his face and, taking a deep breath, plunged again toward the wreckage.

By the time a group of men heard the whistle and congregated around the creek bank, Creag had found Babcock's body, still strapped in the pilot's seat. As he brought him out of the water, the men formed a human chain up the bank. And with his foot slipping occasionally, Creag gradually made it up the bank, with the lifeless body of Elliot Babcock in his arms.

"They've found him. The pilot crashed in the creek." The news spread rapidly, reaching the deputy who left his half-whittled stick on the steps of the Beaumont cabin.

As soon as he disappeared, Alpharetta made a dash out the door and headed toward the still. It didn't matter that she took few pains to disguise her route. She ran the quickest, the shortest way—for time was the culprit.

Rushing into the clearing, with her heart pumping rapidly, her breath coming in uneven gasps, she put her hand over her mouth to keep from crying aloud; for the still lay in ruins. The copper pot was smashed, and the trickling of moonshine saturated the ground. Her father, her brothers were nowhere in sight. Maybe they had gotten away. Alpharetta, hoping it with all her heart, slowly retraced her steps to the cabin.

Chapter 15

In deference to Alpharetta, the searchers laid Babcock's body under the canopy of pines a hundred yards from the cabin. With nothing else to do, the men milled around the clearing while they waited for the ambulance to arrive.

"I can't believe all the excitement," one young man said to another. He lowered his voice and spoke confidentially. "I promised not to tell, but the sheriff said he was on his way to arrest a woman for the murder of her husband when he got the call about the plane crash. Said that would have to wait until tomorrow now."

"Anybody we know?" the other man asked.

"He didn't mention names—only that the police got a letter from her daughter. Seems the woman was having an affair with another man. That provides the motive they were looking for."

Creag Trent gave a start at the confidence. All at once, he saw Belline dropping her letter in the corner mailbox as he drove her to the airport. Could she do such a thing to her mother? There was one way to find out—get his lawyer, Edwards, to inquire on the quiet. With a silent salute to Babcock, he hurriedly left the site, walked to his car parked on the road below, and sped to town, his mind spinning with the revelation.

First Babcock, and now Steppie. He loved her. He wouldn't let them take her. By all that was holy, he swore no one would harm her-or his child.

Creag paced up and down in his office, while he waited for Edwards to call. He had gone over it time and again in his mind as he stalked back and forth to the window overlooking Whitehall Street.

Was it coincidence, a feeling of guilt that had made him think immediately of Steppie when the boy mentioned the sheriff's intention of arresting a woman for murder? And the letter—could it actually have been the same letter that Belline mailed? But she didn't know about them or their night together. Or did she? Had she somehow overheard him when he had talked with her mother?

The telephone rang and Creag rushed from the window to answer it. "Yes?"

"Mr. Trent?"

The voice didn't belong to Edwards. Swallowing his disappointment, he said, "Speaking."

"Mr. Trent, I'm Alvin Bates, with Jergin's Realty. I understand that you're looking for some prime—"

"Not today, Bates. Call me next week." Creag hung up the phone and walked again to the window. As soon as he reached it, the telephone rang again.

"Creag Trent speaking."

"Creag, this is Jim Edwards. I have the information you want."

Creag's hand tightened on the telephone.

"You were right—or at least, partially. The police want to bring in Mrs. Wexford for questioning. Now that's not the same as a warrant for her arrest, but it seems they have some new evidence or information that makes it look pretty black for her."

"How soon are they going to arrest her?"

"Not *arrest*, Creag—"

"I know," he interrupted, "but it's the same thing."

"Well, I understand from"—he hesitated— "my source, that it will be Monday before they get around to it. If it hadn't been for your pilot, it would have been done today. By the way, I'm sorry about Babcock. I know you two were quite close. If there's anything I can—"

"Thanks, Jim. There *is* something you can do. You have my letter in your safe—giving you power of attorney. Take care of things for me if I'm not around for a while."

"Creag, you're not planning—"

"Don't ask questions, Jim. Just keep your mouth shut. I'll get in touch with you later." Creag hung up the phone and ran his fingers through his hair in agitation. He had plans to make and not much time. But one thing he knew—Steppie Wexford would not be at home on Monday morning.

Staring down at his dried but wrinkled clothes, Creag knew he couldn't waste time by going back to Castlemeade Road for a shower and fresh clothes. Instead, he walked over to Herndon's Barber Shop, where he took a shower and sent his clothes out to be pressed.

By the time he drove to Candler Field, the city was dark. Creag automatically stopped for red lights and started again without really seeing the landscape before him. The reporter from the *Atlanta Times* had interviewed him late that afternoon concerning the plane crash. And the argument had begun again—army pilots versus civilians, as if one civilian plane crash could atone for all the military crashes; as if there were any way to equate Babcock's death with any other pilot's death.

Babcock was unique—or had been, in life. Had been. Creag grimaced at the words. It would be difficult to think of the man in the past tense from now on. Creag drove his fist into the upholstery. Why? Why had he been so reckless? If he had waited another hour, the fog would have lifted. But deep down, Creag understood, without really wanting to do so. Babcock loved flirting with danger. That night of the ice storm—the same night Creag had made love to Steppie. Inescapably, their destinies had been tied together and Creag was the link. Alpha—Omega. The beginning, the end. No, not the end. Only another direction—a new flirtation with danger.

He mustn't alarm her. Let her think he needed her help. Call her. Make sure she took nothing with her to indicate she had fled of her own volition. And the baby. What about the baby—the danger? He would have to be careful. She was in her sixth month. If the baby came too soon, there was no chance for its survival.

The upstairs light was still on in the French Normandy house, and Creag, walking to his telephone in the library, called the Wexford number. He hoped that Verbena had already gone to her room over the carriage house, so that Steppie would be the one to answer.

It was ironic. If the black woman had moved into the carriage house immediately after Neal Wexford's funeral, instead of a week later, then he would have given Steppie over to her care during the ice storm.

"Hello?"

"Steppie—Creag Trent."

"Oh, Creag, I heard about your pilot. I'm so sorry. He was the same one who flew Belline to school, wasn't he?"

"Yes. Elliot Babcock. I appreciate your concern."

"I've been worrying about it all afternoon, ever since I heard the news on the radio."

"Steppie, I need to see you."

There was momentary silence at the other end of the line. "No, Creag. It's much too late and I...I've decided that we mustn't see each other again—ever." Her voice quivered. "You've been kind, loaning the money and seeing about Belline, when I needed your help. But it's over. I can manage alone now. And it's best for everyone if we remain strangers."

Her speech infuriated him. Creag, gritting his teeth, countered, "I'll wait until tomorrow morning, Steppie. No longer. I'll come over at eight." He slammed the phone down, snapped off the light in the library, and walked up the stairs.

Steppie looked at the black instrument in her hand. No one had ever slammed a phone down in her ear before. Creag Trent was upset. Babcock's death had affected him unduly. Yes, that must be the explanation. Steppie quietly put the phone in its cradle and walked back into her bedroom. She glanced toward the full-length mirror and then quickly averted her eyes. She needed no reminder of the changing shape of her body.

Grateful for the cooler evening breezes that came with September, Steppie cut off the light, raised the shade, and climbed into bed, where she struggled to find a comfortable position. Eventually, she turned on her side and, clutching the pillow in her arms, went to sleep.

In the deserted cabin at the base of the mountain, the skillet of cracklin' cornbread sat untouched on the cold cast-iron stove. The hurricane lamp, with its wick tasting the last of the kerosene, sputtered and began to go out. Alpharetta, her eyes red from crying, remained in the rocker, the back-and-forth motion producing a hypnotic effect. Her eyelids gradually lowered, and then catching herself with a start, she sat up, opening her green eyes wide.

It was all her fault. Her father and her brothers had been caught because she had been too engrossd in the new dress to watch the road. Heartsick, she didn't bother to replace the kerosene in the lamp. She sat in total darkness—rocking back and forth, listening now to the night sounds coming from the mountain. The howling began—strange, mournful—and Alpharetta drew her shawl around her shoulders. The summer was over, and the hounds of winter were searching for new prey.

Eight o'clock. Steppie, up since six, had spent a sleepless night. She had worried about Babcock , about Belline. And her dreams had turned into nightmares. She should never have allowed Creag to talk her into sending Belline to school by plane. Only one day's difference—and it might have been Belline who was in the wreckage, along with Babcock.

Steppie, with a cup of tea in hand, heard the door knocker. She knew that Creag had ignored her entreaty. What could she do, except open the door and pray that old Mrs. Barber, on the other side, would not see him. She knew she could not keep exposing her unborn child to the risk of gossip.

For herself, it was too late. The questionable death of Neal had put her beyond society's acceptance. Of course, it wasn't obvious yet, because of the period of mourning and her pregnancy, but Steppie knew that after the year was up, there would be no invitations for her—except the occasional family dinner.

Even Axel, Reed, and Julian, with their powerful business connections, had no control over the drawing rooms of Atlanta. Belline had felt it. And for this reason, as well as the others, it was good that Belline had left Atlanta.

Impatiently, the knocker sounded again. Steppie put her cup on the table and walked to the door. Creag, dressed in an airman's pants and shirt, stood on the steps.

"Are you ready?"

"Ready? I don't know what you mean."

He reached out and, with an iron grip locked around her arm, he propelled a protesting Steppie down the steps, toward the terrace, and through the crab apple trees to his own yard.

"Creag, don't you understand? I can't be seen with you. Not now, or ever again."

Creag's long black car waited in the driveway.

"Get in."

"No."

"Steppie, don't argue with me. For your own welfare,

get into the car."

The look on his face chilled her. In alarm, she asked, "What's happened, Creag? What's wrong? Why are you doing this?"

He was silent, shutting the door and walking to the driver's side of the car. "You'll find out soon enough." He started the engine and in all speed he left the house.

"Something's happened to Daniel—the riots in Paris. You were afraid to tell me last night."

"No, Steppie. Nothing has happened to Daniel, or to Belline, either. You're the one in danger."

How could that be, unless…Had the police discovered Neal's murderer? Was she in danger from the murderer, too? She was silent while Creag drove through the city, on past the farmer's market and the fairgrounds and on to the landing field itself, with the hangers on one side rising from the dust of the race cars, getting ready for the afternoon contest.

The plane, sitting apart on the runway, was painted differently from the others—khaki and green, earth colors, blending themselves into the surrounding terrain; camouflaged, like a military aircraft, incapable of being seen from above or below.

Creag drove the car into the hangar itself and parked. Reaching into the backseat, he handed the khaki shroud to Steppie.

"Put it on. It gets cold in the air."

"Creag…"

"Trust me, Steppie," he urged.

What else could she do but trust him, especially with his face set like granite, his strength reaching out in a magnetic flow, paralyzing her own will, her resistance crumbling like some fragile fragment of paper exposed to light and air.

Helped into the plane, Steppie wrapped the shroud around her. Feeling the vibration as the twin motors caught and warmed up, she sat in a rigid position while the aircraft began to taxi down the runway. This was no ordinary plane with room for eight passengers, like most of the aircraft in Creag's fleet. Instead, it had room for just two people—the pilot and co-pilot. Only, Steppie was sitting in the second seat.

Not knowing what to expect, she glanced off and on toward Creag. His aviator's helmet hid the dark golden waves of hair; his attention attuned to the gauges, the indicators. The plane lifted from the ground, soared upward, gaining altitude while Steppie, with the first sudden lift of the wings, caught her breath and clung to the sides of the cockpit.

Down below, small patches of green trees, of red clay earth, formed a pattern, with Liliputian houses in the small squares connected by lines strung from one telegraph pole to the other. The plane leveled off, headed south, and Creag, glancing toward Steppie, shouted above the sound of the wind. "Relax, Steppie."

Abruptly, she looked at her hands and, becoming aware of her tight hold, straightened her fingers, withdrew her hands from the side of the plane, and folded them in her lap. But the feeling of impending disaster stayed with her. Where was she headed? What had caused Creag to become so alarmed that, refusing to let her travel in her own car two days previously, he had now abducted her and forced her into the plane with him? Was the baby of no concern to him anymore? He certainly wasn't concerned about her disappearance, or Verbena's reaction when she couldn't find her anywhere in the house. If he had only let her leave a note, telling where she was going. But Creag hadn't given her time, hadn't even felt it necessary to confide their destination to her.

This was madness. She should have balked. She should have refused to open the door to him. But she had. Now she was going heaven knows where, with the man who professed to be the father of her child.

Chapter 16

On Labor Day, September 2, 1935, as Steppie was busy getting Belline ready for boarding school, a hurricane, with two-hundred-mile-an-hour winds, had struck the Florida Keys without warning. The devastating winds destroyed Henry M. Flagler's dream — the railroad that connected the twenty-nine islands all the way to Key West. At Islamorada on the upper Matecumbe, the last rescue train sent from Miami was swept from the tracks into the sea by one enormous wave.

Every house along the beach in Miami, every hotel within the city was crowded with refugees who had fled to the mainland before the brunt of the hurricane. Now, with the destruction of the railroad, the survivors were stranded with no way to go home except by boat, if they could hire one.

It was in the aftermath of this catastrophe that Creag Trent landed his plane at the airport, with Steppie Wexford as his passenger. Sand and sparse clumps of green — palm trees and palmettos — had taken the place of red clay earth and hardwood trees.

All afternoon, Creag searched for a place for the pregnant Steppie to rest for the night. Finally, he was successful. Not too far from the beach, he found a large, rambling white clapboard boardinghouse with a screened porch facing north, the structure sprawled in wings and ells atop a high brick and stucco foundation.

Exhausted from the plane trip and the search for a room, Steppie half reclined on the wicker chaise of the porch and looked out into the darkness. Overhead, the ceiling fan was stilled; for the hurricane five days before had knocked out the electricity along the coast. Creag, sitting nearby in a matching wicker chair, had the restless look of a man forcibly detained in his journey. He stood and walked up and down the porch like a lion looking for escape. Pausing, he peered into the sky, where clouds obliterated the moon.

"Your room is ready, Mr. Trent." Pepina, a plump, white-haired woman with skin leathered by the Florida sun, stood at the door to the porch. "I'll be happy to show you and your wife to it now."

"Thank you," Creag said. He walked to the chaise. Staring down at Steppie, he said, "Are you ready, my dear?" He held out his arm to help her from the recliner. Amusement, dominating his eyes for a moment, was quickly hidden while Steppie, glaring at him, accepted his aid.

"You found a gown for my wife?" he asked Pepina.

"Yes, Mr. Trent. I put it on the bed."

Speechless at the ease with which Creag claimed her as his wife, Steppie followed the woman who walked ahead, carrying a lamp. Elongated shadows on the wall appeared as the three figures moved down the hall and then merged at the threshold of a bedroom. Two old iron bedsteads, covered by chenille spreads, stood side by side, separated by a washstand that held a lamp identical to Pepina's, plus a basin and pitcher of water.

"I hope this will do," Pepina said in an apologetic tone. "You requested a room downstairs, and this is the only one left."

"It will be fine," Creag acknowledged. Waiting for Pepina to leave, he stood in the middle of the room.

"If there's anything else…"

"Nothing else, thank you." Creag followed the woman to the door and leisurely closed it behind her.

An irate Steppie turned to him when they were alone. "I can't stay in this room, Creag."

"You wish to sleep outdoors with the mosquitoes and alligators?"

"Of course not."

"Then I suggest you make the best of the situation. There's no other room available. And it's just for one night," he added.

"Why are you doing this to me, Creag? In heaven's name, why?"

An almost imperceptible flicker destroyed the outward calm of Creag's features for one brief moment. "I promise to tell you by tomorrow afternoon."

"I don't even have a comb or a toothbrush," Steppie complained.

"But you have a gown," he offered and, walking to the bed, he held the oversized garment up to the light. It was made of heavy white cotton material. "You're fortunate that Papina decided to lend you one of hers. She wasn't so generous to the other refugees."

"I'm not a refugee," Steppie pointed out.

Creag ignored her comment. Pressing the gown into her hands, he said, "You can undress in the bath down the hall, if you like."

She snatched the gown from him and walked out the door. But immediately she was back again. "I can't see. It's dark."

"Then, I'll light the way for you," Creag said, removing the lamp from the table. He walked with a self-conscious Steppie to the small room below the stairs. "I'll wait for you," he said.

Still irritable, Steppie walked into the small closet and closed the door. The only light came from an emerging moon stealing into a tiny window. She would like to have had more light, but rather than ask Creag for the lamp, she began to undress in the dark. She folded her black dress, wrinkled from the long trip, and hid her undergarments between the folds of the dress. Leaning against the wall for support, she removed her silk stockings one at a time. Immediately, she put on her low-heeled shoes again and then struggled into the square-cut, gathered nightgown.

In the obscure light, she could make out a porcelain claw-footed tub in one corner of the room, but there was not enough water for a bath in it. The primitive room was a far cry from her mahogany-paneled, mirrored bath with its lamb's wool carpeting underfoot, and its gold dolphin bath fixtures. All the time Steppie was inside the bath closet, she was aware of the man outside the door, with the lamp in his hands.

Gathering her discarded clothes, she opened the door. With her head held high, she began to make her way back down the hall. The light flickered and she stopped at the sound of Creag's voice.

"One moment, Steppie. You dropped something."

She turned and Creag, with an inscrutable expression on his face, stooped and retrieved a silk stocking from the hall floor. He caught up with her and laid the stocking on top of the bundle Steppie carried in her arms. Without thanking him, she continued her way to the bedroom.

"Steppie…"

Her brown eyes blazed in anger. "If you say anything, I…"

Creag, surprised at her outburst, frowned. He walked to the table, placed the lamp on it, and watched as she turned back the chenille spread and prepared to climb between the sheets of the iron bed. Before she could do so, Creag, on the other side of the bed, jerked the spread and top sheet away.

A brown scorpion, with its slender tail curved in-ward, came alive, moving quickly to the edge of the bed.

Creag, with one rapid flick of his thumb and forefinger, knocked the arachnid to the floor and crushed it under his shoe. One at a time, he shook the spread and sheet in his hands and, placing them again on the bed, he tucked the corners under the mattress. Still saying nothing, he indicated to Steppie that it was now safe for her to go to bed.

"Thank you, Creag," she managed to say. He bowed to her—again in total silence, and Steppie watched while Creag performed the same ritual with the other bed.

An hour later, she was still awake. With its wick turned low. the lamp gave just enough light to outline the other bed where Creag, covered with a white muslin sheet, slept quietly. It had been useless to protest sharing the same room with Creag Trent. Had she not shared the same bed six months previously? And because of it, was in her present state?

Her thoughts returned to Atlanta, to the French Normandy house. And her resentment that Creag had abducted her without allowing her a single word with Verbena overwhelmed her. Looking again at Creag, Steppie got out of bed, picked up the lamp, and slipped out of the room. Earlier in the evening, she had seen the telephone box in the hallway. If she could only get through to Verbena…

Setting the lamp on the hall table, she took the receiver from the box and, standing on tiptoe, spoke into the mouthpiece.

"Hello? Operator?" She waited. The operator didn't respond. Steppie jiggled the telephone and tried again, this time speaking a little louder. "Operator?"

"The telephone line is still down," a voice behind her informed Steppie.

She jumped and let the receiver fall from her hands to dangle in the air. She turned around to see an irritated Creag, dressed in khaki trousers, but minus his shirt.

"I…thought you were asleep."

"So I was, until you removed the lamp from the bedside table," Creag replied. "You might as well come back to bed, Steppie. You can't get through to Atlanta tonight."

He picked up the receiver, hung it in place, and taking the lamp, began to walk down the hall. Steppie had no recourse but to follow him back to the bedroom.

All day long, Verbena had waited for Steppie to appear. She'd gone through the motions of cleaning and dusting, feeding Faust, the cat, and at the same time keeping her eye on the clock and listening for the outside door to open. She had even changed the linen on all the beds, though it was only Saturday and she usually waited until Monday for that chore.

From the bedroom she walked back downstairs to the kitchen and looked again at the bulletin board by the refrigerator. It wasn't like Miss Steppie to go off without telling her, or leaving a note. Yet pinned to the board were merely a grocery list and a reminder to pick up the dry cleaning on late Tuesday afternoon.

Finally, Verbena went to the telephone again and, in spite of her abhorrence of the black instrument, she began to call everyone who might know Steppie Wexford's whereabouts.

"Miss Rennie? This is Verbena. Is Miss Steppie over there?"

"No, Verbena. I haven't seen her since Wednesday. Is anything wrong?"

"I don't know," the woman replied. "She was gone when I came to work this morning, and she's been gone all day. She didn't leave a note for me, like she usually does."

"Maybe she forgot, Verbena. You know, we all forget sometimes. She probably was in a hurry."

"Yes'm. But she didn't go in the car. Her keys are on the chifferobe by her pocketbook. And Wash—he says he didn't take her nowhere either."

"Have you called the Mansour house?"

"Yes'm. Miss Kathryn hasn't seen her. I called all around — to Dr. Julian's, and even Miz Barber next door. It's just like she's disappeared off the face of the earth."

"What about Mr. Reed, Verbena? Did you talk with him, too?"

"I talked with Min-yo. He said Mr. Reed went fishin' early this mornin' with Mr. Albee and the other lawyer fellow. And when I called Dr. Julian, he said Miss Carey went to Milledgeville to visit her mama this weekend. She took Martha, but nobody else."

"I'm sure there's some explanation, Verbena," Rennie assured her. "But if she doesn't get home by six o'clock, then call me back."

"Yes'm." Verbena hung up the phone and tried again to get Creag Trent next door. She waited while the phone rang innumerable times, but there was no answer. As a last resort, she sent Wash to Oakland Cemetery to look around, but he came home in an empty car.

For the rest of the day, Verbena kept busy, even washing the windows on the inside of the house, using ammonia and strips of old newspapers to make them sparkle. But by six o'clock, when Steppie still had not returned, a frantic Verbena called Rennie again.

"Miss Rennie? Verbena. She hasn't come home. What we goin' to do?"

"Don't you worry, Verbena. We'll find her. I'll get Mr. Axel on it right away. And Verbena?"

"Yes'm?"

"Stay in the house tonight. If you hear anything, let us know, no matter how late it is."

Verbena's alarm was infectious and the search for Steppie began in earnest, with Axel and Julian St. John first making discreet inquiries at Grady Hospital and St. Joseph's, in case she'd been in an accident. By ten o'clock that night, the black woman's fear seemed to be well-founded. Steppie Wexford had completely disappeared.

"Do you think we should try to get in touch with Reed?" Julian asked as he and Axel sat together in the red brick house on Peachtree Road.

"There's no telephone at the fishing lodge. Guess we could get the highway patrol, but I doubt Reed would appreciate that. And there's nothing he could do that we're not doing already. Damn it, where could she be?" Axel croaked.

Julian said nothing; for he was thinking of the baby. What a pity if something should happen to the baby. "Neal's murderer could have abducted Stephanie. That's a possibility, you know."

Axel's face turned white. He walked to the telephone. "We'll just have to call the police. I had hoped we wouldn't be forced to resort to that, but if she's in danger, there's no alternative."

The officer on the night desk, not recognizing Axel's name, took down a description of Steppie Wexford, but when Axel gave him Steppie's address, he interrupted, "I'm sorry. You'll have to call the DeKalb County Police. Druid Hills isn't in our jurisdiction."

"But she lives in the city of Atlanta," Axel reminded him.

"We're only responsible for that part of the city that's in Fulton County. We can't help you, Mr. St. John."

Axel, frustrated, hung up the phone and looked in the directory for the number of the DeKalb police. With Julian watching him, Axel grumbled, "I have to call DeKalb County. What if the house were on fire? It would burn down before they decided whose engine to send."

"It's happened before," Julian reminded his brother.

When Axel had been connected to the night desk of the DeKalb police, and repeated the information, the man at the other end of the line asked, "How long did you say she's been missing, Mr. St. John?"

"Since this morning."

There was a brief pause. "We don't usually do anything for forty-eight hours. 'Course if it were a child missing, we'd get on it right away. But with an adult...Tell you what, Mr. St. John. If she doesn't come home by Monday morning, then call us back."

Axel slammed down the phone, walked a few paces, and then changed his mind. "Operator," he said, picking up the phone again. "This is Axel St. John. I hate to bother the governor, but it's rather urgent."

Within a few minutes, Axel smiled. "Eugene?..."

By early morning, with the help of the state highway patrol, the meager information had been pieced together. Creag Trent had filed a flight plan for Mexico. One of the mechanics at the municipal airport had seen a woman with him and the description fitted Steppie Wexford.

"He hasn't broken any laws, Mr. St. John," the captain of the highway patrol informed Axel. "All we can do is check to see if he has your cousin with him. But if he's already left Miami, then he's out of U.S. territory, and there's nothing further we can do."

"Get in touch with the Miami airport," a grumpy, rumpled Axel replied, making no effort to hide his feelings for Creag Trent. "He's kidnapped her. She wouldn't have gone with him willingly."

"It might take a little time. Most of the lines are down because of the hurricane."

Five hundred yards from the clapboard house set on its solid foundation, the shore came alive with the golden sunrise. The debris coughed up by the ocean and the palmetto trees bending to kiss the sand were visible reminders of the recent winds. Lace edges of foam withdrew into the variegated shades of blue, like the gown of an elegant woman disdainfully stepping over the remnants of the storm. Seagulls began their conversations with each other and small crabs burrowed into the sand to hide from their predators. Down by the broken pier, a little brown dog sniffed at a jellyfish discarded by the tide.

The sun, shining into the window through the sheer voile curtain, woke Steppie. As she opened her eyes, she quickly glanced to the other bed. It was empty.

The door opened and Creag, making no attempt to stifle the sound of his footsteps, walked across the room with a tray in his hands. "I brought your breakfast," he announced. The cheerful deep voice filled the room and Steppie's ears.

She winced and, in a voice edged with sleep, complained. "How can it be time for breakfast? I just closed my eyes a few minutes ago."

"No, Steppie. You slept the entire night away. Come on, eat," he instructed, placing the tray upon the bed.

She sat up, rubbed her eyes, and peered down at the breakfast—a cup of steaming coffee, a piece of bread with jam, and one small cull orange, with a knife beside it.

"I don't like breakfast," she said, unimpressed with the fare before her. "Especially coffee."

His eyebrows met in a frown. "It won't be good for you to travel on an empty stomach. Try to eat a little something," he coaxed.

He turned, walked out the door, and left her alone in the room. Steppie wrinkled her nose at the aroma of coffee. She much preferred hot tea. Tentatively, she took several bites of jam-spread bread. Licking her fingers of the jam, she picked up the knife and cut the orange in half. Pulling the slices from the rind, she popped them into her mouth. Surprisingly, the orange was sweet.

Within fifteen minutes, Steppie was dressed—in the same wrinkled clothes she'd been wearing since leaving Atlanta. Washing her face in the cold water from the pitcher made her feel much better. She completed her toilette by running her fingers through her dark curls.

In the hallway, Steppie met Creag. "Good," he commented, seeing her dressed. "We'll be leaving in a few minutes."

"Where to?" she asked.

"The airport," he responded.

Again, she wrinkled her nose. There seemed to be no way she could catch him off guard and get him to reveal their destination.

The same battered Ford that had brought them to Pepina's house waited by the front door. In her hands, Steppie held the small basket of food that Pepina had prepared for them.

"Good-bye, Mrs. Trent. I hope you have a safe journey home."

"Thank you, Pepina," she answered and looked toward Creag. As usual, his face revealed nothing.

By the time Creag and Steppie arrived at the airport, three planes—a Bellanca and two Lockheeds—were already in line, waiting to take off. Glancing warily around him, Creag talked with the mechanic, checked the tires and fuel gauges himself, then hurriedly bundled Steppie into the co-pilot's seat.

The first plane took off, then the second. One more, and then it would be his turn. Creag gripped the pilot's stick. He revved the engines and moved onto the taxiway. As the second Lockheed sped down the runway, a patrol car with lights flashing and siren screaming drove past the wire fencing and came to a stop in a cloud of dust a hundred yards away. With her eyes closed, her hands tightly clutching the side of the plane, Steppie saw nothing. But Creag shut off his radio and taxied onto the runway. Not waiting for clearance, he took off, dangerously close to the departing aircraft, to the dismay of the control tower and the Florida patrolman running toward the terminal.

The plane left the larger land mass behind and soared over the teal-blue waters of the Gulf. Whitecaps glistened in the rays of the morning sun. They were out to sea, following the stepping-stones of lime and coral that made up the out islands. Creag, flying low to survey the damage done by the hurricane, saw the ruined railroad bed, the iron tracks twisted beyond repair. And on Big Pine Key, Steppie spotted a miniature deer, jumping over a fallen tree at the sound of the plane's motors.

A fuel stop in Havana provided the only respite from the long trip. At first, Steppie thought Creag had reached his destination, but that was not the case. So she wrapped the khaki shroud about her, while the plane again lifted its wings toward the sea.

It was Sunday—a day of quiet and rest, when no one that she knew traveled; no one did anything more strenuous than listen to the sermon from the family pew in church and then go home to a quiet family dinner and a long nap. But Steppie had traveled mile after mile, and her Sunday dinner in the middle of the day had not been served on a snow-white tablecloth in the Wexford dining room, with the glazed brown floor tiles covered by a Persian rug. She had sat on a dusty bench by a metal aircraft hangar, and shared with Creag the provisions Pepina had packed into the small basket—that and part of a lukewarm bottle of wine which had made her even thirstier, but Creag had refused to let her drink the water. Using the water to wet the napkin instead, she had cleaned her face of its dust and grime.

Now a dim outline of land appeared—green-gold in the haze, jutting out into the iridescent blue of the sea. They flew over a peninsula where ruins of ancient civilizations rose above the jungle floor.

Steppie looked at Creag and watched his expert handling of the plane as he flew low over the terrain. He indicated to her that they were going to land.

The tangled jungle gave way to a prickly carpet of green, the leaf swords jutting from the body of the plants now row upon row of them, like the yucca in Mrs. Barber's garden. The plane circled the fields in a concentric pattern and at its sweep, a fascinated Steppie saw down below white-clad figures running toward the landing strip, cleared of growth.

The wheels of the plane touched the landing strip and the flaps on the wings broke the speed of the aircraft. It taxied to a standstill before a white stucco building with tile roof. Brown hands reached out in friendliness and help. Creag, accepting their help, climbed out of the cockpit, but he allowed no one to approach Steppie. Walking to the other side of the plane, he held out his arms for her.

"Welcome to Hacienda Dzibilchaltún," he said, his face grave, the tired lines around his burnt sienna eyes revealing the strain he had been under.

"Have we finally completed the trip?" Steppie asked as soon as he had released her.

"Yes." At her questioning look, he announced, "We're in the Yucatán, outside Mérida."

"In Mexico?"

He nodded. Speaking in Spanish, of which Steppie understood not a word, Creag addressed the man standing beside him. Within the span of a few minutes, a carriage arrived. As soon as the two were settled in the back, the driver, also dressed in white, with a tunic over baggy trousers, began a smooth, well-paced journey away from the airstrip.

Steppie knew she should ask for the full explanation Creag had promised to give, but aware of the driver, she decided it would be better to wait until she and Creag were alone. Yawning, Steppie asked instead, "Is that yucca?" She pointed to the plants that grew in every direction as far as she could see.

"No," Creag replied. "They're known by the botanical name, *agave fourcroydes*," he explained. "The hennequen-providing plants."

Seeing the puzzled expression, he explained further, "You know them as *sisal* plants. Their fibers are used to make rope and hammocks and a number of other woven objects."

"Oh."

Creag watched for the first view of Hacienda Dzibilchaltún, the house on the one-hundred-fifty-year-old French henequen plantation that he had purchased when he left Brazil. Its white walls, three stories high, its pediments and arched courtyard, did not disappoint him when it came into view. Magnificent with the patina of years, it rose above the landscape, a palatial symbol of Spanish conquerors and French overlords in Maximilian's time. And yet around the courtyard of the hacienda, the ghosts of the Mayas roamed freely, in features carved in stone and in the dignified, bronzed faces of the *mestizos* who worked each day in the henequen fields.

Creag looked down at Steppie to see her reaction to the house and grounds. But her eyes were closed. The steady sway of the carriage had lulled her to sleep. She was oblivious to the house that Creag had chosen as a haven for her and her unborn child.

Chapter 17

The interior of the hacienda spoke of peace, of time apart from the calendar—past and future were the same. Shutters were drawn to protect the black and white floor tiles from the glare of the late-afternoon sun.

In a bedroom along the gallery of the second floor, Steppie Wexford slept in a teakwood bed. Rococo carving—Spanish in origin—made up the headboard that curved and stopped a mere three inches from the ceiling. The white, cheesecloth netting surrounding the bed protected her from the *jejene* insects, so common in the Yucatán.

Outside, a slight breeze turned the windmills that provided power for the electrical system of the hacienda and pumped the water supply from artesian wells that sprang from underground rivers.

In one shadowed corner of the bedroom, a *mestizo* woman dressed in a white tunic and emerald-green skirt sat in a rope chair and patiently waited for Steppie Wexford to awaken. Slowly, Steppie moved, stretched, and opened her eyes. With a start, she sat up and brushed the netting aside.

The Indian woman stood and tugged at a bell rope. In the distance the bell sounded—a small, tinkling, high-pitched sound, like a sleigh bell. Then the woman bowed to Steppie. *"Buenos dias, señora."*

"Buenos dias," Steppie responded, speaking the only

Spanish words she knew.

The Indian woman spoke again and Steppie, not understanding her, said, "I'm sorry. I don't speak Spanish."

"Neither does Xtyl," the voice from the doorway commented. "She speaks Mayan."

Creag Trent—a very different looking Creag Trent—walked into the room. Steppie stared at him; for he had taken on the appearance of a Spanish grandee from a painting by Goya or Velásquez. She had the feeling that somehow he had managed to step back in time a century or two.

"You look different," she said, her voice hesitant.

"For the better, I hope."

Staring down at her own travel-stained dress, so at odds with his immaculate white shirt, black trousers, and bolero, she replied, "You were certainly busy while I was a sleepyhead."

He smiled. "You needn't apologize for going to sleep. The rest was good for you. That's why I didn't wake you when we arrived. There'll be plenty of time before *merienda* for you to have a bath and change clothes."

"I have no other clothes to change into," Steppie reminded him. "And as for *merienda*, I have no idea what you're talking about."

"Tea," Creag explained. "I seem to remember your aversion to coffee, so you can have tea and cakes and little sandwiches. As for clothes, I think Xtyl can manage to find something for you to put on."

He nodded toward the Indian woman, dismissing her. She moved from the room, leaving Creag and Steppie alone.

With her brown eyes still velvet soft from sleep, Steppie suddenly asked, "Creag, why did you bring me here?"

He could no longer put off telling her. He had promised. Creag looked out the window for a moment and then back to Steppie. There was no way he knew to soften the blow. His voice dredged up the words from the deep recesses of his throat. "The police are planning to arrest you tomorrow for your husband's murder."

Her face drained of all color. She reached out to the carved foot of the Spanish bed to steady herself. "That isn't so. It can't be true."

She looked at him, to find some hint of a cruel joke, but his face told of truth, not lies. "Why?" she asked.

"Someone wrote a letter, accusing you," he answered. "The person evidently knows that the child is mine, and decided to cause trouble by writing the police."

Who could have done such a thing? Who had discovered their secret?

"Belline?" Steppie inquired, fearful of the answer.

"Probably. No one else could have overheard."

"But that happened *after* Neal's death. The baby, I mean."

"It doesn't matter. You can see how the police would have thought they had found the motive, if we were having an affair beforehand."

"I must go back, Creag. To Atlanta. Immediately."

"No, Steppie. You'll stay in Mexico where there is no extradition process. And you'll bear my child. I won't let you sacrifice the child."

He looked at her with a fierceness she had never seen before. "I took an enormous chance in bringing you on such a long journey," he said. "I wouldn't have done it, except that it was absolutely necessary to get you out of the country. For the next three months, I swear you'll be looked after, pampered, your every wish realized."

"Except one," Steppie replied, her voice bitter.

Xtyl chose that moment to return to the room. "Go with Xytl," Creag instructed. "She has your bath ready."

Steppie, numb from the conversation with Creag, submitted to Xytl's ministrations. She sat in the white, high-backed tub and the Indian woman gently bathed her body with a large sponge. Xytl smiled at the protruding stomach and, speaking in incomprehensible words, she gently patted the baby.

With her action, she sealed the kinship of the two women. A nod and a knowing look confirmed, without words, the earth mother, the fertile land, and the mystery of creation. Steppie, who would never have allowed Verbena such liberty at home, felt no embarrassment in the primitive reaction of Xytl toward the baby. For this was another land, another time, not of the present.

She was estranged from all she knew—her family, her home. Steppie tried to come to terms with the sudden turn of events. She was wanted for murder, and Creag Trent had brought her to a foreign country where she was totally dependent upon him.

Belline, Daniel, Rennie. How would her disappearance affect them? Even Verbena. A great sadness overtook Steppie. Belline—the child who had evidently turned on her, wanted to hurt her. She began to mourn Belline.

With a soft gesture, the Indian woman brushed the hurt from Steppie's face. She murmured soothing words that required no translation. And Steppie, feeling the need of comfort, touched Xytl's arm to acknowledge her gratitude.

In the bedroom Steppie found fresh clothes—a cream-colored blouse, lavishly hand-stitched around the neck and sleeves; a burnt orange skirt with voluminous petticoats; and a bright pink apron pinafore embroidered with birds. The black dress of mourning was taken away, and the rainbow colors of piñatas and fiesta clothed Steppie Wexford. But her dark brown eyes betrayed her, broadcasting quietly that the time of mourning was not over.

Steppie left the bedroom. Standing in the tiled entrance hall, Creag watched as she made her way across the gallery. She walked hesitantly down the stairs toward him. She was beautiful, with her dark brown hair framing her large, Murillo eyes, with their long lashes sweeping her cheeks as she looked down.

At last, Steppie had shed her widow's weeds. He was glad. Because of the layers of clothing, Creag had to stare hard before he could detect that she was going to have a baby. The style of dress suited her, with her fair skin, her dark hair and eyes. She could easily be a *criollo*, the Spanish aristocrat whose Castilian blood had never mixed with the Maya or Toltec of Mexico, but had remained pure-bred, a source of pride and haughtiness in a half-breed culture.

"I'm ready to sample your *merienda*," Steppie said with a trace of a smile on her lips.

"So am I," Creag responded.

He led her into the *sala* and almost immediately after they were seated, a servant came on silent feet to bring a pot of steaming hot tea on a silver tray. On the adjacent table, trays of sandwiches and exotic sweets forced Steppie to admit her hunger.

She poured tea into exquisite, six-sided gold cups with brushed golden edges around the gleaming white saucers. Then she walked to the table where she chose for herself a little roll in the shape of a dove. Pumpkin seeds, small pancakes filled with turkey, chocolate and almond sauce, pears, strips of cane filled with sweet syrup lined her plate. Surprised at the variety, she confided to Creag, "I thought I would have only tortillas and black beans to eat."

"Oh, you'll have those later on tonight," Creag replied in a teasing manner. "At dinner."

"I don't think I'll want anything else. I've eaten entirely too much already." Steppie sighed and put down her empty plate. "Would you like another cup of tea?" she inquired.

Creag nodded and watched her pour the liquid,

noting her small hands in their grave, graceful movements.

Almost as if by tacit agreement, neither Steppie nor Creag mentioned their earlier conversation. He was surprised that she had not reacted more strongly to the revelation. Could it be that its import had not registered fully? Creag knew that he had done the right thing by getting her out of Atlanta. And if he married her, she could remain without fear at the Hacienda Dzibilchaltún for the rest of her life. She and the baby. He would change his way of business, remaining in the Yucatán for the larger part of the year and returning to the States only occasionally to check on his interests.

There were problems, of course, that he would have to work through—mainly what to do about Belline and Daniel. But the two were settled for the next several months. His immediate concern was Steppie. He hesitated to imagine what might have happened to her if she had stayed in Atlanta.

Interrupting his introspective thoughts, Creag said, "If you feel rested by tomorrow, you might wish to see some of your surroundings, especially the Mayan ruins."

A sudden clatter caused Creag to look more closely at Steppie. She steadied her cup in its saucer and quickly rose from the sofa. She acted as if she hadn't heard his suggestion.

Abruptly, she said, "Thank you, Creag, for the tea. I think I'll go to my room now."

"Steppie, what's the matter?" Creag hastily arose from the adjacent chair. But she was gone. She fled across the wide expanse of tile, up the stairs, and disappeared from the gallery while he stood and watched. She had been close to tears. That much he had noticed.

Creag returned to his chair and picked up his teacup. But he put it down without drinking, and walked to the table to pour himself some Kahlua instead. For the past two days, Steppie had behaved extremely well under adverse conditions—not knowing where they were going, or why. Now she knew the answers to both. She was entitled to her tears. He would not breach her privacy while she shed them.

His protectiveness toward Steppie blossomed in full measure. He loved her and, during the time she waited for the child to be born, he would do everything in his power to make her forget her unhappiness. And he would forget that she'd had a hand in her husband's murder. He had no way of knowing what had precipitated it. But who was he to judge—a soldier of fortune hired to kill other men?

That evening when the cool jungle breeze swept through the hacienda and whistled down the corridors of ancient Mayan buildings, Creag Trent stood alone in the courtyard and gazed out into the darkness.

Steppie had not come downstairs again after *merienda*, but he was not surprised. Neither was he alarmed, with Xytl looking after her. The gentleness, the timeless integrity of her Mayan ancestry dwelled in Xytl, as in his superintendent, Sayil, who oversaw the henequen plantation and the factory that processed the fibers for export.

Creag threw down his cigarette, ground it out with his boot, and turned to walk up the stairs.

"Creag?"

He recognized Steppie's voice from the shadows. "Yes?"

She moved into view and walked from the porch toward the steps. "I've come to apologize," she said, "for running away this afternoon."

His voice was gruff. "You have no reason to apologize."

"Oh, but I do. I've thought about what has happened and I know you did what you thought was right for the child and me. I realize, too, how inconvenient all this is to you, Creag, and I promise I won't complain or get in your way while I'm here."

A low rumbling began in Creag's throat. Quickly, before he could say anything, she said, "No, let me finish. In return for my promise, I want you to promise me that when I'm strong enough to travel, after the baby comes, that you'll take me home."

In the distance, the cry of a jaguar caused Creag to lift his head. It was closer now—a bad sign.

"I want your promise, Creag."

He faced Steppie again. He saw his plans crumbling at his feet, like the shrine at Uxmal. So she was stronger and more willful than he thought. But three months. She could change her mind in that length of time.

"Creag?"

"On one condition, Steppie."

"What condition?"

"You'll allow the priest to marry us before the baby comes. It's the only way our son or daughter will have my protection by law."

Steppie moved backward, feeling her way with her hand like a blind person. "You would do that—for the baby?"

"Yes."

"I…I'll have to think about it," she responded, her voice almost lost to him in the rustling of trees. She shivered from the coolness of the air.

He saw her shiver, and in a protective voice he said, "Go back inside, Steppie. It's too cool for you out here. I'll see you in the morning."

When she had gone, Creag lit another cigarette. He must be careful not to overwhelm her with his love. Let her find out gradually, until she became accustomed to the knowledge and the feeling. He could tell by her actions that she had no idea he loved her. Perhaps it was best. Let her think he wanted to marry her because of the child. Yes, it was much better that way.

Creag saw the light in her room go out. It was late, time to return indoors.

Off and on during the night, Steppie woke in a strange bed, a strange room, with unaccustomed sounds—the call of a wild animal, the shriek of a tapacamino bird—causing her to sit up. There was something she had to think about. What was it? Creag. That was it. She must make up her mind whether to accept his offer of marriage. The accusation of murder had changed everything. She lay awake, staring at the shadows dancing on the wall. Later, when she shut her eyes, she was no closer to a decision than she had been when she first went to bed.

Chapter 18

Seated at the breakfast table opposite Steppie the next morning, Creag casually inquired, "Have you decided?"

She was dressed that morning in a *huipil,* the white overblouse reaching to her knees and partially covering the lace-edged skirt that hung the rest of the way to the floor.

"Yes, Creag."

"So…"

"For the child's sake, I'll marry you."

Creag leaned back in the chair and sipped his cup of *mate.* It was difficult for him not to show his satisfaction at her answer. "I'll go into Mérida after breakfast, then, to talk with the priest. Do you have any preference as to when you'd like the ceremony to take place?"

"No. I'll leave that up to you."

Creag nodded and forced himself to continue eating. A subdued Steppie picked at the melon on her plate and Creag, seeing her expression, became angry. She looked as if she had just sold her soul to the devil. Well, that couldn't be helped. He had too much to do to worry about her reaction right now. Creag stood as Steppie excused herself from the breakfast room. Then, he too left the table.

Later that morning, Creag rode down the avenue of cypress trees that lined the approach to the hacienda. And Steppie, standing at the window on the gallery, watched him disappear.

In Mérida, Creag left the carriage on the Paseo Montejo and traveled through the square on foot. A shoeblack kneeled on the corner of the plaza and shined the leather shoes of a businessman who sat patiently reading his newspaper.

Creag walked past, taking note of the old familiar sights, the pink and white and blue colonial buildings, and the square peopled with men whose features resembled carvings of the Mayan rain god, Chac, with their long noses extending to their foreheads in a straight line, without indentation.

Finally he reached the cathedral in the middle of the square, built upon the ruins of an ancient temple. Everywhere he looked, the two cultures were inescapably combined — heart of Maya, soul of Spain.

The priest at the cathedral beamed at the sight of Creag. "The news of your arrival yesterday has preceded you, Señor Creag," he announced in careful English.

Creag acknowledged the greeting with a bow. "Then you already know, Father, that I've brought a woman with me this time."

The priest affirmed the information with a smile. "Your wife?"

"Not yet."

The priest's expression became guarded.

"That's what I've come to see you about."

A shared glass of wine, a final cementing of arrangements, and then Creag, with his pockets considerably lighter, left the small office of the priest and headed once again to the square. He had some shopping to do before going back to Hacienda Dzibilchaltún.

On the way home it began to rain. With his large hat protecting him, Creag did not begrudge this last stubborn vestige of the hot and humid months in the Yucatán; for the season was rapidly giving way to a cooler, more pleasant part of the year.

In the afternoon, when the hacienda awoke from

siesta, a refreshed Steppie came downstairs. She had changed her dark, low-heeled shoes for a pair of rope sandals that Xytl had brought her.

As she walked over the cool tiles of the entrance hall, Creag, working in his office, glanced up and saw her. "Steppie," he called, rising from his desk. She paused while he walked out to meet her.

"I didn't realize you'd returned from Mérida," Steppie commented.

"Only an hour ago," he said. "I stopped on the way back to talk with Sayil."

Conscious of the reason for Creag's going into town, Steppie waited for him to speak of his visit to the priest.

"Sayil was getting ready to load the ship with henequen," Creag explained.

Steppie disguised her feeling of disappointment. So he wasn't going to volunteer any information, it seemed, and she was too self-conscious to inquire about the marriage arangements. With nothing else to say, she turned and took a step toward the large teakwood door.

"Are you going somewhere?" Creag asked.

"Out into the courtyard for a walk. I feel the need of some exercise."

She looked well rested, Creag thought, pleased with the way she had stood the long trip. "Would you like to go to the ruins at Dzibilchaltún, instead? You might enjoy the scenery."

"Is it far from the hacienda?" she inquired, warily.

"Too far to walk," he commented. "I'll take you in the carriage, if you wish."

Feeling perverse because of his secrecy, she said, "You remember, I promised I wouldn't get in your way."

A look of displeasure darkencd his eyes. "Let me be the judge of that, Steppie. Would you like to go?" he asked for the second time.

Steppie stared at him before she answered. "Yes, Creag. Very much."

"Then I'll get the carriage while you tell Xytl that you're going."

"How can I do that when we don't speak the same language?"

"Draw her a picture," he replied over his shoulder as he walked from the entrance hall.

Steppie stood in the middle of the tiled floor and tried to decide whether she really wanted to go with Creag, after all. But she did. Swallowing her anger, she retraced her steps and found Xtyl in the gallery upstairs. As if she were playing charades, Steppie used her hands to imitate Creag and the wheels of the moving carriage. The woman smiled in understanding, but before Steppie could leave, Xytl took her by the hand and led her to a chest in the gallery. She pulled out a *rebozo*, or shawl, and gave it to Steppie.

With the shawl across her arm, she left the hacienda and walked into the courtyard to wait for Creag and the carriage.

The sun had come out again, sending its rays through the soft clouds that hung in great billowy pillows throughout the sky. Down the avenue of cypress trees they went, Creag careful to keep the horses at a safe, slow pace.

"What does Yucatán mean?" Steppie asked suddenly.

"Land of Pheasant and Deer," Creag replied. "But there're many other types of wildlife here, too," he went on. "Ocelot, jaguar, turkey…"

"And *jejenes*," Steppie added, brushing her arm as she felt an insect bite her.

"Put the *rebozo* around you," Creag ordered. "Your delicate white skin is a temptation even for the insects."

Steppie glanced quickly at Creag, whose eyes returned to the horses. He slowed the carriage and turned off onto a narrow trail, suitable only for a horse-drawn vehicle.

"The main road goes on to Progreso, the seaport,"

Creag explained. "If we had come a month earlier, we would have gone directly there to a cottage on the seashore. The heat is too oppressive at the hacienda in July and August."

"When I was a child, we went to the mountains each summer to escape the heat in Atlanta," Steppie commented.

She became silent, remembering those carefree days when her greatest worry had been which toys to take to the mountains and which to leave at home. Steppie was so locked into her memories of the past that she saw little of the countryside until the trail widened to a white road and an ancient temple rose out of the tangle of trees, vines, and shrubs.

"The Temple of the Seven Dolls," Creag announced, seeing her interest.

"Isn't that a strange name for a Mayan temple?" a curious Steppie asked.

"The archaeologists named it after they excavated the temple and found the dolls. I'm sure the Mayans had another name for it, but it's lost to us."

Steppie climbed from the carriage with Creag's help. She started toward the temple, but Creag stopped her. "Wait, Steppie," he urged. "There's a *cenote* nearby. I don't want you to fall into it. Stay there until I hobble the horses."

She stopped and, waiting for him, gazed around her to see if she could discover what he was talking about. Her eyes, sweeping the graveled space, saw nothing except a large hole in the ground. Was that what a *cenote* was—merely a hole? She edged closer when his back was turned to her and, cautiously peering down the hole, she saw that it was partially filled with water.

"You'd better be careful," Creag advised, coming to stand beside her. "That's where they threw young virgins for sacrifice to Chac, the rain god."

"Then I would hardly qualify on either count," she

confessed. "I'm safe."

His eyes swept over her. "Safe only from Chac, perhaps," he teased.

Pretending not to notice, Steppie commented, "I didn't realize the Maya were so bloodthirsty. I thought they were gentle people."

"Compared to the Aztecs, they were. Most of the time they sacrificed grain and flowers, but they've been known to use a few humans too, especially during a drought. At least, they gave the victim a fighting chance. If the virgin could swim out of the *cenote*, the priests let her live."

"Oh, that was sporting of them." With an expression of distaste, Steppie turned from the *cenote* and began to walk toward the steps of the temple.

Stone carvings of Chac and other deities lined the way. Steppie reached out to touch one of them and part of the stone disintegrated. She drew her hand back quickly. "It's amazing, isn't it, to realize that thousands of years ago, people worshipped stone idols and built pagan temples in their honor."

"Your Stone Mountain isn't so different from all this, if you think about it," Creag challenged. "Only Chac, the rain god, has been replaced with the Confederate gods of war—Lee, Jackson, and Davis."

Steppie laughed. "I hadn't thought of it in that way."

"There's a primitive recognition in all people, in all ages—the strength is in the rock. We're all 'children of the rock'."

He stooped and picked up a handful of dirt from the jungle floor. "What is dirt—the earth—but crushed rock? It gives us sustenance, and when we die and are buried, we become part of the rock again." Steppie watched while Creag sifted the dirt through his fingers and then brushed his hand against his trousers.

"Your historians say that Atlanta was founded because of the railroad, but that came later. People were attracted first to the rock, the mountain of stone."

Steppie opened her mouth, but Creag stopped her from speaking. "Oh, the citizens of Atlanta might deny that they're influenced by such a primitive passion. That's to be expected. But the rock presides over everything. It's visible from the capitol windows, from city hall, from the bank buildings, and from each church steeple. And the people are aware of its shadow, in everything they do."

Creag looked sheepishly at Steppie. "But that's enough philosophy for today. I merely wanted you to see that the Maya civilization wasn't the only one influenced by stone."

Steppie smiled. "In the wilderness, Moses, the Deliverer, was punished when he struck the rock in anger. He never entered the Promised Land."

Creag's laugh echoed down the long avenue of the temple. "I thought you were going to argue with me. But you actually understand what I'm talking about."

They began to walk up the steps of the temple. "And I felt it, too, Creag," Steppie admitted. "Eleven years ago when the carving on the mountain was dedicated. I was on the ledge, and almost fell to my death. In that split second between life and death, I had this ambivalent feeling, as if a mysterious force within the mountain were calling to me. But then someone rescued me and the feeling was forgotten—until this very moment."

In words barely audible, Creag confessed, "I know. I was the one who rescued you that day."

"You?" Steppie stared at Creag in amazement. "That's impossible. The man was one of Borglum's stonecutters."

"*I* was the stonecutter."

Almost as if seeing Creag for the first time, Steppie examined him with her eyes, tracing the planes of his face—each line, the cleft in his chin, the V-shaped frown line on his brow.

And then she looked at his muscular arms, his

hands, and back to the mouth that showed no emotion.

"I went back later to thank you, but you had gone."

"Yes."

The revelation was so astonishing that Steppie could think of nothing else to say. All her thoughts were centered on that day when Creag had unknowingly changed her life.

They walked along the corridors of the columned temple, but Steppie, unaware of the eons of ghosts that walked with her, felt only the presence of Creag Trent beside her.

Finally, Creag said, "Come, we've been out long enough. Let's go back to the carriage."

Chapter 19

By the time Steppie arrived at the hacienda, the clothes Creag had purchased that morning were all there. Xtyl, smiling broadly, took her hand. She led her up the stairs to the sitting room adjoining her bedroom; then pushed open the door and stood aside for Steppie to enter.

On every chair, on the sofa and the twin pier tables flanking each side of the door, clothes were spread out; beautifully embroidered, loose-fitting, colorful costumes, with shoes and sandals. Yet when Steppie saw the dress hanging on the door to the balcony, the others paled into insignificance.

Made of delicate ecru lace edged with gold, the floor-length dress had an exquisite, transparent long-sleeved silk caftan over it. The caftan was also shot through with gold, and beside it, on the adjacent chair, sat a square headpiece. Six inches in height—exotic, pagan, the intricate gold filigree was set with opals and the same transparent silk, as the dress, attached to it, like a veil. Without being told, Steppie knew it was her wedding dress.

She walked farther into the room and, almost afraid to touch something so exquisitely made, stood before the dress in awe. Xtyl was not so shy. She babbled happily, picked up the headpiece, placed it on Steppie's brow and then motioned her toward one of the long mirrors that hung over the twin pier tables.

Slowly, Steppie walked toward the mirror. The *huipil*

she wore looked coarse and out of place with the headpiece. Only the delicate lace dress would be appropriate with it. She stared at herself in the mirror. The shape of the headpiece was disturbingly familiar. Where had she seen the design before? Quickly, she snatched it from her head; for it was the same shape she had seen on the stone idols at the ruins that afternoon.

Steppie fled from the room, out to the gallery, leaving a puzzled Xytl holding the filigreed headpiece. In her haste to escape, Steppie almost bumped into Creag as he came up the stairs. "You act as if you've just seen a ghost," he commented, touching her arm and feeling it tremble. "Is anything wrong?"

"No. I...I suppose it's a delayed reaction from the afternoon. The ruins must have affected me more than I thought."

Seeing the unrest in her eyes and noticing her rapid breathing, he calmly said, "You mustn't let the past disturb you like this, Steppie. The ruins are just a part of Mexican history, nothing more."

"I think Chac must have followed me home." Her attempt at humor caused Creag's lips to twitch, in spite of himself.

"Impossible. He stays at the bottom of the *cenote*, like all good rain gods—just as Neptune stays in the briny deep."

Her breathing slowly returned to normal. "You have a soothing manner about you, Creag Trent."

Creag smiled. "A hot cup of *mate* will be even more soothing."

"Is it time for *merienda*?"

"Yes. I was coming to find you. Toluca has it ready for us."

Over the cup of tea, Creag casually asked, "Did you find the clothes?"

"Yes, Creag. I should have thanked you immediately," she answered in an apologetic tone.

"I want no thanks," he said, brushing aside her apology. Putting down his cup, he announced, "I saw Father Benito this morning."

She looked up and waited for him to continue.

"He's coming to the hacienda at noon tomorrow."

"I'm not Catholic, Creag."

"Neither am I."

"Then, how—"

"There's no Protestant minister in Mérida. Father Benito is a personal friend, Steppie. He'll perform the ceremony as a favor to me. Then, later, we'll register the marriage with the authorities." He picked up the cup and took a swallow of tea. "If the dress is too long for you, Steppie, get Xytl to hem it for you tonight."

"Yes, Creag."

Steppie did not see Creag for the rest of the afternoon and when she ate her evening meal in the baroque-looking dining hall, the place at the other end of the table was empty.

Creag Trent had left, she supposed, to celebrate his last evening as a bachelor. Was he already regretting giving up his freedom? Steppie wondered. But the marriage was only to give their child his protection, which wasn't the most romantic of reasons for two people to be joined in wedlock.

After she went to bed, dreams plagued Steppie for half the night. She was back again, on the mountain ledge with Neal. She reached out for help and a man grasped her arm. But the man had no face, no identity.

The sun rose slowly over the henequen fields at the Hacienda Dzibilchaltún. Birds sang in the cypress trees and flitted back and forth to the balustrade on the balcony near Steppie's bedroom.

Gradually, as the morning sounds increased, she awoke. Yawning and stretching, Steppie brushed aside the netting, climbed out of bed, and walked across the room to open the draperies. She blinked her eyes at the full impact of the sun. Everywhere she looked, the landscape was bathed in a strange, golden glow.

Today was her wedding day. She was to be married to the man who had saved her from the mountain. Yes, the stonecutter. She had not been able to piece together his facial features in her dream, but Steppie had no difficulty recalling each facet of his face now. Creag Trent. How strange to realize that Creag had held her destiny in his hands, even then.

A nervous Steppie kept to herself all morning, not venturing from her room, but as noon approached she knew that it was past time to get dressed. She rang for Xytl.

Down the avenue of cypress trees Father Benito drove, in a small open carriage pulled by two large bays. His wide black sombrero filtered the sun from his eyes as he drew the carriage to a halt in the courtyard of the hacienda.

The priest's journey through the henequen fields had been duly noted by the workers. One by one, by threes and fours, the men left the fields, went home to wash the dust from their hands and faces, and began their slow descent on the Hacienda Dzibilchaltún. Their *patrón* was taking a wife and he had ordered them to stop working out of respect while the ceremony took place. And for the rest of the afternoon, they would have their own celebration in the sheds—with music and *sangria*, which the *patrón* had provided.

Dressed in the gold lace wedding dress, with the silk caftan over it, Steppie suddenly turned to Xytl. "How I wish I could talk to you, Xytl. A woman on her wedding day should have someone to share her doubts and her fears. He doesn't love me. He's only doing this because of the baby. Did you know that, Xytl?"

She looked at the Indian woman who smiled at her. And Steppie, feeling slightly ashamed for putting into words what she was feeling, sighed and walked into the adjoining sitting room. The only thing left to do now was to put on the headdress.

With deft movements, Xtyl placed the golden headpiece securely on Steppie's head and arranged the folds of the silk veil attached to it. Her bridal dress was now complete.

Steppie's brown eyes stared into the pier mirror at the end of the room. Atlanta, the French Normandy house, the family — Belline and Daniel — all had vanished. Nothing existed beyond the mirror and the woman reflected in it. She stood in pagan headdress and gold lace bridal gown, with the sign of fertility clothing her body, as in the marriage portraits of the Renaissance.

Outside, the sound of music — guitars and the soft serenade of voices — broke the spell of the mirror. Quickly, Steppie walked to the balcony to see what was happening. Down below, the courtyard was filled with workers in white shirts and white trousers, and in front of them stood three men, their eyes lifted toward the balcony, their voices joining with the guitars in a haunting love song. Tears came to her eyes as she listened, but at the knock on the door, she consciously brushed them away and hardened her heart. It wouldn't do for Creag to see her face stained with tears. Steppie let the sheer curtain fall into place and she turned her back to the balcony.

Xtyl cracked the sitting room door open only a few inches. Toluca handed a message to her and Xytl brought the slip of paper to Steppie.

"They're waiting for me, Xtyl," she said, glancing from the paper to the Indian woman.

With her head held high, Steppie Wexford walked out of the sitting room only to pause when she reached the gallery that surrounded the second story of the hacienda. The smell of incense rose to meet her at the top of the stairs. In the black and white tiled entrance hall below, she saw the altar that had been set up, with exotic white flowers banked on each side. And behind the altar, a plump Father Benito waited in his white cassock.

Her eyes searched for Creag Trent. Dressed in black silk, with heavy embroidery decorating his jacket, he stood like some conquistador at the base of the steps. As Steppie descended the stairs one at a time, her eyes remained locked with his. As soon as she reached the last step, he took her hand and led her to the altar.

Toluca and Xytl, watching from the gallery above, made the sign of the cross as the priest began. *"Amadeus...ora pro nobis...gratia in plena."* The Latin words rose above the soft music that drifted through the open door—words older than the conquisitadors who had brought religion to Mexico with a sword.

Unfamiliar with the Catholic service, Steppie felt Creag's hand on her elbow as they knelt for prayer. When the chanting stopped, they stood again. Then, the Latin became Spanish as a more personal portion of the ceremony began. Conscious of the man by her side, Steppie listened for a familiar word, some recognition amid the alien syllables with their lisping consonants coming rapidly, one upon the other.

Father Benito paused and looked at Creag.

"Si," Creag responded.

The words began all over again and this time, when he paused, the priest looked toward Steppie. She felt the slight pressure of Creag's hand upon hers. Quickly, she said, *"Si,"* as Creag had done, but without any idea of what she was promising.

The priest held out his hand toward Creag, and Steppie watched as Creag placed a gold ring in Father Benito's outstretched palm. Steppie's body stiffened. She had forgotten to remove Neal's ring from her finger. What was she to do? She couldn't remove it now. It would be far too obvious.

Her distressed brown eyes followed the movement of Creag's ring from the priest to the man beside her, and with a small choking noise, she gazed into the stern face of Creag Trent, as if to warn him. She couldn't watch his anger. She closed her eyes to avoid seeing it when he discovered the other wedding band still in place. But Creag took her right hand instead, and Steppie felt the circlet of gold placed on the third finger. She opened her eyes in surprise. Was that the Spanish custom—the wedding ring on the right hand?

Oblivious of the emotional turmoil within Steppie, Father Benito pronounced the benediction, placing his hands upon their heads. Amen. Her lips trembled as Creag leaned forward and claimed them for one brief moment. The ceremony was over. Creag and Steppie were man and wife.

Immediately, Creag took Steppie by the hand and propelled her across the entrance hall toward the wide open doors looking out onto the courtyard.

"Where are we going?" Steppie asked.

"The workers are waiting to see the *patrón's* new wife."

With a forced smile upon his face, Creag stepped onto the threshold, the doorway making a suitable frame for the wedding portrait. Amid shouts and applause, a self-conscious Steppie stood at Creag's side as the guitars began a new song in their honor. But even if she had desired it, she could not have escaped. Creag's iron grip encompassed her hand and forced her to remain with him.

When the last note of the song died away, and Creag turned to go back inside, he gradually relaxed his grip. In the courtyard, the jovial crowd dispersed toward the sheds where the cool *sangria* waited for them.

"You will stay, Father Benito, for refreshments?" Creag asked as he returned to the entrance hall.

"Yes, Señor Creag. Thank you. I'll join you in a few moments."

His use of English surprised Steppie. If he spoke English, why had he not performed the wedding ceremony in the language she could understand?

Creag led Steppie into the *sala* and indicated the blue cushioned chair for her to sit down. With his eyes holding some unfathomable emotion, he bent toward Steppie and demanded, "Remove the ring from your left hand, Steppie."

She flushed with embarrassment. So he *had* noticed. She gazed first at her left hand and then at her right. Slowly, with Creag watching her every movement, she twisted the band from her left hand.

He disguised his sense of satisfaction as he took the band and placed it on the adjacent table, just as Father Benito entered the room.

Less than a half-hour after the priest had left, after the refreshments had been cleared from the table and the entrance hall bore no sign of the wedding beyond a fallen white flower petal, Creag accompanied Steppie upstairs and walked with her into the sitting room. A tense Steppie removed the golden headpiece; for its weight was already giving her a headache.

Abruptly, Creag closed the door and, looking at his watch, announced, "I have to fly into Mexico City this afternoon, Steppie. I'll be back sometime tomorrow. For your own safety, I don't want you to leave the hacienda while I'm gone."

A feeling of anger erupted and swept over Steppie at his announcement. So he could hardly wait to leave her now that they were married.

"And I'm supposed to obey you without question, Creag? Was that in the wedding ceremony—my promise to obey?"

"Yes. Among other things."

"Such as?"

"You know the traditional vows, without my telling you."

"To love? To honor? But we both know this isn't a traditional marriage, Creag. Else you wouldn't be leaving me as soon as the priest pronounced us man and wife."

"I have to go, Steppie. I can't put it off any longer. And that reminds me..." He walked to Steppie, gently took her right hand and removed the wedding band. "We'll put the ring where it actually belongs." He placed it on her left hand and gazed into her eyes. "Don't ever take it off, Steppie Trent."

He left the room and Steppie, uncertain of her feelings toward him, heard the door close. The name lingered in the air. Steppie Trent. That was the first time he had called her by his name.

Chapter 20

Flying along the coast of Mexico as it curved and cradled the Gulf, Creag Trent counted off the cities the way that Father Benito counted off the beads of his rosary: Campeche, Coatzacoalcos, and Ciudad del Carmen.

He marveled at the brilliant white sand, the fishing boats and lighthouses, sprinkled between thatched huts and coconut palms; at the azure waters catching the afternoon sun that bleached the walls built to protect the cities from pirate invasion. But too late. No walls had protected the port of Veracruz; for it was here that Cortez had landed and started westward in his conquest of the Aztecs.

On a more peaceful mission, Creag turned inland and followed the route of Cortez. He soared into the clouds over the sand dunes of Veracruz to pass over the Continental Divide, the Cofre de Perote. Below him, the coffee plantations nestled in the valleys between the mist-shrouded volcanic mountains. The route, measured in months by Cortez, was measured in mere hours by Creag Trent. By late afternoon, with the sun in his eyes, he approached Mexico City, the jewel of Montezuma, surrounded by snow-capped peaks of Ixtaccihuatl and Popocatepetl.

If his luck held, Creag would finish his business by the next morning and start back to Mérida before the sun had reached its height. He had not wanted to leave Steppie, but time was running out. With guards posted around the hacienda, and with Xytl inside, she should be safe until he returned.

The golden angel, the landmark that presided over the heart of the old city, came into view. Creag, seeing it, prepared his plane for landing.

Steppie, left alone so abruptly on the afternoon of her wedding day, wandered through the empty halls of the Hacienda Dzibilchaltún. Her pride had been hurt. Forced to appear before Creag's *mestizo* workers as his bride when she was so obviously pregnant had been degrading enough, but the ultimate humiliation had come when Creag abandoned her an hour after the ceremony had been performed. She had seen the pity in Xytl's eyes. A man didn't leave his wife on their wedding day, unless he had no regard for her feelings.

Steppie stared down at the heavy gold ring on her hand. The gold's texture and its weight upon her finger felt alien; she had become accustomed to the feel of the other—Neal's ring. During the ceremony, she had been so worried that the ring would cause Creag embarrassment. She wished it had. They would be even now—eye for eye. Remembering that the discarded ring had been left on the table, Steppie walked toward the *sala* to retrieve it.

Through the windows the noise of the fiesta magnified. The celebration that started at midday had gained in intensity, and the *sangria,* long disposed of, had been replaced with the more potent *tequila.* Eduardo, posted in the courtyard, smiled at the noise. He would like to be there, himself, to dance and sing, to drink a little *tequila.* But alas, he was on duty. He shifted the carbine to his other shoulder and began to make his rounds.

Shadows filled the entrance hall and the lights flickered as Steppie paused. The windmills were silent. Not a trace of breeze filtered into the hacienda. In fact, Steppie realized there had been no breeze all afternoon to provide power for the generator. Steppie quickened her pace. If the lights should go out, she didn't want to be stranded downstairs.

The cushion of the blue chair, filled with soft down, still showed the indentation where she had sat earlier that day. Steppie leaned over and brushed the cushion with her hand to bring it to its former plumpness. Then her eyes searched for the ring on the nearby table.

The ring was gone. Steppie frowned. She held onto the chair as she slowly crouched to the floor and began to look for the ring underneath the table. But it wasn't anywhere to be found. Someone must have moved it. Who? Creag—or Toluca, perhaps?

Frustrated, she rose from her knees and retraced her steps across the entrance hall. She looked up and, for one brief moment, she saw a face peering from the open door of her sitting room. Then it was gone. Annoyed at being spied upon by one of the servants, she walked toward the stairs.

The lights flickered again and then went out, leaving the hacienda in blackness. Exasperated, Steppie reached toward the curved banister. Her eyes would have to become acclimated to the darkness before she attempted to climb the stairs to her room. It would be dangerous to the baby if she fell. While she waited for her eyes to adjust, the heavy teakwood front door, with its nail-studded crosspieces, made a squeaking sound. Steppie, standing in the darkness, froze as the door slowly opened and a figure, dressed in white, making no noise, stealthily moved across the tiles.

Catching her breath, Steppie watched the figure coming straight toward her. He was up to no good. She knew that, but it was too late to escape. Even in the darkness, the man would sense her movement if she attempted to flee before him. Making herself stand as still as possible, she blended into the darkness beside the stairs. The man passed within a hair's breadth of Steppie, his fingers on the banister touching the same spot where Steppie's hand had rested only moments before.

Upstairs, Xytl's voice rose in alarm, and then was silenced. And Steppie, recognizing the danger within the house, fled. She chose the quickest exit—the heavy front door through which the bandit had come. For now, she was certain the man's purpose was to steal the valuable headpiece she had worn that noon at her wedding.

Where were the guards that Creag had told her would be patrolling the grounds of the hacienda? Had they left their posts to join the merrymaking at the sheds? Not knowing in which direction to go, she quickly decided to follow the music; for that was the only direction she was sure of finding help.

At the edge of the courtyard, the guard, with his back to Steppie, sat and smoked a cigarette, his carbine slung over his shoulder. Relieved to see the man, Steppie rushed toward him. "Quick," she said, "there's someone in the house."

He slowly turned and put out his cigarette. Too late, Steppie saw Eduardo bound hand and foot and lying on the courtyard stones. The stranger, wearing the guard's carbine, smiled when he saw her and reached out to stop her escape.

Dr. Emiliano Lopez walked out of the Institute of Medicine with the black bag in his hand. For forty years he had practiced medicine, and in that length of time, he had seen much of life and death. He had once delivered an Indian baby only moments after its mother had died from a revolutionary's bullet; he had been taken, blindfolded, through a mountain pass to care for Zapata himself.

Now he was getting old, and he dreamed of an undisturbed siesta, meals brought to the table while they were still fresh and hot, and most of all, time in the evenings to read his treasured leather-bound books.

He looked at the man beside him. Creag Trent had been entirely too persuasive, assuring Emiliano that he could have all those things and more, if the doctor would be his guest for three months, until the birth of his child. And so, Emiliano, with his own children gone and his wife dead, decided to forsake his empty house, the poorly prepared meals, and accept Señor Trent's invitation.

With his black coat draped over his slightly stooped shoulders, and his proud leonine head turning to gaze straight forward into questioning eyes, Emiliano Lopez gave the appearance of a benevolent old buzzard.

"We'll be at the hacienda in time for tea, Dr. Lopez," Creag assured him as they climbed into the victoria waiting in front of the Institute.

The doctor nodded. "The last time I 'accepted' an invitation of this nature, Señor Trent, I rode a burro through the mountains. It will be much more comfortable, flying over the mountains, instead."

On the return trip, Creag Trent flew away from the sun. The most dangerous part of the journey was the first few hours, and by the time he reached the coast and the white sandy beaches, Creag relaxed and flew low over the water, noting the tranquil turquoise lagoons that mirrored his plane.

The marketplace in Mérida was filled with people, flowers, and fruit, and as he passed over it, he watched Dr. Lopez and his obvious enjoyment of the scenery viewed from above.

Creag saw the green-gold agave fields beyond his right wing, and knew he was home. As some of the workers gathered before the hangar, he eagerly set the plane down on the runway. With a smile, he leaped from the cockpit and reached out to help Dr. Lopez emerge with his black bag. But before he had a chance to get to the waiting carriage, Creag was stopped by Eduardo, standing in his path. He waved the doctor on to the carriage and stayed behind for Eduardo to speak.

All trace of *machismo* had vanished from the guard. With trembling hands, he pressed a large piece of brown paper toward Creag, while his eyes held unspeakable penitence.

"What's this, Eduardo?"

The guard swallowed and his voice, ripped from his constricting throat, formed the dreadful words. "It is a message, señor, from the bandits who kidnapped the señora."

Eduardo, removing the revolver from his holster, presented it to Creag. "You may shoot me, señor, for failing to protect the señora while you were away."

Creag, ignoring the proffered revolver, read the crudely printed words. "We have your wife. If you want her returned alive, leave 100,000 pesos on the steps of the Temple of the Seven Dolls at midnight tomorrow night."

The rage within Creag exploded as he crushed the paper in his hands. Every known expletive he had ever uttered in either Spanish or English now rent the air.

Again, Eduardo pushed the revolver toward the man. "Shoot me, señor. Please," the guard pled.

The pulse in Creag's throat throbbed. "You saw them? You can identify them?"

"*Si*, señor."

"Then what good would you be, Eduardo, as a dead man? Get the horses and meet me back at the hacienda."

"*Si*, señor."

Creag rushed toward the carriage where Dr. Lopez waited. Waving the driver from the carriage, Creag Trent took over the reins. And a sad Dr. Lopez, holding on to his black bag, realized his long-awaited dream of tranquility and peace had once again been postponed.

* * *

Somewhere in the twenty square miles of the Dzibilchaltún ruins, far past the *cenote* and the Temple of the Seven Dolls, Steppie Wexford Trent sat up on a dirty cot. She rubbed the place underneath her right eye where the *jejene* insect had bitten her. She could still feel the fire of its sting, the swelling, angry and red, matching the bites on her arms and legs.

The sound of the plane had awakened her. Creag had evidently come home. What would he say when he discovered she was gone from the hacienda?

The walls surrounding her were vaguely disturbing—dark blood red, with intricate carvings and a terrifying relief of some ancient ruler dropping into the jaws of a death monster. She was inside a pyramid. That much she realized. Steppie, with nothing else to distract her, sat on the cot and traced the cross behind the carved figure. She had no idea that she was seeing the sacred *ceiba* tree, rooted in hell, but with its branches reaching to the heavens, where the *quetzal,* the sacred bird of the Maya, roosted. She only knew that the carving was oppressive, and that the tomb might well become her own. But, no. She mustn't think that. Surely, Creag would pay the ransom.

Steppie berated herself for running into the courtyard. If she had not bumped into the bandit, but had remained hidden in the darkness by the stairs, the bandits would probably have been content with the golden headpiece. Kidnapping her had merely been an afterthought.

Not yet well excavated by archaeologists, the northern half of the Dzibilchaltún ruins was strangled by overhead vines that encroached like some green monster.

Into this mass of jungle growth, Creag and Eduardo rode their horses. Creag had not wanted to bring the man along, but Eduardo's treatment at the hands of the bandits demanded revenge. He would never be able to hold up his head again as a man, unless he countered the humiliation with an act of bravery. Creag understood that, and was conscious at the same time of his own guilt in placing Steppie in a position of danger. He had no intention of waiting until midnight for the bandits to release her. He would find her, he vowed, before the sun had set.

Creag attempted to put out of his mind his anger; for he wanted no emotion to cloud his judgment. Yet, he could feel it smoldering within him, like molten lava waiting to erupt when it could no longer be contained within the bounds of the crater holding it. The bandits would rue the night they had dared to touch his wife.

Each time he had come to the hacienda, Creag had been drawn to explore the Mayan ruins more thoroughly. The Mayan stonecutters of two thousand years ago had produced pyramids and tombs equal to the pharoahs'. Those explorations now proved invaluable. Creag knew that in the wide, wild expanse, there were untold numbers of hiding places, but the bandits had not been smart; for Creag, expert at tracking in the steamy jungles, noticed each vine, each limb that had suffered damage in the bandits' flight.

Behind him, Eduardo's horse stumbled. The man quickly shifted his weight in the saddle and pulled on the reins to lift the horse's head. With his body movement, Eduardo saved the horse from going down. Aware of the blending of horse and rider into one entity, Creag smiled and rode on, his eyes searching for clues as to Steppie's whereabouts.

At the edge of a mass of vines, he stopped and examined a small piece of dark material caught on a twig. He fingered the material—the weaving similar to that of a *rebozo*. According to Toluca, Steppie had been wearing a *rebozo*. But the shawl was not unique. It could have belonged to anyone for miles around. Only it was doubtful that an Indian woman would have entered that snake-infested growth of her own free will.

He put the cloth into his pocket and silently touched the hilt of his knife. For the moment, his gun was useless. He wanted no shot ringing out to broadcast his presence. Ducking his head, Creag urged the horse through the small opening of the thicket.

Chapter 21

Like a heart on the sacrificial stone, the sun lay throbbing on the horizon. Slowly drained of red, it sank into the crypt of the earth and its specter, bandaged in white, took the sun's place in the sky.

Deep within the ruins, Steppie lay on the cot and waited for the hours to pass. Beyond the partially open door, she could see one of the bandits calmly sitting on the stone floor. There was no need to guard her; for she could never have found her way out of the ruins alone.

With the small candle at her feet flickering and casting shadows on the glyphs carved into the stone opposite her, Steppie grew drowsy. Against her will her eyes closed. Like a thief, the sleep that Steppie had fought against now caught her, robbing her of her watchfulness.

Outside, along the stairs leading to the temple altar, the sound of a gun startled the doves that had come to roost in the cote of stone above. They fled their sanctuary with a whirring of wings, and came to rest several hundred yards away in a kapok tree, their white-feathered forms resembling eerie blossoms in the paleness of the moon.

Steppie awoke. Her eyes, struggling to focus, searched for the guard. But the guard had disappeared, and all around her the walls were solid, with no indication that there had ever been an opening in the stone wall. The bandits must have closed it while she was asleep.

"Hello," she called out. "Is anyone there?"

No one answered her.

"Hello?" She rose from the cot and began to walk in the direction of the wall. Something—someone—had caused her to waken. Moving her hands along the far wall, she sought the brief interruption of the stone that would signal where the door had been.

The greasy candle that had provided light in the room sputtered now, and with one last wisp of flame, died in the crude, shallow dish. The premonition of darkness that Steppie had experienced in the mausoleum in Oakland Cemetery became reality. Yet the fear that overwhelmed her then was strangely absent now. Merely shorn of her ability to see, Steppie put her ear to the wall and listened.

She knew that someone was on the other side of the door. "Creag," she called out. "I'm inside, Creag."

The wall slowly moved and Steppie backed away as a small glow of light penetrated the musty room. Relieved, she waited for the opening to enlarge enough for her to escape, and with a quick thrust of her body she went out.

"Creag?"

The smile on her face vanished as she recognized the bandit who had stolen Eduardo's   carbine and had left him tied up in the hacienda courtyard.

He reached out his hand. "We go. Quick."

A   bullet   richoceted   against   the   temple   and reverberated through the stillness. Creag. Now, Steppie was certain. Creag had come for her, and she knew she mustn't go with the bandit.

"My *rebozo*," she said, stalling for time. "I must get it."

"No," the man exploded, pulling at her arm. "Señora, come. Now."

How long would it take for Creag to reach her? The

bandit, evidently wondering the same thing, hurried Steppie in another direction, deeper into the labyrinth of corridors and steps, rapidly passing carved walls that in their hideousness and horror far surpassed the glyphs of the death monster and the *ceiba* tree.

"Please," she said, having lost all sense of direcion. "I have a pain in my side. I can't go on." She leaned against the wall and at the sound of approaching footsteps, Steppie suddenly called out, "Creag, I'm here."

"Steppie?"

The bandit swore, quickly extinguished the lantern he was carrying and, leaving Steppie, crept along the wall toward the sound of Creag's voice.

"He's coming toward you, Creag," she warned.

In total darkness, the two men met, clashed, and fought. Steppie, braced against the wall, listened to the sound of fist against flesh, grunts of pain and anger, one crash, then another farther away, and finally—nothing. Silence permeated the darkness of a thousand years and Steppie, not knowing who had been the victor, who had been defeated, remained silent and still, waiting for one or the other to acknowledge his victory.

Then she heard steps, the heavy breathing of a man coming toward her. Steppie's foot touched the lantern but she had no way to light it, to see for herself which man was edging along the corridor—her husband Creag, or the bandit who had kidnapped her.

A lighted match flared in her face, temporarily blinding her. She gasped at the sudden light.

"Steppie." The familiar voice formed her name and she quickly moved toward the man who had spoken it.

"Creag."

The match went out and Creag, striking another, picked up the lantern and lit it. "Let's get out of here," he said."

Creag held the lantern high in one hand and kept his other hand on Steppie's arm. He retraced his steps past the body of the bandit lying on the stones. They climbed upward until they reached the altar steps where priests once stood and where the virgins came to light the fires for the altar. As they stood before the crucible, the white doves flew from the kapok tree to reclaim their places in the cote of stone.

Creag closed the entrance to the temple behind him. "That should keep the bandits from mischief until Eduardo goes for the police," Creag said.

Creag's whistle between his teeth brought the horse into the open. Yet it took Steppie a moment to see him; for the animal was black as the night. "Can you walk down the steps?" Creag inquired.

"Yes."

He lifted her onto the horse and they began the long journey home. With Steppie in his arms, Creag treated the spirited stallion as if he were a common plow horse, incapable of more than a comfortable, plodding gait.

"Why didn't you speak out, to let me know you had overcome the bandit?" Steppie asked.

"I wasn't sure he was the only one with you, until I lit the match."

"Is Eduardo all right?"

"Yes, now that the bandits are caught and you're safe."

"It wasn't his fault," Steppie answered, worried at the tone of Creag's voice.

"I'm well aware of where the blame lies," Creag replied, his voice somber and stern.

Unwilling to pursue the conversation, Steppie watched the white trail of sand before them. They emerged from the thicket and eventually came to more familiar ground. In front of them, in a line, stood the deities guarding the Temple of the Seven Dolls. And beyond that, the *cenote*. Compared to the demons Steppie had left behind, the rain god, Chac, with his hooked nose, appeared almost benevolent in the moonlight.

Seated at the dining table in the hacienda, Dr. Emiliano Lopez had just been served by Toluca when the noise in the hallway interrupted the tranquility of his meal. He put down his napkin and walked to the entrance hall where Creag stood with a bedraggled Steppie in his arms.

Walking across the black and white tiles to meet them, Dr. Lopez took one look at his patient and rolled his eyes to heaven as he threw up his hands. "*Madre de Dios*," he exclaimed, making no clinical attempt to hide his horror. He reached out and touched the puffy swelling under Steppie's eye and, assessing the other *jejene* bites on her arms and neck, he began to speak rapidly to Creag.

The woman in Creag's arms didn't understand a word that the black-coated man said, but Creag replied in Spanish and then swiftly moved toward the stairs.

"Who was that?" Steppie inquired, her head turned in the direction of the stoop-shouldered man.

"Dr. Emiliano Lopez, your personal physician."

"*My* personal physician?" she said in surprise.

"Yes."

"Did he come from Mérida?"

"No. Mexico City."

Creag opened the door to the bedroom and walked inside.

"Then he must have ridden with you in the plane."

"Yes."

Exasperated with the monosyllables, Steppie prodded, "How long will he be staying?"

"Until after the baby is born."

Creag's information, given in a low, almost dis-interested tone, had an immediate impact on Steppie. That was the reason for his leaving so precipitiously—to fetch a physician who would be with her until the baby arrived. She didn't know why that should make her feel so much better, unless…Steppie smiled. The humiliation she had felt at Creag's abandoning her on their wedding day was now wiped from her mind.

Stopping for one brief moment in the dining room, Dr. Lopez gazed longingly at the plate filled with black beans and rice. He sighed and then walked to get his medical bag. His patient needed him.

Much later in the evening, Creag and Emiliano Lopez sat in the two stuffed chairs in Creag's office and talked. Steppie was upstairs with her bites attended to and her needs catered to by Xytl, who still nursed a small bump on her head.

Dr. Lopez tapped his pipe on the ashtray and prepared to fill it with tobacco. "Don't worry, Señor Trent. Your wife is a strong woman."

"Steppie? Strong?" Creag frowned in disbelief.

"Oh, don't let her smallness in stature deceive you. I've seen it before—this dichotomy between outward appearance and the innner soul."

"I'm afraid you've completely misread her, Dr. Lopez. She allows people to take advantage of her at every turn. Even her own daughter rides roughshod over her," Creag growled.

Emiliano smiled. "Do not confuse goodness of the spirit with weakness, señor. I've seen violence triumph for a time, as you have, but in the end, it is always the same—Zapata, Villa, Lenin—where are they now? Dead by the same means through which they lived—violence."

Emiliano struck a match and drew on his pipe until the tobacco caught fire and began to smoke. "It's good that your wife harbors no ill will for her abductors. She'll get over the *jejene* bites within a few days, and when the time comes, she'll bear you a healthy child."

"If they'd harmed one hair on her beautiful head…"

Emiliano nodded in understanding. "You do well to be protective of her, señor. For she not only carries your immortality within her, but that gentleness that is the hope of mankind."

"Martyr's blood," Creag spat out, remembering the promise he had made unwillingly to Steppie.

"What did you say, señor?"

"She has a martyr's blood flowing in her veins," he repeated. "Did she tell you what she plans to do after the baby comes?"

Dr. Lopez shook his head.

"She's going to sacrifice her happiness—mine—the child's—to go back to Atlanta and answer charges against her. And I promised to take her. I actually promised to deliver her to the police. After tonight, I don't think I can go through with it."

Emiliano's eyes grew sad. "A man does not thwart destiny, señor, for his own comfort." Emiliano Lopez regretfully remembered his half-finished plate of black beans and rice, grown cold in the dining room, while Creag Trent, with his head in his hands, felt the chill of the night air surround him, his eyes recalling the crucible before the temple altar deep within the Dzibilchatún ruins.

Chapter 22

In the small clearing where the Beaumont cabin rested under the shadow of Stone Mountain, Alpharetta climbed into her father's wagon. Picking up the reins, she urged the mules toward the old Indian trail that would take her into town. Beside her in the wagon sat the dark, multi-colored velvet valise. Inside it, she had packed her one good dress, the book of poems, and a change of clothes for her father and her two brothers. There was no telling how long she would have to stay, even overnight.

Since Friday, she had been debating what to do. But with the entire weekend gone, she knew there was only one thing she could do—go to Mr. Axel St. John's brother, who was a lawyer, and ask him to get her family out of jail. She had taken the money hidden under the planks of the floor and tucked the bills in an envelope that she pinned to the inside of her blouse. Surely, Mr. St. John, the lawyer, wouldn't charge her any more than that to represent them.

As the wagon rolled down the hollow with Molly and Maggie, the two mules harnessed to the vehicle, Alpharetta couldn't help but admire the beauty of the cool, crisp morning, in spite of the serious matter that prompted her journey.

The poplars were just beginning to turn gold, Alpharetta noticed, and the other hardwood trees, dappled by the sunlight, promised hues of red and wine and pale yellow as autumn claimed the summer crop of leaves.

On the opposite side of the road, she saw the old man with his spotted dog coming toward her. When they drew side by side, the man tipped his hat. "Fine day, ain't it?" he inquired politely.

Alpharetta smiled back at him. "Yes. A mighty fine day," she agreed.

The dog, running by the wagon, chased a squirrel up an oak tree. The squirrel's tail was stiffly splayed in the air and its small, chattering bark announced displeasure at being interrupted in its gathering of nuts. Judging from the furry coat of the squirrel and its bushy tail, Alpharetta decided it was going to be another harsh, cold winter in Georgia

The man whistled to the dog. Alpharetta, conscious of the slowing of the wagon, tightened the reins. "Git up, Molly! Git up, Maggie!" the red-haired girl urged. She'd never get to town if she allowed herself to be sidetracked by every sight along the way. With a determined tilt to her chin, Alpharetta forced herself to keep an eye on the mules and her mind on her mission to town.

By noon, Alpharetta was hungry. She pulled the wagon to the shade on the right side of the road and stopped for lunch. The mules, glad of the rest, stood still under the trees and did nothing more strenuous than swish an occasional fly with their tails.

Taking the straw basket from behind the wagon seat, Alpharetta climbed down. She spread an old linen cloth on the ground, removed the food from the basket, sat down, and began to eat. Acting as if she were dining with royalty instead of in the presence of two animals, she ate daintily, unhurriedly, and in between bites, she practiced her diction.

"*Get* up, Molly! *Get* up, Maggie!" she repeated, remembering her earlier lapse into the vernacular. The mules pricked their ears for a moment at the sound of her voice, then settled down again to swishing flies.

At the sight of the apple dumpling, she grew sad. It was Conyer's favorite dessert. Alpharetta finished only half of it, screwed the lid tight on the Mason jar filled with water, and began to repack the basket.

From the rock pile at the edge of the woods, a strange noise erupted. Realizing she was entirely alone in the middle of nowhere, Alpharetta listened warily. Suddenly, a man's head popped up from the rocks, and then his body came into view—a rag picker, apparently dressed in his own wares.

"Do you have an extra biscuit, little lady?" the man asked. "Haven't had a thing to eat since day before yesterday," he added. She looked at him again, seeing the leaves stuck to his clothes. He'd evidently been sleeping behind the rocks all the time she was eating her lunch.

Alpharetta, conscious of the money pinned to the inside of her blouse, nodded. "I...I'll leave you the basket," she offered. She laid it on the ground again and fled to the wagon. Totally forgetting her diction, she called out, "Git up, Molly! Git up, Maggie!"

As the wagon pulled away, the man snatched up the basket and disappeared behind the pile of rocks.

By two o'clock in the afternoon, Alpharetta reached the wagon yard. Saturday was always the biggest day for people to come into town with their families, but even now, on a Monday, the streets were filled with people. Alpharetta gazed around her and wondered how long Ben Mark had waited for her on Saturday. She supposed he finally left and went to the speedway when she didn't appear at the proper time.

The red-haired girl removed the flowered sunbonnet from her head. She had always been careful to wear it when she was going to be in the sun for any length of time, whether traveling in the wagon or working in her garden. That way, she had only a few freckles sprinkled across her nose instead of a face full, like Mittie Wilkins, who had been in her class at school. Alpharetta put the bonnet under the wagon seat, unhitched the mules, and took them to the shed, where she turned them over to Caesar, the stable hand, for watering and feeding. She reached into her pocket for change and handed the coins to Caesar.

With the velvet valise in her hands, she hurried along Decatur Street, past the pawn shops and their racks of clothes set on the sidewalks to entice prospective customers inside. The smell of fish frying, the street vendor's singing, the dancing dog dressed in a ruffled collar about his neck, and the people milling around gave Decatur Street the appearance of a carnival.

At the corner she looked up and down the street. When she deemed it safe, she crossed to the other side and walked toward Five Points, the center of the business community, where the five Indian trails had once converged at the springs.

Here the appearance of the city changed from carnival to commerce. The bright, colorful clothes on Decatur Street had undergone a metamorphosis on Marietta Street, like the scarlet tanager, molted of its vivid summer colors and dressed in its coat of gray and black.

While she waited for the light to change, Alpharetta suddenly turned to the man beside her. "Excuse me. Could you please tell me where I can find Mr. St. John, the lawyer?"

"Don't rightly know," the man answered, to Alpharetta's disappointment.

"His office is in the William-Oliver Building," a voice behind her offered. She turned to see a tall black woman with two small children clasped to her side. The woman dropped the hand of one child to point. "It's on Kile's Corner — across the street and down past the drugstore."

"Thank you," Alpharetta called after her. Relieved that she wouldn't have to walk all the way to the Peachtree Trust for the information, she shifted the valise into her other hand, turned right, and proceeded in the direction the woman had pointed.

Named for the two Healy sons, the William-Oliver Building stood on the corner in all its skyscraper glory. Alpharetta walked past the drugstore windows and, glancing upward to trace the entwined names with her eyes, she pushed the main entrance door open and walked inside the vestibule.

ALBEE, ST. JOHN AND GRANT. The lawyers' names leaped out at her from the directory on the wall. Third floor. Alpharetta took note of this, while the elevator opened and released its passengers, who swept past her to the street.

"Going up?" a voice called out.

Alpharetta turned around to see who else had come into the building. The glass reflected her image. No one else was in the vestibule.

"Yes," she answered, picking up her valise and walking toward the elevator.

The man closed the folding iron gate. "Which floor?" he asked.

"Third. Mr. St. John's office."

The elevator began to move and Alpharetta, feeling as if she were in a cage like an animal at the zoo, clutched her valise and held onto the railing beside her. She watched the man's hand on the handle; she listened to the whir of the motor, and when the man stopped the cage, her stomach lurched.

"Third floor," he called out, pushing back the wrought-iron gate.

With unsteady steps, she left the elevator behind. At the end of the long, carpeted corridor, she saw the wide double doors with the names, ALBEE, ST. JOHN AND GRANT, printed in large gold letters. She looked back. The elevator was gone. The quiet elegance of the gold-lettered doors intimidated her. Nervously, she pushed her red hair behind her ears. She had come this far. Despite her timidity, she knew that if she were going to get help for Duluth, Conyer, and her pa, she had to walk the rest of the way down the maroon-carpeted corridor, open those doors, and walk inside. Slowly, she began to walk. But at the last minute before she opened the door, she decided to leave the shabby valise in the corridor.

"Excuse me, I'l like to see Mr. St. John," Alpharetta began.

A woman dressed much the same as Alpharetta, in a white shirtwaist and dark skirt, looked up from her desk and smiled when she saw the girl.

"He hasn't come back from court, dear," she said. "He'll be at least another hour."

Alpharetta swallowed her disappointment. "I've come a long way. Do you mind—if I wait for him?"

"Not at all. If you don't mind the waiting."

Alpharetta looked around for a chair in an unobtrusive corner, but before she could sit down, the woman said, "Oh, no. I'm sure he wouldn't want you to wait out here. Go on in to Mr. St. John's office. It will be much more comfortable for you there."

Surprised, Alpharetta remained where she was standing.

"Go on, dear," the woman urged with a wave of the hand toward one of the innner doors.

Not knowing what else to do, Alpharetta walked toward the door. An adjacent one opened and a man dressed in a dark suit and carrying a briefcase almost bumped into her. He reached out his hand to steady her. "Oh, hello, Belline. How are you?" Without waiting for her to answer, he turned toward the woman at the reception desk. "Miss Gadsen, I won't be back this afternoon. If I have any calls that won't wait, just refer them to my house."

"Yes, Mr. Grant."

Feeling like an interloper, Alpharetta walked into Reed St. John's office. The man, Mr. Grant, had mistaken her for someone else—someone named Belline. Puzzled, she sat down in the tall leather chair and began to wait.

Not feeling free to move around the room or to bring in the valise she'd left in the corridor, Alpharetta listened to the ringing of the telephone and the woman's voice in the reception room as she answered the calls. Each time the outside door opened, Alpharetta sat up, alert, waiting for the door to Mr. St. John's office to open also. It remained shut.

The time passed, and to occupy her mind Alpharetta closed her eyes and began to rehearse under her breath what she would say to the lawyer when he finally did appear—why it was so important for him to represent the Beaumont family; how Duluth and Conyer had never been in trouble with the law before. Surely, he would be happy to get her business. She had almost twenty dollars in the envelope. Slowly, Alpharetta's head began to lean toward the curved wing of the armchair….

Miss Gadsen, looking down at the watch pinned to her shirtwaist, saw that it was time to go. Reed St. John had not yet returned to his office, so she picked up the messages for him, opened his door, and laid the papers on his desk. On her way out, she remembered Belline. With so much coming and going in the office, she hadn't seen the girl leave, but of course she would have gotten tired of waiting and gone.

Miss Gadsen put on her black suit coat, kept the lights on for Hagar, the cleaning girl, and walked out of the offices of Albee, St. John and Grant. She looked in distaste at the mangy valise at the door. Deciding it must belong to Hagar, she hurried down the corridor to catch the elevator before Giles shut it down for the night.

Reed St. John sat in Jim Edward's office several blocks from his own. His hands shook as he re-read Creag Trent's letter.

"You know what this is all about, Jim?" Reed asked.

He looked at the other lawyer, who cautiously replied, "No. Only that my client has gone to his plantation in Mexico, as he does several times a year. Nothing out of the ordinary in that."

"Steppie Wexford, my cousin, is with him."

"Is she?"

"Let's stop beating around the bush, Jim. You and I both realize what this means. Somehow Creag Trent must have found out Steppie was wanted for questioning by the police. He flew her out of the country before they got to her. It doesn't look good at all." Reed brushed back the lock of white hair that had fallen to his forehead. "If she went willingly with him, then that alone would be enough to make her suspect in the murder of her husband and give credence to the accusation that Creag's the father of her unborn child."

"You're overreacting, Reed," Jim cautioned. The younger man stood and loosened his shirt collar. Jim Edwards was the image of a younger Axel, his dark hairline beginning to recede from his forehead. And like Axel, he exuded strength and power that made him seem taller.

"Who's to say that Steppie wasn't afraid to stay in the house where her husband had been murdered?" Jim argued. "The baby doesn't have to be Creag's. After all, he arranged for Belline to fly to school in North Carolina, and Belline certainly isn't his daughter. What if Creag's plan was merely to fly Steppie to a clinic in Mexico where she could have the baby quietly?"

He turned and almost as if he were addressing a jury, he continued: "On the other hand, even if they eloped, that doesn't prove anything. Steppie Wexford is a beautiful woman, and Creag lived next door. What man wouldn't fall in love with her and want to protect her — a widow bearing her dead husband's child?"

"It's a scandal, either way," Reed admitted.

"Axel's and Julian's actions over the weekend didn't help matters," Jim commented.

"I'm well aware of that. But Axel and Julian were genuinely concerned about Steppie." Reed folded the letter, put it in its envelope, and stood to go. "If you hear anything more from Creag, let me know," Reed requested.

Mulling over the day's events, Reed walked down Marietta Street toward the William-Oliver Building. He needed to get the papers he'd left on his desk and the law book on *King v. Mairston* to take home. He looked at his watch and hurried. Min-yo would already have dinner waiting for him.

Chapter 23

Reed St. John climbed the stairs and stood before the wide double doors. Not bothering to take out his key, he pushed the door open, crossed the lobby, and continued to his private office.

Alpharetta, hearing him enter, came alive. She quickly stood up by the leather chair. It had been some time since she'd rehearsed what she was going to say. But when the door to Reed St. John's inner office opened, she held her chin high and watched while the man walked to his desk without looking around.

"Mr. St. John?"

"Belline, what are you doing here? I thought you were…"

For the second time, the name bothered her, but she couldn't afford to put her mind on that. She had more important things to discuss.

"Mr. St. John, my name's Alpharetta Beaumont. I've been waiting to see you on behalf of my pa, Tucker Beaumont, and my brothers, Conyer and Duluth."

"Who are you?" he asked, acting as if he hadn't heard her at all.

"My name's Alpharetta," she repeated. Knowing that she had little time to get all the information out, she spoke hurriedly. "My parents land from Mr. Axel, and on Friday, the sheriff came and took him and Duluth and Conyer to jail for makin' moonshine. I…I want you to get them out of jail, Mr. St. John." She held the envelope containing the money in her hand. "There's almost twenty dollars here, and you can have it all, if you'll only help them. Duluth and Conyer haven't ever been in trouble before—" Alpharetta's lip quivered as she offered the envelope to Reed.

Ignoring it, Reed said, "Alpharetta, sit down. Let's start over."

The girl's uncanny resemblance to Belline startled him. Sitting on the edge of his desk, he took in her long red hair, her green eyes, and neat, schoolgirlish figure. She was young, like Belline, but looking more closely, he could detect a slight difference, also.

"How long have you been waiting to see me?"

"All afternoon."

Reed frowned. At the end of the day, Miss Gadsen didn't usually go off, leaving a client in the office.

"I think your secretary forgot about me," Alpharetta said, as if she could fathom Reed St. John's thoughts. "It really wasn't her fault."

He brushed aside her defense. "You're lucky that I came back to the office for my papers. Now tell me again, Alpharetta—why have you come to see me?"

"To get my pa and my brothers out of jail," she repeated. "The sheriff broke up the still and…and I haven't seen them since Friday."

"Where was the still located, Alpharetta?"

"On the other side of Stone Mountain, on the land my pa rented from Mr. Axel. Will you take their case, Mr. St. John? I don't know anyone else to turn to."

She watched him and waited for his decision. In the silence, she didn't dare say anything while he made up his mind.

Finally, Reed St. John said, "I'll see what I can do."

Alpharetta laid the envelope of money on his desk, as if to seal the contract. Reed suppressed a smile and asked, "Now tell me, has your father ever been arrested before, for making moonshine?"

Fifteen minutes later, Alpharetta, satisfied that Reed St. John would help her, left the office and walked into the corridor. To her relief, the valise was still sitting where she'd placed it. She picked it up, went to the elevator, and pressed the button.

She was still standing at the elevator when Reed, with his briefcase in hand and the law book under his arm, appeared in the corridor.

"You'll have to walk down the stairs," he informed her. "Giles has shut down the elevator for the night."

Alpharetta leaned over for the valise and followed Reed St. John down the two flights of stairs to the vestibule of the William-Oliver Building. She stood, forlorn, looking out onto the street and trying to decide the quickest way back to Decatur Street. Even though it was already dark, she knew she would have to start home. She couldn't spend the night in town; for she'd given Reed St. John the entire contents of the envelope.

Somehow, Reed was reluctant to leave her. "Can I give you a ride, Alpharetta?" he inquired.

"Oh, no thank you. If you'll just tell me the quickest way to the wagon yard on Decatur Street..."

"You can't go down in that section alone, after dark. Don't you have somewhere you can spend the night?"

Alpharetta's chin lifted. "I...I need to get home."

Without understanding his protective feeling for someone he didn't even know, Reed said, "Min-yo, my houseboy, can find a bed for you. Come, you'll go home with me."

"No, I can't do that, Mr. St. John."

"My car is parked around the corner. Come, Alpharetta. I'm your family's attorney now. Do as I say."

He took the valise from her and she had no recourse but to follow him to his car.

Upstairs in the law offices of Albee, St. John and Grant, Hagar, the cleaning woman, set down her turkey-feather duster, and walked to the law library. With the office to herself, she pulled a large volume from the shelf, opened it and, sitting down at the refectory table, began to read where she'd left off the night before.

When Reed drove up West Paces Ferry Road, the house was lit, for once, from top to bottom, with the floodlights shining on the allée of dogwood trees.

Alpharetta's mouth dropped open at the sight. It was the most beautiful home she had ever seen. A regular mansion, suitable for a princess. And she, Alpharetta Beaumont, was going to spend the night in that fine house.

"Won't your wife mind?" she questioned as they turned into the drive. "Your bringing a stranger home?"

"My wife isn't well," he informed her. "It won't matter one way or the other."

He stopped the car and walked around to Alpharetta's side. When she climbed out, he took the valise from the back seat. Min-yo, dressed in a white jacket, with his queue hanging down the middle of his back, met them at the side door of the house.

"Here, Min-yo. Take this young woman's valise and show her to one of the spare bedrooms upstairs. She's going to spend the night."

"Yes, Mr. Reed," he said, his dark eyes speculative as Alpharetta emerged from the darkness.

"And set an extra plate in the dining room for supper."

Min-yo tried hard not to show his excitement at the red-haired girl's appearance. But the idea that Mr. Reed might have hired her to take Nurse Jenson's place pleased him immensely. Debating which bedroom to use, Min-yo led the way up the stairs. Because he wanted to make sure that the nurse knew the young woman had arrived, Min-yo decided to put Alpharetta in the bedroom next door to Lola Jenson.

He turned on the light, set the valise on the floor, and

announced, "Supper in very few minutes."

"Min-yo?"

"Yes, missy?"

"Could you tell me where…where I can wash my hands?"

"You have own bath, missy. Through that door." He bowed and was gone.

By the time Alpharetta walked downstairs with her face washed and the tangles combed out of her red hair, Mr. and Mrs. St. John were already in the dining room.

"I'm sorry," Alpharetta apologized, "to be late."

"We were both late," Reed informed her. He turned to his wife. "Anna Clare, this is the young lady I was telling you about—Alpharetta Beaumont."

"How do you do, Mrs. St. John," she replied, quickly taking her place at the table.

The woman looked as if she had robbed the contents of an old attic trunk for the clothes she was wearing. Even Alpharetta knew that the tiara was out of place. Now she realized what Reed St. John meant when he said his wife wasn't well. Because her Grandmother Rowena had taught her not to stare impolitely, she ignored the woman's dress. "It's quite kind of you to allow me to spend the night," she said.

"Who is she, Papa?" Anna Clare asked uncertainly, as if she couldn't remember what her husband had told her.

"One of my clients, Anna Clare. She lives at Stone Mountain and it was too late for her to travel home tonight."

Serving dinner, Min-yo eavesdropped unashamedly on the conversation at the table. He looked at Alpharetta and he had a feeling that things were going to change for the better in the St. John household.

As Alpharetta finished her dessert, leaving a little of the brick ice cream on her plate, so they wouldn't think she was completely without manners, she remembered the fortuneteller's prophecy. She was spending the night in one of the finest houses in Atlanta, but looking from Anna Clare to Mr. St. John, she realized it wasn't at all the way she'd pictured it. And it was just for one night. Tomorrow she would be on her way back to the cabin at Stone Mountain.

Later that evening, when Lola Jenson walked into the kitchen to get Anna Clare's medicine, her curiosity got the better of her. She knew someone else was in the house. She'd caught a glimpse of the girl on the stairs, and had heard her moving around in the room next to hers. Looking at Min-yo, who was putting the clean dishes in the cupboard, she asked, "What's that girl doing here, Min-yo?"

Min-yo beamed. "Missy come—to take your place, maybe?"

She glared at the Chinese houseboy. "Be careful, Min-yo. You might be the one getting the boot, if you're not careful."

He chuckled as she slammed the refrigerator door and walked out of the kitchen.

Alpharetta folded her skirt and blouse carefully over the chair so that they wouldn't get wrinkled, and climbed into bed. She'd kept her chemise on, in case the house caught fire during the night.

She sank deep into the mattress filled with goose down. It felt so different from the corn-shuck mattress at home. But she would give anything to be in the cabin with Duluth and Conyer and her pa; to lie in the uncomfortable bed in the little room, and by lamplight to be reading a poem from the book Ben Mark had given her. The book of poems was in her valise, but she didn't feel like reading tonight. She had far too much to think about.

When she'd driven up to the St. John house, she had no idea that so much sadness was inside. It never occurred to her, before tonight, that rich people weren't always happy. How lonely Anna Clare had looked in that tattered, old dress, as if all the years had passed her by without her awareness. She'd seen the sadness in Reed St. John's eyes when he looked at his wife. But she admired how he had behaved, not apologizing for the way she was dressed.

Alpharetta was grateful that he'd promised to help Duluth and Conyer and her pa, as far as it was possible. She yawned. She must make certain she didn't oversleep. She had to be up in time to ride into town with the man she'd engaged as the family lawyer.

Retiring for the night in the bedroom beyond Anna Clare's, Reed St. John took the law book to bed with him. But as he began to read the dry legalities of *King v. Mairston*, he realized it was useless. He couldn't keep his mind on the case for thinking about Alpharetta Beaumont.

He still didn't know what had possessed him to bring her home with him. But he had taken great delight in watching her, in measuring her reactions to Anna Clare. The girl hadn't batted an eye as she took in Anna Clare's dress and the incongruous tiara perched on top of her head. She'd been well behaved, kind.

It was a pity that life had turned upside down for her, but of course her father had broken the law. There was no possibility Reed could get Tucker Beaumont off, since he'd been sentenced once before for the same offense. The boys, Duluth and Conyer, were another matter. Perhaps the judge would see fit to send them to the CC Camp instead of making them serve time with their father.

Reed had an uncomfortable feeling about Tucker Beaumont and the strip of land where the still was found. It was the James' property on the other side of the mountain, and he'd remembered the discussion at the bank board meeting. With his affinity for fitting events into a time frame, Reed realized from the conversation with Alpharetta that her father had built the cabin on the land before the board had approved his renting of that land. And Axel was a party to the deal—whatever it was. He'd always known that Axel had two sides to him—the sanctimonious one he showed the public, and the deep, dark side that operated from his ambition and need for power.

A restless Reed finally snapped out the light. He had a busy day ahead of him. His appointments calendar for the morning was filled. Then the Sedgwick hearing came up at two o'clock in Superior Court. That would take the entire afternoon. Still, he had to find time to see Axel and Julian about Creag's letter, to talk with Tucker Beaumont, and somehow fit in Kathryn Mansour, after the disturbing message she had left that day. Yes, all in all, it promised to be a hectic day.

As dawn slowly crept into the corner of the guest bedroom and seeped its way through the shadows, devouring them, Alpharetta sat up. She didn't know what time it was, but the aroma of freshly perked coffee and bacon frying drifted up the stairs and curled under her door—a teasing tantalizing aroma. She hopped out of bed, ran to the bath, and ten minutes later, with her skirt and blouse removed from the chair and smoothed over her willowy figure, she followed the aroma of food down the stairway, through the dining room and into the kitchen, where Min-yo stood at the gas stove with his back to the door.

A few minutes later, Reed also walked down the stairs. He always looked forward to breakfast, his favorite meal. He enjoyed sitting in the kitchen, alone with his thoughts, reviewing his plans for the day over his second cup of coffee; and not having to listen to idle chatter in the dining room. Min-yo, quiet and unobtrusive, served him well and didn't seem to mind Reed's early morning invasion. But woe to anyone else who dared to enter his domain at that time or at any other time of the day.

Reed had not wakened Alpharetta on purpose; for there was no reason for her to go all the way back to Stone Mountain today. She could easily remain at his house until he had some news for her. Setting his briefcase by the side door, he walked through the swinging doors to the kitchen and stopped in surprise. Sitting on Min-yo's stool next to the gas range, Alpharetta was eating a strip of bacon and at the same time listening to Min-yo's explanation of the stove's workings.

At the sight of Reed standing by the kitchen door, she smiled and said, "Good morning, Mr. St. John. Min-yo was just showing me how his marvelous stove works."

Reed stifled a laugh. "Good morning, Alpharetta. Min-yo." He walked to the table and, still amazed, sat down. Overnight, Alpharetta had done what Lola Jenson in three years had never been able to accomplish—gain the Chinaman's confidence and seat herself on the one piece of furniture that Min-yo had never allowed anyone else to sit on.

"Come sit at the table with me, Alpharetta. I have something to discuss with you."

She moved from the position next to the stove and, seating herself opposite Reed St. John, she looked up at him with trusting green eyes.

Chapter 24

"Axel, did you know the man leasing the James property is in jail for making moonshine?"

Reed had come straight from the jail, where he'd arranged bond for Tucker and his two sons, and now he sat in Axel's private office at the bank. He watched his brother turn pale, heard the oath sputtered from his lips.

"When was he arrested?"

"On Friday."

"What about the still?" Axel inquired. "Was it destroyed, too?"

"I presume it was." Reed's eyes narrowed. "You act as if you knew he was operating the still."

"Hell, Reed, the man's a farmer. I don't keep up with what any of them plant or plow under. I leave that to Roosevelt. I just rented Beaumont the land."

"Land which Creag Trent wanted to *buy*."

Axel's bushy eyebrows went up. "How did you know that?"

"Jim Edwards told me. He has power of attorney for Trent, and he inquired about the land again. I assume there's nothing standing in the way of the sale, now that Tucker Beaumont will have to give it up."

"There *is* something in the way," Axel vowed. "Me. I'll never let him buy that land."

"Because of Steppie?"

"She didn't go with him willingly. I know that much.

He's a crook and a common kidnapper."

"Axel, you don't know that," Reed cautioned, realizing that his brother had turned the attention from himself to Creag Trent.

"He might even be Neal's murderer, as well," Axel added. "Have you thought of that, Reed?"

"Creag Trent isn't a suspect. Steppie is."

"Blast that Belline for stirring things up. Why couldn't she just have gone on off to school quietly?"

"I'll admit it doesn't look good for Steppie. But in a way, I'm grateful to Creag for taking her where the law can't touch her."

Axel nodded grudgingly. "The scandal would have hurt us all, having Steppie arrested for murder and standing trial."

"The scandal might still erupt," Reed warned. "Verbena said the police came and searched the house this morning. If they found any evidence to present to the grand jury, she can be indicted for Neal's murder." Reed looked at his watch. "I've got to go, Axel. I have a luncheon appointment." He stood up. "You've told Rennie?"

"Yes. She's relieved, of course, that Steppie's safe. She and Verbena both feared something terrible had happened to her. And in my estimation, it has."

"I'll call you if I hear any more."

"Are you going to get Tucker Beaumont off the hook?"

"There's no way. I've already spoken to Lyle. Tucker will be sentenced, but the two boys will probably be put on probation."

"For how long?"

"It's up to Lyle."

Reed left the Peachtree Trust and walked down the street to the Frances Virginia tearoom, where Kathryn Mansour was waiting for him. And Axel, seated behind his massive mahogany desk, brooded over the loss of the still.

* * *

Kathryn, dressed in a navy-blue suit with white blouse, sat at a table in the corner of the tearoom and waited for Reed to appear. For want of something to do while she waited, she crushed the mint leaves against the tall glass of iced tea and took several sips. She was grateful that Reed had suggested meeting for lunch; for she felt a desperate need to talk. Her bank account was depleted. If she didn't get her financial problems solved soon, she might even be forced to accept old Mr. Epwile's offer of marriage. Kathryn grimaced as she thought of it. She'd been independent too long, coming and going as she pleased. And she'd never met the man for whom she was willing to give up her freedom. Then too, Cyrus Epwile would be aghast if he should ever discover the secret she'd kept for fifteen years, but which now might be broadcast all over the city.

Kathryn looked up, saw Reed, and waved. She watched as he made his way past the tables occupied by women in twos and threes, with only an occasional man sprinkled about the room. Kathryn didn't feel entirely comfortable here, either, but it was the most convenient spot to meet. She knew Reed was due in court early in the afternoon.

"Kathryn, how are you?" Reed inquired, sitting down opposite her in the straight-back chair.

"As jumpy as a cat," she said, seeing no reason to lie.

"Why, what is it?" he asked, suddenly solicitous.

The waitress brought the menus, placed them before Kathryn and Reed. "What will you have to drink?" the woman asked, looking at Reed.

"Iced tea," he replied.

When the waitress had gone, Kathryn sighed. "I guess there's no need to warm up to it. I might as well present you the bloody truth, Reed. I'm being blackmailed— about Belline."

Wearing his glasses to look over the menu, Reed slowly lifted his head and gazed into Kathryn's troubled eyes.

"By whom, Kathryn?"

The waitress brought the iced tea and set it down in front of Reed. "Are you ready to order now?" she asked, looking from Reed to Kathryn.

"I'll have the chicken à la king," Kathryn said, forcing her voice to remain steady.

"The same," Reed said, returning the menu to the waitress.

"Two chicken à la kings. Will there be anything else?"

"No. No thank you."

Reed waited until the waitress had gone. "Who's blackmailing you, Kathryn?"

"Carey."

"Carey?" Incredulous, Reed removed his glasses, put them in his breast pocket, and stared at Kathryn.

"She only asked for money occasionally, that is, at first—when she didn't have enough for a certain dress or pair of shoes. But you remember that day she had her accident, when the baboon got out?"

Reed nodded.

"Well, she was furious. Somehow she blamed me for what happened that day. And she's been draining me financially ever since I…" Kathryn stopped abruptly as Reed's salad was placed on the table.

Kathryn lowered her voice. "Right after that, I went to you to ask for more money from the trust—"

"And I couldn't do anything about it because of the way the trust was set up. Yes, I remember." Suddenly, Reed leaned over the table. "Kathryn, is Tucker Beaumont Belline's father?"

The woman's fork clattered to the table. The waitress, choosing that moment to appear with the two luncheon plates, looked first at Kathryn and then to Reed. She'd been a waitress long enough to know this was no ordinary date for lunch. She dawdled at the next table, straightened the silverware, and hoped to overhear the conversation.

Reed, noticing the woman, said, "Let's eat, Kathryn. We'll talk later."

Disappointed, the waitress moved on to another table.

When Reed had paid the check and left the tip on the table, he walked down the street with Kathryn. "Forget the question I asked you, Kathryn. I had no right to pry. But to return to Carey. If what you said is true, she's guilty of a criminal offense, and you're perfectly within your right to prosecute. But there's a conflict of interest here. You'd have to get another lawyer, since I couldn't enter into litigation against my own sister-in-law."

"I understand, Reed," Kathryn responded unhappily.

"But if you'll allow me to talk with Julian…"

"Reed, I don't want to prosecute Carey—only as a last resort. But I can't afford any more blood money."

"Do you have proof that she's blackmailing you—a threatening letter, even a check?"

"No, nothing except my word against hers. And she would deny it, of course."

"When are you to give her more money?"

"Tomorrow. She's planning on picking it up at two o'clock."

"At your house?"

"Yes."

Reed's mind worked quickly. "Keep the appointment, Kathryn, but don't bother trying to come up with the money. Julian and I will get to your house by one-thirty. Don't worry. Everything will work out."

Seeing the doubtful look on Kathryn's face, Reed repeated, "Don't worry. I'll see you tomorrow." He glanced at his watch. "And not a word to a soul about this, not even Bertha," he cautioned, leaving her on the sidewalk as he hurried toward his car.

At the house on West Paces Ferry Road, Alpharetta left her bedroom to walk down the stairs.

"Alpharetta?"

"Yes, Mrs. St. John?"

"Come to my room and talk with me. I'm lonesome."

"Yes, ma'am."

Anna Clare climbed back into bed, pulled up the sheet and, glancing conspiratorially toward the girl, confided, "I'm not well, you know."

Alpharetta, feeling sorry for her, said, "Would you like me to read to you? I have a book of poems in my room. I could get it, if you like."

"No. I don't like people to read. I want to talk. Did Papa tell you about the time I was presented?"

"Presented?" Alpharetta wasn't certain she understood what the woman meant.

"To society—when I made my debut."

"Oh," Alpharetta replied. Politely she inquired, "Was it here in Atlanta?"

"Dear me, no. At the Court of St. James, in London. I was presented to the *queen.* How old are you, Alpharetta?"

"Sixteen."

"I was two years older when Papa and I sailed for England."

"Mr. St. John?"

"No, I don't think so. It was the other one. Or was it?" Anna Clare frowned. "Stop asking questions that confuse me, Alpharetta. Just listen."

"Yes, ma'am."

"I had a whole new wardrobe. Mrs. Byron made it for me—and the dress with the seed pearls and the lace was the best. How I loved that dress, Alpharetta. Papa said I was the prettiest one at court. He didn't have a title, like the lords and earls, but he was just as dashing as any of them there. I remember the afternoon we had tea in the garden with Lord Cranston. Papa thought I might make a match with him, but he wound up with that horsey-looking girl from Charleston, instead. Of course, she had a lot more money than Papa did. And Lord Cranston was looking for someone to pay the taxes on his estate...."

She stopped and, gazing at Alpharetta, she said, "I think I'l put on my dress now, instead of waiting until tonight. Will you get it for me? It's hanging in the closet." Her face clouded. "If Nurse Jenson hasn't hidden it from me again."

Alpharetta went to the closet and took down the dress the woman had worn to dinner the evening before. She almost tripped on the lace hanging from the hem. Bringing the dress back into the bedroom, she said, "I can mend the lace on the dress for you, if you have a needle and thread."

Anna Clare's eyes lit up. "Yes. Do that, Alpharetta."

"Do you have a sewing box?"

Anna Clare shook her head. "Nurse Jenson took it away from me."

"I'll get it from her," Alpharetta suggested, putting the dress on the chair.

"She won't like it," Anna Clare called after her, "being bothered in the middle of the afternoon."

Nevertheless, Alpharetta went down the hall and knocked at Lola Jenson's door. When the woman finally appeared, she said, "Mrs. Jenson, I'm going to mend the lace on Mrs. St. John's dress. May I have her sewing box?"

Not attempting to hide her annoyance at Alpharetta's request, she replied, "She's not allowed to have any scissors. Mr. St. John was firm in that."

"I'll bring the box back to you when I finish."

Left at the door, she waited for Lola to return with the sewing box. Reluctantly, the woman handed it over to Alpharetta. "You're wasting your time, you know, in trying to salvage the dress. It should have been thrown away years ago."

Ignoring the woman's comments, Alpharetta took the sewing box and went back to Anna Clare's bedroom.

Anna Clare was on her hands and knees, busy pulling clothes out of an old trunk. "It's in here somewhere. I know it is," she commented with a frown.

"What are you looking for, Mrs. St. John?"

"The tea dress. The one I wore in Lord Cranston's garden." She continued pulling out the clothes, strewing them over the pink and beige Aubusson carpet, while Alpharetta threaded the needle and began to sew.

"Oh, here it is," Anna Clare said, smiling as she stood up holding the gossamer white material with the faded blue satin sash. "Now we'll have our tea party—just the two of us. Min-yo can fix some cucumber sandwiches, and we can take them out under the trees." Anna Clare, bright and happy, began to hum under her breath. Her excitement transferred itself to Alpharetta as she mended the lace.

When Alpharetta snipped the last thread, Anna Clare held out the tea dress. "Put this on, Alpharetta." She dismissed the surprised look on her face. "You have to be dressed, too, if we're going to have a party." Anna Clare turned her head and called out in a demanding voice, "Jenson. Jenson, I need you."

Turning back to Alpharetta, she said, "Hurry and get dressed. I'll meet you in the garden as soon as I have my dress on."

Coming into the room, Lola Jenson began to scold Anna Clare immediately. "You can't have your medicine yet. I've already told you, Mrs. St. John. It will be another hour before you get it."

"Hurry, Jenson. Help me with the dress and my hair." Looking anxiously toward Alpharetta, she said, "Get dressed, Alpharetta…" As the door closed, Anna Clare chattered happily. "Jenson, I want you to get Min-yo to fix our tea. I especially want cucumber sandwiches. Alpharetta and I are going to have a party."

Remembering that she had left the sewing box on the table, Alpharetta walked back into the room. "I forgot the basket," she said.

"You might as well leave it. I'll take it with me after I help Mrs. St. John to dress," the nurse replied.

She closed her bedroom door, took off her skirt and blouse and, to humor Anna Clare, dressed in the thirty-year-old dress that the woman had worn in Lord Cranston's garden.

That evening as Reed, later than usual, walked into the house, he heard music from the drawing room. A nostalgia crept over him as he listened. Anna Clare hadn't touched the piano for several years. The notes, hesitant and slightly off pitch, reminded him that he had not bothered to have the instrument tuned in that length of time, either.

Handing over his briefcase to Min-yo, he followed the sound of the music, his footsteps light upon the carpet. Alpharetta, curled up in a blue French bergère chair near the fireplace that contained magnolia leaves, was still dressed in the gossamer white tea dress with pale blue sash. White stockings and slippers completed the outfit, with her red hair pinned to the top of her head. Framed by the richness of the damask draperies, the opulent cushions, and fine old French furniture, she gave a startlingly beautiful appearance — Edwardian in style. Not aware that she was being observed, she sat listening to the music. Reed noticed her faraway look, as if she had been transported to another world.

Anna Clare, dressed as usual in her debutante dress and tiara, sat with her spine straight as memory directed her fingers to the proper notes.

Afraid to startle her by announcing his arrival, Reed

stood back from the doorway until the final bass notes of Beethoven died away. Then he walked into the drawing room.

"That was lovely, Anna Clare," he said, going toward the piano.

Her eyes, looking up and meeting his, emitted a pleased expression. "I'm out of practice," she confessed, "but Alpharetta wanted to hear me play."

Reed looked toward the girl, who had removed herself from the chair at his arrival. "Good evening, Mr. St. John," she said.

He acknowledged her greeting, looking from his wife back to Alpharetta. "If you'll excuse me, I'll be back in a few minutes." Reed left the drawing room, to go upstairs and wash up for supper.

"That *was* beautiful, Mrs. St. John," Alpharetta said, repeating Reed's words.

"Papa always did like to hear me play," she commented shyly, and by this time Alpharetta realized that Anna Clare had lost the ability to discern the difference between her father and her husband.

Reed returned to the drawing room and the three proceeded to the dining room, where Min-yo waited to serve them.

"We had a tea party this afternoon, Papa," Anna Clare began. "We ate little cucumber sandwiches the way we did in Lord Cranston's garden. Only, today I let Alpharetta wear the tea dress. Don't you like it on her?" Without waiting for Reed to answer, she confided, "I'm so glad you brought her home. We had such fun today."

Reed nodded. "Eat your soup, Anna Clare."

She picked up the soup spoon and obeyed for a sip or two.

"Would you like Alpharetta to stay for a long visit?" he inquired.

"Oh, yes. She's a lot more fun than Nurse Jenson."

He noticed the distressed look on Alpharetta's face. "I

had a talk with your father today. We discussed you—and your future. And he's willing for you to stay here with us."

"I can't do that, Mr. St. John. I have to go back home tomorrow. I left the mules at the wagon yard."

"Your father took them this morning, with Duluth and Conyer."

"You got them out of—" Alpharetta stopped, cautiously glancing at Anna Clare.

"Only for a day or so. Your father's going on a"—he hesitated—"on a trip. So he went home this morning to close up the house."

"And Duluth and Conyer…"

"…will more than likely be going in another direction."

"Then I have to go home." Alpharetta half rose from the table.

Reed shook his head. "Your father wants you to stay here. He sees no need in your going back. In fact, he's going to send you the stone chimes and the lamp. He said you'd want them."

She sat quietly for the rest of the meal. While Anna Clare talked, she thought of the stone chimes; how Duluth and Conyer had whiled away the time at the still, making them for her—little pieces of rock from the mountain that sang in the wind with a mysterious melody. She would always treasure them. Surrounded by the scenic French wallpaper, the Hepplewhite sideboard, the sterling silver candelabra, and fine china, Alpharetta realized her life's treasures consisted of only three things—the stone chimes, the hurricane lamp, and the book of poems that Ben Mark St. John had given her.

Chapter 25

Promptly at one-thirty, a grim Julian St. John accompanied Reed to Kathryn Mansour's brown brick house on Briarcliff Road. He had canceled his appointments for the afternoon. What else could he do after being faced with such a serious accusation against Carey?

"If it's true—what you say, Reed—it's my fault. I should never have confided such a secret to Carey."

"There's no need for you to feel guilty, Julian. There must be hundreds of doctors' wives all over the country who've heard such secrets and never used them to injure anyone." Reed glanced at his brother seated in the car beside him and, feeling sorry for him, continued, "It's hard for a man to survive in this world, Julian, without a woman who'll listen to his demons and take his side against them, to share in his triumphs and disappointments."

"Axel seems to be the only one of us to have achieved that. Looks like you and I both struck out."

"We're still operating under English law. Carey's innocent until proven guilty." Reed stopped his car on a side street, and he and Julian got out and began to walk down Briarcliff toward Kathryn's house. Reed wanted no tipoff to Carey that they were anywhere near.

They walked up the sidewalk and onto the porch, and used the door knocker to announce their arrival.

A nervous Kathryn hurried to the door. "Come in," she said, seeing the two men.

"You're alone, Kathryn?" Reed asked.

"Yes. I did as you told me. I gave Bertha the afternoon off. She left right after lunch."

Reed and Julian walked inside, with Kathryn leading the way to the living room. "I've told Julian," Reed began, "about our conversation."

She looked at the tall, ascetic-looking man standing before her. "I'm sorry, Julian."

"So am I, Kathryn."

"We don't have much time," Reed said. "This is what I want you to do, Kathryn…"

She sat on the brown mohair sofa and waited. The living room was the same as it had been for years. True, the walls and woodwork had been given a fresh coat of paint, but the furniture and pictures remained the same. And their positions hadn't changed. She had felt no womanly urge to move the sofa, or rearrange the pictures or knickknacks on the table. Bertha had always presided over the house while Kathryn had spent the larger part of each day in the studio behind the house. Her life was in her canvases, in the images that emerged from the dabs of paint on her palette.

She looked around the living room. It really wasn't a pretty one. Kathryn frowned, and for the first time she examined the pictures on the wall with an artist's eye. What she saw shocked her. They were atrocious. Until this moment, she had never questioned her parents' taste.

At two o'clock, Carey parked her Vickie Ford in front of Kathryn's house. She had come straight from Leonard's shop, and her pleasure at seeing the new fall clothes and realizing that she could now afford the striking black suit with white peplum that he'd put aside for her made her smile.

Remembering her confrontation with the baboon, she looked cautiously up and down the street and searched the shrubbery before she got out of the car. As she walked to the door, Carey smoothed her rust-colored skirt and straightened the black velvet bow on the neck of her white blouse. The door knocker sounded and she waited for Bertha to come to the door. Instead, Kathryn opened it.

"Where's Bertha?" Carey asked without even a greeting.

"She has the afternoon off. She's gone to a funeral."

"Today's not Saturday," Carey responded sharply.

"No. Come in, Carey." Kathryn held the door open for her.

"They don't have funerals in the middle of the week. Bertha's putting something over on you, Kathryn. You ought to be firmer with her. But I suppose you're paying her the full amount for the week, too."

At the look on Kathryn's face, Carey knew she was right. "I always dock Trudie's pay for any time off. You should do the same, Kathryn."

"Have a seat, Carey."

"Well, just for a moment, while you get the money."

"If you're not in a hurry, I was ready to have a cup of tea. Would you care for some?"

A suspicious Carey looked from Kathryn to the porcelain service on the table in front of the mohair sofa. In the past she had often had tea with Kathryn and thought nothing of it. But now it was different. The cookies on the tray looked inviting, and she realized that in her haste to get to Leonard's, she hadn't bothered to eat lunch. Just as the tea kettle in the kitchen began to whistle, Carey made up her mind. "Yes, Kathryn, I'll have a cup with you."

"Then excuse me while I get the hot water."

Carey sat back on the sofa and relaxed. With Bertha out of the house, there was no need for her to be so careful in what she said. And she liked Kathryn. She always had, until the day in the side yard. But she had gotten over her anger at that episode. It was a pity that—

Walking back into the room with the teapot, Kathryn smiled, set it down, and took her place on the sofa. She poured the tea into one fragile cup. "Lemon, Carey?"

"Yes, please. And one lump of sugar."

Kathryn poured a second cup for herself and then leaned against the tall arm of the sofa. "That's a beautiful suit. Did you buy it with *my* money?"

Carey laughed. "As a matter of fact, I did."

"Why, Carey? Why did you decide to blackmail me about Belline?"

Carey reached for a cookie. "I don't really dislike you, Kathryn, but you *did* disgrace yourself in the eyes of society, even if very few people know about it." She took a bite of cookie and continued, "If Julian hadn't raised such a fuss about the money I was spending on clothes, then I probably never would have done it."

"But I don't understand why you feel the need for so many new clothes. You'll never get around to wearing them out." She looked down at her own dress. "I've worn this dress for the past five years and it's still good."

"That's the difference between you and me, Kathryn. When I was younger, my father used to call me his 'little green frog.' Oh, he did it in love, but it hurt because I was ugly. And so I began to dress up with ruffles and bows and ribbons, and fancy hats, so people would notice my clothes and forget about *me*. And I found it worked. I'm nothing, Kathryn, without new clothes. Julian didn't understand this. And that's why, when he stopped giving me the money I needed, I had to find another source. And you were that source, Kathryn."

Carey put down her cup on the tray. "I've really got to go. Martha will be home from school soon. So would you please get the money for me?"

"What if I said I was going to call your bluff, Carey?

That I wasn't going to give you any more money?"

Carey's expression froze. "Then I'll go straight to Belline and tell her that you're her mother—and that she's illegitimate."

"Oh, no you won't, Carey," a man's voice vowed.

A frightened Carey looked up. Julian, followed by Reed, walked into the living room from the adjacent sun porch. Carey stared from her husband to Kathryn and screamed, "You tricked me, Kathryn. You tricked me."

"Let's go, Carey," Julian said softly and reached out toward her, but his wife backed away from him. "Don't you touch me, Julian." Her gaze landed on Reed, directly behind her husband and, becoming more agitated, she screamed, "You're all in this together, every single one of you. You're all my enemies. And you, Kathryn, are the worst one of all."

"I'll get the car, Julian. You'll need some help," Reed suggested. While Julian physically restrained Carey to keep her from running out of the house, Kathryn, white-faced, walked to the front door with Reed.

"I'm sorry, Reed."

"We all are, Kathryn, but Carey's a sick woman. And Julian has to face up to that fact."

Waiting in the hall, Kathryn watched for Reed's car. When he drove to the front of her house and stopped, she went back into the living room. "Reed's here with the car, Julian."

While the two men struggled to escort Carey to the car, Kathryn watched. They drove off, leaving Carey's small Vickie behind. Thoroughly devastated, Kathryn walked down the hall to the back door and headed through the garden to her studio, where she spent the rest of the afternoon. By the time she returned to the house at the end of the day, she saw that the Ford was no longer parked in front.

* * *

Anna Clare's scream from the second-story bedroom

filled the entire Italianate villa. Alpharetta, downstairs in the kitchen with Min-yo, began to run toward the stairs, with Min-yo directly behind her. At the bedroom door they collided with Lola Jenson, who had hurried along the hallway from her own room.

As Lola pushed the door open, Alpharetta saw Anna Clare, dressed in her flowered housecoat and standing in the middle of the floor. She was holding a piece of dingy white satin material with seed pearls dangling from it. Surrounding her feet were scraps of the same dingy material. Anna Clare's debutante dress.

On the table beside the bed sat the sewing box, with the long, sharp scissors in prominent view. Sobbing hysterically, Anna Clare collapsed on her bed and, holding the scrap of material, she curled up in a fetal position, rocking back and forth.

Lola Jenson's eyes blazed in anger as she pointed her finger at Alpharetta. "See what you've done, Alpharetta. I told you Mr. St. John didn't allow her to have any scissors. You were responsible for the sewing box. Why, in heaven's name, did you leave it where she could get her hands on it?"

"But—"

"There's no need to make excuses. It's too late for that. Min-yo, go downstairs and get Mrs. St. John's medicine. And Alpharetta, under the circumstances, I think you should go to your room until I quiet my patient."

With tears in her eyes, Alpharetta looked at Anna Clare, and then to the scraps of material on the floor. With a heavy heart, she obeyed the nurse and walked down the hall to her room.

Reed, sombered by the unpleasant experience with Carey and feeling immensely sorry for Julian, drove home an hour earlier than usual. He didn't feel like going back to the office. It had been extremely nerve-wracking, committing Carey for treatment in the private sanitarium at the north end of town. He recalled Julian's words. Yes, Axel was the only lucky one of the three. Did society do that to Anna Clare *and* Carey — pressuring them into feeling inadequate, driving them to compete for position? Making one grasping and selfish, and pushing the other to decide not to play the game at all?

Alpharetta Beaumont and Hagar, the cleaning girl, seemed to be completely different — both poor, both loyal to family, and without guile. There must be something about the acquisition of money. But, no. Steppie wasn't like that. She had grown up in an atmosphere of affluence, as well. Could it have been her experience as a nurse during the war? Recognizing that German bullets knew no rank or position, but killed at random? Surprisingly she had seemed softer, more vulnerable when she came home from Europe, and she had been loyal to Neal through the years, despite his head injury. Surely, it couldn't have ended the way Belline said, with Steppie shooting Neal on the terrace in cold blood.

He didn't know what to think anymore about people. The longer he lived, the less surprised he was at their actions. He was even surprised at his own, offering Alpharetta a home for the time her father spent in jail. Tucker Beaumont couldn't hope to get off lighter than a year and a day. Lyle had more or less intimated that.

Alpharetta sat on the bench inside Brookwood Station on Peachtree Road and waited for the train. Beside her rested her valise. Her eyes, now dry, still projected sadness and despair.

It was all her fault. Nurse Jenson had made her see that; yet the woman had been kind enough to give her the money for the railway ticket back to Stone Mountain. After what had happened, Alpharetta realized she wouldn't be welcome in the mansion on West Paces Ferry Road.

She should never have forgotten the sewing basket with the scissors in it. Nurse Jenson had evidently forgotten it, too, leaving it on the table where Mrs. St. John could use it. But it was Alpharetta's fault. The box was her responsibility.

Poor Mrs. St. John, cutting up the debutante dress beyond repair, and then weeping inconsolably over it, so that Nurse Jenson had to give her an extra large dose of her medicine to quiet her.

Alpharetta wasn't certain what she would do, once she got home. She'd never ridden a train before, and she guessed she would just have to follow the crowd, and ask for help if she should get lost.

With no perceptible signal, the people around her got up, gripped their handbags, and began to walk out the door toward the tracks. Alpharetta picked up her valise and did the same.

She heard the whistle first—a magnificent sound that heralded the train's approach. She watched as the great iron monester came into sight and moved down the track. The locomotive stopped, spewing out great masses of steam from underneath. And behind it, passenger cars were linked one after the other.

Stepping down from the iron railing of the nearest car, a man in a red hat placed some steps on the ground and then stood beside them to help the passengers descend. They dispersed in all directions, greeted by relatives and friends in clusters. The sound of their laughter, their easy chatter, overrode the sound of steam escaping.

"All aboard," a voice called. The waiting passengers moved swiftly, climbing onto the metal steps, then into the train itself. Alpharetta, holding her valise, moved with them toward the steps.

"Alpharetta! Alpharetta!" Surprised, she turned around at the sound of her name. Coming toward her was Reed St. John, his tall frame towering above the people behind her. She stopped, debating what to do. Should she pretend she hadn't heard him?

"Get aboard, please. You're holding up the line."

"Alpharetta!"

She moved to one side, allowing the other passengers to walk past her. Why had Mr. St. John come to the station? She'd left a note for him. Surely that should have been enough.

His face, unsmiling, severe, looked down at her as he stood over her. "You can't leave, Alpharetta. Here, give me your valise." He reached out and took it from her.

"Mr. St. John, after what happened, I can't stay. I'm sure Nurse Jenson explained it to you."

"I haven't talked with Mrs. Jenson. Only with Minyo. He gave me your note the minute I got home."

"He was supposed to wait until you'd finished your supper."

Reed put the valise in the car and motioned for Alpharetta to get inside, too. As he started the car's engine and backed out of the parking space, he turned to the girl. "Now, tell me what happened, to make you run away."

Alpharetta's chin lifted. "I didn't run away. Under the circumstances, I didn't think that you would want me in the house. I made a terrible mistake, Mr. St. John, leaving the sewing box in your wife's bedroom. Somehow I just forgot it after mending the lace on her dress. And now Mrs. St. John's dress is cut up into little pieces and no amount of sewing can put it back together. Nurse Jenson was kind enough to lend me the money for the railway ticket. She said it would be best if I left."

Reed's frown blossomed into a look of fury. "And you think Mrs. Jenson can speak for me? You should have waited, Alpharetta, until I got home to see what *I* wanted you to do."

"Yes, sir." A chastened Alpharetta, dressed again in her black skirt and white blouse, gazed unhappily out the window as Reed passed Axel St. John's house on his way to West Paces Ferry Road.

"Tell me, Alpharetta, about your grandmother."

Surprised at the change of subject, she glanced at the man who gripped the steering wheel of the car, slowed, and then stopped for a red light at Dead Man's Curve, near West Wesley.

"You mean, my Grandmother Rowena?"

"Yes. Your father's mother."

"Well, there isn't much to tell. I lived with her in Gainesville until I was seven. And when she died, my pa came and got me. And I've been living with him and my two brothers ever since."

"What was her last name?"

"Beaumont."

"No, I mean her maiden name—before she was married."

"She was Rowena Carleton."

"From Atlanta," Reed stated.

"Did you know her, Mr. St. John?"

"Actually not. I've heard a lot about her for years. Alpharetta, my wife was a Carleton, too. So you see, you and Anna Clare are distant cousins. And that's one reason that I can't allow you to leave. You don't have anywhere to go except our house. And I know Anna Clare will want you to stay as much as I do."

"Not after the dress was ruined."

"It wasn't your fault. It was no one's fault. We'll just forget it and try to be more careful in the future. All right, Alpharetta?"

"All right, Mr. St. John."

Min-yo stood at the side door and anxiously waited for the St. John car to appear. As soon as he heard the motor, he opened the door wide and, straining his eyes, peered toward the car. There were two occupants. Min-yo, ecstatic that Nurse Jenson had failed to get rid of

Alpharetta, hurried down the steps to take her valise back into the house.

On the following morning, Tucker Beaumont, Conyer, and Duluth stood before the judge in DeKalb Superior Court for sentencing. The result came as no surprise to Reed. Tucker would serve his year and a day, while the boys were put on probation.

When it was over, Tucker shook hands with Reed. "I thank you for helpin' my family," he said. "It means a lot to me to know that Duluth and Conyer won't go to jail and that you'll keep Alpharetta safe and sound while I'm gone."

While Reed watched, the sheriff's deputy led an unrepentant Tucker away, and Duluth and Conyer walked out to the bus that quickly filled with boys and young men on their way to the conservation camp at Rock Eagle.

Chapter 26

Two months later, at another rail station, Main Terminal on Mitchell Street, Daniel Wexford, newly arrived from New York, took his knapsack from the overhead compartment of the Southern Crescent and walked into the depot.

No one knew of his arrival. The decision to leave Paris had been made in haste, with little preparation beyond acquiring a ticket on the first ship to America with an available berth.

He had watched uneasily as the war clouds gathered in Europe with the rise of Hitler and his Brown Shirts, the insidious persecution of the Jews. Yet Hitler and the rise of fascism had not been the deciding factors in his leaving Paris and the old Vicomtesse d'Arcy. Daniel, reacting intellectually to these happenings, knew that he would leave Europe eventually, but when the disturbing news from Atlanta arrived—the disappearance of Steppie, Belline's treachery, and ultimately the letter from Creag Trent—Daniel's emotions told him it was time to stop his studies at the Sorbonne and head for home immediately.

Tall, blond, and blue-eyed, he stood out in the milling mass of people coming and going through the Atlanta terminal. His clean-shaven face was in contrast to the wrinkled clothes that broadcast the length of time he had traveled by rail.

Daniel walked to the baggage claim and waited for his other cases. When they were gathered, he hired a taxi to take him to the French Normandy house on Castlemeade Road.

Leaning toward the man in the driver's seat, Daniel said, "I need to stop at the Peachtree Trust on my way home. It won't take long."

"Yes, sir."

The cold rain, the grayness of the November day hanging over the city like a pall, gave no welcome to the nineteen-year-old who was neither boy nor man, but caught between the two, with fleeting aspects of both, warring with each other. His large frame forecast the size he was destined to be, but he had not yet attained the flesh and sinew needed to clothe his bones.

Creeping at a snail's pace because of the rain, the driver inquired, "You a stranger in town?"

"No," Daniel replied. "I live here. But I've been away for a year, studying. What's been happening?" he inquired casually.

"Well, the town's in a frenzy right now, gettin' ready for President Roosevelt's visit."

"When's that?"

"On the twenty-ninth. He's drivin' up from Warm Springs. He'll be speakin' at Grant Field that afternoon, while Mrs. Roosevelt will be havin' lunch with the ladies. All the bigwigs have their heads together, plannin' a festive occasion." The driver chuckled. "All except Governor Talmadge. He's on the outs with the President. Said *if* he's in town, he'll come. But nobody expects him."

They stopped talking while the driver concentrated on the road. When the rain slackened, he said, "Guess you heard that Will Rogers got himself killed in a plane crash in Alaska."

"Yes. I read it in a Paris newspaper."

"That where you've been? Paris?"

"Yes."

"I was there once," the driver commented, "back during the war. Had me a cute little French gal," he added wistfully. "She cried when I left."

Daniel thought of the tears that had been shed for him. But they were from eyes old and dimmed by years and grief, from a woman whose four sons had been killed on the battlefields of France.

"All the signs point to another war in Europe," Daniel said aloud. "Hitler's building up his military might and anyone who stands in his way or objects is at the mercy of his bullies."

"And I thought I was fightin' the 'war to end all wars,' " the driver said, shaking his head. "If it happens again, I just hope we'll stay out of it." He thought of his fifteen-year-old son at home. "Let Europe fight its own wars from now on."

The massive bank building with its marble columns had an appearance of indestructibility. The taxi slowed in front, and Daniel, not waiting for it to come to a complete stop, climbed out, ran up the steps and into the rotunda-like entrance. Mr. Cruickshank, the teller, was closing the window as Daniel arrived inside. Walking up to the teller's cage, Daniel said, "Mr. Cruickshank, is my Cousin Axel still here?"

A smile of recognition spread over the teller's face. "Daniel. Daniel Wexford. When did you get home?" His smile quickly disguised itself in a cloud of sympathy.

"Just a few minutes ago. I came from New York on the train."

"I think Mr. St. John is getting ready to leave. You'd better hurry on up to his office if you want to catch him."

Daniel left the teller's cage, walked toward the marble steps with brass railing and, taking the steps two at a time, reached the hallway on the second floor.

Walking out the door of his private office, Axel St. John saw Daniel. Surprised, he stopped quickly and teetered from the sudden change in momentum. "Daniel, what are you doing here?"

"I came home, Cousin Axel. For good. I have a taxi waiting on the street, so I can't stay long. Just came by to find out if the house on Castlemeade Road is closed up, and if you have the key."

"Verbena's there. You won't need a key," he said. Then, remembering that he was Daniel's guardian, he said, "I'll take you home. Do you have any luggage with you?"

"In the taxi."

"Then get it out and dismiss the driver." He reached into his pocket for some bills. "Here, take these to pay him off."

Daniel shook his head. "I have some money left."

Axel put the bills back into his pocket. "Bring your things in, and we'll walk to my car parked out in back. I was just getting ready to leave for the day."

As Daniel disappeared down the stairs to go after his baggage, Axel picked up the telephone.

"Rennie? You'll never guess who just walked into my office....Daniel....That's right. I'm going to take him home now, so I'll be a little late."

Axel listened for a moment to Rennie's voice and then responded, "Well, I'll ask him, but I think he'd rather go on home to get cleaned up and get some sleep. He looks pretty exhausted. Good-bye, dear."

He hung up the phone, took the black umbrella from his desk, and went downstairs to wait for Daniel. His bushy eyebrows pressed together in a frown, making one long, curly slash across his brow. Having Daniel home complicated matters.

They drove along the usual route, from Peachtree to Ponce de Leon. Daniel, sitting in front with Axel, noticed the unevenness of his cousin's driving, his foot constantly pressing down and letting up on the ac-celerator, so that the car, despite its length and sleekness, suffered in dignity, like the runaway car driven by the clown in the circus on the outskirts of Paris. But Axel, unlike the clown, was dressed in a dark business suit with a wool fedora protecting his bald head from the cold.

"I had a letter from Creag Trent," Daniel confided.

Axel's foot pressed down suddenly on the accelerator and then released it. "Reed had a letter, too. A bad business, Daniel, all around."

"Does Belline show any regret for what she's caused?"

"I don't know. She's coming home tomorrow for the Thanksgiving holidays. We thought it better if she stayed at our house." Axel looked at Daniel as he stopped the car at the light at the intersection of Briarcliff. "Rennie's going to have everybody in the family for dinner on Thursday. There'll be a place at the table for you, too. And she wants you to come to supper tonight, as well."

Daniel declined the invitation for supper. "I haven't slept for twenty-four hours, Cousin Axel. All I want right now is to climb into the nearest bed."

"I thought you might feel that way. In fact, I told Rennie that." Axel started up the car as the light changed to green and he continued down Ponce de Leon to Castlemeade Road.

"Have you decided what you want to do, now that you're home?"

"I've thought about it," Daniel replied. "I have several alternatives. But I'll take a few days sorting things out first, before I make up my mind."

Not wanting to appear overanxious, Axel did not question him further.

Verbena had finished up for the afternoon and was getting ready to go to her room in the carriage house when she heard a car drive up and stop. Looking out the window, she recognized Axel St. John's car. What was he doing, coming at this time of day? While she watched, the passenger door opened and the tall, blond Daniel emerged.

Verbena, hardly believing her eyes, opened the door and, despite the rain, rushed into the courtyard.

"Daniel Wexford, you're a sight for sore eyes. But what are you doin', comin' home without lettin' a soul know?" she demanded.

Daniel grinned, dropped his baggage, reached out and lifted Verbena from the ground in a big bear hug. "Verbena, you old crone. You haven't changed a bit. Still telling me what to do."

"You put me down, boy. Ain't proper for you to behave this way, especially in front of Mr. Axel."

He put her down, turned to wave to his cousin who had begun backing his car around the courtyard to go down the driveway. Then taking his luggage, Daniel followed a happy Verbena inside.

"I'll fix you somethin' to eat. You must be starvin'."

"Let me sleep a few hours first, Verbena. The food can come later. What time is it, anyway?"

"Almost five-thirty."

"Leave something on the kitchen table for me. Then you can go ahead and catch the trolley," he suggested.

"I'm livin' in the carriage house now, so I don't have far to go."

"Do you happen to have some of that good sugar-cured country ham?" he asked with a wistful expression.

The black woman laughed. "I sure do. I'll fix you a plate and leave it covered on the table. And I'll take Faust to the carriage house with me, so he won't hop up and eat it. He's bad about that if you're not careful."

* * *

Alpharetta Beaumont looked down at her new green dress and then across the dining table where Anna Clare sat, clad elegantly in a deep teal-blue shantung dress, with a small bow in her gray-blonde hair.

It had been two months now since the remnants of the white debutante dress had been carried off in a sack by the garbage man. Nurse Jenson had put it in the garbage can as soon as Alpharetta left the house for the train station. How surprised the nurse had been to see Alpharetta return to the house with Reed St. John that evening. And she had seemed more than a little disappointed, too.

Pleased that Cousin Anna Clare, as she had been told to address her, had resolved her grief over the loss of the dress, Alpharetta smiled at the woman.

Anna Clare smiled back and turned to Reed. "Papa, guess what Alpharetta and I did today."

He looked from the red-haired girl back to his wife. "I give up. What *did* you and Alpharetta do today?"

"We went for a drive—in the rain. You know how I always liked to ride in the rain."

"Yes. Where did you go?"

Anna Clare frowned and referred him to Alpharetta for the answer. "To Piedmont Park," she replied quickly. "We stopped the car and watched the ducks. Min-yo gave us some bread crumbs for them."

"They were so funny, Papa, waddling up the bank to meet us," Anna Clare joined in, remembering their jaunt now. "Alpharetta said we're going somewhere else tomorrow."

"That's just fine, Anna Clare. I'm pleased that you're leaving the house some."

"Alpharetta says that when the weather gets warmer, we'll go on a picnic," she confided.

"We have an invitation for Thanksgiving dinner, too. Don't forget that."

"Where?"

"With Rennie and Axel. Don't you remember we talked about it last night?"

"Is Alpharetta coming?"

"Of course. She's part of the family now."

"Then I'll go."

The next morning when Verbena let herself into the kitchen with Faust at her heels, she saw the plate she had fixed for Daniel. It was untouched; for Daniel had slept straight through from late afternoon to morning. Verbena sighed, took the plate over to the cat's bowl by the kitchen sink.

"All right, you no 'count cat. Looks like you get the ham." She scraped the contents into the bowl, and the gray Persian, purring his satisfaction, began his fastidious eating of the left-over meal.

After Verbena set the table in the breakfast room, she walked to the refrigerator and took out bacon and eggs. She listened for some sign of activity upstairs, and when she heard the water running in the bath, she put the bacon on the stove to cook.

At the sound of Daniel's footsteps on the stairs, she took the eggs from the bowl, broke them, and began to soft-scramble them the way Daniel liked.

Yawning and stretching his long arms to touch the door frame, Daniel came into the kitchen and watched Verbena at the stove. Without turning around, she said, "No need for me to ask you how you slept."

Pretending he hadn't heard her, he said, "You'd better put on a few more eggs, Verbena. I'm ravenous."

"Figured as much. Already put them on. If you jus' get yourself into the breakfast room, I'll bring your plate to you."

Daniel walked into the breakfast room and sat in the white wicker chair at the end of the table, while Faust hopped up onto the window ledge facing the morning sun and began his daily wash.

Daniel looked around the breakfast room. It was just as if the others would be coming downstairs at any minute to join him—his father, Neal; his mother, Steppie; and his red-haired sister, Belline. They were all together in this room the morning he'd left for Paris a year ago. Even though he was home now, Daniel was overwhelmed with a sense of homesickness as he stared at the three empty chairs.

But change came—sometimes for the better; oftentimes for the worse. Daniel knew that. This past year, for the first time in his life, he had been made to realize that the same things happened over and over. Birth, death, war. Love, hate. Always a circle, and it didn't matter which portion of the arc he entered or how much of the circle he completed before death. The circle would go on without him. Others entered and began the circle of life, experiencing the same joys, the same sorrows.

When Verbena brought his plate and poured his coffee, Daniel looked up at the woman he'd known for almost all his life. "Verbena, sit down with me. I want to talk."

"Now you know that's not proper, Mr. Daniel," she said in a disapproving tone, "me sittin' at the table with you."

Yesterday it had been Daniel; now it was *Mr.* Daniel. He didn't like the subtle change. "Why? You think you're too good to sit with me?"

Verbena glared at him, mumbled under her breath, and pulled out a wicker chair from under the table. She slowly sank into it. Her arthritis had been acting up lately and the slits cut in the sides of her leather shoes attested to the long bombardment of her joints.

"Tell me what happened, Verbena, after my mother left with Creag Trent."

"Two police came," she said, placing the stress on the first syllable. "Acted like they owned the place, lookin' in drawers, pullin' out things in the closets. Said they had a warrant to search the place. Humph!" she said, showing her displeasure at their actions. "They jiggled open the lock on Mr. Neal's desk in the library. I watched 'em do it, and they pulled out that German gun. There was some money in the drawer. They took that with them and gave me a receipt for it."

"They took Dad's gun, too?"

"Sure did. And about a week later, it was in the paper. I saved it for you, Mr. Daniel, if you want to read it. I thought it was terrible, those newspaper people draggin' Miss Steppie's name through the mud, but the only thing Mr. Reed could do about it was keep it off the front page." Verbena's stern expression changed to a smile. "But Mr. Creag was one step ahead of the police. He whisked her right off to Mexico where they can't touch 'er. I don't know what the world's comin' to, Mr. Daniel. But one thing I do know. If your mama was goin' to shoot Mr. Neal, she'd a done it years ago."

She looked over at Daniel. "That's all that happened. Miss Belline went off to school; you came home. And Miss Steppie's with Mr. Creag. But there's some strange things goin' on around here that nobody talks about."

"What sort of things, Verbena?"

"It's not for me to say. But be careful, Mr. Daniel. Somethin's goin' to happen yet. I feel it in my bones."

She pushed herself up from the table and Daniel, finishing his breakfast, felt an uneasiness in Verbena's prediction. He took the small piece of bacon left on his plate, called Faust, and fed the remnant to the cat, while thinking of Belline.

Chapter 27

After riding by car with Celia Wentworth's family as far as Athens, Belline took the train the rest of the way to Atlanta. An hour later, the train pulled into the station. As she got off, Belline saw String, dressed in his dark coat and chauffeur's cap, waiting for her on the platform of the station.

Her three months at Salem Academy had been good ones; for helped by her slight aloofness and aura of mystery, she had portrayed the poor little rich orphan to the hilt, speaking only of her guardian and never of Creag Trent, now her stepfather, who was paying her tuition and sending her a large allowance via his attorney. She looked down at her dark blue fur-trimmed coat with matching muff of white mink. All the other girls in her class were quite envious when she'd returned from shopping with Miss Goldsmith, the house mother.

String, seeing Belline, moved toward her and tipped his hat. "Glad to see you, Miss Belline."

"How are you, String?" she asked, only able to distinguish him from his twin, Wash, by the burn on his left hand that had removed some of the pigment and left a spot as pink as the palm of his hand.

"Had the rheumatism," he replied. "This weather don't help it none."

"Too bad," she said automatically. "Has Mr. Ben Mark gotten home from the university yet?"

"No'm. He's due in sometime tonight. But Mr. Daniel's here," he added.

Belline's blue-green eyes lit up. "Daniel? I can't believe it. When did he come?"

"Yesterday."

Belline's joy at hearing the news suddenly diminished. She was well aware of his fury at her actions. His letter proved that. Reaching into her purse, Belline pulled out the baggage claim as the luggage-loaded wagon passed by them.

"Get my bags for me, String, and I'll go on to the car."

The familiar family car—the Packard V-12—stood out from the rest. Climbing inside, Belline shivered from the cold and spread the plaid lap robe over her to keep warm while she waited for String and her luggage. She thought of Martha and her mother, Carey. It was supposed to be a family secret, Carey's confinement in the hospital for her nerves. But Martha had written her the truth. Carey was caught blackmailing someone. She could hardly wait to talk with Martha to find out the particulars.

When String had loaded the luggage in the back and taken his place at the wheel, Belline asked, "How many are coming to dinner tomorrow, String?"

"Let's see. Mr. Axel and Miss Rennie, you, Ben Mark, Mr. Daniel, Dr. Julian, and Martha. Miss Carey's still in the hospital, but Miss Anna Clare's comin' with Mr. Reed." He counted on his fingers. "That's nine. And oh, the lady stayin' at Mr. Reed's house."

"You mean Mrs. Jenson's coming too?"

"No'm. Miss Anna Clare's cousin. I forget her name. That makes ten. One more than we had last year. I had to buy a bigger turkey," he confided.

It didn't take long for String to maneuver the car into the mainstream of traffic and to reach the red brick house on Peachtree Road. He stopped at the *porte cochère* and opened the car door for Belline.

"I'll put the car in the garage and bring your bags with me, Miss Belline."

"All right, String." Belline, removing the lap robe, climbed out and hurried into the house. "Cousin Rennie," she called out. "I'm here."

When Rennie, in the kitchen putting the finishing touch to the crusts for the pumpkin pies, heard Belline's voice, she wiped the flour from her hands, took off her apron, and walked into the hallway to greet Belline with a kiss on her cheek.

"Did you have a pleasant trip, dear?" Rennie inquired, as if almost three months had not elapsed from the time Belline had left for school.

"It was nice, traveling with the Wentworths," she replied, " but the train trip was boring. I wish I could have ridden with Ben Mark from Athens."

"It was safer for you to come on the train, Belline. You know how fast Ben Mark drives. I worry about him whenever he's in that car of his, and I wouldn't have had a moment's peace, knowing you were with him."

"I'm surprised that the school officials allowed him to have his car on campus."

"He keeps it in a garage in town," Rennie replied in a resigned voice. "I didn't want him to have it, but he said if Ellen Tolbert could take her horse to Wesleyan with her, he didn't see why he couldn't take his Stutz Bearcat. Of course, I don't think it's the same thing at all, but he convinced his father otherwise. Come on in to the fire to get warm. You must be frozen." Following Belline into the study where the large stone fireplace roared with a welcoming fire, she said, "Now tell me about school."

* * *

Bundled in his cashmere coat, an angry Ben Mark walked toward the garage a few blocks from the fraternity house. His father wouldn't be pleased at all with his having to go before the disciplinary board after the Thanksgiving holidays. Breckenridge Smith had been an idiot, smuggling the three girls from Elsie Mae's into the frat house for the party the night before. Now they were all in trouble — the whole fraternity.

Ben Mark had a hangover. His head hurt and his stomach felt queasy, and he didn't look forward to the sixty-five mile trip to Atlanta. But once he got beyond the Athens city limits, he'd open up the car and let 'er rip, like in the race at the speedway the first part of September. He'd won that race, no thanks to Alpharetta Beaumont, who'd stood him up. He'd wasted a valuable hour hanging around the wagon yard that Saturday, until he barely had enough time to get to the race.

Like a cocky bantam rooster, Breckinridge Smith paced back and forth in front of the garage off Milledge Avenue as he waited for Ben Mark.

"Oh, there you are, St. John. Thought you'd never get here. I'm already late, you know."

"You should have taken the train, if you're so intent on meeting a schedule."

"What's the matter? You still mad about last night?"

"Not half so mad as my dad's going to be. He might even take my car from me, especially if I'm kicked out of school."

"There're always other schools, St. John," he stated with a philosophical air. "This is my third in the last two years."

"Shut up, Breckenridge," Ben Mark said, enormously depressed at the information.

By the time Ben Mark reached Highway 78, he gathered speed, slowing down only long enough to pass through the little towns of Social Circle and Monroe. By sunset he was in Atlanta. Dropping Breckinridge at his house on Peachtree Battle, Ben Mark curved around to the light and headed for home.

A subdued Ben Mark sat at the table that night with

Belline and his mother and father. Later, when Axel and Rennie had gone upstairs to bed, Axel reflected on the quiet evening and said, "I do believe the boy's homesick."

"And I thought Belline would be the one," Rennie replied," but school is evidently agreeing with her. Perhaps it was the best thing, after all, for her to go away."

"Daniel called tonight. Belline didn't seem too eager to talk with him," Axel said.

"Can you blame her? She has a lot to answer for. Oh, Axel, I don't know what to do about the girl. She seems totally oblivious to the damage she's done to Steppie. The whole affair has been such a nightmare. Where will it all end, Axel?" Rennie's eyes filled with tears.

Axel, sympathetic, patted her arm. "There, there, Rennie. We can't let it ruin our lives. The only thing we can do is hold up our heads and ignore the gossip." Brightening as he thought of it, Axel said, "But at least one good thing has happened. Tomorrow will be the first time that Anna Clare has been to a family dinner in the last five years. Reed's quite pleased. But he warned me, Rennie. Anna Clare still isn't quite…normal," he said, searching for the right word.

"I understand. I just hope the young people will understand and not laugh at anything she does."

"Let's cut out the light," Axel said. "Tomorrow will be a busy day." In the darkness, he reached for Rennie and she responded willingly, her plump, small body pressed next to his.

The day dawned bright and beautiful, one of those Southern days given to mortals to make them forget the dreariness of winter. The slight frost on the blades of grass turned to glistening moisture and the thirsty sun, eager to drink its fill, dried the leaves, laundering them and leaving them bright and new, while the field mice left their nests to forage for seeds.

It was Thanksgiving. The church bells rang; the city came awake, and in its kitchens, the smells of turkeys roasting, of spicy pumpkin and apple pies baking in the ovens, rose to bombard the noses of those fortunate enough to celebrate the goodness of life. And those less fortunate, who had missed out on the food baskets distributed by the churches, began to line up early in front of Union Mission for their Thanksgiving dinner.

Awakened by the sound of church bells, Daniel got up, put on his robe and, tousel-headed, walked to the kitchen. Verbena, her hat already pinned to her head with a long hatpin, waited to serve him breakfast.

"I'll be off, Mr. Daniel," she informed him a few minutes later as she took her coat from the peg hanging near the kitchen door. "Willie's comin' for me."

"How many children does he have now, Verbena?"

"Five," she replied. "The littlest one was born while you were away. They calls her "Stormy" since she was born the night of the ice storm."

Daniel smiled. "Have a happy Thanksgiving, Verbena."

"You too, Mr. Daniel."

The sound of Willie's car coming up the driveway caused Verbena to rush out the door, and Daniel was left alone.

Waking to the sound of bells in another section of town, Belline had no reason to hurry downstairs for breakfast. It was a fix-it-yourself in the breakfast room, with the coffee and tea kept warm, and toast and sugared doughnuts hidden under large white napkins. String was too busy in the kitchen to serve the usual hot breakfast.

By the time Belline was dressed, she walked to the breakfast room where Rennie and Axel had evidently eaten earlier. Glancing over at Ben Mark's place, she saw that he was as late as she. Just as Belline poured a cup of tea and took a doughnut from the silver tray, Ben Mark walked into the breakfast room.

"Good morning, Belline."

"How's your hangover?"

He jerked his head toward the door and then whispered, "Don't talk so loud, Belline. Somebody might hear."

"Tell me," she said, her voice sweet and soft, "is the Athens moonshine as good as Tucker Beaumont's?"

"No, but it's better than that North Carolina cider you and Celia Wentworth got hold of, I wager."

Now it was Belline's turn to look uncomfortable; for Rennie chose that instant to come into the breakfast room. She smiled at Ben Mark and then at Belline.

"I'm glad I found you both," she said, "because I have a favor to ask."

"What's that, Mama?" Ben Mark asked, anxious to please, today of all days; for he would have to tell them about the disciplinary board before he left on Sunday to return to the university.

"Anna Clare is coming today," she confided. "She hasn't been well for a long time, and I hope you children won't do or say anything to make her unhappy."

Ben Mark said the first thing that popped into his head. "You mean, if she acts loony, just pretend she isn't?"

"Ben Mark!"

"I'm sorry, Mama. But Uncle Reed should have put her away long ago. He would have been a lot happier."

"Our family has never done that, Ben Mark. It would be too heartless."

"Well, *I* think it's catching. Look at Carey."

"Anna Clare is perfectly harmless. And I want you both to promise that you'll be nice to her, as well as to her cousin."

"Okay, Mama."

"All right, Cousin Rennie."

The woman left the breakfast room. Looking at Ben Mark, Belline sat down at the table, broke off a piece of doughnut, and began licking the confectioner's sugar.

Min-yo, interested only in the Chinese New Year and *Ming Ching*, had no desire to celebrate an official occasion that was less than two hundred years old. But he had been given the day off anyway. He removed his white jacket and replaced it with his dark coat with Mandarin collar. His brother, who ran a laundry, would welcome his help that day.

The nurse had left the house after giving Anna Clare her medicine that morning, and now Min-yo waited for the St. Johns to leave before closing the house.

Walking down the stairs with Alpharetta, Anna Clare was dressed in a deep lavender suit with red trim on the hem of the skirt and sleeves. A chic combination, it gave more color to the woman's face than the deathly pale ecrus and whites of her old clothes. Alpharetta had fixed her hair in a becoming roll and the red-haired girl, proud of her accomplishment, glanced admiringly at the woman beside her. She didn't even look like the same woman who had sat at the table that first night in the dingy debutante dress with the lace in tatters.

"You think I look all right, Alpharetta?" Anna Clare inquired timidly.

"Oh, yes," she replied, reassuringly. "Didn't Papa tell you that a few minutes ago?"

Anna Clare smiled. "Yes, he did. And you think so, too?"

"Of course."

They passed the mirror in the hallway and Alpharetta, needing reassurance even more than Anna Clare since she was going to see Ben Mark again, reached up to touch her cheek to make sure the image in the mirror was truly Alpharetta Beaumont. Cousin Reed had been extremely kind, buying new clothes for her, as well as for his wife. The green wool dress with matching jacket trimmed in amber fox fur at the cuffs, picked up the color of her eyes and accentuated the golden red of her hair. She hugged in her memory the words that Cousin Reed had spoken to her earlier. "You look just like the February calendar girl of Mr. Gibson, Alpharetta." How pleased she'd been with the compliment.

Reed drove the car to the door and watched for Anna Clare and Alpharetta. He probably should have apprised Axel of Alpharetta's parentage, but then he would recognize the name soon enough. Actually, he'd been thinking more of Anna Clare and the Carletons. It would be a lot less embarrassing for them all, the fewer people who connected Alpharetta to Tucker Beaumont.

* * *

Waiting for her husband, Carey St. John looked in the mirror at the green hospital gown she was wearing. After her initial rage at being incarcerated in the Brenner Sanitarium by Reed and Julian, she had settled down, done what the doctors had told her. She'd caused no trouble whatsoever; had even pretended to be contrite over Kathryn; for she realized that was the only way she would ever get out. But once she did…

Carey smiled. Only one more day, and she would be released to go home. Julian, acting guilty, had even promised to take her to Grant Field for the President's speech. Of course, as part of the welcoming committee, Axel would be on the platform, while Rennie and Kathryn Mansour were at the luncheon for Mrs. Roosevelt. A perfect day, Carey thought, to get even with them all—Reed, Julian, Kathryn. Especially Kathryn.

"Mrs. St. John," the nurse said. "Dr. St. John is here to see you."

"Julian," she said, turning from the mirror and smiling at him.

"How are you, Carey?" he asked, bending over to give her a kiss.

"A little sad to be missing the Thanksgiving dinner with the family," she confessed.

"Dr. Layfield thought it might be a little too much for you today, seeing the entire family. Sometimes, holidays are not the happiest of times. But I'll come for you tomorrow. I've taken the day off, so we'll have a good day together, Carey."

"That's fine, Julian. I'll be glad to get home."

"I have something for you, Carey, as a homecoming present. It's in your closet at home."

"What is it?"

"Oh, something from Leonard's. He sends his love."

Her eyes became bright at the thought and then she disguised her enthusiasm. "You're sweet, Julian. But Dr. Layfield has made me see there's more to life than new clothes." And something *had* taken precedence in Carey's mind—revenge.

Thrilled to hear her reply, Julian relaxed. "Martha's waiting in the car. We're going on to Axel's. But I'll be here first thing in the morning."

"All right, Julian. Have a good time." She turned her cheek to him for his sterile good-bye kiss and watched as he closed the door to her hospital room.

Julian walked into the central lobby, called for the attendant to unlock the door, and then hurried back to the car where Martha waited for him.

Chapter 28

Hoping to talk with Belline before the others arrived, Daniel deliberately left his house early. The Buick, parked in the carriage house, turned over immediately; for it had been kept in good running condition by Wash, along with Creag Trent's Packard that he'd been instructed to pick up at the airport hangar and take back to the stucco-and-timber house next door to the Wexford residence.

Daniel's trunk still had not come and so he was dressed in the only suit hanging in his closet. The sleeves of the blue coat were shorter than they'd been when he left for Paris. Daniel smiled at the thought. Actually, the suit had remained the same. It was his arm length that had changed.

Daniel drove across town, and when he turned into Axel's driveway he was glad to see that he was the first to arrive. He got out, walked up to the front door, and turned the handle. The door was unlocked and he supposed it had never been locked in the house's lifetime. He doubted that Axel even had a key to fit it. As he pushed open the door, he thought of Paris—the heavy locks on the doors, the security guard downstairs in the apartment house where the Vicomtesse d'Arcy lived. There was quite a difference between that city where thieves freely roamed, pilfering when one's back was turned, and this Southern town whose citizens would be horrified to think some unscrupulous guest had come into the house, unbidden.

"Cousin Rennie," Daniel called aloud, and Belline, hearing his familiar voice, stopped on the stairs for a split second before walking down to meet him.

She was eager to see him, yet afraid too; for Daniel had always scolded her for getting into so much trouble. And she didn't look forward to another scolding for her recent actions.

Ben Mark, stationed in the living room by his mother, hurried to greet Daniel, and as Belline rounded the curve in the stairs and stood on the last tread, she was struck with the contrast between Daniel and Ben Mark. A full head taller than his cousin, Daniel resembled some Nordic god, with his pale blond hair in such contrast to the raven's wing silk of Ben Mark's. While Belline watched, the two stood in the hallway and shook hands like strangers—men, instead of boys, meeting for the first time.

"Daniel?"

He turned, saw Belline. His face, his eyes, cold and stern at first, thawed and with a smile far brighter than the candelabra lights overhead, he drew Belline to him, like a warm fire at the end of a night's journey through ice and snow.

"Daniel," she said again, this time with a delighted lilt to her voice. Belline hurled herself into his outstretched arms. Everything was all right. Daniel was home.

Holding her now at arm's length to get a better look at her, he said, "Belline, I can't believe it's you. You've grown this past year."

"You, too, Daniel," she answered, reaching out to touch the too-short sleeve of his coat.

"Well, don't just stand there eyeing each other. Come on in to the living room," Ben Mark suggested, remembering his manners.

"How's the university?" Daniel asked, walking beside Ben Mark and regretting that he'd lost an opportunity to talk privately with Belline.

Before Ben Mark had a chance to answer, the front door swung open again. Julian and Martha appeared. Then Rennie and Axel, hearing voices, walked up the hallway. All began to talk at the same time, Martha with Belline, Axel and Julian, Rennie and Daniel. Then, as in a new dance, they switched partners; the chatter rose in intensity, spread itself from the hallway into the living room, crescendoed and grew soft with a change of tempo, garlanded all the while by the aroma of ambrosia, pecan dressing, sage, and nutmeg.

"Papa, I think I'd rather go home," Anna Clare said, when Reed parked beside the other two cars and cut off the engine.

He reached over, held her hand in his, and looked into her faded blue eyes. "We'll leave as soon as we've eaten, if you want to, Anna Clare," he assured her.

"Oh, but that wouldn't be good manners. We have to stay at least twenty minutes after a meal, Papa. You've always been firm in that."

"I'm sure everyone would understand, Anna Clare. Don't be frightened."

But it wasn't Anna Clare who was trembling. Alpharetta, sitting on the front seat next to the woman, felt a tremor gather and ripple through her body down to her toes. Unable to prevent it, Alpharetta wondered if her own fear had transmitted itself to Anna Clare.

Nevertheless, the three got out of the car, followed the same path as the others to the front door. The sound of voices beckoned and Alpharetta, stepping inside, hung back to allow Reed and Anna Clare to precede her.

Abruptly, all conversation ceased; all eyes turned to the threshold where Reed, Anna Clare, and Alpharetta stood.

"What is *she* doing here?" Belline's voice, harsh and shrill, pierced the silent air as she spied her look-alike who had invaded the family circle.

While Belline's question hung in the air unanswered, an embarrassed Rennie rose from the sofa to greet the woman dressed in purple. "Anna Clare, how nice to see you."

"May I present Anna Clare's cousin, Alpharetta Beaumont," Reed said, first to Rennie, then to Axel directly behind his wife.

"How do you do, Mrs. St. John? Mr St. John?"

Axel's eyes bulged at the sight of the girl, so like Belline. Unable to help himself, he openly stared first at Alpharetta, then back to Belline, who, by this time, had also risen from her chair.

"I don't believe it," Axel finally said.

"Neither do I," Daniel joined in. But Ben Mark, with a sudden alertness, a sense of anticipatiion, walked directly toward the girl dressed in green.

"It's good to see you again, Alpharetta."

"Thank you, Ben Mark. It's…good to see you, too."

"You already know each other, Ben Mark?" Rennie inquired, surprised.

"Yes, Mama."

"Well, how nice. Alpharetta, this is Daniel Wexford," Rennie said, acknowledging Daniel on her right. "And Belline…"

"If you'll excuse me, I think I'll go into the garden for a breath of air," Belline said, whirling past Alpharetta without speaking to her and rushing into the hall.

"Belline," Ben Mark called, hurrying after her, leaving a completely baffled Alpharetta facing Daniel and no one else.

"Anna Clare, do come and sit down. We're so happy that you could come today." Rennie, nervously fingering the red flower pressed to her throat, motioned Anna Clare to a seat. No one noticed Anna Clare's confusion, for her reaction was the same as the others in the room—all except for Reed, who walked to the bay window and began to converse with his brothers.

With the appearance of the girl who looked identical to Belline, the air had become electrified, full of tension that in one short moment had swept through the room like the unnatural silence preceding a storm. Ben Mark and Belline had both recognized her. That was certain.

Martha, the youngest, almost completely ignored so far, came up to Alpharetta. "Hi, I'm Martha. It's amazing how much you and Belline look alike."

Rennie, not knowing what else to do, led Anna Clare to the sofa and, seeing the lost look on her face, took her hand and consoled her.

"Belline, come back," Ben Mark called, seeing her hurrying past the courtyard to the garage. With a long stride, he finally caught up with her. "Where do you think you're going?"

"I don't know, and I don't care. But I *do* know I'm not going to spend Thanksgiving Day with a...a moonshiner's daughter," Belline vowed.

"How do you know that's who Alpharetta is?"

"Because you told me, yourself."

He could see the distressed look on his mother's face. She'd worked so hard for the day's success, and he realized if it were to be salvaged, then he was the one who had to do it, to keep the peace.

"You took me seriously?" he asked in a teasing voice.

"Of course. That day in the cemetery. I told you I saw her and you said her father made the best moonshine in Georgia."

"Well, I dunno. *Your* father made some pretty good bathtub gin, I'm told."

"What?"

"Oh, come on, Belline. *Everybody* made it at one time or other. I was just being smart that day. You're so naïve.

You believe everything anybody tells you."

"I don't."

"Yes, you do. You heard what Uncle Reed said. She's Anna Clare's cousin. A poor cousin, but she's family, too, Belline. Else my uncle wouldn't have her in his house, or bring her here for Thanksgiving. Come on back in the house, Belline, and stop acting like a spoiled brat just because you two resemble each other."

Undecided, she stood with her hand on her hip. "I suppose it is rather silly," she admitted. "But I never liked to see anybody wear the same clothes as mine. And I guess I *do* resent it, that she has the same hair color, the same features."

"I think it would be fun to have a double. There're definite advantages. If you got into trouble, you could blame the one who looks like you." Inwardedly, Ben Mark would have welcomed someone who could go before the disciplinary board in his place on Monday.

"Yes, it could be fun, at that."

Ben Mark laughed. "Think how you could confuse people. Why, you might even have Alpharetta go back to school and you could stay in Uncle Reed's house for a while."

"Ugh. I don't think I'd want to be around Cousin Anna Clare all day. School is preferable to that." Belline's eyes narrowed and then lit up. "I have a much better idea, Ben Mark. Something to do with this weekend."

"I thought you wouldn't let a golden opportunity for intrigue pass you by." He glanced at her sideways. "You ready to go in?"

"All right." Belline smiled as she thought of Breckinridge Smith. Rennie didn't approve of him. She thought he was much too worldly for Belline. But now she'd found a way to see him without Rennie's censure.

Relieved to see that Belline's animosity had vanished, Rennie went into the kitchen to help String. Within a few minutes, with everyone watching, Axel stood at the dining table and expertly carved the turkey.

The extra leaf had been put in the table, extending it to seat the ten people comfortably, but its fine dark wood was hidden completely by the embroidered white linen tablecloth. Rennie, seated at the opposite end of the table from Axel, saw that they were evenly divided—five older people, five younger people. And yet, the younger ones seemed to overwhelm, to take up more space. Perhaps it was the way she'd seated them.

She always liked to have a man, then a woman, but realizing that Anna Clare would feel better if Alpharetta were beside her, she had foregone her preferred seating arrangements. She put Daniel opposite Belline, so that Belline would not be staring directly into Alpharetta's face. It had been unnerving to see such a close resemblance, and while Rennie had been in the kitchen, her mind had been on the two girls. Alpharetta was related to Anna Clare through the Carletons. Neither Steppie nor Neal was anywhere on *that* family tree, yet Belline and Alpharetta looked as if they could be twins. Seeing String appear at her side with the plate, Rennie gave up trying to figure out family ties and turned her mind to the dinner.

But Axel would not be sidetracked. He kept thinking, digging into his memory until it dawned on him who Alpharetta Beaumont really was. A dark, murderous urge to throttle Reed, who sat at his left, came over him. How dare he bring Tucker Beaumont's daughter into his house. The carving knife hit bone, and Axel, shifting position, began to carve the other side of the turkey breast.

"Alpharetta, have you lived all your life in Atlanta?" Rennie inquired politely.

Before she had a chance to reply, Reed answered for her. "She lived in Gainesville, Rennie, with her grandmother."

Alpharetta looked at Reed as he spoke. His manner told her that he did not wish her to talk about her father or brothers. "But she's dead now," Alpharetta added sadly. And Belline, watching her, remembered Alpharetta crying in the cemetery—and the hearse. Belline's head lifted and her eyes sought Ben Mark. Under the table, his hand pressed hers, while his attention returned to Alpharetta. Not realizing he'd held his breath for Alpharetta's answer, Ben Mark relaxed, began to cut his meat, and to dip into the congealed cranberry and nut salad on his left.

Rennie, still trying to place Alpharetta in the Carleton family, all at once realized who she was—the granddaughter of Rowena Carleton. She sat silently at the table and recalled the scandal that took place at the Exposition in Piedmont Park in October of '88, when the Carleton girls, with their father, had been invited to inspect the large air balloon due to go up that afternoon. Rowena, always the more daring, had stepped inside the gondola and then the straps holding it down broke. It wouldn't have been so bad, except that the man explaining the workings of the balloon was inside, too. And when the balloon came down an hour later in Tom Acree's pasture by the Chattahoochee River, Rowena's reputation was ruined. The only course left to her was to marry the man—Alvin Beaumont.

"Papa?"

"Yes, Anna Clare?"

"I'm not hungry."

A stifled giggle at the other end of the table brought a censuring look from Julian, and Martha lowered her head to take an undue interest in the plate's blue and white design.

"You don't have to eat everything, Anna Clare," Reed assured her.

"Can I take my bread home for the ducks?"

"String can give you a whole basket of bread for the

ducks, Anna Clare," Rennie offered, and Anna Clare, happy at the thought, smiled.

"Daniel, tell us about Paris," Julian broke in, and the small talk began again, with the subjects of Steppie and Carey assiduously avoided.

At the end of the meal, when the adults had begun to walk back to the living room, Alpharetta remained beside Anna Clare. But Ben Mark's voice asked, "Alpharetta, we're going upstairs to the recreation room. Would you like to come with us?"

Shyly she responded, "I think I'd better stay with Cousin Anna Clare."

"That's all right, Alpharetta," Reed broke in. "Go on with the young people. I'll see to my wife."

She wanted to protest, to cry out that she didn't want to go with them, but it was too late. Ben Mark had taken her arm and was propelling her toward the stairs, where Daniel, Martha, and Belline had already gone.

"Why did you stand me up?" Ben Mark inquired, speaking softly, so no one else could hear.

Her heart missed a beat. "There…there was an accident," she said.

"I waited for you for over an hour at the wagon yard that Saturday."

"I'm sorry, Ben Mark."

"There's only one way you can make amends."

Her sober green eyes, matching the green of her dress, looked up at him. "How?"

"By going with me tomorrow to the President's speech at Grant Field."

"But you have to have tickets to get in."

"That's no problem. My father's on the committee. I can get an extra ticket from him."

"Cousin Reed may not…"

"Oh, stop the pretense with me, Alpharetta. Remember, *I* know who you really are. You're no more related to Anna Clare than I am to President Roosevelt. I heard what happened to your father—that he got caught. Was that why you couldn't meet me?"

"Hey, Ben Mark, what are you two talking about so secretively?" Martha called out, watching them from the head of the stairs.

"Oh, nothing that you'd understand, Baby Face."

With one last whisper, he said, "I'll ask Uncle Reed to let you go."

"All right, Ben Mark," Alpharetta said, suddenly happy at the thought that even though Ben Mark knew about her father, he wanted to be with her.

Chapter 29

Early on the morning of November 29, as Dr. Julian St. John drove to the Brenner Sanitarium to get Carey, President Franklin Delano Roosevelt arrived in Atlanta from Warm Springs, Georgia.

The streets were jammed with thousands of visitors who had come from all over the Southeast. Starting from Fort McPherson all the way to the heart of the city, a solid ribbon of humanity lined the streets and waved. No Caesar ever entered Rome under a more welcoming banner than President Roosevelt enjoyed in Atlanta on that bitterly cold day. Yet one man was conspicuously absent. Govenor Eugene Talmadge, disillusioned with the New Deal administration, sent word from his farm in Telfair County that he was spending the day "hunting and farming — hunting something to plant that there's no processing tax on."

In the northwestern section of the city, Alpharetta stood at the window of the house on West Paces Ferry and watched for Ben Mark's Stutz Bearcat along the allée of dogwood trees. The bare branches moved back and forth with the wind and Alpharetta was thankful for the warm, beautiful brown coat that rested on the chair.

Everything had worked out as she had hoped and prayed it would. For the first time since she'd come to the St. Johns' house, Alpharetta was going to spend an entire day with Ben Mark. Nurse Jenson was already taking care of Anna Clare, who had remained in bed, for the Thanksgiving dinner the day before had exhausted her.

Although she was concerned about Anna Clare, her heart yearned for the dreams that had sustained her for the past several years. But then, thinking about it, she grew sad. She knew that Ben Mark St. John was beyond her reach.

"Don't get your hopes up, Alpharetta Beaumont," she said aloud, glancing in the mirror at the stranger. "It can't last any more'n a soap bubble."

Properly subdued by the thought, a pensive Alpharetta picked up her coat as the familiar Stutz Bearcat roared down the allée.

* * *

"I'm ready, Julian." Carey, walking downstairs, was dressed in the smart black wool suit with white peplum that Leonard had sent her and that Julian had paid for. Disguising her sense of anticipation for the moment when she would confront Belline and, at the same time, destroy Kathryn's cloak of respectability, she put her arms into the dark Persian lamb coat and picked up her purse.

The President's motorcade made its first stop at the corner of Techwood Drive and North Avenue, where the first low-cost urban housing project in the nation had just been completed. Axel, as a member of the welcoming committee, stood in the small, protective cadre around the President as he unveiled the marker commemorating the historic event. It took only a few minutes. Then they all climbed into their cars and, with the police escort screaming the way, the procession continued the few blocks to Grant Field, where fifty thousand people jammed the stadium. Outside, just as many more congregated to catch a glimpse of the President.

"There they are," Ben Mark shouted above the band playing the snappy martial music. Thinking that the President had arrived, an excited Alpharetta looked first at the empty platform draped in red, white, and blue. Then she saw the direction Ben Mark was pointing. Down below, nearer to the platform, in the reserved seats, Alpharetta recognized Belline and Daniel, Cousin Reed, Dr. Julian St. John, and Martha. With them was a woman she had never seen before.

Shyly, she looked back at Ben Mark. He had given up his seat with the family so that he could sit with her. She hugged that fact to her heart. For the rest of her life, no matter what happened, she would always remember this day.

"Who's that next to Martha?" Alpharetta inquired.

"Oh, that's Aunt Carey, Uncle Julian's wife. Look, Alpharetta. I see my father. Right behind the mayor."

The band struck up a different tune, and the fifty thousand people stood in homage as the President of the United States, followed by the mayor and the welcoming committee, took their places on the platform in the middle of the athletic field.

"I didn't know he was crippled," a sympathetic Alpharetta said, watching the President's slow, painful journey.

"He had infantile paralysis," Ben Mark explained. "Only, he was a man when he came down with it. But that's why he spends so much time at Warm Springs."

They remained at attention as the band began to play "The Star-Spangled Banner," the song officially adopted as the national anthem only four years previously. When the music was over, the crowd sat down again in one concerted movement.

Switching places with Martha, Carey took the chair next to Belline and whispered, "It's too bad your mother couldn't be here. But I understand she's helping Rennie with the decorations for the luncheon."

Puzzled at Carey's comment, and mindful of the mayor's shuffling his papers prior to speaking from the platform, Belline hurriedly corrected her. "*My* mother is in Mexico, Carey." She was evidently worse off than Martha had intimated.

"Poor child. You've thought all these years that Steppie was your mother, haven't you? But the truth is, you were adopted as a baby, just like Daniel."

"I don't believe you."

"Ssh," the voice down the line quieted the two. With her small, sharp teeth covered by the lingering smile, Carey pretended to turn her attention to the mayor.

The thousand demons that Belline had wrestled, denied, chained to her subconscious—her doubts, her fears—were unleashed with Carey's words to crowd into her head. She suddenly felt dizzy, sick. Was Ben Mark right that day in the cemetery when he'd suggested that she and Alpharetta might be sisters? But no. Carey said her mother was helping Rennie. Today.

Carey, watching for some sign that her words had sunk in, saw Belline nervously twisting the fur on her white muff. She was ready now to voice the words that she had rehearsed for two months.

"It's Kathryn Mansour, if you're wondering who your mother is, Belline. Julian delivered you. But Kathryn wouldn't reveal your father's name."

"No!"

Not aware of what was occurring on the platform, Belline held her hands over her ears to block out Carey's malignant voice. She stood abruptly, the white muff falling to the ground. Unwillingly the center of attention, Belline fled from her seat in the stadium. She began to run through the crowd, as if all the demons were trailing her. Daniel, too far away to overhear the conversation, saw that Carey had upset his sister dramatically. He, too, left his seat and hurried to catch up with her.

"Belline!"

Breckinridge Smith, who had lost his admission ticket in a poker game the evening before, stood near the gate and watched, hoping to slip inside when the guard looked the other way.

"Belline!" he called also, but she passed by without seeing him and rushed into the street. A car slammed on its brakes and Breckinridge shuddered at the screech of tires on the pavement. But Belline, paying no attention to the car, crossed directly in front of it to the other side of the street. Miraculously, she wasn't touched.

While the driver sat, shaking at the narrow escape, Breckinridge took the same path, his coat tail flapping against the front fender. But Breckinridge was no more successful in catching up with Belline than Daniel was. She disappeared into the crowd.

Back inside the stadium, Julian leaned toward Carey. "What was that all about? Where did Belline go?"

"I told her, Julian," she crowed. "I told Belline the truth. I've been waiting for this day for two months." Her eyes, triumphant, gazed into his. "I've finally gotten even with Kathryn."

Seated on the platform with his heavy coat wrapped around him, Axel felt the cold wind graze his bald head. But he didn't mind the discomfort. With a sense of self-importance, he cast his eyes toward the members of his family. He knew they must be proud that the St. Johns were represented on the dais with the President of the United States.

He frowned as he saw the two empty seats. What had happened to Belline and Daniel? They'd been there only a moment ago. Incredulously, he watched as the rest of the family stood up and began to file from the stadium. The President hadn't finished his speech, yet they were all leaving. Axel became enraged at their embarrassing behavior. With his cheeks turning red, he glued his eyes to the back of the President and listened intently, at the same time praying that no one else on the welcoming committee had noticed.

When the speech was over, a baffled Axel traveled back to Fort McPherson for the luncheon, as an official member of the entourage, while Rennie, Kathryn, and the other women entertained Mrs. Roosevelt at the Woman's Club. Then, she flew on to New York to keep a speaking engagement while Mr. Roosevelt headed south again to Warm Springs.

It was later that afternoon when Axel discovered what had happened on that disastrous morning of November 29 at Grant Field. It seemed that Carey had gone berserk again.

The sun had set. Belline, standing on the street and looking up at the brown brick house on Briarcliff, finally walked onto the porch and knocked. Her lips were blue from the cold, and her red hair, usually so neat, was tangled and windblown, for she had not only lost her muff, but her matching hat, too.

Kathryn Mansour turned on the hall light, walked to the front door, and opened it.

"Come in, Belline. I've been expecting you."

Kathryn led the way into the living room and Belline, refusing at first to take off her coat, stared into Kathryn's eyes—blue, slanted—trying to find some resemblance to her own.

"I don't look like you, do I?"

"No, you don't, Belline."

"I look more like my half-sister, Alpharetta."

"Yes."

"I stood at the train tracks for a long time today, trying to get up enough nerve to throw myself in front of the engine."

At her confession, Kathryn said, "I did the same thing, Belline, sixteen years ago. But I'm glad I didn't succeed. Just as I'm glad you came to *your* senses today."

"Wasn't it a terrible embarrassment, Kathryn, coming to our house and being reminded constantly that I was your daughter?"

"You were never my daughter, Belline. Now, that may sound harsh for me to say. But from the moment you were born, *Steppie* was your mother. I gave you up when you were only five hours old. Steppie fed you; she took care of you when you were sick; she played games with you when you were bored. But more important than all of that, she loved you, Belline. You were *her* daughter. You're still her daughter, and don't expect me to feel guilty or penitent for giving you up. You fared much better with Steppie than you would have with me. I'm just not the maternal type."

Belline's blue-green eyes filled with tears. "But she can't love me any more. Not after the terrible things I did to her."

"You're wrong, Belline. She still loves you. She always will."

"Oh, Kathryn, what am I going to do? My life is ruined."

The woman reached out and stroked her hair. "No, your life is merely beginning. If you're worried about other people knowing about your birth, they won't. Julian has put Carey back into the sanitarium. He and Reed are the only other ones who know. Not Axel, or Rennie, or Ben Mark, or even Daniel."

"What about Alpharetta and…and her father?"

"Neither has any inkling that you are related to them. And we'll leave it that way, unless you want to tell them."

"No, I'd prefer not to."

"Write your mother, Belline. She needs your love right now in her life."

"But what can I say?"

"You can start off by telling her you're sorry." Kathryn smiled. "Now, have you had anything to eat?"

Belline shook her head.

"I'll fix you some left-over turkey and dressing. And then I'll take you back to Rennie's. All right?"

"All right, Kathryn."

Rennie and Axel were both relieved to see Belline when Kathryn brought her to their house an hour later. She immediately went to her room, and on Kathryn's advice, no one questioned her on her whereabouts that day, or why she'd left the stadium in the middle of the President's speech. They knew it had to do with something that Carey had said, and that was sufficient.

Kathryn drove home, put her car in the garage, and walked into an empty house. For a long time she stayed in the living room and, sitting on the sofa where she had faced Belline, she let the tears flow. She had ached to take Belline in her arms—her little, spoiled, haughty daughter—to comfort her, to hear the word "Mother" on her lips, but it would have been the worst possible thing for Belline. No, it was better to deny her own longing, her own need, so that Belline's character could be strengthened.

Through the blur of tears, Kathryn noticed that the pictures on the wall were still hideous. Tomorrow she would begin to replace them.

Chapter 30

On the fiesta of the Virgin of Guadalupe, December 12, 1935, Steppie awoke early at the Hacienda Dzibilchaltún. She had spent an uncomfortable night, yet no one had been any more pampered than Steppie, from the time Creag had rescued her from the ruins.

Dr. Lopez, Xytl, Toluca—all had been at her command. Steppie was embarrassed by all the attention given her, especially having Xtyl sleep in her room for the past two weeks, in case she should need help in the night. But Creag, her husband, had insisted.

Sitting up in bed, Steppie saw that the cot in the corner of the room was now empty. She swung her feet to the side of the bed and waited a few seconds to regain her equilibrium. Then she slowly stood by the heavily carved bed. As she reached for her robe at the foot, she felt a sudden pain. Surprised, Steppie sat down again on the side of the bed. A brief sense of anticipation caused her to look down at her gown. She could hardly remember the time her stomach had been flat. But it was past time for the baby to be born. Could labor be beginning? No, she'd had false alarms before. This was probably just another one.

The door to her bedroom opened and Xytl, appearing with the breakfast tray, smiled and walked toward the bed. Curiously, Steppie had lost all appetite, a curious thing. When Xytl came later to remove the tray, most of the food was untouched. Answering the questioning look on Xytl's face, Steppie waved her hand for the Indian woman to take the tray back to the kitchen.

An hour later, when Steppie was bathed and dressed in a white, loose-fitting garment embroidered with red and aqua threads about the sleeves and neck, she felt a second pain. And from that, she knew that the time was approaching for the baby to be born. She hugged the knowledge to herself. The feeling was too new for her to share it yet. When the pains came closer together, there would be plenty of time to alert Dr. Lopez—and Creag.

She hadn't seen Creag that day, except through the curtains as he'd left on his horse for the henequen factory. How busy he had become in these last months. She hardly saw him anymore, except in the evenings at mealtime, and even then, Dr. Lopez was always with them.

As she waited now for the birth of their child, deep in the pagan ruins of the Maya, far from Atlanta, Steppie remembered that other time—the day of Belline's birth. She had been so thankful when Neal had agreed to adopt Belline. Steppie had named her in Kathryn's house when, as a nurse, she had stood beside Julian and received that tiny, mewing miracle the moment she was born. She'd loved her the instant she saw her, and regardless of Belline's betrayal, she would always love her, as David had loved Absalom and grieved for him.

Brushing a tear from her eye, she picked up the embroidery and continued the intricate stitches that Xytl had taught her.

Her memories of the past didn't stop with Belline. Like a reincarnation of an earlier life, Steppie dredged up the memories of the war, when she and Kenna, Neal's sister, had been nurses in France, dedicated not only to caring for the wounded, but searching for Neal, missing in action for over two years before he was found—when the Americans had finally retaken St. Mihiel after those years of occupation by the Germans.

She would never forget seeing Neal on the hospital train with the two-year-old Daniel in his arms. Unlike her instant love for Belline, a feeling of desolation had accompanied the first sight of Daniel; for she'd immediately thought he was Neal's love child. But she had been wrong, and her depression vanished, supplanted by a vast love and feeling of protection for that small victim of a harsh and bloody war.

Love child. Was that what this baby, waiting to be born, would be called? But no. There was no love involved in its conception. She had no way of knowing *what* Creag felt the night the child was conceived — the night of the ice storm. He could have denied his part so easily. Instead, he had taken full responsibility, even married her so that the child would have his name.

A name. Steppie had been afraid even to think of a name for the baby, in case the gods learned of it and snatched the baby from her. With a start, she realized she was becoming as pagan as Xytl.

Later, when Steppie refused the luncheon tray, a worried Xytl left the sitting room. Within a few minutes, Dr. Emiliano Lopez put aside his leather-bound book and trudged up the steps to check on his patient.

Sitting on the sofa, Steppie laid her embroidery on the table. She gripped the arm of the sofa as her muscles contracted. She held her breath and closed her eyes, not seeing Dr. Lopez as he entered the sitting room from the other door.

"Señora?"

His voice went unheeded until the pain passed. When Steppie opened her eyes, she saw the doctor standing befor her, observing her. "The pains have started?"

"Yes, Dr. Lopez."

"Shall I send for your husband?"

"No, please. You and I both know how long it takes for a child to be born. He'll be home in plenty of time."

"I understand. Sometimes husbands only get in the way," he confided.

Steppie was shy, even now, with the man who was her husband. She could not bring herself to send for him.

By late afternoon when Creag Trent appeared at the hacienda and was met at the door by an excited Toluca, Steppie was sitting up in the Spanish bed with its headboard that reached to the ceiling. Behind her were propped two plump pillows with snow-white embroidered cases.

Creag dashed up the stairs and, without knocking, entered the room. "Steppie!" He seemed unsure of himself, as if this were an alien experience.

"Yes, Creag?"

"Toluca told me the baby's coming. How do you feel?"

"Impatient. I've waited so long. Nine months, to be exact."

He looked at the white-haired doctor for reassurance. "The baby will come in its own good time, señor. You might as well find something to do," Emiliano advised him. "It will be a long evening."

But Creag sat down in the chair beside Steppie's bed. "I thought I might sit here awhile—in the bedroom with my wife." His face was enigmatic. Yet, by his actions, he showed that he was not to be pushed out of the bedroom before he chose to leave.

"In that case," Dr. Lopez said, "I'll go downstairs for some *mate*. Come, Xytl," he commanded, motioning for the woman to accompany him. He paused and turned to Steppie. "I'll be within calling distance at all times."

When the two were alone, Creag, acting as if he and Steppie were conversing politely at the dinner table, said, "The factory has been extremely productive this past week, Steppie. Sayil will begin to load—"

He stopped as Steppie reached toward the side of the bed for something to hold onto. She felt his large, masculine hand grasp hers. A sense of protection encompassed her—an echo of the past, stirring memories of the same hand that had saved her from the mountain. As her pain subsided, her hand relaxed and she began to pull away, but Creag continued to hold it. Surprised, she looked at the man leaning forward in the chair and searching her face.

"Better now?"

"Yes."

"As I was saying, the ship will be loaded tomorrow. Everyone is observing fiesta today."

It was strange that she felt as she did, so aware of this intimacy in the touch of hands—the first deliberate physical contact beyond the courteous hand at her elbow to guide her down the stairs when she had become heavy with child.

"You know this is the fiesta day of the Virgin of Guadalupe?"

"Is it?" she inquired, keeping up with the polite conversation.

Creag nodded. "And I'll bet no one has bothered to tell you about her."

She had never seen this side of him—sweet, caring. Usually, he'd been somber, overbearing, but not now. It was as if he had embarked upon a plan to entertain her, to take her mind off her labor.

She shook her head. "No. But you can tell me, if you wish."

She didn't hear everything he said. The words were plain enough, but her mind was attuned to her body. Though spoken from the chair beside her, the words seemed to come from a great distance.

"It was four hundred years ago when the virgin first appeared to a poor Indian, Juan Diego," Creag began. "No one believed the vision at first, especially the priest.

And so the virgin told him to gather the roses on a barren hillside, wrap them in his mantle, and take it to the bishop. When he unfolded it, the roses had vanished and in their place was the figure of the virgin impressed upon the cloth. It's in a golden frame over the altar of the church, and today thousands of barefooted *mestizos* will be crossing the plaza on their knees and saying a prayer with each step."

Creag's fingers tightened on the small, slender hand. "It's a good sign for our child to be born on the fiesta of Mexico's patron saint."

"The child may not arrive by midnight, Creag," Steppie reminded him.

Creag frowned. "How long have you been in labor?"

"Since this morning."

A concerned Creag, cognizant of Emiliano's return, stood up and leaned over to kiss Steppie on the forehead.

"Dr. Lopez, may I see you outside for a moment?"

"Of course, señor."

A tired Steppie watched while the two men disappeared together into the gallery and closed the door.

She dozed, awakened only by the arrival of another pain, harder, lasting longer than the one before. Then she went back to sleep.

Time passed. It grew dark outside and the lights came on. Steppie's confession that she had borne no other children meant that her labor would be longer, more dangerous than Dr. Lopez had anticipated. Worried, he stood beside the bed and noted the baby's lack of progress.

"You must try, señora," he encouraged her.

"I'm so tired," Steppie whispered, for her voice had lost its strength. Xtyl took a cloth and wiped the perspiration from her brow. She smoothed the wet tendrils of hair from Steppie's face and changed the pillowcases, but nothing seemed to help.

Another hour passed. Then another.

"I was mistaken, señor," Emiliano's sad voice said. "She is not as strong as I thought. She's rapidly growing weaker."

Creag, standing in the shadows, keeping vigil with the doctor and Xytl, moved toward the bed.

"Is there nothing you can do?" Creag demanded.

"It is up to God and the señora — whether she lives or dies."

Creag refused the doctor's fatalistic pronouncement. He had not traveled all the way to Mexico City for a doctor to preside over the deaths of his wife and child. He had brought Dr. Lopez to the hacienda to deliver a healthy baby, to care for his wife. Creag grasped both of Steppie's hands in his, as if to transfer strength from his own body to hers. And in one desperate play to reach Steppie, he leaned down and said, "Steppie, listen to me. You've got to fight. You can't give up now. I love you. Oh, God, Steppie, I've loved you from the moment I saw you on the mountain. I didn't marry you just to give the child my name. I married you because I wanted you for my wife."

His voice, low, anguished, held all the pathos of a man who sees his dream vanishing at his feet. "Please, live, Steppie. For *me*. I need you so."

Her eyelids fluttered open. "Creag?"

"Yes, darling."

"Don't…let me go."

She clung to his hands and he willed his strength to her as she fought for survival. He felt her hands tighten, her body tense, and for the first time in the past four hours, Dr. Lopez became hopeful.

Creag, murmuring to her, coaxing her with endearments, remained at her side, while Dr. Lopez attended her.

"Now, señora. Bear down. Now. More. More."

With tears in her eyes, Xytl continued wiping the perspiration from Steppie's face. A few minutes before midnight, Steppie screamed. Her hands loosened on Creag's. Her travail was over.

Holding the baby by its heels, Dr. Lopez spanked it and the tiny voice, weak at first, protested its harsh passage into the world with an increasingly indignant sound.

"You have a daughter, señor," Dr. Lopez informed Creag. But Creag had no eyes for the baby. He merely nodded as Xtyl took the child.

"My wife will be all right now?"

"*Si,* señor. After she rests."

Creag remained at her side into the small hours and, finally assured that Steppie would sleep the rest of the night, he walked to his own bedroom. The child had been born on the patron's saint day, after all. The virgin's name would have to be one of the names given to the child, that is, if it were agreeable to Steppie.

Too tired to remove his clothes, Creag took off his shoes and stretched on top of the muslin counterpane, where he slept until he was awakened in the morning by a baby's crying.

He sat straight up, rubbed the night's growth of beard on his chin. He stared down at his clothes. And then he smiled. He was a father.

Hurrying, he bathed and shaved; for he realized he had taken only a fleeting glimpse toward the baby. He had no idea what his daughter looked like.

Steppie, dressed in an emerald- green silk caftan, lay in bed and held her child. As Creag stood in the open doorway, he watched her dark head lean over the blanket; he heard the soft whisperings as she talked to the baby. Somehow he felt like an intruder. It might be better to come back later. He had just turned on his heels, so as not to disturb them, when Steppie looked up.

"Creag?"

Hearing her voice, he stopped.

"Come and see our baby. She's beautiful."

Slowly he walked toward her. He had no words to greet her, to tell her what pain, what anguish he'd experienced. He merely looked down at Steppie and watched as she removed the blanket around the baby.

The first thing he saw was the small cleft in her chin. "Good heavens," he said, reaching up and touching his own. "I'm so sorry, Steppie."

She laughed aloud at his reaction. "She's perfect, Creag," Steppie assured him.

"But what an inconvenience. I've cut myself a thousand times."

"It won't bother the baby. *She* won't be shaving, Creag."

He laughed. "No, I guess not." He became silent for a moment. "She has all the prescribed things, like fingers and toes?"

"Yes—all except a name. I was waiting for you to come this morning, so we could talk about it."

He reached out and touched the baby's hand. "Since she was born on the virgin's day, I'd like one of her names to be Maria. You can add anything else you'd like."

"Then I'll call her Maya-Maria, if that's all right with you."

"Maya-Maria. Yes, I like that. Very much." His eyes grew serious. "Thank you, Steppie for our child." He cleared his throat; for his voice had grown unsteady.

Grateful to see Dr. Lopez enter the room, Creag stood up from the edge of the bed where he'd been sitting. "Good morning, Emiliano," he said, his voice recovered. "Will you join me in a few minutes for breakfast?"

"*Si*, Señor Creag. Just as soon as I've taken a look at my patients."

Chapter 31

The days in the Yucatán passed like fireflies, each one beautiful, with a shimmering phosphorescence that mimicked the delicate fragility of happiness.

Steppie watched Maya-Maria grow. The double name had always been a Southern custom that indicated the roots of a child—a careful blending to include both sides of a family in another generation. This Steppie had done in naming her daughter Maya—an obeisance to the stone through which the roots had sought sustenance from underground springs; and Maria—the lofty vision that caused all eyes to lift to heaven. A suitable coupling, Steppie thought—a child of the rock and of heaven.

Steppie blossomed with the days she lived—in love, for love, with love. She knew that she had only these three months from December to March—no more. And sometimes as she nursed her child at her breast, she remembered those words that Creag had spoken on the night the baby was born. He loved her; he'd always loved her; yet it was his sorrow that had wrenched the confession from him, and forced her to remain alive. His voice had been stronger than the one in the distance, calling her from the cote of stone high above the temple, where the doves in the twilight sun flew on wings of gold.

It was late in the evening when Creag walked into the bedroom that Steppie occupied alone. Only a few moments before, Xtyl had taken the sleeping baby into the sitting room that now served as a nursery. The small bed, carved in the same design as the rococo Spanish one in the master bedroom, had the place of honor in the middle of the sitting room, with cheesecloth netting to protect Maya-Maria from the *jejene* insects.

With her mind still on the baby, Steppie turned to face her husband. Seeing his troubled expression, she asked, "What is it, Creag?"

"I have a letter for you, from Belline. Eduardo brought it from Mérida."

He watched pain mar the beauty of her eyes, but quickly erasing her reaction, she held out her hand for the letter, the first communication she'd received from her fifteen-year-old daughter in months.

She sat in the chair by the light and slowly read it, her face alternately showing her joy and her sorrow. Creag made no comment while she read. He merely waited. Finally, she held it out for Creag.

"Belline knows — that Kathryn is her natural mother."

"Who told her?" Creag inquired.

"Carey, Julian's wife."

Now it was Steppie's turn to remain silent as Creag scanned the contents of the letter. "…I went to see Kathryn that night. She made me see that I'm not her daughter at all, but yours. I've done such terrible things to you. Can you forgive me, Mother?"

He folded the letter, put it back in its envelope. His face was grave as he spoke. "It's a little late, isn't it, to ask your forgiveness."

"She's still a child, Creag."

"A vindictive child, Steppie — who thinks she can erase everything with an apology."

The light caught the subtle ferine luster of Creag's brown eyes, stripped the thin veneer of civilization from him in the same length of time that it took for lightning to divest a tree of its bark. "You're not going back to Atlanta, Steppie."

She lifted her head. "You promised, Creag."

"That was before the baby came."

"The bargain was made, Creag. I expect you to keep your side of it."

"We'll talk about it later." He stalked out and down the stairs. In the courtyard of the hacienda, he looked up at the stars while he smoked a cigarette and wrestled with his thoughts.

Blast Belline's letter. He should have kept it from Steppie for a while. But no, he couldn't do that, any more than he could cause time to regress.

Everyone else had become impatient to leave— Emiliano Lopez to go back to Mexico City; Father Benito to make his pilgrimage to Rome; and Sayil to visit his mother in Palenque before the busy season began. All had gone. He had sensed a sudden restlessness in Steppie, too, as she read the letter that reminded her of the outside world.

Was Creag Trent the only one content to let time stop—like the Maya, who had measured time more precisely than any civilization until the measurement, itself, became the important thing and time ceased to have any meaning?

Creag lit another cigarette but only smoked half before putting it out. With a resolute set to his jaw, he walked back into the hacienda.

Surprised to hear the bedroom door open again, Steppie looked up to see her husband. "Is anything wrong, Creag?"

He stared at her in the white batiste nightgown and saw the Spanish bed behind her. He had not slept in his own bed for the past five months; for he had willingly given it up to Steppie.

"I presume you've already decided when you wish to go back to Atlanta?"

Yes, in March," she replied, trying to disguise her emotion. "Maya-Maria will be three months old then."

One month. In one month he was to give Steppie up, hand her over to the police. There would be a trial; for Jim Edwards had sent him word that the grand jury had already indicted her for the murder of Neal Wexford.

He held out his arms for Steppie, and shyly she came to him. He brushed her hair from her forehead and touched her cheek. "Is there nothing I can do to persuade you to stay here?"

Tears sprang to her eyes. "No, Creag, I *must* go back, even though I'm afraid. I've never run away from anything in my life."

His arms tightened around her. "You realize we have so little time together?"

"Yes."

"I want to love you, Steppie," he whispered. His lips found hers, and the passion that he had kept under control was ignited, not as it was the first time, but with a tenderness that made love the sweeter.

Self-consciously, Steppie pled, "Xytl's in the other room."

"Then she'll be extremely pleased to note that I've finally claimed my wife. Besides, it's unnatural for a man to give up his own bed."

Steppie felt her feet swept from the floor by an impatient Creag, who obviously was willing to wait no longer to consummate the vows spoken before Father Benito and God.

A quickening of the blood, a breathlessness caused Steppie to become alert as Creag carried her to the bed, cut off the light, and held her in his arms.

The moon cast a silver glow over the dark cypress trees that nodded in the breeze and, accompanied by soft murmurings that stirred the curtains at the balcony, found its way into the bedroom to spin a silver web around the carved Spanish bed.

Rising from the dark wooden floor, the scent of jasmine and lavender teased the memory with an earlier time when love had invaded the heart.

Softness of flesh, warm to the touch, a gentleness of hands, and a quiver of ecstacy bound one to the other, as Creag made love to the woman at his side—slowly, each movement recorded by Steppie forever, to remember when love was lost and she was a woman alone, not sleeping in a man's arms or comforted by the warmth of his body, but surrounded by bars of steel—cold, desolate, impersonal.

She reached out to touch the cleft in his chin where the finger of the gods had branded Creag—a sign of favor, completely different from the mark of Cain that some men wore on their foreheads, or suffered in their hearts.

They slept, woke again in the night, touched each other. Desire fanned to flaming heights never reached before. By morning, they lay wrapped in each other's arms—a new creature made whole from the two, whose souls had wandered the earth in search of completion, perfection, finding it at last in the jungled ruins of the Hacienda Dzibilchaltún.

The teasing finger outlining Steppie's mouth awakened her.

"Good morning, Mrs. Trent."

Sleepily, she murmured, "Good morning, Mr. Trent."

The sound of a baby's cry in the next room caused Steppie to sit up quickly. "The baby. Xytl will be bringing her in here for breakfast. You must get up at once, Creag."

Creag leaned back against the bed, his arms reaching behind him in a lazy, stretching movement.

"Why?"

"It will be embarrassing if Xtyl finds you in this bed."

"Embarrassing for whom?" he inquired.

It was too late. The door opened and Xtyl walked into the room with Maya-Maria, who screamed her hunger in lusty anger. Steppie's face turned red, but Xtyl, halting an imperceptible moment before giving up the baby to Steppie, pronounced something that satisfied her immensely in the speaking, although it was not understood by Steppie. The Indian woman left the room with a smile.

As soon as she was gone, Steppie put the baby on the bed. "Watch her for a moment, Creag, until I get back."

When she returned, Creag had a mournful look; for Maya-Maria was crying, her cherub face distorted, despite Creag's effort to quiet her. "She acts as if she hasn't had anything to eat all night," he commented, knowing well that Xtyl had given her a feeding of goat's milk at two in the morning. Creag, concerned for Steppie's welfare, had insisted that his wife not be wakened in the night to feed the baby. Now he had another reason to add to the first.

He watched as Steppie climbed back into bed and put Maya-Maria to her breast.

"Don't you have work to do?" she asked archly, trying to disguise with a bantering tone her embarrassment at being so closely observed.

"I've decided to take a holiday. In fact, I *may* stay in bed all day."

Steppie laughed. "Well, you'll be alone. Because I plan to get up for my own breakfast as soon as the baby finishes hers."

"Toluca could bring us breakfast in bed," he suggested. But before she had a chance to answer, he added, "I know. You don't like crumbs between the sheets."

In no hurry to remove himself, Creag sat up, with the pillow at his back. In two months, his daughter had changed, even as to hair color, for the dark fuzz had turned into gold curls, more similar now to Creag's coloring than Steppie's.

And if he had ever doubted that the baby was his,

there was the evidence of her small chin.

"Do you want to go into Mérida later today?"

Steppie's eyes turned from the baby to Creag. "Yes, I'd love to. Dr. Lopez told me about the market and the Montejo mansion. I want to see it all before…"

Quickly, Creag said, "Then I'll shave and get dressed and meet you downstairs for breakfast."

Excited at her first venture into the town of Mérida, Steppie dressed carefully in the elegant blue silk dress that was a part of the wardrobe presented to her by Creag after the birth of Maya-Maria. With the dress, she wore a silk shawl, light in color, since the serviceable black *rebozo* had been left in the temple. With her dark hair parted in the middle and coiled into a chignon at the nape of her neck, she could easily be mistaken for a true señora, Creag thought.

Despite her trepidation in leaving Maya-Maria for the first time, Steppie was determined to have a perfect day. She listened to Creag eagerly, watched their progress, punctuated the air with questions. Directed by the same driver, Hermanito, who had met the plane when she'd first arrived at the hacienda, the horses trotted smartly down the crushed-rock road that gleamed white in the sun.

"How old is the town of Mérida?" Steppie inquired, remembering the ancient towns of France—especially Toul, where she had been stationed at one of the hospitals during the war.

"It depends on whose calculations you use—the Spaniards' or the Mayan's," Creag began. "Actually, Francisco de Montejo, the Spaniard, is credited with founding the present city fifty years after Columbus discovered America."

Steppie laughed. "And that's in dispute, too, isn't it?" she said, "as to who really discovered America? I could never understand the dates I had to memorize in American history. On one test, I put down two dates for each question—the earliest time known when land or gold was discovered, and then the later date when the white man discovered what the Indians had known for centuries. Miss Budden was incensed, and I almost flunked the course."

"You'll see that same arrogance when we reach the Casa Montejo," Creag informed her, amused at her confession.

"What else are we going to see today," Steppie asked, "besides the casa?"

"We can go to the museums, or to the municipal market. There're a lot of interesting things for sale. Would you like to buy a tiger-tooth necklace?" he inquired suddenly with a grin.

"I think I'll pass on that."

Riding into the city, which was the capital of the state of Yucatán, Creag and Steppie came into the shaded main square, the *Plaza Mayor*, with its colonial buildings in white and pastels. They climbed out of the carriage and began their journey on foot—two carefree people, who drew smiles from those they passed.

At the entrance of the mansion built by the Spanish conquistador, Steppie saw the arrogance Creag had mentioned—the two stone figures of Spanish knights, each with a haughty foot upon the neck of an Indian bent low in subjugation.

For a long time Steppie stood, looking at the figures. "Not much has changed in four hundred years, has it?" Steppie commented.

"No. The statues could just as easily be Mussolini and the Ethiopians," Creag replied. "Or Hitler and the Austrians."

Seeing the sober look on Steppie's face, Creag said, "Let's forget the outside world. For today, there're only two people—you and me. And I think I'd rather show you the amusing animal figures that served as street signs in the 1600s." Creag took her hand and they left the Casa Montejo behind.

They wandered through the marketplace where Steppie saw the display of tropical fruits—melons, bananas, papayas. Along the Paseo, the city sparkled with cleanliness.

"Are you getting hungry?" Creag inquired. "We could stop for lunch, if you'd like."

She glanced down at her watch in surprise. "Yes, Creag. I was so busy looking at everything, I didn't realize it was past time to eat." All at once, Steppie felt ravenously hungry.

They found a little place off the main plaza, shaded and secluded. "Pedro serves the best *papadzul* in Mexico," Creag informed her as he waited for Pedro, himself. "What would you like?"

"Something wrapped in banana leaves," Steppie replied immediately.

"Pork or chicken?"

"Pork, I think."

"*Cochinita pibil*," he said, nodding his head. "We might start out with gazpacho soup, and then progress to the pork. And perhaps a sweet and coffee. All right, tea, instead," he acquiesced, laughing at Steppie's grimace at the suggestion of coffee.

Later, when Creag sat sipping his *Xtabentum*, the honey liqueur with absinthe, and Steppie her fruit juice, Pedro appeared again. As a courteous proprietor, he said, "You and the señora have enjoyed the meal, *si?*"

"*Si*, Señor Pedro. Very much. *Gracias.*"

As they left the small café, Creag asked, "Now what, Steppie?"

"I think we'd better go back to the hacienda, Creag. The baby…"

"Xtyl can manage with the goat's milk if you're uncomfortable about Maya-Maria."

"Not uncomfortable about the baby. Just… uncomfortable, Creag," she confessed with a slight embarrassment.

Creag, glancing at the fullness of her breasts, understood. With his hand reaching for hers, they walked back to the tree-lined plaza where they had left the carriage. The driver, sitting in the shade and sharing a pitcher of *sangria* with a friend, hastily got up from the S-shaped bench when they appeared.

A half hour later, Steppie and Creag arrived at the hacienda. The day had been a stolen one, when time had stood still for two people in love.

From that moment, Creag was aware of time racing along. He saw the days ripped from the calendar, passing too fast, until the dreaded day in the early part of March arrived when he was forced to keep his promise.

Steppie stood on the airstrip at the Hacienda Dzibilchaltún. Xytl, Toluca, as tall and thin as Xtyl was short and plump, Eduardo, Sayil—all were there to tell them good-bye.

"Take care of things, Sayil, while I'm gone," Creag said, shaking hands with his overseer. "And Eduardo, thank you."

With his carbine slung over his shoulder, the guard grasped Creag's arm in one final salute as their hands met. "God go with you and the señora."

"Xtyl?" Steppie's voice showed the emotion she felt at leaving the woman. "I know you can't understand the words I speak, but I'll say them anyway. You've meant a lot to me, Xytl—both you and Toluca." She leaned over and kissed Xtyl on the cheek. Completely surprised at Steppie's display of emotion, the woman quickly touched her cheek with her hand.

"Come, darling. It's time to take off."

Steppie climbed into the cockpit and held out her arms for Maya-Maria, wrapped in a *rebozo*.

As the plane lifted its wings, Steppie saw the miles of green-gold agave plants in neat rows, their spiked stalks holding within them the wealth of the Yucatán. She didn't look back at the hacienda. It was too painful. But if God willed, she would come back someday, to walk among the ruins of the Maya, to look into the *cenote* without fear, to watch the doves fly from the temple to the *ceiba* tree, while Chac, the rain god, encased in stone, guarded the long corridors of centuries past.

Chapter 32

Later that night, in a suite at the Fontainebleau Hotel in Miami, Steppie faced Creag as they began their evening meal. Maya-Maria, after an uncomfortable, fretful trip, had finally gone to sleep in the crib provided by the manager.

She watched Creag as he lifted the metal cover from the chateaubriand, then served a portion onto Steppie's plate and another onto his own.

His face contained such anguish that Steppie, wanting to comfort her husband, commented lightly, "This is quite a change from Pepina's white clapboard house on the beach."

Taking his cue from her, he smiled. "We'll still have to be careful of scorpions. But at least we'll worry about only *one* bed tonight, instead of two."

"I was shocked, you know, sharing the same room," Steppie recalled.

"I gathered that. And I'm sure that if you could have reached Verbena by telephone, it would have been the last night we ever shared a room together."

"I'm glad now that the telephone line was down." Steppie began to eat silently, thinking of the months she had spent with Creag—the hacienda, the ruins, the trip into Mérida—the memories etched deeper than the face of the man she had been accused of murdering, the man she'd lived with for sixteen years—Neal Wexford.

"Creag, what's going to happen when we get back to Atlanta?"

He picked up his glass of rosé and held it to the light while he formulated an answer. She watched him until he set the glass on the table.

"Tomorrow or the next day, you'll turn yourself in to the DeKalb County Sheriff, with Reed and Jim Edwards accompanying you, of course."

"And bond? Will they arrange bond for me?"

"If the judge approves it."

"You mean, there's a possibility that I might be denied bond? That I'll be separated from the baby?" This had never occurred to her and the alarm showed in her eyes. "Won't the judge take into account that I'm nursing my baby?"

"I'm sure he will, Steppie. Reed and Jim Edwards will do everything in their power to persuade him."

Creag, noting the fatigue that had taken away the luster of Steppie's brown eyes, reached across the table and touched her hand. "It's not too late to turn back, Steppie. Tomorrow morning, we could head south...."

"No, Creag. I must go on to Atlanta."

In the middle of the night, there was no Xytl to get up to feed the hungry baby. Waking at the sound of her cry, Steppie climbed out of bed and walked barefooted across the floor to the crib. She lifted Maya-Maria from the crib and, sitting in the small rocking chair, she whispered softly to her as she nursed.

Creag reached out his hand, seeking the softness of his wife, even in sleep. But he was alone in bed. He awoke with a vast sense of loneliness. Looking toward the end of the room through diffused light, Creag received a fleeting impression of madonna and child. Steppie's dark hair, grown long, hung over her shoulders and a tiny hand closed over a loose strand. His wife. His child. A premonition of the days ahead caused Creag's skin to prickle—the same feeling that he'd sensed when taking Belline to the airport. He awoke fully and sat up as if he'd never closed his eyes during the night.

He watched Steppie's every move, saw when she put the baby back in the crib and cut off the light. She had no business walking across the room barefooted. But she was already back in bed. He reached out, taking her in his arms, and they slept that way until morning.

Deliberately putting off leaving Miami as early as he should, Creag had the mechanic go over the plane carefully. He wanted it to be late when they returned— too late for Steppie to present herself to the sheriff. She was entitled to a good night's rest before thinking of the next ordeal. And so it was almost dark when the plane reached Candler Field. Lights framed the runway as Creag set the plane down and lowered the flaps to break the speed, while the whine of the engines and the feel of ground under them brought a frightened cry from Maya-Maria.

Steppie, gasping from the sudden shock of winter, climbed out of the plane. The windswept apron of concrete, free of trees, suctioned the cold, the wind reaching out, flapping the khaki shroud and threatening to tear it from her. Quickly, she covered Maya-Maria's head and ran toward the familiar long black Packard that waited in the distance.

"Wash, what are you doing here?" she inquired, as her gardener-chauffeur stepped out to open the car door for her. "How did you know we were coming?"

"Mr. Creag called Mr. Daniel from Miami," he said. "We was awful worried about you, Miss Steppie. It's a bad time to fly."

Even as the car door closed, Steppie heard another voice. "Hello, Mother."

She looked up and her face betrayed her happiness. "Daniel. Oh, Daniel. Let me look at you."

She laughed and touched his hand. "I think you've grown this past year. Yes, I'm sure of it."

He smiled. "Two inches, in fact."

"Hello, Daniel."

"Creag." Daniel held out his hand to Creag Trent. And looking from her husband to her son, she saw that Daniel was no longer a child, but a man—reacting as a man—without animosity toward Creag.

In the deserted Peachtree Trust building, a frantic Axel St. John sat at his desk and carefully went over the figures. The building was cold and Axel, removing his gloves, dipped his pen into the inkwell, with stiff, icy fingers. Even as he wrote the altered amounts, they looked fishy to him. He sighed. He would just have to find another unused account to conceal his embezzlement.

He was still angry with Tucker Beaumont for getting caught and cutting off his best source of extra money. The sale of moonshine had been extremely lucrative and Axel had profited without any dangers inherent in making the stuff—until Creag Trent's pilot crashed his plane at Stone Mountain.

At first, it had been relatively easy, switching funds from one trust to another, and then reversing them when the heirs called for an accounting. It had been a godsend, too, when Neal had been murdered—for it allowed him to transfer Steppie's dividends to his own account, and close out Neal's, except for a few dollars. But that day when Steppie appeared at the board meeting had scared him. If she had called for an official accounting in front of Reed, he would have had a lot of explaining to do. Just as he would if the bank examiner slipped up on him.

Axel had been able to keep one step ahead, but now it had finally caught up with him and he desperately needed to find a way out. He walked to his files, pulled out the Exeter trust papers. He ran his finger down the list of properties until he came to a small hotel on the coast. Yes, he would put that up for sale and switch the money received to the Benham fund, which he had dipped into far too heavily, with the heirs apt to return to Atlanta in the next few months. He would advertise anonymously, as he'd done in the past, with the post office box number instead of the address of the bank. It wouldn't do for too many people to see the bank's name in all the sales he'd made lately.

Feeling better, now that he'd found a possible way out, he cut off the light in his office and left the building. Rennie would be worried about his working so late. Thinking of his wife waiting at home for him, he smiled as he walked to the car.

Having solved one problem, his mind began to gnaw on the other one—the murder trial. But there was really nothing to worry about. No jury in the world would convict Steppie for the murder of her husband.

Jim Edwards, Creag's lawyer, was not so sure. He sat in the library of Creag's house on Castlemeade Road and, together, the two men discussed Steppie and the procedure for the next day when Steppie would turn herself over to the sheriff.

"How serious is the evidence against her?" Creag asked.

"Extremely bad, Creag. The ballistics expert has proved that the bullet killing Neal came from the gun in the desk drawer. I have a copy of the coroner's report, too," he continued. "There were no powder burns on Neal's body. He was shot from a distance, so that means there was no struggle for the gun, no way it could be called an accident. The gun damns, yet it's our only hope of defense, too, because all the fingerprints had been wiped clean by the time the police confiscated it. If it weren't for Belline testifying that she saw the gun in her mother's hands that night, then we could go with the idea of a burglar that Neal claimed to have seen—that the burglar took the gun from Neal, started to run, and then realizing that Neal could identify him, changed his mind and shot him. Then he put the gun back into Neal's hands to make it look like a suicide."

Creag got up from his chair and walked to the window. "But there was somebody in the garden, Jim. I saw him from this window that night."

Jim looked at Creag suspiciously. "Why didn't you come forward with that information at the inquest last March?"

Creag turned from the window and Jim could see the unhappy look on his face. "Because…I heard Steppie talking with him a few minutes earlier, before Neal came out on the terrace."

"And after Neal was murdered, you thought Steppie had set it up."

Creag nodded.

"In light of the money the police found in the drawer, it might be better for you to forget it."

"Why?"

"If there were any hint of an accomplice, the D.A. might connect it to a possible payoff, but that something went wrong and Steppie decided to kill Neal herself."

Creag swore as he remembered the episode of handing over two thousand dollars to Steppie for Belline's expenses and tuition. She had protested and had tried to return half of it to him.

"I gave that money to Steppie, myself," Creag confessed, "in late August."

Now it was Jim's turn to ask why.

"As a loan. She was selling her furniture to meet her bills."

"You have proof—that it was a loan?"

"She gave me an IOU—"

Jim Edwards brightened at the information.

"—but I tore it up."

Creag watched disappointment erase the look of hope on Jim's face.

"I wish I'd never brought her back."

"It might have been best, Creag, for her to have remained in Mexico."

"She refused, Jim."

The lawyer stood up. "Well, I've got to go. Reed and I will come by at ten-thirty tomorrow morning. You'd better get some sleep. It'll be a long day."

He walked with Jim to the front door and when the attorney had gone, Creag, not nearly so trusting as the majority of Atlantans, locked his house and walked across the mass of vines and rhododendrons to the house next door, where Steppie and the baby were already asleep.

By early morning, Daniel, Wash, and Verbena had all been put to work on behalf of Maya-Maria—stocking a supply of milk formula, getting the crib down from the attic, and seeing to the diaper service.

Promptly at ten-thirty, Stephanie Wexford Trent, accompanied by Creag, Jim Edwards and Reed St. John, left the house on Castlemeade Road for the DeKalb County Courthouse. With a look behind her, Steppie saw Verbena holding the baby in her arms, crooning to her one of the ancient songs that Steppie remembered from her own childhood—songs never written down, but a part of that African heritage, uprooted and transplanted to the American South.

Assured that Steppie Trent would not attempt to leave town, Judge Harvey Madison set bond, and in the early afternoon Steppie returned home. Now the legal wheels began to revolve. While Reed and Jim grilled Steppie relentlessly in preparation for her defense, Kennesaw Thompson , the district attorney, was just as active preparing her prosecution.

An austere man, bespectacled, with thin, graying

hair, Thompson was an evangelist with one mission in life—to stamp out sin and bring the guilty to justice. He was convinced of Steppie's guilt and he would have no hesitation in sending a woman to the electric chair.

"If we let her get by with this, no husband in DeKalb County will be safe," he said to his assistant. "We must destroy her reputation on the first day by painting her as a fallen woman, but we have to be careful how we do it."

"The fact that she didn't wait a full year before remarrying will prejudice the jury to begin with," Darrel Hood replied. "And then, there's the baby."

Kennesaw Thompson frowned. "But she's not on trial for remarrying. Or having the baby." He toyed with the pencil while he thought. "Reed and Jim both know that if they don't call any character witnesses in her defense, then we can't attack her character directly."

"That shouldn't be any problem for you, Kennesaw. I remember what you did to Harry Chiles on the witness stand."

"But I can't use the same tactics. If I appear to be bullying the poor woman, especially if she's attractive— and I believe she is—then the jury will become sympathetic to her. We can't allow that to happen for one moment."

"What if her lawyers don't allow her to appear on the witness stand at all?" Darrel asked.

"Then I can't cross-examine her. It's as simple as that."

Steppie was exhausted. Still, Jim and Reed continued questioning her, even though the lights were on and the aroma of dinner floated through the hallway from the kitchen.

"Now, Steppie, let's go over this again. Did Belline hear you arguing with Neal?" Jim asked.

"Yes, although she didn't hear what we were arguing about."

"But she saw you with the gun in your hands?"

"Yes. She accused me that night of murdering her father."

Jim groaned. "Reed, have you talked with Belline lately? Do you think she's going to be hostile to her own mother when she's called as a witness for the prosecution?"

"She wrote the police, Jim. That's about as hostile as you can get."

"I had a letter from her. She asked me to forgive her," Steppie offered.

"It's too late for that," Jim argued. "We will just have to find some way of discrediting Belline, to convince the jury that she lied."

"But she didn't," Steppie replied. "It was true. I had the gun in my hands when she came onto the terrace."

"But you didn't shoot him."

"No, I didn't."

"Then we'll try to prove that Belline was hysterical that night."

At Steppie's look, Jim added, "It's the only way. Would you rather spend the rest of your life at the Women's Prison in Reidsville?"

"No. But I don't want my daughter hurt at my expense."

Creag appeared in the doorway and began to walk toward Steppie. His hand reached out to draw her from the chair. "Gentlemen, my wife is tired. Let's call it a day, shall we?"

Seeing the two men rise to their feet, a grateful Steppie joined Creag in walking them into the hall and bidding them goodnight.

"I had no idea they would still be here," Creag said to Steppie.

Knowing that while she had been secluded for the afternoon with the two lawyers, Creag had gone to Oakland Cemetery to pay his respects to his pilot, Steppie said, "You found Babcock's grave?"

"Yes. The monument is well made. I forgot to thank Jim for that just now."

"He'll be back tomorrow."

Verbena met them at the base of the stairs. "Miss Steppie, the baby's crying. I think she's hungry."

"All right, Verbena. Thank you."

As the black woman went into the kitchen to check on the evening meal, Creag and Steppie climbed the stairs. When they reached the bedroom, Steppie felt Creag's arms drawing her to him. With a hurried kiss, he murmured, "I love you, Steppie Trent. Don't ever forget it." He released her so she could take the wailing baby from the crib that had once held Belline.

She had two weeks at most, to switch Maya-Maria to the milk formula; for once the jury was selected and the trial began, Steppie would be separated from the tiny baby that she held in her arms.

Chapter 33

"Gentlemen of the jury, you have been selected to sit in judgment, to decide whether Stephanie Wexford Trent did willfully and with premeditation shoot Neal Wexford, war hero and community leader, on the night of March 4, 1935, at his home on Castlemeade Road, County of DeKalb," the district attorney began.

"I intend to present evidence that said Stephanie Wexford Trent took the murder weapon, a German Luger, from her husband's desk and, after a domestic argument, did follow him onto the terrace where she pulled the trigger. I intend to produce witnesses, even from her own family, to show that Stephanie Wexford Trent was the only other person on the terrace at the time of Neal Wexford's death, that only one shot was heard—the shot that killed Neal Wexford.

"Gentlemen, when I have proven, beyond a shadow of a doubt, that said Stephanie Wexford Trent is guilty of the crime of which she is accused, I ask you to return a verdict—murder in the first degree."

Kennesaw Thompson, sweeping his eyes along the jury box, noted with satisfaction the twelve men chosen the previous week. He'd made certain that half of them were veterans of the Great War. Former soldiers would identify with Neal Wexford, and by the time the trial was over each man would feel as if *he* had been killed by the Trent woman.

At the harshness of Thompson's charge to the jury, a surprised murmur filled the courtroom. Steppie, sitting at a table between Jim Edwards and Reed St. John, felt Reed's hand tighten on hers. She turned her head to seek out Creag, who was in the second row with Daniel. In the third row, Axel and Julian sat together. They sat on the hard benches like members of a bride's family declaring their allegiance at a church wedding. Only, Steppie was on trial for murder with judge and jury and a district attorney who had just asked for the strongest verdict—murder in the first degree. And in the row directly behind the district attorney's table sat Belline Wexford, her young face mirroring her extreme unhappiness.

Like a participant in a nightmare, Steppie watched Jim Edwards rise to make an opening statement in her defense. Until the last moment, Jim and Reed had debated whether to waive this right. But feeling that it would be worse to have no defending statement at all, Jim proceeded.

He faced the jury and said in an earnest, relaxed voice, "My client, Stephanie Wexford Trent, stands accused of a crime she did not commit—could not commit because of a vow she took almost nineteen years ago. For those of you not familiar with her story, let me tell it to you briefly.

"She became a nurse and went overseas during the war, to search for the very man she is accused of killing. And when she found him, sick and injured, she remained in France until he was strong enough to travel home. She married him, knowing that he might not ever be well again. And then she began a lifetime of devotion and dedication to him. Many of you were soldiers, and I don't have to remind you of the selfless angels who worked in the field hospitals, who rode the hospital trains, and yes—who died in the line of duty, as bravely as any soldier bearing arms."

Watching the faces of the jurors, Kennesaw Thompson saw some nodding in affirmation. He had a new respect for Jim Edwards. In less than one minute, he had negated the prosecution's advantage over the jury. But that was all right; for his evidence was secure. He had nothing to worry about.

"...Stephanie Wexford Trent, fortunately, returned from the battlefields unhurt. Instead of accusing her today of a crime completely foreign to her nature, we should all thank her for her life of dedication and service."

Edwards changed stance, indicating a new direction. "Now, there are some who would condemn her for not observing certain of society's unwritten rules, but remember, gentlemen of the jury, the woman before you is accused of murder. No other considerations should cloud your judgment. The evidence to be presented is circumstantial. There were no witnesses to Neal Wexford's death, nothing to point the finger at the defendant. I ask you to remember this as you hear evidence that in no way proves Stephanie Wexford Trent suddenly became another person, acting in direct opposition to her belief that life is precious."

The prosecution began with the coroner's report, and then the ballistics expert was called to testify. When the name of Belline Wexford was called, a hush swept over the crowded courtroom. Those fortunate enough to find seats sat straight and watched for the daughter to come forward.

"Belline Wexford." The name sounded again and she stood. Looking apologetically at her mother, she walked slowly toward the stand.

Sitting beside Axel, Dr. Julian St. John watched Belline. Somehow he felt guilty; for he'd long ago recognized the Electra complex at work, with Belline's vying for her father's attentions, to Steppie's detriment. Yet he thought she would outgrow it when she became interested in boys her own age. It was a fact of life that little boys fell in love with their mothers, while little girls coveted the attention of their fathers and looked on their mothers as rivals. Julian had seen it over and over. But Belline was in a position to destroy her mother, once and for all. And if she had any regrets, it was too late.

"Do you swear to tell the truth, the whole truth, and nothing but the truth, so help you God?"

"I do."

"Please take the stand."

She walked to the witness stand and sat in the chair.

"Please state your name and your relationship with the accused."

"Belline Wexford. I—I'm her daughter."

Kennesaw Thompson, looking toward the court recorder, said, "Let the records show that the witness looked in the direction of the accused. Now tell me, Belline—and don't be nervous—you were in the house the night of March 4, 1935, when your father was murdered?"

"Yes."

"And you heard your mother and father arguing loudly that evening?"

"Yes."

"What about, Belline?"

"I...couldn't hear. I was upstairs."

"Do you have any idea what they *might* have been arguing about? Another man, perhaps?"

Jim Edwards rose. "Objection."

"Objection sustained," the judge ruled.

"But you heard the shot."

"Yes."

"Tell the jury, in your own words, what you saw when you ran onto the terrace."

"My...my father was lying on the stones and...my mother was bending beside him."

"What did she have in her hands, Belline?"

She looked toward her mother and then back to the district attorney. "Don't make me answer that, Mr. Thompson," she begged.

"You're under oath to tell the truth. What did your mother have in her hands?"

"The…the gun."

Kennesaw Thompson walked over to the exhibit table and picked up the German Luger. "Was it this gun, Belline?" he asked, carrying the weapon over to her.

"Yes."

Kennesaw, drawing out the dramatic moment, walked slowly to the exhibit table, laid the gun in place, and came back to face Belline in the witness stand. "Now, Belline, tell me about the conversation you heard later, between your mother and Creag Trent."

"I don't remember."

"Then, let me refresh your memory, Belline, with your sworn statement." Taking a few steps to the prosecution's table, he held out his hand for the paper that Darrel Hood presented to him. He put on his glasses and began to read. "Creag Trent and my mother were lovers. I heard them talking about it on the morning of August—"

Reporters rushed from the courtroom to begin the next morning's headlines. But the questioning continued and by the time Kennesaw Thompson ended his interrogation, the damage to Steppie had been done and Jim Edwards could not erase that fact.

Feeling bereft, Creag paced up and down in the library of the Wexford house. He glanced toward the desk where the police had found the gun. As he paced, the telephone rang again. It had rung almost incessantly from the time he'd gotten home. And Verbena, more aware than ever that the instrument was nothing but a monster, answered it warily. Soon she knocked on the library door.

"Mr. Creag, Mr. Edwards is on the phone."

He picked up the extension in the library. "Creag, here."

"Creag, this is Jim. Would you look in the desk drawer in the library downstairs and see if you can locate five hundred dollars? Your wife informed me that she had put a thousand dollars of the money you gave her in the drawer, but the receipt shows that the police took only five hundred. Either someone pocketed the rest of the money, or it's still hidden in one of the drawers. Oh, by the way, the key to the locked drawer is in the small box behind the first drawer on the left."

"Do you want to wait, or shall I call you back, Jim?"

"I'll hang on while you look."

Creag laid the phone down and began his search of the desk. He looked in all but the last drawer and, after unlocking it with the key, he removed the papers inside, went through them, and put them back.

"There's no money in the desk, Jim," he said, picking up the phone again.

"Well, thanks, Creag."

"Jim?"

"Yes?"

"How is Steppie?"

"Upset, of course, at Belline's testimony. But she'll be all right by tomorrow. I've got to go. See you at the courthouse in the morning." Jim hung up, leaving a puzzled Creag staring at the desk. Finally he returned the key to its box and went upstairs to bed.

The house seemed empty without Steppie and the baby. Kathryn Mansour had taken Maya-Maria to keep her during the trial. And Steppie, with her freedom curtailed now that the trial was underway, was spending her second night behind bars.

In the middle of the night, Creag sat straight up in bed. His mind, even in his dreams, had been on the missing money. Someone must have gotten into the desk after he'd taken Steppie to Mexico.

All at once, Creag became excited. It was a farfetched idea—the type that often comes in that twilight period between dreams and total wakefulness. But it was possible, logical. What if there were *two* guns—the one that Neal took on the terrace and the one that had killed him. And what if they had been switched? Would that not be a perfect way to dispose of the murder weapon? By placing it in the desk of the man who'd been murdered?

Creag got out of bed and almost stumbled over the empty crib as he groped his way to the window. If the man he saw moving about the garden was actually the murderer—Thinking of the plausibility, he became discouraged. There were too many holes in the theory. Still, if it could put a reasonable doubt in the minds of the jury, it was worth a try. He would talk with Reed and Jim about it tomorrow—and take another look at the gun on exhibit.

The trial was not going well for Steppie. Unless something unforeseen were to crop up, the district attorney would probably wind up his case in a few days. Then it would be up to the jury to decide Steppie's future, to determine whether she was guilty or innocent in the death of her husband.

During the recess of the trial at lunchtime, when Reed had gone back to his office, Creag and Jim received permission to examine the gun. Creag didn't know what he was looking for exactly, but he held the gun up to the light by the courtroom window. Tiny scratches on the band at the muzzle of the barrel were barely visible in the light. His finger traced the almost invisible marks while his mind began to speculate freely on what he felt through his fingertips. Like a sudden jolt, he remembered the ambush in the jungle, when the man beside him had been picked off without a sound. Creag's eyes widened. He looked down again at the gun. A silencer, of course. The same as in the jungle.

"Jim, this gun has had a silencer on it."

"So?"

"Don't you see? If the murderer used a silencer to kill Neal on the terrace, then the shot I heard, the shot Mrs. Barber heard, came from the other gun—the one Neal fired and that Steppie took from him."

"You're grasping at straws, Creag."

Creag acted as if he hadn't heard Jim. "Tell Steppie I love her, and that I'll see her tomorrow morning." He handed the gun carefully to Jim and hurried from the courtroom. And on the way out, he took Daniel. He would need help in the search.

That afternoon, Creag and Daniel began an almost impossible task. In the tangled mass of vines and rhododendrons between the two houses on Castlemeade Road, they started a careful search for the bullet that Neal might have fired from his gun. There was no guarantee that the bullet even existed. Still, Creag had to pursue the idea.

The wind died down and the afternoon sun filtering through the trees, shone on the dry leaves near the terrace where Faust, the cat, was playing.

Looking toward the cat, Daniel walked over to the animal. "Well, Faust, you seem to have been more successful than both Creag and me. At least, you found *something*." He leaned down and picked up the piece of string that the cat was batting around.

"What did Faust find to play with?" Creag inquired, stopping his search for a moment.

"Just a piece of string," Daniel replied, smiling. He started to throw it down again when Creag stopped him.

"Just a minute, Daniel." He walked over, looked at the string and said, "We'd better keep it."

"Sure," Daniel said, handing it over to Creag. As

Creag wrapped it around his finger and stuffed the small ball into his pocket, Daniel laughed.

"Watch out, or you'll be as bad as Cousin Axel's butler."

"Why do you say that?"

"That's how he got his nickname," Daniel informed him. "He couldn't resist picking up bits of string wherever he went. When Ben Mark and I were little, if we needed string for our airplanes or kites, all we'd do is go to String. He'd reach in his pocket and give us as much as we needed."

Creag went back to his search amid the vines. He had measured the distance from the end of the terrace where Neal had fallen. The ballistics expert had testified that Neal had been shot from the other end of the terrace, judging from the penetration of the bullet. So if Neal shot at an intruder and missed, then the bullet would have gone only so many feet beyond the terrace. But Creag had spent the entire afternoon looking in that direction, and both he and Daniel had been unsuccessful.

Now, if the intruder had not been at the end of the terrace at all, they had been wasting their time. Creag trudged to the spot where the cat had been playing and, narrowing his eyes, he stared at the terrace, approximately twenty feet away. Ten feet less than the witness for the prosecution stated. While Daniel continued in the arc they had mapped out, Creag began to search amid the leaves.

The wind, rising and sweeping across the golf course, sang an evensong as the sun dropped below the horizon. Soon the wooded area was completely shadowed. With a sense of disappointment, Creag said, "We'll have to quit for the day, Daniel. It's getting too dark to see anything. Maybe we can get up tomorrow, with the sun."

"All right, Creag."

They walked into the house, cleaned up, and within

a half-hour, were sitting in the breakfast room where Verbena served their supper.

Glancing across the table, a subdued Creag said, "Daniel, did your father ever reuse the brass casings to his gun, and load them with half-powder?"

"Not to my knowledge, Creag."

"Did you know anybody who had a Luger, besides your father?"

"Lots of people. Even Cousin Axel." Daniel grinned and in a confiding tone, he said, "Ben Mark told me his father used to get too many gin and tonics under his belt, and then decide to have target practice in his backyard. The neighbors complained of the noise and Cousin Rennie got so mad at him she told him she was going to leave him if he didn't put up his gun. I guess he put it up for good."

To Creag, Daniel's words were like a vast explosion in his brain. "Daniel, I believe you've given me the key to your father's murderer."

Chapter 34

The trial resumed the next morning. Steppie stared nervously over her shoulder at the empty place beside Daniel. Creag had promised to come, but he had broken his promise.

Dejectedly, she sat at the defendant's table, and with each witness called by the prosecution, her situation looked bleak. She no longer listened to the questions by Kennesaw Thompson or the cross-examining by Reed. Jim Edwards, who sat beside her, kept his head down, staring at the paper in front of him.

It was a few minutes before noon, when the prosecution, taking the court by surprise, rested its case in *the State v. Stephanie Wexford Trent.* Jim, stung from his lethargy, sat up. He turned to Steppie.

"You'll have to address the jury, Steppie, declaring your innocence. We have nothing else to lose."

Steppie had refused to change her plea and there would be no bargaining with the district attorney. He'd already won his case. She looked again at the empty space beside Daniel. Even Creag had deserted her at the last.

"I can't, Jim."

"You must." He stood up and, taking her by the elbow, forced her to rise from her chair. Slowly, with tears in her eyes, she walked toward the jury.

"Jezebel," a woman's voice called out.

"Order," Judge Madison cautioned, rapping his gavel in emphasis. The echo of the wood was answered by the creak of the door at the back. Steppie looked and saw that Creag had come after all. Lifting her head bravely, she stopped before the jury box.

Creag did not take his seat. Instead, he rushed toward the table for the defense, whispered in Jim's ear, and handed a slip of paper to him. Only then did he walk to his seat.

Steppie had not taken the witness stand during the entire trial. Even now, what she had to say was an unsworn statement, spoken only to the jury and not subject to cross-examination.

"Gentlemen of the jury," she began in a slightly unsteady voice. "Like you, I have heard the case presented against me. And like you, I would consider anyone with such evidence against her, guilty. There is only one small statement I wish to make. I did *not* kill my husband, Neal Wexford."

She looked into the faces of each one of the jurors and she saw in their manner that they had already made up their minds. There was nothing further she could say.

Jim Edwards stood and when Steppie walked back to the table and sat down, the attorney requested permission to approach the bench.

"Your Honor," he addressed Judge Madison, "I have just been handed new evidence that will clear my client of the charges against her. I request a recess of court until tomorrow morning, so that certain witnesses can be subpoenaed."

The judge looked at Kennesaw Thompson and back to Jim Edwards. "The request is granted. I declare a recess of this court until nine A.M. in the morning."

"Thank you, your Honor."

In the private chambers of the courthouse, Jim faced Creag. "Now, what's this all about, Creag?"

"The German Luger on exhibit as the murder weapon

didn't belong to Neal."

"What?"

Creag had requested that Reed St. John not be present for the meeting. It would have been too awkward. Creag began with the search that he and Daniel had started the day before, and his decision to contact the gunsmiths in town. He'd finally located the right one on Decatur Street at eleven-thirty that morning. And he proceeded to give Jim the details.

"I walked into Gresham McHenry's gun shop...." Creag began.

"May I help you?"

"Yes. Do you design custom-made silencers for guns?" Creag asked.

The man behind the counter looked at him for a moment before answering. "Occasionally. Most of the time, though, I get them through the Parker-Haile Company in England. They make them to fit just about any gun. Which gun do you have in mind? I might already have it in stock."

"A German Luger."

Gresham McHenry laughed. "You're out of luck on that one. Won't work very well. You see, the gases escape from the breech. Now, if you want one that's totally silent, I'd suggest a broom-handle Mauser...."

"Have you ever made a silencer for a German Luger?"

"Only once, because the man insisted. A stubborn sort of fellow. Told him it would only muffle the sound."

"Could you give me his name? He might be willing to sell."

McHenry stared hard at Creag and scratched his head. "I dunno. I really shouldn't give out names of my customers."

Creag didn't take his eyes from the short, stocky man. He stood still, not a muscle moving in his face. Finally, McHenry, breaking eye contact, said, "Wait a minute. I'll go back and see if I still have it on file."

When Creag had finished, Jim Edwards slammed his hand on the table in glee. "And you say he had regular target practice in his backyard?"

"Yes. And there's something else. Daniel found this about twenty feet from the terrace." Creag pulled out the string. "It's the distance one would be, if shooting with half-powder shells.

"Jim, Axel and his man, String, were in this together. I talked with Wash this morning and he confessed that the night Neal was killed he and String had swapped places. While String supposedly went gambling, Wash was at the St. Johns', serving dinner."

"But Steppie said Wash had returned to work on the azalea bed," Jim argued. "He stayed past dark. Even Mrs. Barber testified at the inquest she saw him leave before she heard the shot."

"Don't you see? That wasn't Wash. It probably never occurred to either Steppie or Mrs. Barber that it was his identical twin, String. He could easily have left the car on the next street and doubled back in less than five minutes through the woods at the rear."

Jim nodded. "It's possible. And if String became a suspect, he had an alibi at the time of the murder. Now the thing to do is find *Neal's* German Luger." Jim suddenly stood up. "We'll get a warrant to search Axel's house immediately."

* * *

Axel St. John left the DeKalb County courthouse and drove along Ponce de Leon toward Peachtree. He didn't know what he was going to do. Tomorrow Steppie would be declared guilty of killing Neal, regardless of Jim Edwards' last-ditch efforts to save her. He hadn't meant to harm Steppie. His head felt as if it were in a vise being squeezed tighter and tighter. Maybe if he had lunch, he would feel better. And then he would be able to think.

He walked into the Commerce Club and hung up his coat and hat. Abner, the waiter, showed him to a table by the window. Men nodded to him as he passed by, some with sympathetic looks, others deliberately bland, yet all cognizant of the trial coming to conclusion.

Each dish that Abner brought him, from the chicken and rice to the macaroon ice cream, Axel ate, like a man condemned to die, allowed to select his last meal.

He lingered over coffee, something that he seldom did, and then he merely sat, staring out the window until Abner came again.

"Anything else I can getcha, Mr. St. John?"

"No, nothing, Abner." Axel rose slowly from the table and, leaving his car parked in the garage, began to walk toward the bank. They wouldn't be expecting him, but there was no other place he wanted to go.

The walk in the fresh air cleared his head somewhat, and he was glad he'd left the car at the Commerce Club, even though he would have to pick it up later that afternoon.

For a moment, Axel stood on the sidewalk and gazed intently at the powerful façade of the bank—*his* bank, with the columns that were a legacy from the Greeks, the brass-trimmed front door. He walked up the steps, was greeted by one customer and another until he'd made his way to the center of the marble floor, where he stared down at the reproduction of the rare Roman coin, raised slightly, edged with gold. *Montalcino, ascendi, 1556.*

"Mr. St. John." The stealthy whisper from the corridor attracted his attention. He looked up and saw Mr. Bussey beckoning to him. He left his position and walked toward his assistant. "What is it, Mr. Bussey?"

The man's eyes darted toward the stairs to the second floor, then returned to Axel's face. "The bank examiner came after you left for the courty courthouse. He's still upstairs. I just thought you should know."

"Thank you, Mr. Bussey."

Axel turned, but instead of going up the stairs to his office, he retraced his steps across the marble floor, walked out the front door, and headed for his car still parked in the garage at the Commerce Club.

A sense of desolation came over him. The examiner would find the discrepancies. No one had wanted to buy the hotel on the coast. And when the magnitude of his embezzlement was discovered, the bank would go under. He was ruined.

Axel retrieved his car. He drove along Peachtree and by the time he came to that area near 10th Street called Tight Squeeze, he saw String, his butler, walking rapidly down the street. Axel pulled over to the curb, rolled down the window, and tooted the horn.

"Where are you going, String?"

Seeing Axel, the man crossed the street, opened the car door on the right hand side, and climbed in. "Take me to Decatur Street, Mr. Axel. We's got to get away. The police are swarmin' all over the backyard."

"What?"

"Jus' turn around, Mr. Axel. You can't go back. They's found out what we did to Mr. Neal." String reached into his butler's white coat and pulled out the German Luger. "Here's Mr. Neal's gun. I don't want nothin' more to do with it. When they started searchin' the house, I figgered that's what they wuz lookin' for."

Leaving the curb, Axel almost hit a car passing by. He slammed on his brakes, waited for the other vehicle to pass, and then pulled into traffic, turning to the right to go in the opposite direction of his house farther out on Peachtree Road.

String left the Luger on the front seat, got out, and melted into the carnival-like atmosphere of Decatur Street. It would be difficult for the police to find him in the honeycomb of back alleys, shanties, and the mass of humanity drifting in and out, never revealing the identities of its individuals from one day to another.

For Axel, it was impossible to disappear. He drove haphazardly, going in no particular direction. It was all Creag Trent's fault. Axel remembered the way he'd come into the courtroom that morning and handed a slip of paper to Jim Edwards before Steppie had addressed the jury.

Trent had been his anathema from the moment he'd come to Atlanta. Wherever the man went, whatever he ventured, Creag Trent had brought Axel trouble, challenging his position of power. Even Creag's losing his best pilot and one of his airmail planes had caused Axel to lose even more—the moonshine still near Stone Mountain. That day, when the still was broken up, began the rapid deterioration of the empire it had taken Axel years to build.

But he had won in one respect. Creag Trent had never gotten his hands on the James property at Stone Mountain.

Like one coming out of a trance, Axel became aware of his surroundings. He was almost at Stone Mountain. He continued driving and stopped the car at the base of the mountain. Putting the gun in his coat pocket, he left the car and began to trudge toward the mountain itself. He stood and looked up at the carving on the scarp—of Lee, Jackson, Davis. He'd been on the commission that had fired the first sculptor, Gutzon Borglum; for the man had discovered that a half million dollars was missing from the memorial fund.

Axel heard the sirens in the distance. The police had followed him. He continued walking, until he reached the other side of the mountain that had been scaled hundreds of times, where the path was worn smooth into the rock. And he began to climb toward the top. The wind whistled through the caves as the bull horn magnified a voice below.

"Mr. St. John, this is the police. We know you're up there."

Creag Trent, standing below with Reed and Julian St. John, Jim Edwards, and Daniel, listened for an answer. It came unexpectedly, reverberating over the quiet countryside — the loud shot of a German Luger.

The gun, falling down the incline, bounced against rock, clattering all the way down the side of the mountain. But there was no sign of Axel St. John.

One hour later, the old man of the mountain, who'd made a career of rescuing animals and people trapped on top, had been summoned by the police. Creag watched as the man began to climb, with a length of rope over his shoulder and a pick in his hand.

"Daniel, are you going to stay here?"

"Yes, Creag. I can get a ride home with Cousin Reed."

"Then, Jim and I will leave. We have a busy day in court tomorrow."

At twilight, when Axel's body had been brought down from the mountain, Reed and Daniel drove back to town.

"Rennie will take this awfully hard. She always loved Axel — from the time she was a young schoolgirl," Reed reminisced, his voice sounding tired and older than his forty-eight years.

"And he loved her just as much. You could always tell when we were together at family dinners," Daniel added.

They made no mention of the grief Axel had caused — the murder of Neal, the trial of Steppie. And when they reached town, Daniel went to his empty house while Reed drove on to his office.

The lights in the William-Oliver Building were on and Reed glanced down at his watch. Hagar would be cleaning the offices. Muffled by the heavy carpeting, Reed's footsteps went unnoticed as he walked into the double doors of Albee, St. John and Grant. The feather duster, Reed noticed, lay beside his messages on the receptionist's desk. The messages were printed in neat letters, not his secretary's handwriting.

Reed walked to the law library and as usual, Hagar had her head in one of the law books. But the office was clean. He had nothing to complain about.

"Hagar, did you take these messages?"

Seeing him, she stood up. Her eyes were serious. "Yes, sir. The phone kept ringin' and ringin' and finally, I answered. I knew you'd be back. Mr. Bussey said he'd been tryin' to reach you all afternoon. He wants you to call him, no matter how late. That's his number on the paper."

The idea had been incubating in Reed's mind for a long time. He knew tonight wasn't the right time to speak of it, yet he felt a need to do something humanitarian. Maybe it was his guilt about String—the black man's unquestioning obedience to Axel, even though it meant killing a man and covering up the murder. Anticipating her answer even before he spoke, he looked closely at the cleaning girl.

"Hagar, how would you like to go to Spelman College?"

She looked as if she had been stung across the cheek. "*Like to* isn't in my vocabulary, Mr. St. John. *Have to* governs what I do."

"No, I'm serious, Hagar. If I paid your tuition, would you go?"

"I have to work."

"You could still work at night, while you go to school during the day."

"I couldn't pay you back for a long time," she argued, trying to hide her eagerness at his suggestion.

"That wouldn't be required. Although you could never be a lawyer, you might become a teacher."

"I'd like that, Mr. St. John."

"Then we'll talk about it in a few days."

He walked into his office and put in a call to Mr. Bussey, Axel's assistant at the bank. Later, when he'd hung up, Reed sat for a long time at his desk. It was even worse than he'd suspected.

Finally, at the knock on his door, Reed looked up. "I'm leavin' the building now, Mr. St. John."

He got up from his desk. He needed to pay his respects to Rennie. "Then cut out the lights, Hagar. I'm leaving, too."

By nine o'clock the next morning, the courtroom was packed. The crowds milled around the entrance, and spilled over onto the lawn with its Civil War cannon, where over a half century before, General Schofield had marched by direct orders from Sherman to destroy the Georgia railroad between Decatur and Stone Mountain. The county seat was even older than the city of Atlanta in Fulton County which, like Adam's rib, had been taken from DeKalb, given its breath of life by the terminus, and now outstripped in power and prestige its mother county.

As Judge Harvey Madison took his place on the bench, a tremendous hush came over the courtroom, like a collective intake of breath.

Jim Edwards stood. Gresham McHenry, the gunsmith, took the stand. And on the exhibit table lay two German Lugers, identical except that one was more battered-looking than the other.

When the gunsmith had been sworn in, Jim Edwards began. "Mr. McHenry, as you can see, there are two German Lugers on the table. One is the weapon that killed Neal Wexford a year ago. But its ownership is in question. Can you make a positive identification of either gun? You have the court's permission to approach the exhibit table. But remember, you're still under oath to tell the truth."

Gresham McHenry left the witness stand. He picked up one gun and then the other, balancing them in his hands and peering closely at them. He laid down one and, holding the other, he said, "This is the gun belonging to Axel St. John, one of my customers."

"Let the records show that Gresham McHenry is holding Exhibit A — the murder weapon."

From that time on, it was difficult to keep order in the court. A recalling of witnesses wove an entirely different story, with Wash, the chauffeur, and Creag Trent as the last two to testify.

Kennesaw Thompson, sitting at the prosecution's table with his assistant, looked exceedingly glum as the judge charged the jury. The twelve men, filing from the jury box to a sequestered room, looked just as surprised at the morning's outcome as the men and women crowded in the courtroom.

Creag took his place behind Steppie as they waited for the jury. In one hour, the door opened and the jury returned to the box.

The judge, addressing the foreman, asked, "You have reached a verdict?"

"We have, your Honor."

"Will the defendant please rise and face the court?"

"Your Honor," the foreman began, "we, the jury, find the defendant, Stephanie Wexford Trent, not guilty."

Overjoyed, Creag took Steppie in his arms and kissed her in the courtroom. Pandemonium reigned, with the photographers flashing their bulbs in the faces of Steppie, Creag, Jim Edwards, and Daniel.

Less than an hour later, having observed the legal procedures, Steppie walked out of the judge's chambers and into the corridor of the courthouse with her husband at her side.

Now the halls were empty. Steppie paused at the open door of the quiet courtroom, the rays of the midday sun magnifying the dust particles suspended in the air. Her eyes swept over the jury box, the rows of benches where hostile spectators had sat for days, waiting for her demise; where she, herself, had waited with resignation to be sentenced for a crime she had not committed. But then, reprieve had come when she least expected it, with Creag's last-minute evidence. Only, Steppie did not, even now, feel completely free.

As her eyes took in the rest of the courtroom, committing it to memory, she suddenly knew why; for at the end of the second bench, Steppie saw a figure, forlorn, forgotten. She drew in her breath and pain showed itself in her face.

A protective Creag touched Steppie's arm. "Are you ready to go, darling?"

"I…Wait for me, Creag. Please."

He looked from Steppie back to the open door, to the slight movement inside the courtroom. Then he understood.

Steppie walked into the room and, as she slowly closed the heavy door the figure in the shadowed corner looked up.

"Belline?"

"Mother?"

The voices were little more than whispers, delicate threads that, if wound too tautly, could break, leaving no path to the heart.

But then, voices were no longer needed; for Steppie's actions showed the heart, itself, forgiving, loving, compassionate. She held out her arms to her daughter. And Belline, her face tear-stained, left the bench and rushed to her mother's side, words of remorse tumbling one over the other. "I didn't mean to hurt you, Mother…."

"I know, Belline. Hush now; it's all right."

"But it isn't. I'll never forgive myself. I've been so hateful to you."

"That's in the past, Belline. When we leave the courthouse, we'll never speak of it again."

They stood in silence, their arms regaining the feel of kinship between mother and daughter. The healing had begun.

Finally, they broke apart and Steppie looked toward the closed door. "Creag is waiting to take us home."

But Belline, with a rueful smile, shook her head. "You go on, Mother. Daniel will take me back to Cousin Rennie's. She needs me—with the funeral and all."

Steppie hesitated. "Daniel's waiting for you?"

"Yes. In the square. And Mother? Could you—could you thank Creag for me? For finding my father's murderer?"

Steppie looked closely at her daughter. Despite the stubbornness, a new maturity now clothed Belline. And Steppie knew at that moment that they were both free.

Steppie nodded and left the courtroom to rejoin Creag.

Chapter 35

Dressed in his chauffeur's cap and black uniform, Wash stood across the street near the waiting car. He tipped his cap as Steppie approached from the courthouse.

"It sure is good to see you out, Miss Steppie," he said, opening the door for her.

She acknowledged his greeting and, in a quiet, subdued voice, said, "I...I'm sorry about String."

"He never woulda done it, if he hadn't needed the money so bad. Somehow I jus' knowed he was goin' to get into a heap o' trouble, messin' with that bunco gamblin' ring."

Creag climbed into the back seat with Steppie. They both sat, watching until Belline came out of the courthouse and got into Daniel's car parked in the square. When Daniel and Belline disappeared down Clairmont Road, Creag turned to Steppie.

"Well, darling, are you ready to make peace with your *second* daughter?"

Steppie's dark eyes shone with joy. "Yes," she whispered.

Creag leaned toward the driver. "Take us to Miss Mansour's house, Wash."

"Yes, sir."

The engine purred and the long black car left the square.

There was so much to say to Creag; yet Steppie realized it was neither the place nor the time. And so she reached out, touched Creag's hand and, in an attempt at normalcy, said, "I hope Maya-Maria hasn't been too much trouble for Kathryn."

Creag took Steppie's hand and tucked it into his larger one. "I expect she turned her over to Bertha."

They rode the rest of the way to Briarcliff in silence.

When they reached the Mansour house, Bertha, as usual, answered the door. She smiled and waved them on to the art studio in the backyard.

"Miss Kathryn has the baby with her," Bertha informed them.

Surprised, they walked along the stepping-stones, past the fig tree and bird fountain, until they reached the studio where the large oak tree gently waved its branches over the skylight.

Kathryn sat at her easel with her back to the door. She was busy talking softly to Maya-Maria, who lay on a white bearskin rug at Kathryn's feet. With coos and gurgles, Maya-Maria answered Kathryn, who was putting the final touches on her canvas. It was all there— captured in oils—the baby-wide brown eyes, golden curls, and the small shadow on her chin.

"How did you get such a willing model, Kathryn?" Creag inquired.

The woman turned around, looking from Creag to Steppie. As she slowly laid down her brush and wiped her hands, her eyes showed her joy at seeing Steppie.

"Oh, it was easy. I bribed her with a bottle of warm milk and a promise to take her for a stroll in the buggy."

"Well, I'm sorry you'll have to break your promise to her," Creag said, laughing. "You see, we thought we might take her for a ride ourselves. Home."

Kathryn, glancing toward Steppie, said, "Well, what are you waiting for? Are you afraid to pick up your own child?"

"She might not know me," Steppie replied sadly.

"Then, it's time for you two to get reacquainted. Go on, Steppie."

She hesitantly walked to the bearskin rug and gently picked up the baby in her arms. "Maya-Maria," she whispered. "I thought I'd never see you again."

The canvas shifted on the easel and Kathryn, straightening it, said, "I'll go and tell Bertha to pack the baby's things." She left the studio and the baby.

"I'm glad Kathryn didn't paint the usual bear-rug picture," Creag commented. "I'd hate for my daughter to pose in the nude."

"Oh, Kathryn would never..." Recognizing the teasing in his voice, Steppie stopped and smiled at Creag.

With a light blanket around Maya-Maria, Steppie and Creag walked back to the house. Wash took the baby's things to the car.

"Kathryn, I don't know how I can thank you," Steppie said as they stood on the curb.

"Oh, the pleasure was all mine. I'm going to win the top art award in the spring show, you know, with Maya-Maria's portrait. Then I *might* think of giving it to you as a present. Or I might hang it in my own living room."

One block from Kathryn's house, Maya-Maria began to coo and squeal. Steppie, delighted at the sound, said, "I believe she's beginning to recognize us again."

Creag reached out, touched the tiny chin. "We won't rush her. We have all the time in the world."

From Briarcliff, the car turned on Ponce de Leon. Passing the Druid Hills Golf Club, Wash made another left turn onto Castlemeade Road.

With a questioning look at Creag, Steppie saw that the gardener-chauffeur was pulling into the driveway belonging, not to her own house, but to the stucco-and-timber house beside it.

"Last night, Daniel and I moved the crib and all of your belongings to my house," Creag informed her. "We decided that he was old enough to have his own quarters, especially now that he's going to become a businessman."

"Oh?"

"I'll tell you about it later."

That evening, Verbena constantly grumbled about cooking on an unfamiliar stove. "If you'da let me cook on the stove I'm used to, the dinner would'na been burnt."

"Verbena, how would you like some extra help?" Creag asked.

She eyed him suspiciously. "You tryin' to tell me I'm gettin' too old to do my job, Mr. Creag?"

"Not at all. Only there're *two* houses to take care of now. I thought you could rest a little easier from now on, if we got someone to do the housework in both houses, and another cook for this house.Then all you'd have to do is cook for Daniel."

Verbena squinted at him as she placed her hands on her hips. "I goes where Miss Steppie goes," she informed him. "Let somebody else do the cookin' for Mr. Daniel. He's like every other boy I ever saw. He'll eat anything put before him. Don't matter if it's cooked good or not. But now, Miss Steppie's different. She appreciates my cookin'."

"All right, Verbena. You win." Creag laughed. Then he became sober. "The St. Johns are coming over tonight. I'd appreciate it if you would serve us some of that carrot cake of yours and coffee later in the library."

"Yes, Mr. Creag. You can depend on me." Mollified, she ambled out of the kitchen.

Creag sat in the library with Daniel, Julian, and Reed St. John. The seriousness of the discussion caused the V-shape of Creag's brow to become more pronounced.

"We think Neal stumbled onto Axel's embezzlement

at the bank. That, or his moonshine partnership," Reed informed Creag.

"And there's no way to save the bank from ruin?" Julian inquired.

"None that I can think of. Axel evidently had been dipping into the funds for years, but always managed to put them back until this past year," Reed answered. "Now, it's too late."

Up to that point, Creag had merely listened. Now it was time for him to speak. "Steppie has stock in the bank that should pass on to Daniel and Belline," Creag mentioned. "I'd hate to see it go up in smoke. Now, if I were to buy Axel's share, repay the debts, would that be agreeable to you two?"

He looked from Reed to Julian; saw the incredulous expressions on their faces.

"You have enough collateral to do that?" Reed inquired.

"Not collateral. Cash," Creag replied.

Astounded, Julian said, "You're taking a pretty big chance, you know."

"That's nothing new," Creag informed him. "Is it agreeable to you?" he asked again.

"Of course. You know it is."

After Julian and Reed left, Daniel, apprised that he would be expected to learn the banking business, walked across the terrace to the French Normandy house. Creag went upstairs.

It was late. Steppie, dressed for bed, leaned over the crib and tucked the blanket around the sleeping baby. Creag came to stand beside her.

"She's been through so much for a tiny baby," Steppie said regretfully, her eyes still on Maya-Maria. "...moved from pillar to post."

"But she's home now. Just as you are, Steppie."

Creag led her from the baby's crib to the massive, intricately carved bed with its dome-shaped headboard.

Steppie stared in awe at the headboard and looked back at Creag. The dome was a replica of Stone Mountain in all its splendor, carved, not in stone, but in wood with Borglum's design of Lee, Jackson and Davis, and below them, the Confederate Army — cavalry, artillery, infantry — marching around the mountain.

"Did you carve this, Creag?"

"Yes."

"From one of Borglum's models?"

"Yes. With one addition of my own."

"What?"

"Look closely, Steppie. On General Lee's shoulders."

She could so easily have missed that tiny addition to the overall design. It was a woman, dressed in a fur-trimmed coat with a cloche framing her dark hair, and perched saucily upon the general's shoulders.

The laughter in her eyes matched his, until they grew serious. Then she was in Creag's arms, and kiss for kiss, their bodies were saying what mere words could not—of vast need, passion, love.

Two days later, as the soft, sweet scent of wild azalea wafted over the quiet avenues of Oakland Cemetery, Axel St. John was laid to rest. Only the family was present—Rennie and Ben Mark, their faces closed to grief and disbelief at what had happened; Reed St. John and Anna Clare and Alpharetta stood next to Julian and Martha; and beside Creag stood Steppie, with Daniel and Belline a little apart from the rest.

When the brief service was over, the families got into their long, black, chauffeur-driven limousines and went home, their maids in crisp white aprons, their butlers in pristine white coats meeting them at the door.

Tragedy and scandal had blown the doors of the power mansions open for a season—for outsiders to catch a brief glimpse. Now those heavy, wooden doors guarded by stone lions, sphinxes, and whippets, slowly swung shut. And inside, the secrets of power continued to be transmitted in the oral tradition from father to son, mother to daughter, as with the druids of old.

In the primeval forest of oaks called Druid Hills, Creag Trent, in his ascendancy, gazed down at his sleeping daughter, Maya-Maria, and with love in his heart he held out his arms for Steppie Wexford Trent, his dream become his reality.

About the Author

Whether sailing the Danube or the Rhine, exploring World War I trenches in France, or giving voice recitals in Budapest, Madrid, or Singapore, Frances Patton Statham has combined two careers and two loves—music and writing novels.

She graduated *magna cum laude* from Winthrop University, holds a master of fine arts degree from the University of Georgia, and an honorary doctorate from World University.

Author of sixteen novels, Statham has won numerous awards in fiction, music composition, and community service. She is listed in such biographical works as *International Who's Who of Writers and Authors, World Who's Who of Women,* and *Personalities of the South.* She lives in metro-Atlanta, Georgia.